The Caretaker of Secrets Faith

A.T. Geiger

Mountain Peak Press LLC

An imprint of Mountain Peak Press LLC

Bonney Lake, Washington.

For more information about special discounts for bulk purchases, please contact the author at atgeiger.com

First Edition December 2024

Manufactured in the United States of America

Library of Congress Control Number: 2024924228

ISBN 978-1-961910-03-4 (Paperback)

ISBN 978-1-961910-04-1 (eBook)

Content Guidance

This novel may be emotionally challenging to read. It explores themes such as violence, child endangerment, abuse, loss, and grief. Please read with care. Although *The Caretaker of Secrets (Faith)* is inspired by true events, some names, characters, and incidents are products of the author's imagination and have been dramatized or fictionalized.

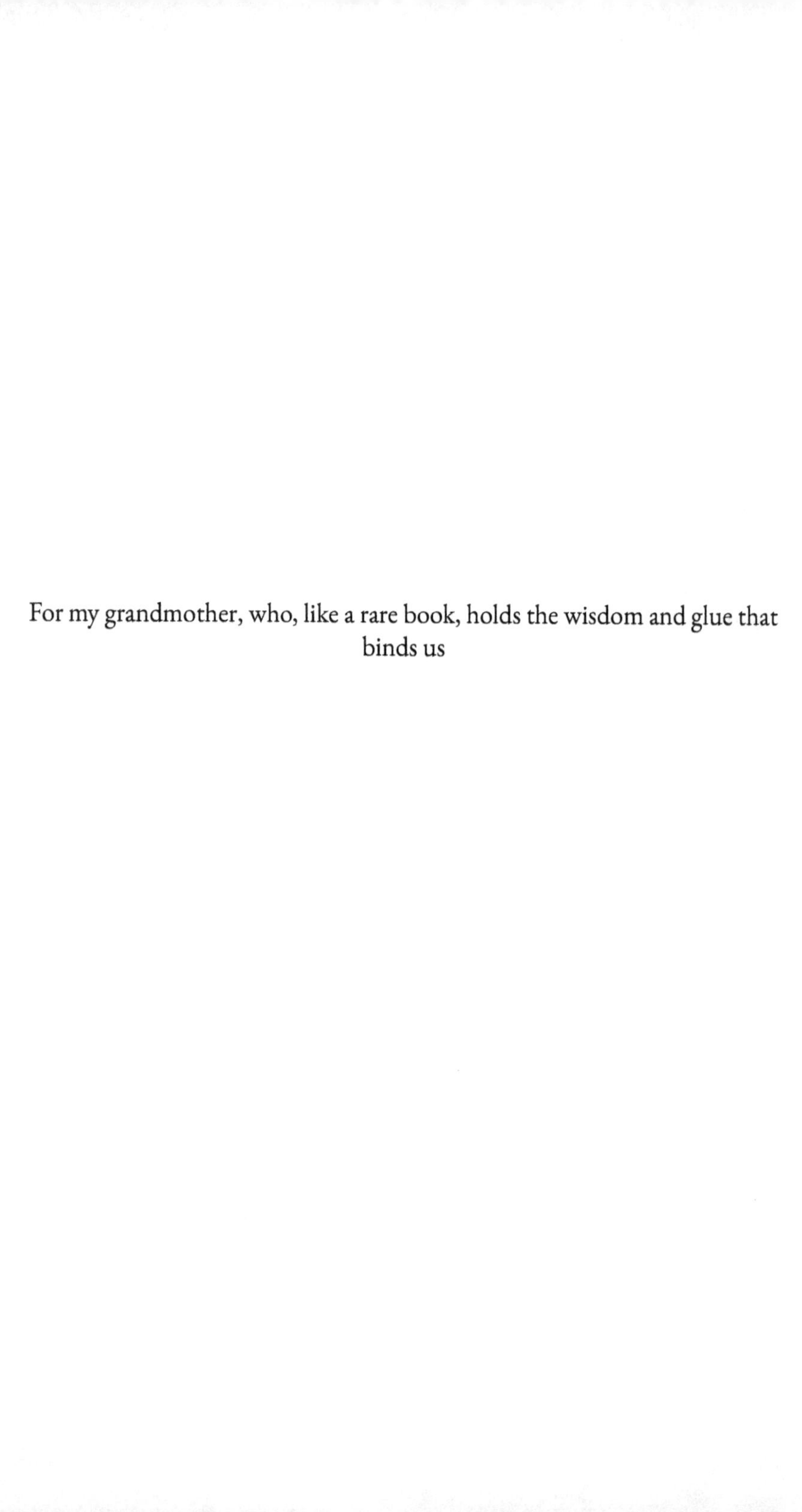

For my grandmother, who, like a rare book, holds the wisdom and glue that binds us

Prologue

Dark, wet whorls of matted hair clung to her tiny head while curious dark blue eyes stared back into mine, as if daring me to choose her over him. Maybe some young mothers could look away, but I didn't dare. I memorized every finger and toe, every fine, delicate detail of her perfect little body—silky skin like cream, a button nose, and pale pursed lips making soft, mewled cries like that of a kitten.

How could I ever forget her?

"It's a selfless act of love," he said, trying desperately to console the inconsolable.

I couldn't bear to look at his face as mine became wet with anguished tears, mimicking my daughter's tears. Her face was contorted in confusion, wondering why I didn't give her what she needed.

Milk?

Security?

A mother's love?

Already a blurred question.

The nurse took her from me all too soon, and like a frayed seam, my heart tore apart as I watched my child's arms fling wide—searching and needing the warmth of her mother's arms, arms that lay limp against the bloodied bedsheets.

It was the hardest decision I had ever had to make.

A mistake that would never be mended.

Chapter 1

Sam 2005

Great. The killer of all joy: traffic.

The low evening sun hovered at eye level, blinding me as I sluggishly drove north on Highway 167. I snapped the visor down to block its glare before taking a reluctant glance at the clock above the dash. Groaning, I bit the inside of my cheek, a nervous habit that often left the tissue there raw. Not even a Bon Jovi song on the radio could help my mood, not when I found myself oddly relating to the lyrics of "Livin' On a Prayer": *Gina works the diner all day working for her man, she brings home her pay, for love.*

Bless Gina. She and Tommy were holding on and were supposedly halfway there, but did she ever find the silver lining after a life of struggles? Was love enough? Did fairytales persist after the prince rescued you?

"Really. What happened to Gina and Tommy?" I blurted out in the car, though no one was there to answer.

Feeling tired of living on a prayer from day to day and worried I would be late for work yet again, I flicked the radio off in a huff, gritted my teeth, and dug my nails into the steering wheel. It finally dawned on me that today—Monday, October 31st—was Halloween, which explained why there were seemingly a million cars on the road, driving at a snail's pace. I imagined droves of parents rushing to find the perfect neighborhood to appease their children's sugar cravings while I suffered in grueling traffic. I would have loved to trade places with them and go door to door saying, 'Trick or treat?' As if on cue, my stomach growled as an image of a candy bar came to the forefront of my thoughts. I hadn't eaten for hours.

To be a kid again, without a care in the world, sounded divine and dreamy. At twenty years old, I was beginning to learn that 'adulting' often meant a life without treats, and what remained was one trick after another. The joke seemed to be on me—a struggling-to-stay-afloat, full-time college student who still lived with her parents and had little to no time for adventure because she worked till midnight at a filthy restaurant run by a relentless, perverted boss. I had come to terms with attending classes and working fourteen arduous hours a day. But with the realization that my days as a carefree adolescent were over, doing grownup things felt far more bitter than sweet.

"Welcome to heaven, said no adult ever," I said, again to no one.

Adulting did have a silver lining. First, I was grateful to have a job that paid for my college tuition and helped pay for my first car, which I had long dreamed of, and proudly made a down payment a few months ago. Second, college and work kept me away from home. You'd think at twenty, I would have adjusted to my parents' determination to keep their marriage alive despite the endless screaming matches I had witnessed since infancy. But their marriage was the real reason I had wanted to grow up quickly. Adulting brought me one step closer to flying the coop and living blissfully alone in peace and quiet.

Well, not totally alone. The last part of the silver lining was Liam, who, like Gina's Tommy, only needed to hold out his hand and promise that we would make it. And I believed him. Liam was the circle that made my world round, the sane one who held me safe and whole, and the reason I bothered to wake up each day. With his lips the night before still on my mind, he was the only positive thing pushing me past that Monday, which had stolen me away from him.

Monday nights were supposed to be a much-needed night off, but I'd been forced to cover for someone who had called in sick. So here I was, looking toward the next exit, wondering whether back roads would be faster, because I couldn't be late again and risk getting fired. Making a quick decision, I swerved my baby—a 1990 teal-green Honda—onto the offramp and prayed for a miracle.

At the end of the exit, an older homeless woman paced back and forth, holding up a bent piece of cardboard that read HELP ME, PLEASE. She wore a dirty, oversized, tattered jacket with jeans that had likewise seen better days. Clearly, she wasn't equipped for Washington State's cold and wet weather. Although this was a rare dry and sunny evening, October's chill was still crisp, and temps would drop to the low forties by nightfall.

With only two cars in front of me, I thought of the woman's dire situation and contemplated what to do. I didn't know her backstory or hardships, but I suspected that 'adulting' wasn't her specialty, either. I didn't want to be late, but at the same time, I didn't want anyone to starve or freeze to death. So, with only one car ahead of me now, and the woman's pleading, pale blue eyes connecting with mine, fate and choice decided for me. As I looked more closely, I realized she had no fingers on her right hand.

I drove my car within a few feet of her before rolling down my window to hold out a few dollars. The light ahead turned green, and the woman seemed to panic, as if I would drive off before she had a chance to grab the money with her good hand. In horror, I saw her trip at the exact moment we were connecting, just as the wind picked up our hopes and dreams and blew the bills into a field behind her. As she hobbled after it with what appeared to be a bum knee, failing terribly to stop the wind from blowing our money farther away, I glanced at the clock again and cursed before pulling over and jumping out to help her.

"Here's to living on a prayer," I said to myself as I gathered flying money.

"Sorry," she said after I fetched and handed over the few dollars I could find. "I'm a veteran and haven't much mobility, what with my arthritis and this stupid stump of a hand."

Guilt washed over me. Here I was, complaining and feeling sorry for myself about school and work, when this poor woman couldn't find a job even if she wanted to. I wanted to stay and talk, to tell her I understood her disease, as I had once taken care of someone with severe arthritis. But if I stood there any longer, I probably would have also found myself without a job.

"I'm sorry for your ... your plight," I called behind me as I ran back to the car in a mad rush. "I do hope you can have a warm meal tonight. Have a blessed evening!"

My decision to take the back roads seemed the best choice. With no cars in front of me, and ignoring the speed-limit sign that read thirty-five, I tried to compensate for lost time by pushing my car to sixty. I took a glance in the rearview mirror and gasped. As often happened, between attending class from 7 a.m. to 3 p.m. and my shift starting at 4:30 p.m., I hadn't found time to freshen up in between, except for a quick change of clothes.

With one hand on the wheel, I wiped black mascara smudges from under my eyes and pulled a stick of Maybelline Sun-Kissed from my purse. Lipstick always made me feel better, making my lips look more proportionate to my other sizable features. I blamed my father for the not-so-feminine nose that seemed to clash with the narrowness of my face. I was grateful my mother had given me green-blue eyes that made me look wide awake no matter how tired I felt.

When a black hatchback appeared out of nowhere and pulled out in front of me, I instinctively dropped my lipstick to grab the wheel with both hands. It hit the floor, but not before rolling down the front of my white button-up work shirt, staining it taffy pink. I hit the steering wheel with the palm of my hand in exasperation. "Oh, come on."

I pinched the bridge of my nose and debated taking an Advil for the dull throbbing in my head, produced either by my failure to find time for dinner or the fact that I had stupidly pulled my thick, curly brown hair too tightly into a ponytail.

With the restaurant only five minutes away, I carefully used my left knee to steer the wheel while trying to braid my hair. Finished, I put both hands safely back on the wheel and looked into the mirror again to admire my handiwork. Not satisfied, I pulled down a few strands of hair to frame my face with a wispy look.

"There," I told myself, feeling slightly better. "That will have to do." When I finally looked up at the road ahead, my heart lurched forward at the sight before me.

"Shit!"

The car in front had come to a dead stop.

I gripped the steering wheel in terror and slammed the brakes to the floor with all my strength. The pedal vibrated violently, disagreeing beneath my feet, and I knew the impact was inevitable. I squeezed my eyes shut and instinctively stiffened.

The sick sound of metal on metal reached my ears at the exact moment my body slammed forward. When the airbag did not deploy, my head hit the steering wheel briefly before the seatbelt dug into my left shoulder, yanking me back into my seat with a jolt when the car came to a complete halt.

It was over as fast as it started.

The dormant headache now pulsed like an active volcano about to explode. With my eyes still tightly shut, my hand unsteadily found its way to my forehead, where I felt a bump beginning to form at the hairline. I slowly opened my eyes to look at my fingertips but felt relief when I noted the absence of red.

Before braving a look up to survey the damage I had caused, I thought of Liam's last words to me the night before. He had pinned me against the wall, giving me his best kiss yet, leaving my lips wet and swollen. "Knock 'em dead tomorrow," he said, knowing I had a stressful test that morning and had an added night shift to follow. It never occurred to me that his last words might hold some foreboding truth. So, I prayed to God no one was hurt.

I prayed no one was dead.

I expected to see my car on top of the other vehicle, but it wasn't. The momentum had pushed the other vehicle a whole body's length away from mine. The trunk had been crunched inward and cracked open a foot, with a bent license plate that was still legible. I had to reread it a few times to be sure that my head injury wasn't affecting my ability to make sense of things. Nope, it said what I thought it did: 3WYS4FN. But I doubted either of us was having fun.

I could see the male driver was talking to someone in the passenger seat. Although I had never been in an accident before, talking seemed a good sign, meaning, thankfully, no one was dead. With noodles for legs, I stepped out of my car and cringed on seeing the damage to my front end. My hood was crunched in and a few inches ajar as well. I swallowed down the sick feeling in my gut and held back a slew of emotions. My first car was one thing I had taken pride in; it seemed to prove my worth as someone who could make something of herself. But I shouldn't have been surprised. I've always been good at screwing things up.

Just as I reached the other car's front door, a skinny guy around my age with a mop of curly dark hair and wearing a baggy shirt and ripped jeans stepped out. He greeted me with vacant, saucer-like eyes, homing in on me accusingly.

And rightfully so.

"Dude, what the hell?" he said with such force it felt like a slap to my face. He threw his arms wide to display the mess I'd caused. "Really. What the hell."

"I am so, so sorry. I, um ..." I squeaked, bending forward to peek inside his car to see if his passenger was all right. At first, I thought the cloud of smoke was coming from the car, but then the smell of skunk hit me. They must have been smoking dope before I hit them. "Uh, are you okay?" I asked. "I am so sorry."

The passenger, who appeared to be the same age as his friend, glared, "Yeah, I'm fine. But what *were* you thinking?"

I wasn't, clearly, but I didn't say so. I would have gone to my grave before telling anyone I was playing with my hair in the rearview mirror before crashing.

Curly Mop in front of me rubbed the back of his neck. "So, are you gonna explain what just happened? I mean, here I was, stopped with my blinker on to take a left, and BAM."

The words were lost on my tongue as tears pooled, threatening to tumble. "I know. I am so *so so sorry*. I just assumed you would keep driving straight and didn't expect you to stop so suddenly. I wasn't paying attention. I feel … I feel just awful. *Really*."

He flared his nose, letting out what looked like a stream-line of steam. "No shit, you weren't paying attention. *Jesus*."

"What can I do?" I asked as we stood awkwardly while his friend rummaged inside the glove box. He spoke to someone on a cell phone, which I could only presume was the police.

Curly Mop crossed his arms. "Bacon is on its way. I hope you got insurance."

"Yes, I have insurance," I said. "But what … what is *bacon*?"

"Really? The pigs? You know, *cops*?"

"Oh, yeah. Of course. Sorry. This is my, um … this is my first accident. I'm not quite sure what to do."

He spoke to me as if I were a child. "Well, we are calling the cops right now to file a police report, and then we need to swap insurance, okay? Simple. But while we wait for the cops, I need to assess the damage you caused to my car."

"Right. Okay," I said, feeling like a complete loser.

We surveyed the damage to his car together. "I know my car looks like a piece of junk," he said, kicking his bumper, "but now my car *really* looks like crap. This is going to cost you."

"Sorry."

"Yeah. You've said that already." He turned to face me. "Look. I don't mean to be rude, but this is a *big* deal. My neck hurts, I have a headache already, and it looks like my car is nearly totaled. I'd be surprised if I could drive it home. And now that I think of it, maybe I should go to the hospital."

My eyes widened. "I am sorry. And I know I keep saying that, but I don't know what else to say or what to do, for that matter. Should I call an ambulance?"

He looked down at his watch. "I'll go later when I have time. For now, let's go back to our cars and wait for the cops."

"Sure."

I was relieved to be safely back inside my car and away from Curly Mop. He was obviously furious, and again, who could blame him? As I pondered what he meant about the accident being a big deal, a line of impatient cars drove around us. The looky-loos slowed to catch a glimpse of the guilty at-fault—me. I turned my face away in shame, sliding further down into my seat.

After the adrenaline wore off, I called the restaurant to tell them I'd be a tad late. For once, I had a genuine excuse. After that, I decided to call for my own backup.

The line trilled twice before he answered in his usual playful, sexy voice, "Hey, you."

Upon hearing his voice, my guard dropped, and all the bottled-up tears finally fell free. "Liam," I choked, barely getting the words out, "I got into a car wreck. I hit someone, and it's all my fault. The cops—"

"What?" His voice, sexy a second ago, was replaced by one of panic. "Samantha. Okay, okay, slow down. First, tell me, are you hurt?"

I could almost envision Liam pacing the floor as I looked in the rearview mirror to examine the damage to my forehead. I felt terrible scaring him like this, especially since he once lost a friend to a drunk driver. I may not have been intoxicated, but what I had done was just as careless.

"Sam, answer me. Are you okay?"

"There is only a small bump on my head. Nothing is bleeding."

Liam let out a long-repressed breath. "Oh, *thank God*. Okay, what about the driver? Did you check on them? Are they okay?"

"Yes, and they seem okay. But the guy I rear-ended is pissed. I mean, I would be too, but I'm freaking out. They called the cops, Liam."

"It's going to be okay. Calling the cops is all part of the process, so don't freak out. If you're not hurt and everyone seems okay, take a deep breath. Can you do that for me? Just breathe."

"Okay. I am breathing."

"Where exactly are you?"

As I relayed my location to Liam, I heard the sirens approaching and quickly sat up straight. "Liam, the cops are here. I have to go. I'll have to call you later."

When a stout man in his thirties with a bushy, upward twisting mustache approached my car, I quickly rolled down the window. His concerned eyes took me in before asking, "Ma'am. I'm Officer Ryan. First and foremost, have you sustained any injuries?"

My voice shook along with my head. "I don't think so."

"Good. And the others? Did you talk to them?"

I looked out through my windshield and nodded. "They seem to be okay, well, except for the driver, maybe. He stated that his neck or head hurt. Or both?" I rambled on, "I didn't mean to hit them. It happened so fast, and it was an accident."

"Yes. Accidents happen. Hence, why they call them accidents." The officer pointed to my glove box. "Can you please provide me with your license, registration, and insurance card?"

I couldn't stop my hand from trembling as I reached over to open the glove compartment. My life spilled onto the floor as I scrambled to find the proper paperwork. "Sorry," I said, rummaging around as more items fell to the floor: a plastic fork for eating on the run, a few tampons for emergencies, and a ton of pens for school and for writing down the patrons' orders at work. I nervously laughed, holding up a few pens, "Need some pens?" When he didn't laugh, I quickly looked down at the task at hand. "Sorry," I said, wiping my nose. "The papers are here somewhere. Is it bad I'm not sure what the papers look like? This is my first accident."

"Miss. You're flustered. It's expected. Please take your time."

When I handed him what he needed, he looked at my license and read, "Samantha Carey, twenty, born on December 19th, 1985, from Puyallup, Washington?"

"Yes. That's me."

"Says you are five-six, brown hair, blue eyes, weighing one-twenty-five?"

"Yes. Still me."

"All right, Samantha, stay in your car while I gather a full report from the other driver. From my point of view, it is pretty obvious that you rear-ended the vehicle in front of you. Do you deny this?"

"No. It was my fault."

"Do you remember your speed when you hit the other vehicle?"

"I remember driving around thirty but then slowed down to twenty-five after slamming on my brakes."

"All right. Thank you for the information. Be right back."

My mind was consumed with worry about how I would pay for the accident. I didn't have any large sums of money saved up. I had used everything in my bank account for books, tuition, and my latest car payment. While I waited for the officer to return, and to avoid a complete panic attack, I went to the one happy place that calmed all the storms in my mind:

Liam.

Chapter 2

Sam 2005

Before Liam, I didn't believe love even existed. I didn't know you could feel so much for another person that nearly every cell in your body hurts at the thought of ever losing them. It was over two years ago, at the tail end of summer, before our senior year in high school. Our worlds collided at a pivotal moment when I was on the road to disaster. I was the lost drunk girl at parties, and he was the sober knight who saved me from destroying myself.

At the time, I was taking care of a bedridden senior woman named Jane—my first-ever job—one I would never forget. She was mysterious, and at first, I believed I might be working for a murderer. But I soon found out the truth, as I became the caretaker of her secrets and she mine. Jane had demons of her own to conquer, along with a million regrets like mine. But it was Jane's stories and our unlikely friendship that ultimately led me to Liam. Jane would have called our meeting *fate*. 'Like when the stars align, the moon controls the ocean with purpose, and two hearts wouldn't dare question the what-ifs; that is called fate,' she once said.

I remembered my first real date with Liam as if it were yesterday. I was still recovering from losing Jane when Liam had an idea to cheer me up. From then on, whenever the world pressed me too far down, I would remind myself of that first date, and suddenly, I was on my feet again.

"Are you still not going to tell me where we are going?" I had curiously asked him after driving almost an hour that late September evening two years ago. The windows were down, blowing my long hair every which way, but I didn't care. Summer was almost over, and I wanted to enjoy the last bit of warm weather before fall.

He gave me a slow, mischievous side glance as he drove down the freeway into Bremerton. "If I told you where we were going, I'd have to kill you."

I was still getting to know him, but there was something about the grin on his clean-shaven face that made me want to bite his seamless jawline. "Good thing I brought my pepper spray. A girl can never be too careful," I said.

I watched his side profile muscles twitch as if he were trying to devise a clever rebuttal, but instead, he flicked a finger toward an upcoming highway sign. "Last summer night before they close the gates."

I hurried to read the sign quickly before we passed it. "Really?" I said, clapping my hands. "I've never been to a drive-in theatre before."

"I know it's a far drive from Puyallup, but when you mentioned you loved movies so much, I figured you had to experience this just once. Hence why I borrowed my dad's truck instead of driving my car."

It was near dusk, and after Liam paid the attendant sitting in a small booth, we pulled into the lot. They were playing two movies, *Uptown Girls*, with Brittany Murphy and Dakota Fanning, and some other comedy called *Grind*. "Do we just park anywhere?" I asked, looking around at all the cars aligned in perfect rows before the largest screen I had ever seen.

"Well, typically, big trucks like this have to sit in the way back. We don't want to block the view for smaller cars." After Liam fiddled with his radio to tune and sync us to the movie's audio, he exited the truck and opened my side of the door. "Ready?"

I couldn't help but laugh when I noticed that our clothing matched. We both wore white T-shirts and blue jeans, except mine had holes in the knees. I took his warm hand in mine and squeezed it. "This is so fun," I said, jumping down. "I've always wanted to do this, ever since I saw the musical *Grease*, where they all meet up at a drive-in and sing and dance."

"I hope you're not expecting me to sing or dance." He laughed. "Might ruin the night." Liam led me to the back of the truck bed and opened the top to reveal the ultimate setup—a blow-up mattress, pillows, and blankets. "So that's two dreams I've made happen for you? Looks like I'm nailing it."

I knew exactly what he was referring to. We were still only friends at that point, almost two months ago, when he took me to the most beautiful reading spot, under a willow tree beside a creek. I had mentioned that I loved trees and books, and one of the things on my summer bucket list was to find the biggest willow tree around and read underneath it. No one had ever done something like that for me. It was the first time I'd felt seen and heard.

I looked up and past Liam's tall, athletic frame before finding the gold and green in his hazel eyes and smiled. "I'd say you are nailing it. But now I feel bad because I haven't really done anything special for you. What's on your bucket list?"

Liam effortlessly lifted me up and put me down on the lowered truck gate before grabbing my legs to wrap them around his hips. He laced his fingers around my back and leaned in close to me. "Are you serious?"

I threw my arms over his shoulders and took in the smell of him. "Yeah. I want to know your dreams and what makes you happy."

Liam sighed and laughed all at once. "The moment you took a chance on me, my dreams came true, Samantha."

I cocked my head to the side. "So it was that easy?"

"Yep. Well, okay, there is one more thing that would complete my ultimate dream."

"And what's that?"

"I have yet to kiss you."

One lock of summer-blond hair just above his eyebrow fluttered in the breeze, and I moved it aside for a better look at the hypnotic eyes that had been melting me for weeks. "So, what's stopping you?" I asked.

"The stars."

I pulled back and looked up at the sky, disappointed it wasn't fully dark yet. "You won't kiss me until the stars come out?"

"Nope."

"Darn it. Patience is not a virtue I really have."

"It's not?"

"No."

Liam pulled me closer to him, and just when I thought we would finally kiss, after weeks of getting to know each other, his lips skipped mine and met my ear instead with a whisper. "Too bad. Looks like I will have to teach you the art of patience."

I pushed at his firm chest and laughed. "*You* are a tease. But that's fine." I crossed my arms. "Come to think of it, I'd like to add something else to my bucket list."

"And what's that?"

"I'd like our first kiss to come only *after* we see a shooting star. Let's see how well *your* patience lasts."

"Okay. I'm fine with that." He swallowed as if swallowing the lie before adding, "Totally doable."

"Even if we don't see a shooting star tonight?"

"Trust me. We will see one. Now, go," he said, pushing me toward the pillows. "Get into bed, and don't come out of this truck until I return."

"Wait," I said, climbing under the covers. "Where are you going?"

"Snacks. I'm going to get snacks."

I bit my lip in anticipation before asking, "What kind of snacks?"

"Chocolate, salty, sweet, you know, the good stuff."

"Peanut M&Ms good stuff?"

"Obviously."

I gave the man a saucy look. "I didn't think I could like you any more than I already do. Hurry back," I said.

"So sweets do it for you?"

"You have no idea."

"Noted."

I meant it when I said I didn't have any patience. After waiting five minutes, I climbed out of the truck and snuck to the bathroom to ensure my hair was in place. After applying lip gloss and popping in a cinnamon breath mint, I went to get a sneak peek at what exactly Liam was purchasing. I laughed when it was his turn in line and he pointed to too many snacks to buy. I had never complained about having too many treats, but I worried that I was too nervous to eat anything, knowing we would be sharing kisses for the first time.

After an entire summer of getting to know Liam as friends, I already loved everything about him. He was funny and playful and liked to banter, as did I. We were equally stubborn, often fighting over who was right or wrong, usually over the dumbest things like which route was quicker to the freeway or how much salt is too much salt on fries. And I couldn't deny the attraction, either. I initially didn't see him as anything but a friend since we could be nearly polar opposites. He liked country music; I didn't. He loved basketball; I knew nothing about sports. I loved reading; he hated it. He liked the heat on full blast in the car but it dried my eyes out. The list went on, but something changed along the way.

"Opposites attract," he had said when we finally caught feelings. And he was right. Liam was everything I wasn't. But that was the beauty of it all. He was teaching me to be more sporty. I was teaching him to enjoy rom-coms over action films. He was teaching me not to take things so seriously. I was teaching him to use chopsticks and to try vegetables for once. It was because we were opposites that I liked him so much. "I suppose we could never be bored of each other," I had told him late one evening, after talking on the phone for hours.

But now, on this first real date, Liam seemed to be all I could think about. It was a little scary, how much I liked him, and we hadn't even kissed yet. For crying out loud, I knew I was in too deep if I was too nervous to eat snacks. And because the only thing I could think about was his lips on mine, it made me wonder. Like, would the kiss seal the deal? Would the kiss reveal him to be my soul mate? What if kissing Liam felt like I was kissing a friend or, worse, a brother? What if he was a terrible kisser? Would I lose him as a friend if this kiss didn't pan out?

I was in the middle of contemplating all the things that could possibly go wrong when Liam turned around and spotted me at the entrance. He growled, "Hey. What did I say." He briskly walked toward me, and I jetted toward his truck, but he was closing in on me fast. "I thought I said stay in the truck, Missy," he called a few feet behind me.

I stopped, turned, and laughed when I saw his arms full of everything but the kitchen sink. "Well, I had to go the bathroom, so sue me."

"Don't get smart with me, or—"

"Or what?" I threatened back. It was always a game with Liam, and I loved to test him. "Also," I said, grabbing the overflowing bag of popcorn and a jumbo pack of Peanut M&Ms about to spill from his arms, "it's a good thing I came to check up on you. How could you carry all this stuff to the truck alone?"

He shrugged and nearly dropped the balanced pop and candy on top of the pizza box, which smelled divine. "I mean, you said you liked snacks, so I had to get you everything, to be on the safe side."

I shook my head. "Yes, snacks are a passion of mine, and I often hoard and hide them under my bed, but really? I can't eat all this."

"We could try."

When I noticed a steaming pretzel with cheese hiding behind the bag of candy, I couldn't help myself. I leaned in and softly kissed his cheek. "Okay. We can try and eat all this. But don't get mad at me when I get fat."

"Fat?"

Liam knew that word held a different meaning for me. I had told Liam a little about my dysfunctional family dynamics after he heard my parents arguing in the background during a phone call. Embarrassed, I joked that it was fun growing up in a home with a father who monitored everything we ate, especially my mother, because he didn't want her to gain weight. When Liam stayed silent on the other end of the line, I went into damage control and quickly tried explaining how I could never figure out my father's need for control. Whether it was because he grew up in a chaotic home without rules or just had a real fear about keeping his family in optimal health, either way, I told Liam I assumed all men would be mad if their women gained weight.

But now, at the drive-in, the look on Liam's face suggested he had something to say on the matter. Liam turned to a bench at the side of the building and piled everything onto it. Once his hands were free, he grabbed the popcorn from my hands and placed it on the bench too.

"Oh, so no more snacks now? You don't want me fat, huh?" I joked.

He slipped his thumbs into the belt loops of my jeans and wrapped his fingers around my hips before slowly pushing me toward the wall. His face was inches from mine. "Oh, we are definitely eating *all* of that. You don't go home tonight until every single bit of it is gone. And we are *not* your parents. There is no guilt here. You could eat an entire truck filled with ice cream, and I would like you more for it. Do you understand?"

It baffled me that my heart could turn to liquid at the same time it solidified, whole and healed. I swallowed. "I understand." There was a long beat before I noticed him looking down at my lips. I swallowed and glanced up briefly at the starless night sky before finding my way back to the golden caramel in his eyes that zeroed in on me. "I just saw a shooting star," I said.

His eyes never left mine as he pulled my body to him. "Liar," he breathed.

I fell under a spell of confused wonder when his lips finally claimed mine. There was an urgency in that kiss, as if the end of the world was approaching. Yet time stood still. It was a reckless fire, yet somehow, the flames were contained and harmless. I felt like I was drowning in an ocean of waves, only to realize that I could breathe underwater. I might not have seen a shooting star that night, but it was as if an entire meteor shower of colors exploded within me. And it scared me, too.

The memories of that first date all but vanished the moment my car door flew open. Liam dropped to his knees before me, and I sighed in relief as his strong hands cupped my face. "Don't ever do this to me again, Samantha," he said in a pained voice as he begged me, "Promise me."

I sat in the driver's seat and stared into somber eyes flecked in green and gold. "I promise."

He pulled me into a bear hug. "I don't ever want to get a call like that again. I can't ever lose you." His kisses reached every corner of my face and stopped above the small bump on my head. "Does it hurt too bad?" he asked, slightly brushing his lips across that tender spot.

"*Ouch*. Yeah. Just a little."

Liam's sandy blond hair tickled my cheek, and all I could think of was losing myself in its softness, anything to help me escape from the grim reality I was facing. I had no clue what the accident would end up costing me, and I didn't want to know.

"Here," Liam said, throwing his jacket over my shoulders. "You're shaking. Let me shut the door, and I'll get in on the other side." Once he hopped into the passenger seat, he handed me my phone. "You'll need to call your work and tell them you can't come in. You might have a concussion."

"No, I'm fine," I said, putting the phone back into my purse. "And I need to go to work tonight. They're short-handed. Plus, I seriously could use the extra money, especially now that this happened."

"What?" Liam's eyes turned a shade darker. "You're joking. Sam, please. I'll pay you for tonight's tips and wages. Don't go to work tonight. You just got into an accident. Don't be stupid."

"One, I am not stupid," I said defiantly. I glanced ahead at the wrecked car before me. "Okay, maybe I was stupid today, but I'm not taking your money. And honestly, my head only slightly hurts. I'll take an Advil at work."

"Why are you so stubborn?"

"Please don't be mad. I know you care about me, but please try to understand that I have no choice. Just be here for me right now, okay?"

Liam threw his head back against the headrest and sighed before facing me. "Fine. But just know, you drive me nuts sometimes."

"I could say the same," I said, nudging his shoulder.

He leaned in for a kiss, and I marveled at the softness of his full lips and how they often left me with a lulled feeling. For a moment, they had done their job, and I had forgotten my problems and my mistakes. When we reluctantly pulled away from each other, he chuckled. "Remember when I kissed you for the first time?"

I laughed, knowing he was trying to distract my thoughts. "How funny, but I was just thinking about that night before you got here. How could I ever forget that starless night full of shooting stars?"

He chuckled. "I lost count of how many we didn't see."

"Remember when the employee had to come over to your truck to tell us that the movie was over, and you said, 'What movie?'"

"Well, it's true. How could any man remember anything with those things distracting me," he said, running his thumb over my bottom lip. "But I do remember one thing. I'll never forget how, after our very first kiss against the side of the snack shack, you suddenly had the strangest look on your face before you turned away from me. I was so scared you were about to tell me that you hated the kiss and that it was over before it began."

I closed my eyes and reached into my mind, pulling my happiest memory into the light again. "I have to be honest. Our first kiss not only left me floating high in the clouds, but it scared me. I was scared of falling too hard after being so high up. Imagine feeling nothing for so long, and then one magical kiss shows you a glimpse into what forever looks like." I opened my eyes and found him staring at me. "Forever sounded scary, you know?"

"And now?" Liam asked, looking concerned, like he did that first night.

"Now, forever doesn't seem long enough. I want an eternity of kisses with you."

Liam's features softened. "Eternity sounds not nearly enough, though."

My heart hopped and skipped a beat. "I'll tell you something, Mister. If there weren't a console between us, I'd jump over there right now and— "

Liam interrupted and nodded toward my door's window. "I don't think that guy would approve."

When the officer knocked on my window, I jumped before rolling the window down. "All right, Ms. Carey," he said. "We're all set. Here is the Exchange of Information Sheet so you can call your insurance company and start the claims process." He handed me the paper and held up another. "And this is the infraction ticket for causing the collision. Unfortunately, it's my department's policy to cite all drivers causing a collision. And since you were the sole cause of this accident, you are receiving a ticket today."

"Okay. I understand."

"Be sure you turn in these forms within fifteen days." He tipped his hat. "Sorry about your day, Miss Carey. And please, in the future, stay safe."

"Thank you, officer. I will."

My head swarmed with all the information, especially when the ticket said I owed $186.

I held the papers up to Liam. "Head injury or not, this ticket is why I have to work tonight."

"Sam. Why don't you just let me pay? It's not too much."

"Please don't do that."

"Do what?"

I wasn't sure what I hated more, having no money or Liam offering to pay for things. He didn't realize he made me feel like a charity case. Liam's family owned their own business, so his worries were not like mine. Liam was fortunate to have his parents pay for his car, insurance, college, and an allowance for whatever else he wanted. I knew my parents wished they could help in the same way his parents did, but it was financially impossible for my blue-collar family, with their many debts—which were the cause of so many arguments. Securing my future was solely up to me.

"You know I hate when you offer me money, like I'm some lost cause."

"Stop. You are not a lost cause."

"Fine. But just let me do this myself, okay?" I laid my head on his shoulder. "Thank you for offering to help, and truly, you are the sweetest." His grunt indicated he wanted to argue further, but I stopped him. "Do you know how much I love you? You mean the world to me. Forever and always."

"Change the subject if you want, but just know that someday I'm going to marry you, Samantha Carey, and then you'll have no choice but to allow me to take care of you. For eternity and thereafter."

"You'd have to have a job first if you want to take care of anyone," I said, a little too dry.

Liam seemed offended by this as he leaned back and away from me. "Obviously."

My comment was meant to be playful, but I suppose there was some truth behind the dry inclination. I held onto a bit of jealousy because Liam wouldn't have to work until after college. He had no clue what it was like for us ordinary, simple folk. Sure, work and school were all I had known since I was fifteen, and I was used to that, but I didn't need him to feel sorry for me, like I was some peasant in the street wishing for a handout. I didn't need his charity, nor did I want him to think I needed him to take care of me. He would know this if we were on the same playing field, but we weren't.

"Sorry," I said. "I'm not complaining that I have it harder; I just meant you are lucky right now."

"I know I'm lucky," he said, "but don't make me feel bad about it. You know my parents don't want me to work for their business yet. They want me to focus on getting better grades while I have this partial basketball scholarship."

It was true; his parents had these hopes and dreams that he would transfer from the local college to a big university with better basketball recruitment opportunities. Liam was talented, so I understood the plan. I, too, wanted all his dreams to come true. But as much as he wanted me to stop making him feel bad for having an easy life, I didn't want him to make me feel bad for having a harder one.

"Look, I don't know why we're even fighting. So, let's not. Okay? You love me, and I love you. Now, how about we see if my car starts, huh?" We both held our breath as I slowly turned the key. When the engine purred to life, I smiled. "Oh, thank God. Small blessings." I kissed his cheek. "Okay, I gotta run. I'm already an hour late for work."

"That's a good sign," Liam said as we watched Curly Mop drive away with ease.

"Fingers crossed. He mentioned he had to go to the hospital later and that this was a big deal or something."

"It will be fine. Don't worry about him. Your insurance will take care of it all."

"I hope so. Anyway, thank you again for coming to my rescue tonight. You really are my knight in shining armor."

Liam turned to face me. "Even if I don't have a job yet?"

"If Gina worked at the diner all day, working for her man, then I think we can make it too. After all, Bon Jovi knows best."

It took a moment before Liam got it. He laughed, "So we are living on a prayer now, are we?"

"We'll give it a shot."

Chapter 3

Sam 2005

Malbec's Place was a façade. The worn-down restaurant claimed to be a high-end steakhouse, but deep down, it was no more than a prestigious poser. Sure, their twenty-nine-dollar aged Wagyu Kobe Beef steaks were all the rage, but mostly because they smothered them with such generous amounts of garlic butter that no one questioned the quality. And while the kitchen was no better than a bathroom at one of those grimy gas stations where they were always out of toilet paper and nobody washed their hands, the people working there were just as disgusting as the greasy carpet everyone's feet stuck to.

The fact that we recently had to call an exterminator when a guest said they had felt something run across their foot said a lot. But we all knew why the manager kept the lights dimmed so low, and it wasn't for the ambiance. The place was like a table with three legs. And as the management had no intention of improving anything, something was sure to give.

I walked through the back door to find one of my managers waiting for me. Kristen was relatively pretty: in her late thirties, with ringlets of chestnut hair that she wore extra crispy from the ton of gel she used. Her tall, super-toned body was a huge plus. But her smile, which never seemed to reach her eyes, fell short. It often gave her a cold, careless, and unapproachable expression.

"Samantha," Kristen said, waving her hands frantically. She hopped from one foot to the other while wringing her hands. "Oh, thank God. Finally. We are super swamped and need you out there right now, so hurry if you can. Also, Shelly's been covering your section for you, so check in with her for the run-down."

Of course Shelly would cover for me. She was the epitome of what it meant to be a selfless friend. I didn't think I could last alone at the restaurant for more than a day without her.

"Okay. But what about taking the wine quiz before I step onto the floor?"

The restaurant had a stringent policy on spirit knowledge. Servers weren't allowed to work on the floor until they knew in detail all twenty-six wines and the ten specialty drinks they offered. So, before each shift, one of the managers randomly chose five drinks to quiz each server about. We had to know what region the grapes were from, the maker, the type of fruits added, the smells, the depths, notes, and balance, and finally, which drinks paired well with what dish. Our test was like taking the SAT times ten, which always made me anxious.

"We don't have time for that right now."

I was more than relieved. Our knowledge of those drinks was imperative if we wanted to continue working there, and if we couldn't recall a drink or screwed up on the verbal test, we lost out on some good money. I was beyond relieved to receive a 'get out of jail free' card, especially after being rattled by my fender-bender.

As I stored my purse, Kristen cleared her throat. "I forgot to ask. Are you okay? I'm sorry. I should have asked you how you were first."

"No, it's fine. I'm okay. My car still drives, and so did the other person's, so that's good news." I tied my black apron over my hips and checked the pockets for all the necessary items: a pad of paper, pens, and spare cash for change. "It just sucks, is all. I guess I have to—"

"Sorry to interrupt you, Samantha, but we desperately need you on the floor. Let's talk later, k?"

"Oh, yeah, totally."

She paused before leaving the room. "Just a side note, but it's important you come to work wearing clean clothes." She pointed a sparkly-purple polished finger at my shirt. "Whites need to be white. Your blouse has pink stains on it. And fix your tie before jumping on deck, please?"

"Of course," I said, turning to the body-length mirror that hung near the back door. There was no way to get the lipstick out, but I hurried to adjust my tie and check my uniform before presenting myself to the guests. My black slacks, white long-sleeve button-up, and black tie all seemed intact, minus my brain cells. I still felt unsettled by the accident.

I quickly sought out Shelly to relieve her of my section of tables. She noticed me and nodded toward the sidebar, mouthing silently, 'Talk?'

We huddled in the corner of the dining room before Shelly's eyebrows drew inward. "Hey, Sammy, you poor thing. How bad was the accident?"

"Without a doubt, it was scary. I wasn't paying attention, and of course, it's my fault."

"Oh no."

I didn't realize how badly I needed to tell someone the truth. "Listen. I am only going to tell you this because you won't judge me, but I was looking in the mirror doing my hair." Shelly's eyes widened, and I hung my head. "I know, so stupid. I hate myself right now."

"First, you are not stupid. You had a moment of stupidity, is all. And that is why they call them accidents. But next time, you won't be distracted, right?"

"Right."

Shelly pointed to my head. "Does your head hurt? It looks kinda swollen."

"I'm not hurt too bad. The other guy said his neck hurt."

"Well, I'm glad no one was injured. Especially you. I can't lose my wing woman here in this travesty of a place."

Shelly was eight years older than me. She was a young mother with three children who often treated me as her fourth child. I didn't mind when she played the mothering role, as it never came from a nagging place. My friend always treated me as her equal, and the age gap never bothered me. We were often mistaken for sisters because we had the same brown curly hair, except hers was slightly shorter than mine.

"Oh," I said, pulling out a small bag of crumbled cookies. "I thought your kids might want these, but they got a little smooshed. They must have flown down to the floorboards in the accident, and then, when Liam got into the car, he must have accidentally stepped on them."

Shelly laughed and squeezed my shoulders. "My little rascals will eat just about anything. We can put these over some ice cream, like a crumbled cookie topping."

"Good." I looked at Kristen glaring at me from across the room, nodding for me to get on with it. "Okay, I'm getting the eye from Kristen. Quick run-down of my tables?"

"Right. So, the couple at table seventeen are eating dessert now. Table sixteen, with all the rowdy men, are about to order drinks, so it's perfect timing. Oh, and beware. They seem to have an overly flirty agenda. And the family at table fifteen is eating appetizers, with their dinner orders already placed." Shelly pointed to the hostess, who walked past with more guests. "Looks like Lydia is about to seat your fourth table."

"You're a lifesaver, Shelly."

"You would do the same for me. I got you."

Shelly was right. When we got to table sixteen, and I introduced myself as their new server, the men were obnoxiously flirtatious. "Oh, wow, boys," one of the men joked. "We've got two hot waitresses. Do you suppose the restaurant could throw in a third? One for each of us?" He laughed too loudly while banging his hand on the table, and a few guests glanced our way.

If there were such a thing as an internal eye roll, mine rolled straight out of my head. I forced a smile just before the boys ordered another round of Fireball shots. *Great.* My night would be a long one. Sure, I was used to this form of behavior, and for the most part, generous tips followed, but on this particular night, I had forgotten to take medication, and my head began to pound as the men spoke loudly at me.

Forty minutes passed before Shelly peeked her head over the five-foot wall that hid the computers. I was in the middle of entering a guest's order into the kiosk when she asked, "How are you doing, girlfriend? I wanted to make sure you're not dying on me. I keep seeing you rub your forehead."

"Surviving. But the family at table fifteen is worse than those buffoons at sixteen. The kitchen overcooked the dad's steak. I won't be shocked when they hold back my tip tonight." I let out a sarcastic laugh. "And like it's my fault. Anyway, I will ask Kristen to offer them a free dessert. You know she's too cheap to comp their steak."

As Shelly counted out change for one of her tables, she shook her head. "I wish when this happened, we servers didn't have to share so much of our tips with the crappy cooks at the end of the night. I mean, it's not our fault when they overcook the steaks. It should affect their tips, not ours."

"Exactly. Hey, speaking of back-of-house, what's Bad Rep's mood like tonight?"

Bad Rep was the nickname Shelly and I had given our disgusting kitchen manager, aka Brad Repp. The guy was a walking hormone—hitting on anything with two legs, or even a third leg, if such an option existed. He was possibly the worst manager ever.

Shelly looked behind her before returning a whisper. "Tonight, he's acting rude as hell. I don't know; I mean, why is he hitting on me again? Do I look like some desperate woman on a bad rebound?" I gave her a sad look, and she rolled her eyes. "Yes, I know I need a bad rebound, like months ago, especially after all the crap my ex put me through, but I would never get on with someone like Brad Repp."

"Same. I can't seem to shake his ickiness off of me every time he gives me the 'meet me in the back' look."

"Right? He is so gross. He actually said to me tonight that I couldn't keep playing hard-to-get and that constantly denying him was getting a little old."

I paused in the middle of entering orders. "*Ew*. Surely, he knows beefy beer guts and balding sleazebags aren't a thing women like. I mean, sure, his face isn't as hideous as his heart, and he *is* about your age, Shelly, but you're like a ten to his negative twenty when it comes to the looks department."

"Honestly, Sam, I may need to be a little more plain with him and tell him to stop harassing me."

"You should. And why wait? Have that talk tonight. But let me be there when you do this, okay? I want to see his face when you tell him. I'll be your backup support if you need it."

"You're right. Why wait for another onslaught of torture? Okay, meet me back in the kitchen around closing time?"

"Got it." I winked. I finished entering my orders into the computer while Shelly just stood in a silent daze beside me. "You're thinking too hard, Shelly. Don't tell me you're thinking about backing out now."

"I'm not," she said, sounding doubtful.

"Look, no one has ever told Bad Rep to back off. Just think. You'll be making history tonight. You'd be doing ALL women a favor."

I had never told Shelly how truly awful it was for me as well, with how often Brad approached me at work and harassed me. My friend had enough on her plate, with her nasty divorce and now being left as a single mother. If she knew all the things Brad had said to me, it would only stress her out more. Plus, I didn't want her to fight my battles because I didn't have enough guts to do it myself. I only hoped she would fight for herself and save me by default.

"The problem is," Shelly said, "he is technically our manager."

"True, but ignoring him seems to increase his antics. I think he literally gets off when we ignore him."

Shelly tilted her head. "You gotta wonder what makes him be this way in the first place."

I shrugged. "Maybe it's his divorce last year that did him in. Maybe he hates his ex so badly that he needs to degrade all of us to feel better about himself. Either way, you're the single one, and right now, you're numero uno in his black book."

"Lucky me," she sighed. "Still, I don't know."

I moved out of the way for Shelly to punch in her table's order and thought about my recent run-in with Brad. If Shelly needed a nudge to tackle our problems, I needed to at least come clean with one of my incidents with Brad. "I didn't tell you what he said to me last week."

"What?"

"So last week, he pulled me to the corner of the kitchen and asked me if I was a … " I paused to try to find any word besides the one Brad used.

"What? What did he ask you?"

"It's too gross to repeat. And I didn't get what he meant at first, so I just stood there like an idiot as he walked away laughing."

Shelly crossed her arms. "Tell me what he said."

"Fine," I said, feeling dirty all over again as I whispered the grotesque words into Shelly's ear.

She pulled away as if my words burned her. "NO-HE-DID-NOT."

"Yep. The worst part was that he asked me this in front of all the cooks, who were all too eager to clue me in on what that meant. You know that movie *Carrie*, where she stands in the shower naked while everyone laughs at her? Well, I know how she feels now."

Shelly's chest moved up and down like I'd seen her do when disciplining one of her kids after they had done the unthinkable. "That does it. I've had it." Shelly put a hand on my shoulder. "What did Liam say when you told him all this?"

"What?" I nearly yelled. I ducked behind the plexiglass and said quietly, "I didn't tell Liam. He would freak the hell out. But look, I've been able to avoid Brad like the plague ever since. So now I'm fine," I lied.

"Well, whatever you feel about it, I'm sick of it. They don't pay us enough for this crap. It has to stop. *Tonight*."

A wave of relief washed over me. If anyone could put a stop to Brad, it would be Shelly.

The wave of relief turned into a wave of guilt as the night dragged on. The knowledge that Shelly would soon be tackling this big sack of crap all alone didn't sit well with me. The memory of my accident earlier seemed like a distant dream when the clock on the computer showed ten p.m. I bit the inside of my cheek while looking over the tables to see if Shelly was nearby.

I had just finished filling all the salts and peppers on my tables and still needed to vacuum my section, along with another thirty minutes of kitchen chores in the back. The restaurant was too cheap to hire a professional cleaning crew, so we always had a ton of tasks. There were front-of-the-house chores and back-of-kitchen work, so by ten p.m., my feet felt like sausages with a heartbeat. I wouldn't be home until almost eleven.

With the vacuum hung up on the sidewall, I walked into the kitchen, where Shelly had rearranged coffee mugs and drinking glasses in perfect lines along the shelved walls above the drink station. Steam rose around her face from a crate of glassware that had just come out of the hot, oversized dishwasher. "I'm so glad this shift is over," she said, looking exhausted. "I still have to go home and make tomorrow's school lunches for the kids, and I have at least eight loads of laundry to tackle."

"I feel you. Even though I have tomorrow off from work, I still have school in the morning. I still need to study for at least two hours before bed. They say you can retain and memorize more just before you sleep, but I'm so sleep-deprived that I'm tempted to start drinking again." I nervously looked around the room and asked, "By the way, where is he?"

Only a few others remained cleaning the kitchen as I helped Shelly put away the cups, and she leaned in close. "I think Brad's in the office with Kristen. Those two are acting weird together. It may only be my imagination, but I swore he swatted her butt earlier, and she laughed. What are the odds those two are humping?"

I made an *ick* face. "If she can't see what a sleaze he is, then they deserve each other."

While Shelly cleaned out the coffee pots, I cleaned the soda fountain. When we finished, we stood side by side, making small talk inside a tiny kitchen nook where we rolled silverware into napkins. When Brad walked in, I grabbed Shelly's hand and placed it over my racing heart.

She patted the top of my hand. "Don't worry. I've decided to go easy on him."

I squinted and nodded in half understanding. "*Right*. Kill with kindness. But hey, before the kill, will you maybe not mention me at all? I just …"

"Sam, I get it. You don't have to worry."

Brad eyed us from afar. "*Ladies*. You know it turns me on to see you two roll the silverware like that." He shimmied his way over, biting his lip just before picking up a roll of silverware. He eye-measured the roll before slowly running his hands from its top to bottom. "Yep," he said, nodding with a satisfied wink, "it's about this size, too."

Shelly looked at me, and I nodded in encouragement before she kindly retorted, "Brad. I am sorry, but you need to stop being so gross. It's wearing me thin."

"Oh, come on. You don't enjoy my humor? You're single and divorced. So am I. What's the harm." He nudged my arm. "I bet Sammy here knows we'd make an adorable couple. Right, Sam?"

My nose instinctively crinkled upward before I shook my head too hard. "*Uh*, no, I don't think so."

Shelly tilted her head. "I am sorry if you can't read my body language, but us, together? That's not on the horizon. We will never be together, Brad. You are my manager, and that's all you will ever be. So … so let's stop trying, okay?"

Brad looked at Shelly cynically and laughed. "Wow. Okay. Sure." He shook his head. "What's up with you? Bad night, Shelly? Didn't get the tips you wanted?"

"No, that's not it at all. I just thought you could chill out on the comments you're always making. If I am being honest, it makes coming into work a little uncomfortable."

"*Oh, Lord*. Seriously? I'm just playing with you both." Brad elbowed me again. "Someone's in a bad mood. Sammy, help your friend out here and give her a Midol."

Shelly crossed her arms with a look that said 'killing with kindness' wasn't going to work. "*Wow*, Brad. Awesome. Just because I inherently have a vagina, you automatically go there? Just stop."

A bead of sweat dripped down the back of my neck as the air in our tiny space evaporated. I was a runner, not a fighter, and moved a few feet away to pretend to grab more silverware.

Shelly started to roll her silverware at a brisk pace. "You know something, I wasn't in a bad mood, *Brad,* until you came sauntering up in here with your sick, perverted, and degrading mind that one could only presume is working solely with your southern parts."

Brad puffed air out through his thin lips. "Shit, Shelly, when someone pays attention to you, it's a form of flattery. Obviously, you have a lot of pent-up anger from your divorce, and maybe I'm just trying to help you get laid. There. I said it."

My eyes and mouth flew open.

"See?" Shelly said, slamming her roll down. "This is exactly what I'm talking about. You know nothing about my divorce, and who I sleep with is none of your business."

"I know you ain't sleeping with anyone, Shelly. That's why I'm interested in you, and I just thought we could have fun with it. No strings attached. But now? Now you're acting like my ex."

"Then I feel bad for your ex. But let me lay it out for you, Brad. I am NOT into you, and we will *never* sleep together. I'm sorry if you got the wrong impression, but try to take note that when someone ignores you, that is a clear sign they are not into you."

Brad tossed a napkin of silverware onto Shelly's pile of finished ones. "Fine. Whatever. Your loss, and duly noted." Brad turned on his heels and walked away, but his face was as red as the ketchup bottles on the counter when he passed by me.

For some reason, I had a feeling my egotistic boss's embarrassment wouldn't slide nor be forgotten. I touched Shelly's shoulder. "You okay?"

Shelly blinked in shock but gave me a weak smile. "That was more than awkward."

"At least it's over."

"I don't know why I waited so long to set him straight."

"I have to say, watching you handle him tonight was amazing. You are one badass momma."

Shelly laughed. "I don't know about that, but let's get the hell out of here before I have to see his face again."

Everyone was sleeping by the time I walked into my parents' house. Even though the clock in my room showed eleven p.m. on the dot, I picked up the phone and called Liam. He always waited up for me to make sure I arrived home from work safely.

"Hey, you," he answered with a sleepy voice.

"Hey, yourself. Were you sleeping?"

"Yes, and no. How was work?"

"Work was blah. You sound tired. I should let you go."

"Not as tired as you sound."

I fell onto my bed, fully dressed and too tired to shower or brush my teeth. "I am so glad I have tomorrow off. Also, I'll need to figure out how to submit my claim to the insurance people tomorrow."

"I can help you after we both finish classes. Did you tell your parents yet?"

"No. They were sleeping when I got home, which is just as well. I'm too tired to get into it with them. My mom would have made some comment that I inherited my father's driving habits, and then he would have snapped back, saying that all her backseat driving didn't help me get any better. At some point, after hours of fighting, they would have forgotten what the argument was all about in the first place. So, it was a blessing that they were asleep."

"So, you'll tell them tomorrow?"

"Yeah, probably around dinnertime. I parked at just the right angle so they can't see the front of my bashed-in car." I bolted upright in bed. "I have to tell you about Shelly at work."

"Wait, tell me if your head is all right? I mean, not mentally; we all know you're a little crazy."

"*Ha, ha.*"

"But physically, how do you feel?"

"The head is fine. I told you it was just a baby bump. But a customer asked how it happened, and after I told her, she gave me a pretty good tip. So there's that."

"Still, I think you should have gone to a doctor. Anyway, go ahead; what were you saying about Shelly?"

"Oh, yeah, Shelly put our kitchen manager in his place tonight. The scene was sort of epic."

"Like how?"

"So, I may have never mentioned this, but we all call him Bad Rep instead of Brad Repp because he harasses all the women at work. Anyway, Shelly had just about had it with him, and I got to watch the beautiful scolding scene unfold from the sidelines. It was scary and lovely."

"Well, good for Shelly. But did he take the conversation well?"

"I don't quite know. Guess we'll have to wait and see."

A beat passed before Liam asked, "Has Brad ever harassed you?"

I paused and swallowed. "Not really." My lie sat heavy in my mouth, and suddenly I was parched. I knew he would be upset to learn that I had never told him about Brad's advances or that I didn't ever stick up for myself. I wasn't strong like Shelly. Growing up in a home that was more than confrontational, I had learned that sitting quietly in the background was the easier way out.

"Okay, but Sam, you said he harasses *all* the women at work. I may be partial, but out of every female there, I'd choose you every time. Makes it hard to believe he hits on everyone *but* you?"

"Well, I'm considered taken and undatable, so ..."

"Yes, you *are* taken." Liam laughed. "Sorry if I sound irritated; it's just that I wouldn't be too thrilled to know some idiot manager was making moves on you when they know you have a boyfriend. But I'm confused. Isn't Kristen your boss? How is Brad your boss, too?"

"He's like third-down on the totem pole. We have a few general managers whom I have never met. They oversee all the restaurants in the Pacific Northwest or sub for house managers who go on vacation. Kristen is our house manager, the boss of almost everyone but the general managers. And last is Brad, our back-of-house 'kitchen' manager, who deals with servers only if it has to do something with food."

"Gotcha. Still, it surprises me about this guy."

"I know. That's why Shelly took care of it. You don't need to worry."

"I believe you, but if this weirdo does anything shifty, you better tell me or your other boss."

"Okay," I said, yawning. "Look, I'm sorry, but it's almost midnight, and this has been the longest day of my life. I still have to study before getting up super early for school, and actually, we both do. I'll call you after my classes?"

"Sounds good. Hope tomorrow gets better for you. Love you."

"Love you more."

Chapter 4

Sam 2005

I woke up tempted to break my alarm. After only five hours of sleep, I questioned how much longer I could stand being the lead in the movie *The Night of the Living Dead*. By nine a.m., if someone had pulled the fire alarm in my Anatomy and Physiology class, which I was already behind in, I would have stayed seated, unmoving, and burned alive.

My longtime friend Emily sat beside me in class, wearing a pink turtleneck that complemented her lovely, long, strawberry-blond hair and green eyes. As for myself, I hadn't even had time to check if my black-and-white sweater was inside-out or not. She gently nudged me and whispered, "Long night at work again? Your eyes look a little bloodshot this morning."

Our instructor droned on about the anatomy and optical functions of the eyeball just as I rubbed my heavy blue ones. "You haven't heard? Blood-filled eyes are all the rage right now. It's fashion suicide if you are not staying up till two in the morning memorizing twenty-six pages of the eyeball."

"Pass." She laughed. "Red eyes *and* red hair would make me single forever."

"Yeah, well, then count yourself lucky. Even with all the late-night studying, it will be a miracle if my squirrel-of-a-brain can remember half of the irrelevant nonsense in this fat book."

Emily was studying to become a nurse and truly needed the class for her future, unlike me, who only wanted to have a career as a dental hygienist. The class was a waste of my time. But Emily knew my struggles and sympathized. "We can study together, if that helps you?"

"Thanks, Em. You're always trying to fix the broken. One day, you will become the world's greatest nurse. However, I doubt you'd want a study partner whose only time to study is from eleven p.m. to two in the morning."

"I don't know how you do it."

"I secretly thrive on torturing myself," I joked. "But really, what bothers me the most about this Anatomy class is that is has nothing to do with the dental hygiene program I am trying to get into. Why would someone need to memorize every bone in the body or be required to know all about the eyeball to clean and floss someone's teeth?"

"I have no idea. Many of the prerequisites seem like a waste of time and money."

"Exactly. I swear, colleges don't care about our future. It's all about racketeering, extortion schemes, and political gains." Emily's bright green eyes widened at the level of my voice, and I brought it down a notch. "Sorry. I just sounded like my father there."

"But we gotta play the game to get ahead, right?"

"Sad but true. But if the dental hygiene program wasn't so competitive to get into, I wouldn't have stress so much about trying to maintain a perfect GPA." I finished jotting down the notes displayed on the whiteboard and sighed. "The sad part is, I had a near-perfect grade-point until this class. Now, I don't know if I will be good enough to get into that program. And I certainly don't have the time or money to change careers. Plus, I don't have a plan B." I looked at my friend. "Do you have a plan B?"

"No. This is it, I'm afraid. And I get it; I would freak out, too, if I couldn't get into my nursing program after paying a few years into it. I've had this career planned since I was five and taking care of all my baby dolls, remember?"

I laughed. "I still remember coming over to your house for the first time in the seventh grade. When I first saw you had a row of dolls sitting at the end of your bed, I was ready to question your maturity level. But then, when you pulled out a serious tray of pretend needles and said you were practicing how to draw blood so you could be a nurse one day, I knew you were going places."

Emily laughed. Thanks to you, you became my first alive patient, besides my parents."

"Well, it was a good tradeoff—me, pretending to be your blood donor in exchange for you hinting to Carter Morgan to ask me out."

"Those were fun times."

"Yeah, but look at you now; you're two years closer to becoming the best nurse in town."

When our instructor paused and glanced in our direction, we turned to the next page in our eighty-pound book with foreign title called, *Vitreous Humor*, except there was nothing humorous about it. I silently cried inside when the following picture showed twenty-one labels of a diagrammatic view of the eyeball.

With the instructor's back to us, I leaned into Emily's ear again. "This is a bunch of jibberish. I can't even pronounce some of these words."

"True. But are you almost done studying? We only have three days left before another big test."

I swallowed after flipping through the thickness of each chapter. "If they say perspiration and perseverance go hand-in-hand, I'm sweating profusely. I've studied my ass off, but I don't think my brain can contain this much info in just two days. I need at least one or two more solid weeks to get an A." I shrugged. "Truthfully, I'd probably be a head a little further on the weekend if it weren't for the lack of concentration at home."

"Your parents fighting again?"

"Let's just say if it weren't so cold outside, I'd go out to my car and study in there."

"Can you study at work?"

"No. Work is too busy and crazy to study. I often wonder how other people maintain full-time jobs AND go to school and *still* get a 4.0."

"I wouldn't know. If it weren't for my scholarships, I'd be in the same chaotic boat as you."

"I wished I had worked a little harder in high school. A scholarship would be great, right about now. But if anyone deserved a scholarship, it was you. Do you remember Martin Solinsky?"

"Yeah. What about him?"

"Your nose was so flat into a book all of high school that when you walked on stage at graduation, I overheard him ask someone, "Who is that?""

Emily smiled. "Yeah, my social calendar was non-existent."

The teacher grabbed a plastic eye model and passed it around. When the thing came to me, my fingers were like butter, and the egg-like puzzle slipped through my hands. It landed on the floor, scattering pieces all around my white Converse high-tops. Emily tried to help me pick up the pieces off the floor, but I waved her off. "It's okay, Em. I think I can put this together myself. How hard is it to put Humpty Dumpty back together again?" Everyone patiently waited for me to assemble the pieces for passing around, but I finally had to give up. "Here, take it, Em," I said, feeling like a fool. "This class is going to be the end of me."

Emily put the parts back together with ease before asking, "Why don't you look for another job? One with fewer hours?"

"Because there are no other evening jobs." I wiggled my eyebrows. "Unless I sell myself on the side of the road."

"Yeah, but you'd have to like what comes with that kind of trade."

"You mean, a ton of money?"

"No. Syphilis, Chlamydia, genital herpes, gonorrhea, and several other venereal diseases."

"It's not a terrible trade-off," I joked. "Anyway, an evening restaurant job will have to do. I need the money to pay for my car payments, insurance, school, and books. And on the bright side, I won't go into student debt. I know all too well that debt is one of the major arguments between my parents. They fight like two badgers in a barrel, and I am determined to be nothing like them."

"Well, school and a job has left you with a ton of stress *and* has left you without a social life. That's not good for your mental health. So, how about to help you release those happy endorphins, you, me and Heidi meet at the Trellis Café for lunch today, instead of eating in the cafeteria?"

"This is why I love you. You are so smart."

My favorite restaurant made you feel like you were eating at Grandma's house. With walls covered in pink and yellow flowers, lace doilies, delicate teacups, and an array of delicious finger sandwiches with homemade scones smothered in sweet Devonshire cream and jelly, I'd be the first in line at the Trellis Café if they posted a room-and-board sign out front.

I sighed happily when entering through their antique door. The bell chimed, alerting Minnie, the establishment's eighty-year-old hostess, that a customer arrived. She smiled before waving me in further. "Hello, hello, Samantha. It's been a while." She nodded to the back and gave me a warm, wrinkled wink. "I sat the girls in the back corner, where you normally sit."

"You're the best, Minnie."

Minnie adjusted her lace-collared blouse, crooked underneath her pink knitted sweater, and frowned at me. "You look skinny, hon. Are you not eating? I tell you, all that running around you kids do. I couldn't keep up if I tried."

"I'd say you could keep up with me. You get plenty of exercise running around here, Minnie. You are my idol. But to make you happy, how about I order a whole BLT sandwich instead of a half." When she didn't look satisfied, I tried again when I saw what was listed on the chalkboard. "And I'll add a cup of potato-carrot soup with a fat scone on the side."

"That's my girl," she said, pinching my cheek.

I found my friends deep in conversation, with their heads together. I couldn't help but note how totally opposite the two were, not only in appearance but also in personality. If Heidi was piss and vinegar, Emily was a catheter full of sugar. Emily, the green-eyed strawberry blond, stared intensely into Heidi's conspicuously dark, cat-like eyes that complemented her signature sleek, 1950s-style black bob with bangs. My girls were the butter to my scones. I had met my wild, fiery, and untamable friend Heidi in third-grade camp. As for sweet-tempered and innocent Emily, whose sunny disposition reminded me of a basset hound, we had been friends since junior high.

I slipped into a honey-colored chair with a floral blue and yellow cushion and asked, "Heidi looks like she swallowed a canary. What's the scoop?"

"Oh, I was just informing Emily about the recent—Matt and his *apparently* new girl."

Matt was perhaps my best friend—well, until Liam. One could only assume we naturally grew apart the moment I fell hard in love with Liam, which unfortunately, had happened not long after Matt confessed that he had loved me ever since the seventh grade. It had been a little awkward for my boys to be in the same room ever since. Still, I could honestly blame my distance from Matt on us attending different colleges, work responsibilities, and me making Liam my top priority. Did I feel bad? Yes. I honestly missed Matt. But things had changed and where we were now was out of my control. Life happened. We were adulting now.

I asked, "Who's the recent girlfriend now?"

Emily filled me in and then added, "Heidi thinks he is serious about this one."

I laughed. "Matt? Serious? Since when is he serious about anything?"

"Exactly!" Heidi took a sip of her black coffee, which matched the look of her entire ensemble from head to toe: black combat boots, black tights under a black skirt, and an oversized black sweater. The only color on her was her lips which now stained the rim of her coffee cup. "Really," she said, "they barely know each other. Did he mention this girl to you, Sam?"

"Oh, are we not speaking her name?" I laughed. It made sense why Heidi was irritated. She was the only one that still hung out with Matt at parties, ever since I took the sober journey. The two seemed good buddies after I had introduced them two years ago, so if Matt was busy hanging with someone else, that left Heidi bored. "It's been a month since I spoke to Matt, so no, I don't know of her," I answered.

"I haven't heard anything either," Emily confessed.

"It seems this skank has her claws in him, and we don't even know if she is good for him," Heidi grumbled. "You two should find out more."

"Well, I'm not worried about it. I'm really happy if he has found someone special," I said.

"I suppose you don't care about your best friend anymore, now that you have Liam." Heidi patted my leg. "Have you and Liam, you know ... changed your mind about doing the nasty?"

Having already explained myself to my nosy friend plenty of times, I rolled my eyes. "Sorry to disappoint, Heidi, but no. We're still holding out until marriage."

She rolled her eyes. "Yes, I know, I know. The born-again virgin. Still, it's just weird you are, quote-unquote, 'holding out' when you two have already done the deed."

Emily came to my defense. "I don't think it's weird. Don't listen to her."

"Thanks, Em. I am glad *one* of you understands. But yes, Heidi, we *technically* did do it once. But what's so wrong with me wanting a fresh start or having something sacred and meaningful to look forward to?"

Heidi slowly stirred her Coke. "I'm not saying it's a bad thing. It's just so ... so boring. I just think it's a waste of time when clearly you both want to jump each other's bones. I see how you two act around each other, so I can't understand all the torturous waiting."

"Well, you are not me," I said.

"Nope. I'm more like *Goldilocks and the Three Little Bears*. I need to make it my life mission to try out all the sizes until finding one that fits *juust* right."

"You're sick," Emily laughed.

I shook my head and laughed, too. "Girl, you do you. But to put it in perspective, and by the way, my choice has nothing to do with religion, because no little piece of legal paper will change how Liam and I feel about each other. Besides, I feel like we are already married. I love and want no one else but Liam. But the truth is, waiting makes it special when the big day comes. Plus, ever since my mission trip to Mexico two years ago, I'm on a new path. No more parties. No more drinking. I just want to feel good about myself. I like having control over who I am."

"Sam ... no fun," Heidi said, pointing a black polished finger at me.

I crossed my arms. "Hey, even if I am still trying to figure out who I am, I'm still fun. Well, okay, maybe not fun lately ever since adulting. But that's just it. I don't want to end up like my chaotic combative parents. Sure, they say they love each other, but every impulsive decision they've ever made has brought them closer to their demise: debt because using a Visa helped pay for everything during hard times; two unplanned pregnancies because they lost control; jobs they hate because now they have kids to support. The list goes on. Plus, sex wasn't in the cards with my last boyfriend, so why change that now? And even if Liam and I slipped up once, I regretted it mostly because it shows I didn't have control or willpower. So, what does that say about me?"

Our food arrived, and Heidi took a bite of her quiche. "Who's to say you can't control yourself again? Like, all I'm saying is, don't beat yourself up if you two mess up again. No one is perfect."

"No. I get it. Believe me, the waiting is hard, especially since I know Liam is 'the one', but this goal of mine is not impossible." I blew on my soup before taking a bite and swallowing. "I just want to follow through on my goals for once in my life. Plus, I think waiting makes for a stronger foundation in a relationship. I want Liam to be my forever, not a maybe-for-now."

"I don't see anything wrong with goal setting, Sam," Emily said. "I mean, look at me, I have chosen books over boys. I'm still a virgin, and I really don't care what anyone thinks about that."

"Emily ... no fun," Heidi said, pointing a finger at her. "Seriously. How am I friends with a non-drinker and two supposedly-virgins?" She shrugged. "Whatever. I'm in both your corners as long as we can be done with these boring speeches." She picked up a pickle and waved it in my face. "And for the record, I was only thinking of poor Liam. All that waiting has got to be getting *harder* and *harder*."

While Emily nearly choked on her iced tea, I shook my head at my friend. "Will you put that thing away before you assault someone?" When Heidi took a gruesomely large bite of her pickle, I had to laugh. "You know, I worry for whoever marries you, Heidi. You are going to eat him alive."

"But of course," she said with a wicked laugh.

Emily pulled her long hair back into a ponytail before taking hold of her sandwich and then zeroed her green eyes in on Heidi. "Speaking of men, Heidi, have you mentioned to Sam how you might be interested in someone?"

"No. Because like I mentioned, he is off-limits."

"Oh, *so* mysterious," I said. "Please tell me who the guy is so we can warn him about what he's getting himself into if he goes your route."

"All I can say is that he is way more fun than you two bores. But it doesn't matter. He is off-limits."

"Married?" I asked.

"Something like that. Now, look. Let's talk about anything else but mine and Emily's loveless lives. I'm over it." She looked to me. "Anyway, Emily mentioned it will take weeks before they fix your car?"

I was shocked that Heidi didn't want to discuss a guy with us. She was the most open-ended book I had ever read. The girl could talk with her grandmother about sex positions and one-night stands without missing a beat. But if she didn't want to talk about this one mysterious guy she liked, then I didn't want to push her. Heidi was scary when backed into a corner, so I didn't push further. "I had planned on fixing my car, but since I desperately need it for school and work, I've decided I'll have to fix it in the future. It runs fine."

"Wow. You go years without a car, and just when you finally can afford one, you wreck it." Heidi patted my shoulder. "Your tombstone should read, Car Problems."

"Yep. Story of my life."

Spending my only day off from work to deal with my first-ever insurance claim went something like this: "So to clarify, you weren't paying attention?" asked a stranger named Jan. "May I ask what you were doing?" asked nosy

Jan. "And he said his neck hurt?" Jan questioned in a foreboding tone. "Well, then. This doesn't look good," snapped judgy Jan.

I hung up, wishing Liam was home from basketball practice to cheer me up. And because I had a few hours to kill before I broke the news to my parents about my accident, I drove to Alice's—the senior Jane had asked me, just before her passing, to befriend and visit. Fulfilling my promise to Jane was easy enough, since Alice always put a smile on my face. And I never let too many days pass between our visits. For one, being seventy-eight, Alice wasn't getting any younger, and I knew all too well how life was fleeting. And two? It was simple. I had grown to love Alice as I once did Jane.

I first met Alice in the nursing home where Jane had lived, but when Alice's arm healed, she was able to move back home to her tiny rental. She lived north of me, alone, on a ridge called Milton. It overlooked the town where I resided, a farming valley called Puyallup, Washington. It was a compact, charming town with a long history as home to a Native American reservation and a forty-five-mile river that flowed from the glaciers on majestic Mount Rainer, of which Alice had a pretty view. When Alice realized I lived down in the valley, below her hill, she said she was practically my guardian angel, winking down at me.

And one could describe Alice Clark as an angel—a sweet, pure-as-they-come, seventy-eight-year-old woman with a heart of gold—who came straight from the quirky side of heaven. If an evil murderer came knocking on her door, she'd probably only hit him over the head with her Bible before inviting him in for a snack and leading him straight to Jesus in less than five minutes. And I especially loved how she often switched out first names with adoring pet names instead, like 'soul', 'love,' and 'child.'

The woman also had an infectious laugh, often cracking up at her own jokes. She never took life too seriously. And, unlike Judgy Jan at the insurance company, Alice was someone you could talk to without an ounce of discomfort. Not only was she a good storyteller, but she was also a great listener. It was as if Alice's mission in life was to bring others peace, love, and joy. Come to think of it, there was no one like Alice Louise Clark.

I pulled into Alice's driveway and parked in front of her small beige Rambler. Her home lacked luster; it looked deserted from the outside, but not because we were nearing winter, with oak and maple leaves blowing all around, but because Alice lived a very simple life, almost like a nun. They say a home is a reflection of who you are, but that wasn't true for Alice. The outside of her home reflected the inside—homely, dull, nothing too extravagant—which I found odd since Alice's spirit and inner charm embodied every color of the rainbow. I once asked Alice why she didn't decorate or liven up the place, and she simply replied, 'Child, those things are merely worldly things and bring me no joy. Nothing in this world compares to the treasures of heaven.'

A spare house key lived under a rock by her front porch, so I let myself in. "Alice? It's me," I called out.

It was futile, and I suppose a form of habit that I announced my presence at all, since my friend was deaf in one ear and partially deaf in the other. The first time I'd visited her at her home, she told me not to bother knocking or ringing the doorbell because she couldn't hear me even if she bought the world's most advanced hearing aids. Her current ones were outdated and didn't seem to work at all sometimes. I once asked why not buy an upgraded pair, and she waved that silly notion away, saying, 'Because if the Lord planned to heal me, he would have done so already.'

So, while we all waited for Jesus to heal Alice, we had to yell back and forth like we were at some overly crowded football game rooting for opposing teams. It was one thing for me to have to scream for Alice to hear me, but for a while, I couldn't figure out why Alice was yelling at me in return. I finally figured it out. Alice was like many who spoke too loudly while wearing headphones. She just simply couldn't hear herself talk. I often left Alice's with a headache, a hoarse voice, or both, but it was worth it. She made me laugh, and I loved her.

I found Alice sitting in her green electric-powered recliner, watching one of those Christian channels playing twenty-four hours of praise and worship. She looked like a gracefully aged Rapunzel, with her stark-white braided hair that hung past her hips because she believed God didn't want us to cut our beautiful hair. The bright, blue-eyed woman was tall, too; five-foot-eight with size eleven sock-feet that always hung past the recliner's footrest. And with a sturdy, thick middle, she walked as if on a mission to save the world.

Alice didn't see me enter, nor could she hear me, but I stood momentarily and admired her peaceful, content smile as she bobbed her head side to side, singing along with the gospel choir on the television. I knew she could barely hear the television, but she watched intently and mimicked every single person's facial expression, copying whatever mood was depicted on the screen.

The corners of Alice's eyes must have finally caught me inching forward, so as not to startle her, but she froze before promptly laughing. "Land sakes, dear child. You startled me."

I laughed before shouting, loud enough for her to hear me, "I wish you could hear the phone ring or the doorbell, Alice! I'd hate to give you a heart attack whenever I come around unannounced."

"No, no, love. It's always a good surprise to see you." She tapped her chest with her good arm. "Besides, this heart is gonna tick till I'm a hundred. You watch and see."

Like I said, when I first met Alice two years ago, she shared a room at a nursing home with Jane. Although unlike Jane, who was there permanently, partly due to the part I played and still had much guilt about, Alice was only there to recover from a fall that injured her right shoulder. But even after rehabilitation, two years later, Alice still claimed her arm was stiff and some-times useless. Other than that, Alice proudly lived alone and, surprisingly, managed to care for herself quite well.

She waved me in to sit down. "For Pete's sake, come sit and wrap yourself up with that there," she said, pointing to a tattered tan blanket. "Why is it every time I see you, you have no coat on?" I grabbed the quilted blanket and wrapped it around me as Alice continued, "You know it's nearly winter, right? Where I came from, in Canada, now *that* was cold. If I left the house without a coat this time of year, my father would have my ears, he would."

"What did you do for fun in Canada if it was so cold all the time?" I asked.

"What didn't I do? As a kid, I loved everything that started with the letter 'S'—swimming in the summer, and skiing, and ice skating in the winter."

"Wow. You were active. I like skiing, too, but not so much swimming or ice skating."

Alice wore a finicky hearing aid only in her "good" ear. She tried to adjust it while the apparatus made a loud, high-pitched scream. "Dang, this thing! Whistles for no reason." She fiddled with the gadget before asking, "Tell me what's going on in your neck of woods down there. You staying out of trouble?"

Oh boy, where to begin, I thought. "Well Alice, in a nutshell, I was stupid and got myself in a car wreck yesterday. And it was my fault."

"*Oh dear.*"

"I know. If Jane was still with us, I could almost see her shake her head, saying, 'Have you learned nothing about my accident? If you don't care about the little things in life, it will all spill over into the most important.'

"*Ah*, that woman. She would say something like that."

I smiled, thinking of Jane; a bittersweet smile, if anything. Whenever I thought of her, a pang of regret ached at my ribcage. There were so many things I would have done differently if I had known what the nursing home did to one's spirit. But I tried not to dwell too much on that. I couldn't go back and fix it, so, I tried to remember all the good memories over the bad. "I miss her. I miss Jane wagging her finger at me," I told Alice.

Alice smiled. "I know you do. But I'm sure grateful she introduced us before she left. You've become like a granddaughter to me, dear girl."

"Thanks, Alice. I am grateful, too."

"As for college, well, it's hard, but I'll get through it. I love my Literature class. Writing is a favorite of mine, but this year, they forced me to take an Anatomy and Physiology class. It's pretty intense. There is a lot to study, but insufficient time because of work."

"I'm sorry. I do hope you catch a break, child."

"Yes, a break *would* be splendid."

"I'm sorry, but did you say, *suspended?*"

I laughed and wondered how much of what I said she actually heard. I tried again, but louder this time, and slower so she could read my lips, "I said, *splendid*."

"Blended?"

I yelled louder, "No, *splendid*."

Alice gritted her teeth when her hearing aid acted up again. "I'm about to throw this thing in the trash."

"Maybe it needs a new battery?" I realized, like always, it would be easier if she talked rather than trying to decipher what I was saying, at least until her hearing aid worked properly. And because my friend loved to tell stories, I asked her, "Alice, if you don't mind me asking, is there a story behind why you lost all your hearing in that one ear?" I pointed to her ear and spoke slowly and clearly, "What happened? How?"

She stopped fiddling with the useless apparatus and instead, placed her hand on the ear where she was deaf. She rubbed her ear softly, as if the memory alone made it ache. "I suppose I lost my hearing because of meanness, inconvenience, and a trumpet."

Chapter 5

Alice 1923-1937

I don't like to talk about folks in a negative light; it's not my nature, but I always wondered how a person acquires such meanness. Is unkindness something folks are born with, like some inherited trait that descends upon each generation unbidden, or is it learned simply in the form of example? Perhaps we all have a bite in us, and it becomes more prominent amongst those faced with life challenges that leave them with little room for self-control. I'd like to believe a person's reaction is never caused by one thing alone. No, I think my father's meanness must have come from all the above reasons.

Let me clarify: Daddy wasn't a terrible father who beat us every day. For the most part, he was a decent, giving, and loving father. But he had a mean streak that appeared out of nowhere if a forgetful child egged him on. I don't think my pa's hardness came from his father, though, as I remember my sweet Grandpa Albert and how he used to sit on that store's front porch where he rocked us in his unique chair, singing to us kids while he fed us freshly picked strawberries dipped in Grandma Nora's thick whipping cream.

Maybe my father's lack of patience and stern discipline came from my grandmother. Grandma Nora was a stickler for obedience. I can remember that for sure. Of course, most children learn lessons by making mistakes. But my grandmother always ensured you received double in whatever lessons needed learning, like that icy cold winter day when I didn't heed her warning not to go outside during a snow flurry.

Doing nothing was hard for my six-year-old self. Having to sit there idly while watching all the fun happen through a big-picture window was like waiting for Christmas morning. My eyes cast anxiously upward in awe at the thousands of tiny, soft flakes falling from heaven, and before you knew it, I was sneaking outside for a quick adventure. As fun as the snow was, my regret came later when I tried to come back inside the house. The front doorknob froze itself stiff. You should have seen me panicking, thinking, 'I can't let Grandma see me out here! She'll have my ear!'

I'll never know why I thought it would be a good idea to melt the doorknob with the saliva in my mouth, but you could imagine my fright when my tongue stuck to that frigid iron handle like glue. The icy doorknob peeled the top layers right off my licker like a newly skinned chicken before supper, and you'd think that was a lesson in itself for a little one like me. But Grandma Nora wasn't satisfied. My tongue wasn't the only thing that got skinned that day! Now, I'm not trying to make excuses for folks who hurt and discipline children too harshly; still, maybe my father was severely strict at times because he never had the opportunity to experience life as a child. I'm sure Grandma Nora made sure of that.

My father, Joe Aldworth, grew up in Waterloo, Ontario, Canada, with a town population that, at the time, was a little over 2,000. Yet, as small as the city was, he kept busy working at his daddy's grocery store, located just on the outskirts of town. He had worked there since he was a small, skinny boy of five, right up into his teen years. But one of my father's skills included playing the trumpet, and this gave him the idea to quit working for his unyielding mother and travel from town to town, playing for his supper while also giving him the chance to meet someone special.

Of course, playing the trumpet town to town didn't leave him much money to save up, so Daddy settled in British Columbia, in the southwestern part of Canada, where he worked for a logging company along the Powell River. There were plenty of times when my father's thoughts floated down the river along with the logs, with daydreams of falling in love.

Because my daddy was an excellent jazz musician and singer, the town band hired him to play the trumpet on his nights off. One night, my mother, Helen Grey, saw eighteen-year-old Joe Aldworth playing in the band. She said she fell in love at first sight, even if my father wore two different-colored socks that evening. They got married in the backyard of Grandad's apple orchard, with Daddy singing to his bride:

It's just an apple-blossom wedding,
Underneath the sky above.
It's just an apple-blossom wedding,
I wed my apple-blossom love.'

Soon, my parents moved back to Kitchener, Ontario, next to Waterloo, where they had my sister and brother. But in 1926, it was in Unity, Saskatchewan, where they chose to have me. By the time I turned eleven in 1937, and after many life struggles, the Great Depression forced us to move to another small city called Flin Flon, in Manitoba. Flin Flon was built on a rock and was mainly a mining town that offered many families secure jobs mining zinc and copper. This place was my favorite because of its name. The city inherited its silly nickname from a fictional character in a book, Josiah Flintabbatey Flonatin—what a tongue-twister! I crack myself up whenever I try to say that name three times.

When I think back to my childhood, I don't remember exactly when my father's mean streak came to a head, but certainly, the Great Depression played a part. Most kids don't see all the things adults struggle with on a daily basis, but I suppose that with three kids to support, having to work a dayshift and play in the band in the evenings to earn extra cash, well, my father was pretty stressed and tired.

And yes, Joe was strict, which made us kids relatively well-behaved. We knew better than to cause a stir or ruffle any feathers, especially after one of Dad's long workdays. We learned to tread lightly when he was in a foul mood, like we would on the spring ice of Lake Athapap. But sometimes, no matter how good you were, you might find yourself on thin ice without a good reason. I lost my hearing late the night my father arrived home to find an unexpected guest at our dinner table.

Earlier, on my walk home from a friend's house, a gentleman asked if I was the daughter of Joe Aldworth. He said he knew my dad from elementary school and that they were old pals. We chatted a bit before I had the grand idea to invite the nice man over for dinner and surprise my father with a visit. I thought my actions were most hospitable, assuming Daddy would be thrilled.

My father acted politely during our late dinner and seemed in high spirits as he strolled down memory lane with the fellow. His friend asked him to play a song, and he kindly obliged. As I looked around the cheerful room, I was so proud of myself for orchestrating this special occasion for everyone.

If I could, I would have patted myself on the back for such thoughtfulness. By the time the gentleman left, the moon was high, and the hour pushed near midnight. We were all spent. But none more so than my father, who was exhausted after a long day.

Dad's true feelings about the situation surfaced immediately after the man's departure. He pulled me to the back room where he polished his trumpet. "Why did you do that, Alice?" he asked. The muscles in his jaw worked overtime, and his eyes narrowed. "Who said you could invite strangers into my home? Do you pay the bills?"

Of course, I was taken aback by his calm coldness and tried to defend myself: "I'm ... I'm sorry, Daddy. I thought you'd be happy he was here. He said he knew you, and you two were old pals from school."

"Who cares if someone *thinks* they know me, girl. You don't just invite whoever you want. This is *my* home. I decide who to allow inside." His ears turned red, and his voice grew tighter. "Tonight, I had to waste my time entertaining and feeding a man I don't even know. And as for your mother, she went without a full portion of dinner just so there was enough to go around."

"But I thought—"

I wasn't expecting his short fuse to blow like that, and I wished afterward I had moved quicker when my father picked up his trumpet by the handle. As he struck me heavily with it on the side of my head, the solid blow felt like a bomb exploded. As pain ripped through my ear and blood dripped from the side of my head, I saw a million musical notes dance before my eyes.

"The problem was, you didn't think. That was the problem, you stupid girl."

I discovered days later that the man I invited over was a stranger just looking for a handout. But because my father couldn't quite remember if he knew him, he just played along instead of being rude. Either way, the infection I got in my ear lasted days, but I didn't speak of it nor complain, not once. I knew we didn't have enough money to see a doctor, and it was what it was. I lost my hearing from it, and from that day forward, it never returned.

But I did learn a valuable lesson, one I continued to learn throughout my life. One may never quite know where a person's meanness stems from, so it is better to second-guess yourself when making decisions, because what you think might be suitable for all may be a terrible inconvenience for some.

Chapter 6

Sam 2005

Alice shrugged when she noted my reaction to her story. "It's fine, dear. That was a long time ago. I've forgiven him."

I blinked a few times before asking, "Was your father always that mean?"

"Oh, no. What happened was a rare incident. But one I'll never forget. How could I? Whenever my hearing aid acts up, it's tough not to think about that unfortunate event that night long ago."

"I'd have a hard time forgetting such a thing, too. Did he feel bad, at least?"

"Dad wasn't perfect. Sometimes, people do things they regret, and I knew he regretted his actions by the way he tried to make up for that incident many times. Like the generous gifts on my next birthday, when he bought me a wristwatch and a bike. I don't know where he got the money, but after the Great Depression, he never worried about splurging on us kids. I knew he loved us."

"Well, I am happy you still have some hearing left in the other ear."

"Barely. This ear competes with the other and wants to give up on me, too." She laughed.

"Speaking of birthdays, when is yours?"

"November 19th, 1926. I will be seventy-nine!"

"Oh, my birthday is on the 19th, too. But next month, in December."

"Is that so?"

"Since your birthday is in nineteen days, how about I come by right after school and bring you something special?" I knew not to bring houseplants to Alice. I had once bought her an indoor African violet like the one Jane gave me, thinking it would bring a little color to Alice's living room, but the poor potted plant died the next month. So now, I don't buy her house plants.

Alice raised her hand. "No, no, no. I don't want you to spend your money on frivolous presents. Use the money on yourself; you need it, dear."

"I don't work until four-thirty that Saturday when it's your birthday, so maybe instead of a gift, how about I pick us up a late lunch? You can't balk at a little snack."

"Well, I never say no to a good meal!"

"What's your favorite food?"

"Oh, let me think. All right. Do you know of the Thai restaurant by Safeway? They have the best walnut prawns. Let me give you some money for that."

"No. That's okay," I said. "I want to buy *you* something for your birthday, so let it be, and let's focus on celebrating you!"

"I wish you wouldn't spoil me, Sammy girl. But all right. Just this once."

I stayed with Alice as long as possible to avoid the inevitable with my parents and hoped it didn't turn into an argument. When I arrived home, I peeked around the kitchen corner to find my mother busy cooking dinner while my father sat on a stool a foot away, reading a motorcycle magazine. "Mom, Dad?" I said before fully stepping into the room.

My parents were both nineteen when I was born and had just turned forty the year before. Having such young parents has its advantages and disadvantages. The good was that both my parents understood my generational struggles, since it wasn't so long ago that they made the same stupid mistakes. The drawback was that they often acted shocked when I messed up—as if they thought I should have learned from their past messes.

My mother stood over the electric range, stirring something. When she tucked a shining strand of light brown hair behind her ear, I noticed she must have recently highlighted it with shades of caramel and blond. She glanced up with pale green eyes that were complemented by her new look. "I'm making one of your favorites, Sammy."

I started with compliments. "Love the hair, Mom." She smiled as I looked inside the pot of split pea and ham hock soup and took a big whiff. "This smells amazing."

She covered the pot with a lid and threw open the oven. "And, look, I even made your favorite homemade drop-biscuits to accompany dinner."

"Wow," I said while bending down to take a peek. "I don't know if I quite deserve any of this amazing dinner, though."

My father set the magazine down on the counter. "What do you mean? You're not hungry? Because that would be a first."

"No. I'm starving to death; it's just that, well ... yesterday, before work, I got into a little fender bender." While both my parents gasped, I hurried to go on, "And, yes, the accident was my fault, if you're wondering. I wasn't paying attention to the car in front of me when his car stopped suddenly, and it all just happened super fast."

"Oh, my God." My mother quickly set the soup spoon aside. "Were you or anyone else hurt? Why didn't you tell us yesterday? Why didn't you call me?"

My father's eyebrows drew inward. "Yeah, why are you only telling us this news now?"

I went into damage control and explained everything as best I could before my mother lightly let into me, "So you say you've got it all under control, huh? Well, fine, but either way, this whole thing bothers me, that you couldn't tell me sooner or even wake me up last night."

"I'm sorry. I just didn't want you to worry and then be unable to go back to sleep."

"Next time, wake me, please. I'm just glad you and those you hit weren't hurt."

My father stood, pointing to the front door. "All right, let's go outside and see the damage you caused to your new car."

Just as we headed outside, Liam pulled up in his black truck—a birthday gift from his parents a year back. The red Mustang he drove in high school didn't suit his tall frame, anyway, and I told him so after he borrowed his father's truck on our first date, saying, "This truck looks sexy on you."

"Is this a good time?" Liam asked when he made his way over to me.

"Just told them the news," I whispered in Liam's ear while my father checked under the hood. "They aren't freaking out like I thought they would."

"That's good to hear."

We watched as my father closely examined the car while mumbling sarcastically, "You did a number here, girl. The whole front end needs replacing.

Good thing you have insurance." He sighed and shook his head. "I'm going inside to eat and try and forget about all this. I don't have the energy to deal with this."

Liam kissed my cheek. "Surprised to see me?"

"Yeah. Don't you have basketball right now?"

"Practice ended early, so I thought I'd pick you up and take you to dinner."

"*Ugh.* So sweet of you, but my mom just made my favorite. I don't want to leave and make her more irritated at me, so let's eat here and save a buck. Then go for a drive after?"

"All right. Deal."

We needed a relaxing drive to digest the most amazing dinner my mother cooked. I rested my head on Liam's shoulder and closed my eyes while we listened to the playlist he'd made for me. It was labeled SAM'S PMS PLAYLIST, which, even though it wasn't that time of the month, it suited me fine, especially after dealing with the tense atmosphere at the dinner table. I had a feeling my parents' sudden silence was about something other than my accident. Per usual, I imagined that while Liam and I were outside, my father had said something to my mother like, "How many biscuits are you going to eat tonight?" Either way, I was glad Liam drove me out of there before an argument could ensue.

"Do you want me to go anywhere specific?" Liam asked as we drove around aimlessly. "Or we could stop and get dessert somewhere?"

"You know I'm like a ninety-year-old after eating—lethargic and comatose. Plus, I'm too stuffed to eat dessert. Could we just drive to Decoursey Park and snuggle? Listen to music?"

"Sounds good to me."

The park was across the street from Clark's Creek, where my sister Stephanie and I used to splash around when we were children, fishing for crawdads during the summer months. But now, the place had a different feel, one that offered privacy to young adults like Liam and me, seemingly stuck between worlds, still living at home when we were more than ready to move forward as adults. After high school, Liam and I had talked about moving in together and getting married right away, but his parents insisted we both finish college before heading down that road. That was hardly what we wanted to hear—being told no as adults—but Liam felt he needed to concede to their wishes since he was their only child and didn't want to disappoint them. I didn't make a fuss about it. I knew that, either way, one day we would marry and grow old together.

After Liam parked, we climbed into the backseat so we could snuggle more comfortably. He covered my legs with his jacket and asked, "Better?"

I rested my head on his chest and sighed, "Perfect." It was already dark, and our only light came from a streetlamp a yard away. I stared at its soft glow and pondered our future. "Liam, when we get our own place someday, do you think we could buy an oversized plush couch with an ottoman so we could stretch our legs out and do this every night? And maybe one of those heater blankets that you can plug in to stay warm while we watch old reruns of *Friends?*"

Liam brushed a fallen loose curl away from my eye and tucked the strand behind my ear. "All right. that all sounds like a reasonable request." He took my hand in his and examined our entwined fingers. "What else would we have?"

My fingers softly roamed in and out of his splayed palm while I thought about his question. "Maybe in the backyard, we could string little lights across a basketball court so you could play ball at night with our kids. We could put my piano in the living room, and I could play some of the songs I made for you?" I said, looking up at him.

Even in the low light in the car, his eyes seemed to flicker when I spoke about our forever future together. "I'd like that very much. And maybe we could have a dog named Ralph?"

I laughed. "Ralph?"

"What? You don't like the name Ralph?"

"Not to hurt your feelings, but no. What about Ollie or Chewy, if it's a little Chihuahua? I like the idea of a small white dog with a grey-blue nose."

"Chewy sounds cute. But I thought we'd get a great big husky with different-colored eyes, like you."

"A husky? You know they shed like crazy, right? And being that I'm a clean freak, I don't know if I could handle all that hair everywhere. Remember my Aunt Lucy, with her yellow Lab? Every time I left her place, I felt part Lab myself with all that hair sticking all over my clothes."

"Fine. A little dog will do. But promise me no cats."

"No cats." I laughed. The music played on low, and after a long, silent thought, I asked, "Liam? Wouldn't it be amazing if we were there already?"

"Where is there?"

"Married, in a place to call our own, and with a little white dog named Chewy?"

"Yes. Anywhere with you sounds amazing. It will happen one day. I promise."

A Montell Jordan song came on next, and I rolled my eyes and laughed before quickly sitting up to change it. "I can't believe you purposely added this song to my PMS playlist."

Liam pulled me back so I couldn't switch out the song. "But it always makes me smile. Plus, who doesn't like the one and only Montell Jordan? 'This Is How We Do It' is a classic, for your information." He sang along to the song just to annoy me. "I know you secretly like it."

"Oh yes, I just *love* songs that are sung way out of key the entire time," I said sarcastically.

"Did it ever occur to you I play Montell Jordan's songs because I, too, sing out of key, and if the artist is singing out of key and we all are singing out of key, then you can't make fun of me?"

"I have never made fun of you when you're singing," I scoffed.

"Oh, really?" He folded his arms, looked forward out the window, and pouted. "Don't think I don't see you make that squinty face of yours every time I'm singing a song."

I scratched the side of my head and sucked in my lips guiltily. "Okay, so I've noticed you sing a little off-key. It's fine. No biggie. I still love you."

He faced me again. "Then say you love Montell, too."

I laughed. "You're joking. You seriously want me to say I love Montell Jordan?"

"Affirmative. Say it now, or this," he said, waving a finger between us, "*we* can't work. I can't live my life knowing you hate hearing 'This Is How We Do It.' Because if you don't love how I do it, how *I* sing, maybe we aren't a match, Samantha Carey."

I knew he was playing with me just to annoy the crap out of me, but I played along anyway. "You're really gonna make me say it?"

"Say it now, and *maybe* I will reconsider marrying you."

My mouth flew open, and I let out the biggest laugh. "Oh, so if I don't say what you need to hear, all bets are off?"

"That's right. And don't think I'm joking."

I glared at him, bit my bottom lip, and hesitated long enough to make him think I would risk our future together before saying something so ridiculous. "You, kid, are one sick weirdo," I finally said before caving. "Fine. But paybacks are a bitch. I don't know when, but you might regret this one day." I rolled my eyes and blurted it out as fast as possible, "I love Montell Jordan. There. Happy now?"

"Wow. It doesn't sound like you love him *or* me. That was pathetic. Can you say it a little louder?"

When I tilted my head and raised my eyebrows, indicating I would do no such thing, he opened his door in a threatening manner, like he was about to leave me. It was a pathetic attempt. I grabbed his arm. "*Stop.*" I cleared my throat and swallowed before I cupped his stupid face, which I adored too much, with both hands. "I. LOVE. MONTELL JORDAN. And I love this stupid song. And I love *you*, Liam Becker. Tone-deaf and all, I love all of you."

He shut the door, seeming partly satisfied. "Then, if you truly love me, and you love Montell Jordan, will you allow me the honor of singing this song to you?"

If I laughed at him now, the charade would only continue longer than I could manage. It was easier to suffer what came next rather than fight the urge to roll my eyes once again, so I smiled sweetly at him and widened my eyes big-like to try to stop the tears of laughter from spilling out at him. "Please. *Please* will you sing this song to me, Liam? I would love that so much."

"I thought you'd never ask," he said, leaning forward and over the console to turn up the volume enough to make the windows shake. The worst part was how he started the song all over again, just to torture me.

My cheeks hurt by the time he was finished with the loud and theatrical display of rapping and off-key singing—if you could call it that. I grabbed my ribs. "Thank God that is over," I cry-laughed. When he gave me a half-squinted glare as if questioning my comment, I hurried to remedy it. "I mean, thank God that is over so I can do this ..." At that, I gave him a juicy, saucy kiss just to shut him up. There was only so much I could handle of these little fun games Liam liked to play.

"Maybe I should sing more, if these kinds of kisses are my reward."

"Let's not."

"Oh, I nearly forgot. I have a small treat for us," he said, leaning forward between the front seats.

"*Ohhh*?"

"Don't look until I give it to you."

I sat back and closed my eyes while I heard him digging inside his console. "If it's chocolate, I'm yours forever."

"Maybe. But why you gotta ruin the surprise?"

"Because I'm impatient. Also, whatever the surprise, may I ask how long it has been sitting in your console? Is it old? Because I'm not eating anything old."

"No. It's new, I promise. Found it." Liam sat back next to me. "Okay, now open your eyes." Both of his hands were behind his back. "Pick which hand. If you choose wrong, you'll just have to watch me eat them all."

I didn't even know what 'them all' meant, but I had a sixth sense when I was in the same room as chocolate. "No way!"

"Well then, choose correctly, and you won't have to suffer."

I bit the bottom of my lip before tapping the top of his left hand. "Okay, that one."

A playful smile reached his eyes before he showed me his empty hand. "Bad deal for you." He held out the other hand. "Guess these Peanut M&Ms are all mine to eat."

He went to open the bag, and I lunged for it. "Give me half, or I will murder you."

"Sorry, Sam. You lost the deal."

"You are really on one tonight."

"Only because I like you feisty."

Typically, Liam wasn't the ticklish type, but because I needed that chocolate stat, I had to try anything. I flung forward and dug my fingers into his flesh, only to find myself out of breath without the results I needed. "Why are you never ticklish?" I asked, totally dumbfounded.

"You mean ticklish like you?"

His fingers barely touched my ribs before I screamed and begged him to stop. "Okay, okay! You know how much I hate to be tickled. It's the worst form of punishment. If I had a choice to be eaten by a shark or to be tickled to death, I'd choose the shark every time."

"Well, you started it. How about another kiss, and then you can have a treat? But only one."

"Like, I get one piece of chocolate for every kiss?"

"I'll take that deal."

My glare accompanied a smirk before I huffed, "Fine. I'll oblige."

Liam opened the bag and held out a shiny red one. "Okay. I'm ready for that kiss."

My quick peck to his lips was over in a millisecond. "Okay, gimme," I said triumphantly.

"Um, no! That was a lousy kiss. I expected something just as sweet as this chocolate," he pouted.

"Hey. You didn't specify *exactly* how good the kiss had to be. That's on you." When he didn't look like he would budge, I succumbed. "You are testing me with all your ultimatums tonight, but I will oblige on this last bargain." I slid my body slowly up his before hotly breathing in his ear. "Prepare for the best kiss of your life."

"Oh, yeah?"

"Yep, although you may not survive it."

"I'll take that chance."

I gave it my all because, hey, it was chocolate.

The kiss lasted a long minute, and I laughed when Liam sat back and blinked as if in stunned silence. "That good, huh?" I asked him. "Now give me one of those chocolates before I clock you."

Liam rewarded me with one well-deserved candy but then quickly demanded, "Now hurry and chew that. I'm ready for the second kiss."

"I'll take my time, thank-you-very-much," I said, allowing the M&M to melt in my mouth ever so slowly.

He thrummed his fingers impatiently on the backside of the seat. "Seriously? I need to develop better contracts when making deals with you." When I finally chewed and swallowed, he crossed his arms. "Done yet?"

"I guess," I said coolly.

Without waiting, Liam's hungry and eager lips reached mine.

The kiss was different this time. As our tongues lazily tasted traces of velvety, rich, salty, and sweet, and the kiss deepened, it left my head spinning high above my body, lost in a place of space and time where no amount of oxygen could bring me back down to earth, which was fine because it was too dangerously good to come back down.

The second M&M never came.

There was no oxygen in a world of need and want. Liam tore at my shirt while I fumbled to unbutton his. Our hands roamed over each other with desperation for a long while before I took an agonizing pause to peek outside the window. Luckily, the glass glistened in a blur of condensation—blocking anyone from seeing us inside.

"Liam," I said, practically begging.

His hair was sticking up in disarray, and his eyes remained closed as he kissed my neck. "*Hmm?*"

"I think I'm dying."

His lips found my ear. "Me too. But in a good way."

"So, do you think, maybe ..."

He opened his eyes and asked, "Maybe what?"

"*You know.*"

He kissed my bottom lip. "Sam. Did anyone ever tell you it makes you almost irresistible when you pout?" He laughed after I attempted to make a long, sad, sulky face, like my sixteen-year-old sister Stephanie often did whenever she needed money that my parents couldn't give. "*Oh, no.* You can stop all that. I said your pout was *almost* irresistible. But if you're asking what I think you are asking, unfortunately, I'll have to decline. I made a promise to you, remember? You said, and I quote, 'Promise to hold me to my word, even if I say I am dying.'"

I sank into my seat. "I did say that."

"That you did."

"But it's just ..." I sat up quickly. "Well, maybe we can rethink that whole deal? We love each other, so what the heck are we waiting for? Heidi is right. This is so stupid."

"You're only saying this now, but you'll regret it later. I *know* you."

"*Ugh.* Why are you the sensible one right now?" I joked. "And I did warn you at the very beginning of this relationship that I was impatient. This was bound to happen."

He smiled and handed me my shirt. "Look. Don't get all whiny and make me regret taking you to our favorite spot." Liam pulled my face close to his to lighten the mood. "I *will* marry you, in less than two years, and we will be happy that we both waited. Two years will come faster than you can blink an eye. I promise."

"Not fast enough," I said while blinking excessively to prove my point. "No, but really, will you be honest with me?"

"Always."

"Is it enough that we don't? I mean, are you at all a little irritated by the notion, because, quite frankly, I am regretting this whole decision, and Heidi seems to think I'm a weirdo loser for coming up with the idea to wait."

Liam took a long sigh. "Look, I know this is hard; trust me. You are so freakin' hot, Sam. But it's okay. *I'm* okay. I only want to be close to you, just like this. I promise we don't have to be any different, and I don't need anything more. So stop worrying about me. Besides, we have something to look forward to when we get married, right?"

"Yeah, I guess."

"How about another M&M? Will that help?"

I playfully rolled my eyes. "I suppose that will suffice. But just to warn you, I'm so irritable that I may bite your finger off."

Chapter 7

Sam 2005

I hated Wednesdays as much as I hated celibacy. Since I worked Wednesday through Sunday, my Wednesdays were like everyone else's Mondays. After a long day at school, I hurried home before my work shift started to meet the insurance adjuster, but by the time he left, I was almost three minutes late to work.

My boss, Kristen, met me at the back door. "Sam. This can't keep happening. You are late again." She shook her head. "I'm sorry, but I will have to write you up the next time you come in late."

I didn't even bother to tell her why I was late. It was a futile point.

Kristen continued, "Also, just FYI, the sea bass special is 86'd."

At least half of my customers would be disappointed, so I asked, "How could we run out of the bass before the dinner shift?"

"Brad made a minor mistake and forgot to order the fish for the next shipment. It's a setback, but we'll expedite it for tomorrow's dinner. For now, steer the people towards the chicken if steak isn't an option."

"Okay."

I spotted Shelly near the condiment station, wiping her trays down. "Hey, Shelly. Did you hear they 86'd the bass?" When Shelly looked up at me, I noticed the rims of her eyes were red. "*Whoa*. What's wrong?" I asked.

"It's nothing."

"Shelly. You've been crying. Tell me what's wrong."

She whispered, "Meet me in the bathroom ten minutes after you set up your area for dinner. I don't want anyone to hear me."

I never worked so fast to set up my section. After polishing the wine glasses, setting the silverware out, and rearranging my section, I quickly went to the bathroom to find Shelly. I only had five minutes to spare before my boss would be quizzing me on the wine test, so I hoped whatever was bothering Shelly wouldn't take long. I was already on thin ice with Kristen.

Shelly was the only one in the bathroom when I shut the door behind us and asked, "Okay. Tell me. What's happened?"

"You just missed a shit show before you got to work, Sam." Shelly's chin quivered. "I was standing at the counter, waiting for the cook to put some extra sauce into a ramekin, when Brad came up beside me. I could tell he was already in a foul mood."

"Probably because he messed up big-time and forgot to order the bass for tonight."

"Yeah, maybe. But anyway, when the cook handed me the alfredo, Brad asked what the sauce was for. I told him an early-bird customer complained there wasn't enough sauce on their pasta. Brad got all bent out of shape and was like, 'You're going to charge them for that extra sauce, right?' And I was like, 'No. Why would I, when the chef didn't put enough on the pasta in the first place?'

Then Brad lost it. Like, Sam, he *lost* it on me. He freaking just started yelling at me in front of everyone, saying, 'If everyone asked for a side of sauce, Shelly, and no one charges for it, then the back-of-house budget gets all effed up, and that is *my* responsibility!' Then he said, 'If you don't charge them for the sauce, I'll have to write you up and then take it out of your paycheck.' I was so mad that he was being unreasonable that I was like, 'This is so silly, Brad. Their pasta is dry.' I mean, the argument was so dumb, Sam, but then he says, 'God, do I have to explain everything to you? Just do what I asked, and don't argue with me.'"

"I have a feeling there's more."

"Oh yeah. Brad literally took the sauce from my hand and slid it across the counter. The ceramic smashed into the wall and made a mess everywhere before he got in my face and said, 'Now, go and tell your customer there is a charge for the sauce. And someone clean up this effing mess!' I mean, his face was so red that even the veins in his neck were sticking out. And for what, Sam? An extra side of sauce?"

"What the hell, Shelly? That's not cool."

"Sam, I'm telling you, I know why he's treating me this way. He wants to embarrass me as much as possible because I embarrassed him in front of you the other night."

"Why does this not surprise me? I had a terrible feeling that he wouldn't let it slide."

"Right?"

"*Ugh.* What a freakin' lunatic. I am so sorry, Shelly. If I had been here, I would have grabbed Kristen and told her he was losing his shite out on you for no reason."

"That wouldn't have done any good. Kristen and Brad are like best buds lately. Haven't you noticed?"

"I guess, but what are you going to do now?"

"I already ordered another side of sauce and just paid for the sauce out of my pocket. I didn't want the customer to get all mad at me with a charge that makes no sense." Shelly wiped her eyes. "I can't believe I'm letting him get to me this much. You must think I'm pathetic."

I pulled Shelly into a tight hug. "You are not pathetic. You are an amazing, smart, single mom raising three kids on her own and hustling to make ends meet. You're just worn out and don't deserve Brad's constant bullcrap. Look, stay your distance from him. He obviously needs time to get over the rejection and learn how he is a level-ten loser."

"Yeah, a loser who is out to get me now." Shelly pulled a list out of her pocket. "But hey, here's a cheat sheet of drinks you'll be tested on tonight. And beware, Kristen may ask if you know the Black Cadillac and the Whiskey Wild specials. I think she threw that one at me because she's bored."

"Thank you," I said, taking her cheat sheet before grabbing her by the shoulders. "Now listen to me. You go back out there with your head held high, and don't let this low-life maggot get to you, you hear?"

I was grateful for Shelly's cheat sheet after skimming over it. My brain had already forgotten two of the cocktails on it, and if the drinks weren't already stressing me out, I now needed to avoid Brad at all costs, especially if he was in a blood-sucking, sabotaging mood. I didn't want to get in his line of fire tonight, or ever.

Kristen found me as I exited from the bathroom. "Sam. Ready for your test?"

For a split second, I thought about purposely failing the test so that I could go home, but I needed the money, and I needed to help keep an eye on Shelly. "Sure," I said.

After I passed the five-minute test, Kristen gave me a thumbs-up. "You get the green light to work the floor."

"Lucky me," I said under my breath.

Five minutes later, the hostess sat my first customers—an elderly couple just in time for the Early Bird Special. They were adorable and had me laughing, but I worried about Shelly in the back of my mind. I hurried and put their order in at the kiosk before making my way to the back kitchen to grab the cute couple's soup. My heart dropped when I saw Brad standing alone near the kettles of soup. I couldn't avoid him even if I tried.

"Sam," he said with a heavy bite.

I stood beside him but tried to avoid eye contact as I grabbed the spoon inside the kettle of chicken noodle soup. "Brad," I said in return.

Brad interrupted me in mid-pour. "Wait. Make sure you don't grab so much of the solids from the bottom."

Darn it; he caught me. I always grabbed the chunks of meat and veggies at the bottom for my seniors. I replied, "Okay," before adjusting my portions.

Brad wasn't satisfied. He scooted closer to me while his hand covered and coaxed mine for guidance. "Here, you want to grab some of the chunks at the bottom and then add the broth at the top. We don't want to be left with just broth at the end of the night and have none of the hearty stuff left for our late-night customers."

"*Oh*. Gotcha," I said, feeling incredibly awkward. I could finally breathe when he removed his hand from mine, but his eyes watched my movements closely as I carefully filled the next bowl. Some of the soup's broth splashed onto the counter, and I cringed.

Brad pulled out a kitchen towel that hung from his waist. "Here. I've got it. I don't mind when things get a little wet," he said, slowly wiping the counter for me. I stood silently, cutting fresh bread to accompany the soup, all the while wondering if he was registered as a sex offender. "So. You still dating that boyfriend of yours?" he asked.

"Liam? Yeah."

"You two have dated for how long again?"

"*Um*, almost three years."

"You ever get sick of him?"

"No. I like him just fine."

As Brad leaned in, he glanced over his shoulder before whispering close enough that his lips touched my hair, "You know you're top ten here, right?" I remained silent in our uncomfortable proximity while he continued, "I'm just saying, maybe you need someone a little older, you know … like, to show you what you're missing."

I wasn't scared of him, but still, I instinctively took a step back at the implication of his words while trying not to make a face of pure disgust. "*Uhh*," I said, clearing my throat with what sounded like an uncomfortable cough/laugh. "I'm not missing out on anything. But thanks."

"Hey," he said, grabbing my wrist when I tried to give him a wide berth as I passed. "Don't be too quick to say no, because I'll tell you something." He rubbed his rough thumb in circles over the thin skin on the inside of my wrist. "If *only* you gave me a chance, girl, *mmm mmm*," he said, shaking his head and licking his lips. "The things. I would do. To you."

The contents in my stomach wanted to exit my body, and I was sure my face was the color purple when I nearly dropped my tray. But what was worse was Brad's sick smile that gloated in unadulterated satisfaction. I looked around me to see who had just heard him, but everyone seemed too busy to notice anything amiss. Was this man bored or just joking to get a rise out of me? But I knew better. He actually thought there was a chance that I would take him up on his offer.

I would have to add this one to the long list of gross things Brad had said to me. And sure, for all the times I couldn't stomach the way Brad made me feel, I wanted to tell him he was scum beneath my feet. It would have felt so cathartic to get that off my chest, but I couldn't find the courage to say anything at all. I wasn't ready for a full unpacking at the moment with all that had been going on at home and school.

But, oh how badly I wanted to quit my job at that very moment. I wanted to tell my sick idiot of a boss to go screw himself. And I wanted so badly to slap his face, just to feel an inkling of satisfaction. But I did none of these things. Instead, my verbal rebuttal seemed to stall and die in my mouth as I stood there looking incapable, weak, and pathetic. The least I could do was tell him I wasn't interested, not now, not tomorrow, and not ever in a million years, but I didn't say a single thing when Brad brushed past me, laughing at me as I stood there in a dazed stupor, stuttering over the words that never made it past my lips.

At that moment, I realized what was worse than having little to no self-control. It was having zero willpower to fight and stick up for yourself.

And I was disgusted with myself.

When another server came to grab a bowl of soup, pulling me from my unconsciousness, I quickly tried to shake off Brad's words, though they seemed to embed themselves beneath my skin like a million eight-legged, blood-sucking ticks. My recovery was only superficial; internally, his words left my mind slimy with the dirty images he so badly wanted me to imagine.

And I needed a shower.

A ten-hour, scorching hot, soapy shower.

I don't know how, but I somehow managed to carry my tray of soup and bread out to my customers with a plastered-on smile. When finished, I quickly looked around to find Shelly and found her standing over the kiosk alone, plugging in an order. She had been through a lot with Brad already, but I needed to get the ick out of my system before I died.

"Shelly. I think I might throw up," I said quietly.

Shelly stopped typing mid-order. "Oh, no. Did you eat the artichoke dip that was left out? I told Ian he should throw it out."

"That's not it."

"Okay. What then?"

"Brad has apparently gotten over his rejection from you and has now moved on to someone else."

"Oh, great. Who's the lucky girl?"

"Me."

"*No.*"

"Yes."

"But you have a boyfriend, practically happily married. He knows this."

I swallowed. "Yeah, but it didn't stop him from saying what he just said."

"Tell me what he said *exactly*."

I repeated Brad's exact words and watched Shelly's face contort into what looked like rage. "And I just froze and stood there like an idiot, Shelly. It's like I have a disease. Analysis paralysis or something."

"Analysis paralysis?"

"I just made that up, but it's where I know I need to take action, but I can't because I overanalyze and overthink everything to the extent of paralyzing myself."

"Well, you need to take a pill for that disease. You should have immediately thrown the hot soup in his face, Samantha."

"I ... I wanted to, but his remark threw me off. I couldn't find my voice at that horrifying moment. Even if I could go back, I'm still not sure what exactly I'd say. I mean, he is a terrible boss, but still, he's my boss. It's not like I am scared of him, but—"

"But you're too scared to do anything because you need this job."

"Yes. I don't want to risk losing it by saying anything."

When Shelly shook her head at me, I looked down at my notepad with a long order I should have put into the computer five minutes ago. "Shelly, I'm not like you. I'm too embarrassed to say anything. Liam was right—I'm a wimp when it comes to sticking up for myself. When we were skiing last year, a man completely knocked me over, and I nearly busted my knee. When we saw him at the bottom of the hill, he looked at me without saying sorry, and it was Liam who had to put him in his place. I can't fight my own battles. If I had a few shots, maybe I could, but I don't drink anymore. Besides, if I say anything, Brad's just going to treat me like crap, like he's doing to you right now. I can't handle him flipping out on me in front of all these people."

Shelly gently gripped my arm. "I love you, but if you don't do anything about it, I will. This is *not* okay, Sam. It's one thing when this dirty thirty-year-old targets someone like me who is eight years older than you, but I am NOT okay with him talking to you like that."

"What would you have me do, then?"

"You don't have to do anything. I'm going to Kristen about this. I have had it with how he treats all of us girls here. We're like pieces of meat to him, and he's using his power as a manager to get away with his disgusting behavior."

"Look, I know you want to help me, Shelly. I know you are sick of his crap as much as I am. But can we just hold off a while before you go to Kristen? Just wait a bit before we go this route?"

Shelly shook her head at me again. "You are just prolonging your own torture."

"I know. But please, just let me think about it before doing anything rash."

"Well, don't think too long. Otherwise, Brad will keep saying and doing whatever he damn well pleases."

"Okay." I tried to lighten the mood and bumped Shelly's shoulder with mine. "I love that you would go to bat for me. You're like my real-life Babe Ruth."

"Yeah, well, I wish more than anything I could hit Brad with a 96-mile-an-hour curveball right in his soft spot."

"Same."

For the rest of the evening, I avoided any possibility of finding myself alone with Brad again. I knew Shelly was right and that we should tell Kristen before it got worse; otherwise, he would most likely continue to torture me *and* others with his sick innuendoes. On the flip side, if I said anything, my job was at risk, which left me with an uneasy feeling in my gut. And like any trapped bird in a rose-thorned cage, it didn't matter. Whatever direction I chose to fly only left me pained without an exit.

It was late when I arrived home after work. After taking a longer shower than usual, I called Liam to say goodnight before he went to bed. Unlike him, I still had three hours of studying for the upcoming Anatomy test. I would be lucky to be in bed by two in the morning.

"Hey," Liam said, answering the phone.

"Hey, yourself," I groaned after massaging the bottom of my right foot.

"You sound tired."

"Just a little. It's eleven, and I still have three hours of studying. I'll be dead for school tomorrow morning." I lit a pine-scented candle next to my bed, hoping the forest smells would bring me to another place in time altogether.

"I feel bad for you, babe."

With the lighter still in my hand, I flicked it on and off. "Hey, I have an idea. Do you want to have a bonfire tonight? I have a lot of kindling," I said, glaring at the books on the floor. My eyes were already heavy, and I knew it would be hard to see the words on the pages.

"Kindling?"

"Never mind." I contemplated telling Liam about what my sick boss said but decided against it. Instead, I flung myself onto my bed and asked sarcastically, "How was your evening playing ball with the boys?"

"It was fine. Look, you sound tired. Want me to call you tomorrow?"

"No."

"Well, it sounds like you had a rough night, and if so, I'm sorry. But hey, if it makes you feel better, I bombed tonight's game against Highline. My shots were poor, and our defense sucked."

"Oh, I'm sorry," I said without any emotion.

"And then, because I was so mad, I was driving home a little too fast while turning my wheel up that really tight corner by my house and ended up skidding my truck into the ditch. Now I have to replace a tire and fix a dent."

"*You* have to fix it?" I scoffed. "Or do you mean your parents will pay for everything, and you can just go on your merry way?"

"What's your deal, Sam? I can just let you go if you just wanna talk tomorrow."

I exhaled deeply, wishing I could sleep for two weeks straight. "I'm sorry. I am just tired and irritated."

"Irritated with me?"

I couldn't stop myself. "Am I irritated that you losing a basketball game and running into a ditch that you technically don't have to pay for will probably be the biggest problems you will ever face? No. I am not irritated about that. I am actually happy you don't have to have real struggles like most of us. But it just proves how different we are, and it makes it hard for me to have any sympathy for you at times, which then makes me feel like a shitty girlfriend."

Liam let out a long sigh through the phone. "You're right. My problems are nothing compared to yours, and I'm blabbing on about a flat tire. I am sorry I said anything, and I'm sorry for being tone-deaf. You've obviously had a bad day, and I—"

"Stop," I said, feeling like an ass. "Don't be sorry. I'm sorry. I'm the one being spiteful and jealous. I just wish I were you sometimes."

For a moment, I quietly stared at a galaxy of stars, aka the tiny asbestos popcorn bumps that coated my ceiling with glitter. My parents had long wanted to resurface our old 1950s ceiling with something more modern and health-conscious, but I always fought them. I liked counting the infinite constellations that occupied my mind whenever my parents fought in the room beside mine. But now, the glittering stars above me took on a whole new meaning. The largest of the textured fibers that clumped together seemed to triple in size like large, round mounds, reminding me of my building problems.

Finally, I asked Liam, "I don't suppose you'd wanna run away to a simple, faraway place with me? There's a movie coming out in December called *Narnia*, and from what I gather, all we have to do is open a closet that will lead us to a magical snow-covered forest. You can build a fire for our tiny cabin while I forage for acorns, chestnuts, and wild cranberries. Can you make that happen for me? Pretty please?"

"Or, we could just head to a tropical island where we won't freeze to death?"

"Okay," I said. "As long as it's anywhere but here." I pretended to smooth out the ceiling with a wave of my hand, imagining that I could start over fresh. "Or we could magically disappear—start over—start fresh. You know, like a clean slate of new beginnings—no mounds or problems to suffocate us."

"Sam. Either you are super tired, or something's wrong. I know you." When I said nothing, Liam tried again, "Talk to me. Why are you irritated?"

Before I knew it, I sat up and spilled the beans. While I paced the room, which grew hotter by the minute, I didn't realize how upset I was until my rant included a full two years' worth of Brad's womanizing rap sheet targeting me, Shelly, and every woman that worked with us. When I finished, and the end of the line went silent, I thought I had lost my connection to Liam.

"Hello? You still there?" I asked.

"I'm here," he said, sounding far away.

"Well, did you hear everything I said?"

"Oh, yeah, I heard what you said perfectly clear. I'd like to know why I am just *now* hearing all this?"

"Well, I—"

Liam interrupted, "Scratch that. Because, more importantly, do you plan on doing something about it? Like reporting this asshole to the higher-ups, or at least having your friend Shelly do it for you, like she offered?"

I hesitated before answering, "I'm not sure yet, Liam."

"You're not sure? Did I hear that right? Sam, you better do something about it, or I will," he threatened.

I didn't like his tone. I had never done well with anyone telling me what to do. In fact, it made me want to do the complete opposite. "Liam, don't make me regret telling you everything. And for your information, what you are suggesting is not that easy, and I don't—"

"Not that easy? Bullshit. All you need to do is walk into your main boss's office and tell her that your kitchen manager is a full-on, level-ten perv. He's getting away with sexual harassment, Samantha."

"You don't think I know all this? Liam, you have to see the bigger picture. What if Kristen doesn't believe us? Or what if Brad only gets into a bit of trouble and continues working alongside us? Or, even worse, Brad finds out I turned him in, and then he is out for my blood. And there is no way I could continue to see his stupid face after that."

"Then quit. Why do you want to work for them, anyway?"

Again, it was just like Liam to have no clue about the real world. He knew nothing about real struggles. I took two deep breaths, but I knew my next words would come out snarky no matter how much I loved him.

"Quit? I'm sorry, but I don't get the luxury of having my *parents* pay for my car, insurance, *or* college. So you see, I have no choice, Liam. Since I pay for everything myself, I can't just up and quit my job. It's too risky. Unlike you, I have responsibilities and pressures you will never understand."

"You act like you could never find another job. Restaurants are probably hiring all the time."

"Not for fine dining, they aren't." I pinched the bridge of my nose while wondering how one person explains the ins and outs of work life to someone who has never held a job. "Fine dining positions are hard to land, Liam, especially one that is so close to my home and college. I'm already late to work most weeks. I'd have to drive forty-five minutes to an hour if I wanted to find another fine-dining restaurant. Secondly, I can't make the money I make at Malbec's Place compared to some regular local dinky restaurants where you wear hats and sing "Happy Birthday" every two seconds. And last but not least, let's not forget my recent accident that may or may not cost me money I don't have. So, no, I can't take a pay cut right now."

"Fine, then. But do you want to know what *really* needs to happen, Samantha?"

"Enlighten me, since you sound like you have all the answers."

"I come to work with you and beat the living pervert out of this guy. I think that would solve everything; don't you think?"

My mouth dropped open. "You can't be serious."

"Try me."

My parents were sleeping, so I had to whisper my fury into the phone. "I knew I shouldn't have told you about Brad. Something in my gut told me you would freak out."

I frantically began cleaning my room, which I often did when angry, and just as I bent over, punching my two decorative pillows into submission, Liam hissed his fury at me in return, "Why wouldn't I freak out, Samantha? Did you expect me not to be pissed about a guy that keeps harassing *my* girlfriend? And it's not like you're even my girlfriend."

I stood erect at this. "You don't consider me your girlfriend? What?"

"No. Because, at this point, I already see you as my wife. My future. This guy is basically messing with my wife!"

There was a short pause on Liam's end, and I could almost imagine him running an angry hand through his thick bed-head hair. "Let me ask you this, Sam. If the roles were reversed, and *my* boss lady was all over me, telling me she wanted me in all kinds of sexual positions, what would you do? And be honest here."

I stopped dusting the framed photo of me and Liam in my hand, remembering the moment the picture was captured. Some random person took it for us a few years back as we stood high and entwined on top of the Space Needle in Seattle, celebrating our first anniversary under bright moonlight. You couldn't even tell it was us in that image, as strong winds had blown most of my hair over both our faces. You only saw the flash of the camera capturing my stupid, happily-ever-after smile plastered across my face as Liam's side profile softly whispered words that brought goosebumps all over my skin that night.

'Me and you. Forever.'

My response to Liam's hypothetical question about another woman trying to have sex with him came out hot and quick. "I'd slash the slut's tires before lighting her car on fire."

"Exactly."

I sat down heavily on my bed. "I get why you are mad, Liam, but we both need to calm down for a moment and think rationally here."

A minute passed before Liam broke the silence. "All right. I'm sorry for yelling. I guess I'm just blown away by how this dirtbag thinks he can get away with his actions. And, mostly, I'm worried about you, okay? You are already going through a lot with the accident and also trying to get into the dental program, so the thought of him harassing you while you are trying to work your ass off makes me see red."

"I know you're worried. And you are right—Shelly and I should tell the manager. I just need a couple of days to think about how to handle this situation, okay? But what I don't need right now is worrying about you showing up at my work and causing a stupid fight. Like you said, I have enough on my plate right now."

"I know. I'm sorry. I guess I'll have to trust whatever you choose to do. But of course, I want you to bury this freakin' guy ten feet under the ground, Sam."

"I get it; I do. But it's more complicated than you think. Just ... just give me a couple of days to think about it, okay? Man, you and Shelly are stressing me out."

"I'm sorry I'm stressing you out."

"It's fine. I'll be fine. Look," I said, retaking a loathing glance at my textbooks on the floor, "I'd love to keep talking, but if I don't at this exact moment hang up with you, then I won't pass the biggest test of my life, which is in two days."

"Okay. I hope you get some sleep after you study. Call me tomorrow?"

"Okay."

"I love you, Samantha," he said in an emphasizing guilty way, like he was making sure I truly knew these words on a deeper level, even after our spat.

"I know. And I love you, too."

My brain couldn't settle down for the next three hours to focus on the task. Each anatomy word in the textbook seemed to blend with Brad's words in the back of my mind, and eventually, it all sounded like some foreign language about sex positions. Memorizing tests had always been a struggle, but now, after my fight with Liam about the Brad situation, my accident, and total sleep deprivation, it seemed studying was near impossible. As tears of frustration threatened to destroy the flashcards in my hands, I called it a night and threw my textbook across the room, blaming Bad Rap for everything.

Friday's test rolled around, along with the many heavy rocks at the bottom of my stomach, and of course, I was dead last to finish the one-hour test. I approached the teacher. "Ms. Clancy?" I said, holding my test high in the air. "So … I'm pretty sure I failed this thing." I tossed my paper on top of the other twenty tests in a box and tried not to hyperventilate. "I'm in a predicament, and I need some advice."

Ms. Clancy was in her late fifties. She had shoulder-length salt-and-pepper hair and kind green eyes that made her look younger.

"Here, sit down," she said, pulling up a chair beside her. "You're probably being too hard on yourself and did better than you think, but let's take a look, shall we? Normally, I wouldn't correct these papers until next week, but I can do it for you just this once."

I held my breath and waited patiently for what I already knew. Every time her blood-red pen marked up another failed question, it felt like a small cut in an already open wound. I needed a B or higher, because even if I didn't score the A that I needed, I could possibly make up the grade with extra credit.

The teacher removed her bifocals and smiled gently. "Sam, it's not as bad as you think."

"What?"

"Yeah, you came in at seventy percent. You didn't fail. You passed. Your grade may not be the best score, but at least you passed."

My heart sank. "Ms. Clancy, maybe you didn't know this, but I'm trying to get into the Dental Hygiene program. I have to obtain a 4.0 GPA."

Her smile quickly faded. "*Oh.* I see. Then that *would* be a problem." Ms. Clancy gently placed her glasses on the table. "Well, this would mean that from here on out, the remainder of your tests must be flawless."

I let out a false laugh. "That's kind of an impossible feat. Is there anything I can do to bring my grade up for this specific test?" I asked.

"I wish there were, Sam, but no. Unfortunately, and I hate to be the bearer of bad news, but today's test was just the tip of the iceberg. If you're struggling now, it's only going to get harder. We still have a major test on the entire body and all its functions, then a hands-on quiz dissecting a cat and ending with the big final, which counts for more than half your grade. The final is everything you've learned for the entire year."

All the air left my body. "So basically, if I can't cut it now, I'll have no chance to achieve the grade I need for this class."

"Never say never, but yes, the tests will eventually become more and more challenging."

"Then, I'm not sure what else I can do. I don't have much time to study because I work in the evenings, and my memory skills are not the best with all that's happening. Do you have any suggestions?"

"Yes. This type of dedication will take blood, sweat, and tears. But don't give up, Samantha. Find every waking moment to study if you can. And try to clear your mind of any distractions. If you do this, you may find yourself accepted into that program after all."

I replied with little hope, "Sure. Thank you for your time, Ms. Clancy."

Chapter 8

Sam 2005

A little over two weeks passed, and I did everything possible and spent every waking moment studying between my shifts at work. Liam understood when I told him I might never see him again, which was the biggest curse of all. Without him to keep me sane, part of me was missing. I ached for his smile. I ached for his touch. And I ached for his hazel eyes that took me in like I was more than just empty space, a speck, a dot, a grain of sand in this vast, big world of problems. The saying, 'You always want what you can't have,' totally made sense to me. Because now, without him, I wanted him more than ever. He was the air I needed to live and breathe, and I simply didn't know how much longer I could go without my person.

As for what to do about Bad Rap, I explained to Liam that I wasn't mentally capable or in the right mindset to confront Kristen about him just yet. Of course, he wasn't thrilled with my decision, but he understood that school needed to be my main focus for now. But, if I was candid with myself, I wasn't prepared to do anything drastic pertaining to Brad, not only because of school but because I was too scared of the unknown outcome and the ramifications of that. I feared what my future looked like without a job. I had worked for over a year as a hostess before they finally let me become a server. The thought of Brad taking that opportunity away from me wasn't something I wanted to imagine.

As for Shelly, it was in the middle of my busiest and most stressful school week when she decided she wanted to talk to Kristen about Brad. With my blood pressure to the ceiling from weeks of pressure, I nearly went into cardiac arrest with her news. I knew I was the worst friend ever when I told Shelly that if she planned on turning Brad in, it would have to be *her* side of the story and *her* story only. I couldn't take part. It was just one more stress that would push me into Looney Tune Town.

I sensed Shelly was disappointed in me, but she promised not to mention my name during the meeting. Her promise didn't bring relief, not when guilt tore at me as I sat on the sidelines while my friend revealed her hour of truth. I paced the floors at work, waiting to hear the verdict as Shelly poured her heart out to Kristen.

So I was more than puzzled when Shelly explained what had transpired in her meeting. Apparently, Kristen remained emotionless and asked Shelly not to mention the issue to anyone else. She said she needed time to contemplate Brad's fate.

Two days later, before Kristen called Shelly into her office, I gave Shelly a thumbs-up. "You got this. I have a feeling the news will be in your favor."

"I really hope so," she said, wringing her hands.

After she walked into the office and softly closed the door behind her, I said a silent prayer that Brad was a goner. We all deserved to work in an environment where we were treated with respect and revered as equals, without feeling like an object being picked and plucked over.

I walked around the restaurant in an uneasy daze until I realized I had managed to avoid Brad my entire shift. I asked the hostess at the front, "Hey, Alyssa. Where is Brad tonight?"

She gave me a wicked smile while wiping down a menu. "Poor guy. He called out sick tonight. The flu."

"Is that so," I said, a little too excitedly.

"Right? He's so gross. I hope he has it coming out at all ends."

I knew Shelly and I weren't the only ones suffering from Brad's advances. I looked at the hostess in sympathy, thinking she couldn't be barely seventeen yet, and here she was, already experiencing the real and ugly truth of what it's like to be a woman.

"Anything out of that man's mouth alone could give you a bad case of chlamydia. Try to stay clear," I said.

She laughed. "Agree. I'm just happy we all finally get a day pass from him spreading his venereal diseases."

"Same."

To keep busy while I waited for Shelly to come out of Kristen's office, I frantically cleaned my section and guiltily went ahead and cleaned Shelly's area, too. Just as I finished both our side jobs in the back kitchen, Shelly finally came out. Her face was crimson, and the muscles in her jaw clenched on and off like a vein with a heartbeat.

She passed by me with her head held high. "Meet me in my car."

"Crap. Okay," I said.

I quickly clocked out, grabbed my belongings, and rushed outside to find Shelly sitting in her car a few spaces from mine. I opened her passenger door and sat down beside her.

She stared straight ahead at a brick wall while she spoke. "You were right, Sam." Before I could reply, she hit her steering wheel with the palms of her hands. "Nothing. Voicing my thoughts has accomplished nothing!"

"Why? What happened in there?"

"Ask me how many days Kristen suspended Brad."

"Suspended?"

"*Yep.*"

"Three. Three days, Sam. It's like a vacation for him."

I gulped. "Why?"

Shelly turned to face me. "I told her everything—how Brad hits on every single one of us, how he's made vulgar comments for years, how he treated me poorly because I said no to him, and how degrading he is to women. I thought Kristen would have a little more sympathy because she's a woman, but no. She had the gall to tell me that Brad is as harmless as a hound, and yes, even though his jokes are sometimes obscene, he means no harm. She said she already spoke to him this morning, and he promised he would 'refrain' from any more sexual comments once he returned."

"That would explain why he wasn't here tonight. Wow. So, today is Brad's first day of suspension?"

"Yes."

"But you were in there forever. What else did she say?"

"I kind of zoned out from the shock, but Kristen more or less went on to say stuff like, 'Oh, you know how guys are,' and blah, blah blah. She even laughed and said if I only got to know him, I'd see what a good guy he was and that everyone deserves a second chance. She said all of this was to be kept between me, her, and him and that to expose this further than the four walls of the office would only make me look like I had malevolent intentions, which wasn't healthy for the workplace as a whole."

"You're saying that Brad got a small slap on the hand, and we still have to see his ugly face in less than two days?"

"You got it."

This was exactly what I feared, but I didn't say as much to Shelly. She, too, knew there was this chance that nothing would change. "Shelly, I am so sorry."

Shelly sat motionless except for her chest, which heaved up and down.

I continued, "Do you think he would have received more punishment if I had come forward with you?"

"Ha! Not by a long shot."

"Why do you say that?"

"Because it was evident that he and Kristen are 'close' buddies. She resorted to some asinine excuse that she couldn't overlook his good qualities for a few bad ones. I laughed sarcastically at that and asked Kristen, 'Like, what good qualities are we speaking of?' and she said that Brad was 'exceedingly loyal to his friends,' and he was the one who got her the manager's position here at Malbec's. So, you see, the odds were already stacked against us. Those two are as tight as a floozy's tube top."

"So, Kristen didn't take your accusations seriously at all?"

"Nope."

"Well then, I doubt three days of skipping work will change Brad's behavior."

Shelly started her engine and blew out a long, drawn-out breath. "Look, kid, it is what it is. What's the use of freaking out? I had my little meltdown just now, but we have to move on from this. I gotta get home to the kids. Little Maxwell will most likely be waiting for me to tuck him in, and Kenton lost his first tooth while I was working tonight. I just want to go home and pretend that my actual job was that of a tooth fairy."

"Okay," I said reluctantly and stepped out of the car.

Before I shut the door, Shelly leaned over the console and ducked her head lower to see me. "Hey. As long as you and I stick together, we will be okay here. We are all we have. And even though we still have to see Brad's ugly face, let's hope and pray he stops his antics for good. Heck, you and I may even finally live a life of peace and quiet in this shithole."

I leaned in so my face was two feet from hers. "Sure. I'll pray for that. And who knows? Maybe Brad will become a changed man after all this."

Shelly and I looked at each other briefly before bursting out laughing. I was still holding my sides when I got into my car and drove home, all the while thinking our odds of a peaceful work environment were the size of Brad's brain. Nanoscopic.

I returned home late to find on my bed a formal-looking envelope with my name on it. "Oh, God," I groaned after noticing a law firm's name in the return address. There was a note next to the envelope from my mother, saying she almost opened my mail but changed her mind. "I didn't want to overstep, but please wake me up if necessary," she wrote. My heart raced while I quickly tore open the envelope.

After reading the letter, I slowly sat down on my bed, perspiring from every pore. It was a statement of legal claim from lawyers who represented someone named Randy Jergins. I didn't fully comprehend what was being said, but I knew this wasn't good. My parents were sleeping, and I didn't want to wake them, so I quickly called Liam instead.

He answered on the second ring. "Hey."

"Liam, I got this formal letter from my insurance company and a copy of something from another insurance company. I'm not sure what the hell I'm reading exactly."

"Okay. Take a deep breath. What's the letter say?"

"From what I gather, I think this claim is from the guy I hit, Randy Jergins. It says it is for one hundred and fifty thousand dollars, plus legal costs and interest, which is way the hell more than my liability limit." I ran a shaking finger across the next paragraph. "And it says, 'Should this claim be successful, you would be personally responsible for any amount awarded by the court in excess of your policy limit. As your insurer, we have assigned you a defense lawyer.'"

"What the hell?"

"Right? And then, Liam, the statement continues on about how a lawyer will contact me to discuss the case in detail." I was feeling light in the head, worried I might faint. "Liam, am I being sued?"

"You sure it said one hundred and fifty thousand dollars?"

"That's what it says." Sweat pooled down my back, and I wheezed out, "Liam, tell me what to do. Is this Randy guy seriously milking me for all I've got? Or all I don't have?"

"How much does your insurance cover you now?"

"When I first got insurance, I didn't want the full coverage because the full amount was too expensive. So, I got fifty thousand dollars for each person injured and fifty thousand dollars' worth of coverage for property damage. So, my coverage isn't enough for this lawsuit. I'm a hundred thousand short."

"Did you show this to your parents?"

"No. They're sleeping." I tried not to cry. "They must have seen the envelope was addressed to me and just put it in my room. If I woke them now and they saw this, they wouldn't be able to sleep ever again."

"I'm coming over to spend the night. I'll park down the street so your parents won't see my truck. Go and unlock the front door, okay?"

"*Uh-huh,*" I murmured.

"Sam, in the morning, we'll go our separate ways to school like normal, and then after school, you will call your insurance company for more clarification. You can talk to your parents when they get home. Also, I think you should just skip work this one time. Tell them you have a bad stomach bug or something."

"I don't think I need to lie about my stomach. I'm already sick."

"I'm coming," Liam said and then hung up.

Twenty minutes later, when Liam climbed into my bed, my tears spilled over his chest. Not tears from the feeling you get when someone has done you wrong, but tears from knowing it was all your fault. I did this to myself. The accident was avoidable, and now the punishment was all mine for the taking. Whatever heartaches came from this, I deserved it.

A careless mistake.

A STUPID, careless mistake that was just the tip of what was to follow.

The next day, I went about my classes like a zombie, barely able to compute anything the teachers talked about. When I finally dragged myself home, there was a message on the answering machine from a woman named Cecilia Smart, introducing herself as my assigned lawyer.

"You better be smart, Cecilia," I said to no one as I dialed the number she provided.

Promptly, a mannerly, formal-sounding woman with a stuffy nose answered, "Hello. Jacob and Jacob Law Firm."

"Hello. I'm Samantha Carey. I'm calling for a Cecilia Smart?"

"One moment, please."

A minute passed before I heard, "Hello, Ms. Carey?"

"Yes?"

"Thank you for returning the call, Samantha."

"Sure, but can you please tell me what's going on? First, I'm confused about why I am being sued for so much money. The guy I hit didn't seem that hurt, and his car wasn't totaled or anything. He drove off and everything. Second, I only have a few thousand dollars in my account. How am I to pay for all this?"

"I can understand your concerns, Samantha. That's why I am here to help you. Usually, in cases like this, the amount the plaintiff is suing for is exaggerated. I can't one hundred percent guarantee it will be less than that, but most likely, we will settle for less than half of what they are demanding. Your current insurance coverage could cover that amount."

"But what if it goes over the less than half?"

Ms. Smart cleared her throat. "In the event that Mr. Jergins is awarded over the amount that your policy covers, then yes, unfortunately, you are responsible for the remainder."

"I just don't get what there is to sue for."

"I understand this is all confusing. However, I have thoroughly reviewed everyone's statements and examined Mr. Jergins's medical claims, along with the police report and the report on the damage that occurred to each vehicle. First, I can tell you that he won't receive much for his vehicle. His car is an older model, and even though the insurer assessors deemed it totaled, his vehicle was only worth eight thousand."

"How can his car be deemed totaled? Sure, the back was dented in, but he could drive away without issue. The engine wasn't totaled or anything."

"The report from the autobody shop determined his vehicle at a total loss."

"Okay. But that's only eight thousand. What about the rest?"

"The plaintiff is suing mostly for bodily injuries, like pain and suffering, loss of work, plus compensation for his future medical bills."

"But he didn't seem hurt when he got out of his car. He was rubbing his neck, but he didn't look hurt. What about the other guy in the car? Is he going to sue me, too?"

"To answer your first question, Samantha, sometimes in a car accident, the injured persons are initially in shock, so it isn't until much later that they realize they are more injured than anticipated. Mr. Jergins has submitted extensive documents from his medical records stating he has substantial neck injuries. And to answer your second question about his passenger, luckily, the young gentleman walked away without harm. He has not brought forward any claim."

I roughly ran my hand over my face. "Oh, my God."

"Samantha, I know this seems overwhelming for someone like yourself. Not a lot of young folks find themselves calm and collected when facing a lawsuit of this magnitude. But let's take this one day at a time. Try to trust us on our end. We do hundreds of cases like this every year, and I assure you we will do everything we can to ensure you will not incur a fraction of these costs they are asking."

"Thank you," I said, feeling the prickling sensation of tears behind my eyelids. "So, what's next?"

"I will contact you with a date for when you'll come in for your verbal deposition."

I felt like a complete idiot. "What is a deposition?"

"Depositions are a vital part of the litigation process. This is your recorded oral testimony. It is done under oath but comfortably out of court, in a nearby office. Mr. Jergins will do the same so that we may compare testimonies."

"We will be in the same room?"

"No. Your deposition will be just you, me, your attorney, the court reporter, and Mr. Jergins's counsel representing him. You may never have to see Mr. Jergins in person if we settle all this out of court."

"I hope we don't go to court, and I sure as heck hope he doesn't get the full amount he's asking for."

"Then we're on the same page. I will email you a list of things *not* to do in your deposition. The list is a little tongue-in-cheek, but you'll get the gist of what to say. If you have any questions at all, please call me any time. I'm available almost all business hours."

"Thank you, Ms. Smart."

After hanging up the phone, I banged my head lightly but repeatedly onto the cool kitchen table. "You-are-so-freakin-screwed-Samantha. Stupid-stupid-stupid." I tried to stay calm by telling myself that no one ever died from a lawsuit, but it still felt like a knife sat wedged deep into my back, and I couldn't breathe. I wasn't dead—well, at least not *yet*, as I still had to talk to my parents when they arrived home after work. They would kill me for sure.

Maybe I should make a last will and testament? I'd have to give my car to my sister, and the measly money I had left in the bank could go to Shelly and her three kids. That's all I had. I supposed that before my death, I could write Liam a note, a death request, giving Liam full permission to kick Brad's ass for me. The last part seemed most appropriate and worth dying for.

"Back to reality, Sam," I told myself aloud while picking up the phone again to call in sick for my evening work shift. I had to, even though I needed the money more than ever now, especially after I imagined myself hanging upside down as this Randy Jergins shook out whatever I had left in my pockets. But I needed this one night off from work to hash things out with my parents.

Kristen didn't sound too pleased to hear me skipping work. "Well, you don't sound too sick."

"Well, I have never felt sicker," I said, and I meant it. Part of me took some satisfaction in knowing she would have to scramble for a sub. It served her right for siding with Brad and not having Shelly's back.

With three hours remaining until my parents came home, I paced the living room like a madwoman, biting my cheeks raw. Finally, I paused to glance at the calendar, only to realize the date—Alice's birthday. "Mother of God! MY LIFE," I yelled. Our Chinese pug, Otis, jumped, and his face scrunched in even more than it normally was when I slapped my hand against the calendar. Feeling sorry for him, I threw him a biscuit before rushing out the door to grab Alice the birthday lunch I had promised her.

The front door to Alice's home was unlocked this time. But before I entered, I slapped both sides of my face to snap myself out of the dismal mood I was in. The fact that my day was ruined didn't give me the right to ruin Alice's birthday by dumping all my problems on her. Before entering the living room, I put on a smile and yelled, "Happy 79th birthday, Alice!"

Alice shot upright from her chair and clapped her hands with joy when she saw me. "Oh, wonderful! WONDERFUL! I have been looking forward to seeing you today."

I smiled and kissed Alice's cheek. "Wow, you don't look a day over thirty, Alice."

"Oh now, stop that nonsense," she said, waving my words away. Then she winked. "Maybe more like thirty-five, dear."

"Of course, of course," I laughed. Maybe spending time with Alice was all I really needed when my spirits were so low. Alice was the medicine for anyone's aches. Well, that and food. I held up in the air the bag of goodies I bought. "I got us a very late lunch from that Thai place you mentioned."

"Yummy. I've been fasting all day, knowing you'd be bringing me some delicious pad thai and shrimp. I don't know what's worse for us: the noodles or the sugary sauce they drench them in."

"Both." I laughed. "But today, we are celebrating, so we won't be counting our calories."

"Well then, if we aren't counting calories, after we eat this splendid meal, shall we have some of that Cherry Jubilee ice cream I have in the freezer? I even have sugar cones."

"Boy, are we spoiled today, Alice. Do you want me to put your lunch onto a tray?"

"That would be lovely."

While I prepared our plates, Alice asked, "So what's been happening in your neck of the woods, dear?"

I lied a little. "Not too much. I've been working a lot, and school is just okay."

"What?"

I realized Alice couldn't hear me from the kitchen, so after bringing the tray to her, I repeated what I had said. "Just working a ton, and school is just all right." Wanting to turn the conversation away from myself, I asked, "So, what kind of jobs did you have back when you were my age?"

She watched my lips closely and repeated what I said to ensure she heard correctly: "What job did I have at your age?"

"Yes."

She sucked up a long noodle and swallowed. "All my life, I worked. At ten, my first job was babysitting. Someone always needed a babysitter, and since I wanted to save up for a swimsuit to learn how to swim, it wasn't long before I had enough money for two swimsuits, a swimming cap, and goggles. Took me a year, but I was so proud of myself."

"That was some good babysitting money for a ten-year-old." I looked down at my plate with disinterest as my stomach pinched in pain.

Alice replied, "That kind of money was a lot back then. Unfortunately, my mistake was asking my pa for swimming lessons."

"How's that?" I asked while forcing down a small bite of the sweet, sticky noodles.

Alice shook her head. "He said, 'The only way to learn how to swim, Alice, is to sink or swim.' Before I knew it, there I went, flying five feet in the air as he threw me into the lake. He wasn't lying; I learned to swim within that frightening fifteen seconds that I thought I was drowning."

"*Oh, geez*, Alice. That was quite mean of him."

"Maybe. But it got the job done." Alice took a small bite of her shrimp and talked between bites. "After years of babysitting, in 1943, I got my first real job on my seventeenth birthday, working with my father at Hudbay's Mining; I helped build aircraft products, which were essential in the war effort. World War II wouldn't end for another year or more, but women were working in factories all over Canada to help keep those war materials in abundance."

"Wow. It sounds like a fascinating first real job."

Alice shyly smiled and looked down at her hands. "It was fascinating mostly because I met the man of my dreams while working there. *Frank*," she sighed.

I was more than relieved to hear Alice talk about her life rather than wallow in pity with my own. Anything to keep my mind off my current situation. I nodded and encouraged Alice to continue. "Falling-in-love stories are my favorite. I need something to cheer me up, so since I'm not working tonight, tell me about this Frank character."

Chapter 9

Alice 1944

I had worked exactly a year before I turned eighteen at the Hudbay's Mining Company in Flin Flon, where this particular company mined zinc and copper. During the war, the company created a subsidiary company called Emergency Metal Ltd., which helped build and supply metal products for aircraft parts. So, as I was helping to build airplane parts for the war, it was then that this gorgeous, twenty-one-year-old fellow named Frank Clark finally took notice of me. Of course, I already knew of *him* because all the gals I worked with pointed him out.

Anyone could see why Frank was someone they'd talk about. He was a lanky six-four, beautiful, tall tree you wanted to climb. He wore his thick, honey-blond, wavy, soft hair slicked back to avoid falling in his bright, light blue eyes. Now, if a fellow had wonky teeth, I probably wouldn't look twice, but with Frank's perfect, wide, white smile and those deep-as-the-ocean dimples, well, I was a goner. A for-sure goner.

It was November and near the end of the year, and all the factory workers were feeling worn out from a grueling year of production. So, to keep the workers' morale up, the company decided to put on a dance for all their employees. Everyone was excited and talked about who was going with whom. I remember hearing that Frank asked Dorothy Thompson, but then, for some reason, he changed his mind. And, could you believe it? He asked me instead.

I'd never been introduced to him or even spoken to Frank before, so I was a little shocked when, as I waited my turn in line to clock out from my shift, this large hand tapped my right shoulder. I almost choked on my saliva after I turned and found those blue eyes staring back at me. "*Oh,*" I said.

He was a handsome man. I stood motionless, gawking, and nervously ran my hand over my hair. I'm sure I looked like a ninny, with my hair a mess from wearing a work cap all day. And I was in my most natural state, as I never wore makeup at work.

Frank laughed. "Sorry to startle you."

"That's quite all right."

"It's Alice, is it?"

"Yes. And you are Frank?"

Frank's smile widened, as if welcoming me to the pearly white gates of heaven. He held out his hand. "Frank Clark. I am sorry not to have introduced myself sooner."

I was more than weak in the knees as I continued to shake his warm, sizeable hand in mine. He tipped his head upward, suggesting I should look over my shoulder. I turned around to find I was holding up the line. "*Oh!*" I said and hurried forward to clock out. I didn't dare turn back around. I was internally at war with myself, wondering whether I should continue the conversation or not. I had no clue why this man would want to talk to me.

Frank tapped on my shoulder again. "Alice?"

I whipped around eagerly. "Yes?"

"This may be out of the blue and even late notice, but you see, tonight there's the dance. I'm sure you already know about it and probably already have a date." I didn't have a date. I planned to go with a few of my girlfriends, but I let Frank continue. "And even though you don't know me, I would be more than delighted if you would join me in tonight's festivities—that is, if you don't already have plans or a date?"

I thought to myself, by God, what would he want with me? I was taller than most women—five-foot-ten, with feet as long as a football field. And I wasn't the skinny type, either. I got my curves from my momma. The only thing we had in common was the same hair color and matching blue eyes. But, whatever the reason, he had noticed *me*. To say I was thrilled to be asked to the dance by the infamous Frank Clark would be an understatement.

I could only nod *yes* while watching Frank's smile spread across his face, even more prominently than before.

"Splendid!" he said. "How about I pick you up around seven tonight? Will that be all right?"

"Yes, yes, thank you," I said in a daze, still feeling like someone might wake me from a beautiful dream at any moment.

Frank called my name again as I was near the exit. "And Alice?"

"Yes?"

"I don't suppose you have an address for me to pick you up?"

I slapped my forehead. "But of course! Silly me." I quickly wrote my address down on a small piece of paper in my purse. "There you go. Plum forgot that important information," I said, feeling like a complete goof.

Frank tipped his hat and winked. "Tonight, at seven."

I almost swooned right then and there.

That night, I spent two hours preparing for the dance. I wanted to look spectacular. However, with the war going on, almost all makeup products were too pricey and made with low-quality ingredients. Sometimes, they weren't available at all. So, Momma and I did everything to recreate an array of beauty products. First, we applied sugar water to my dampened hair, helping it set after we curled it. Then, we pulled my long curls into a pretty chignon at the nape of my neck. For makeup, we steeped rose petals in water to produce a bit of color for my cheeks and lips and added a bit of soot from the fire to make eye shadow.

But what to wear was the most agonizing question. I went back and forth before deciding on the right dress. I didn't want Frank to be disappointed that he'd chosen me instead of Dorothy. Though the dance was near winter, and I had to wear a coat until we were inside the dance hall, I finally selected a short-sleeved, bright yellow floral dress just below the knees. Most girls would be wearing darker colors for that season, but my mother had always dressed me in dresses of spring-yellow ever since I was little. She made nearly all my dresses, and come to think of it, I can't remember if I wore any other color dress. Either way, my mother said I would stand out like a daisy amongst the wintergreen and plum-colored Hellebores.

Frank picked me up that evening right on time. He wore a sharp grey suit and a matching tie, but when I looked down at his shiny black shoes, I couldn't help but think his feet seemed to belong to the one and only Frank Harty, the chief clown for Billy Smart's Circus. I thought to myself, by God, if we ever marry, our children's feet would be enormous! For a moment, doubts clouded my confidence, not because of his feet but because I felt so out of Frank Clark's league. And it didn't help when I got nervous. I often talked too much when Nervous Nelly showed up. Lord above, if there were such a muzzle, I would have needed it on myself that evening.

I blabbed on and on. "Awfully nice car you got here, Frank. You been driving this car for long?"

Frank glanced at me with an odd expression, probably because the car was neither new nor in the best shape. "Uh, well, no ... a year, maybe?"

"Well, it's sure a nice car. I don't drive just yet. My neighbor and friend, Shirley, drives me to and from work. You ever met Shirley? She works with me."

When he spoke, I noticed his profile was even more handsome from the side view. "That is kind of your friend to drive you. And no, I don't think I know of this Shirley."

"I suppose I should learn to drive soon," I said, "but driving scares me. To tell you the truth, I don't care if I never drive. However, I can change a tire. I've seen my father do it a thousand times. Do you know how to change a tire?" I asked Frank.

Shut your pie hole, Alice, I said to myself.

Frank laughed. "Why, sure, I can change a tire. But it's good to know I have an expert here for all my future tire-changings. You will come in handy someday."

My cheeks reddened at the mention of a possible future with Frank Clark. I tried to save myself from speaking any more rubbish. "You must think I'm nuts and bolts for talking too much. I'm blabbing myself silly, so feel free to shut me up any time."

Frank didn't seem to mind that I'd become a blabbermouth when he said, "I like how you got lots to say." He looked at me under the glow of the street lights, and I swear his cheeks turned a hue of rose. "I know I haven't said it yet, but yellow is your color. A true ray of summer and sunshine."

I had to look out the window so he couldn't see me smiling from ear to ear like some ninny. I'd only been on a few dates, but with Frank, he somehow managed to fill my stomach with thousands of drunken dancing fireflies. He didn't know, of course, that I'd had a little crush on him for months. To have Frank pay me a compliment was a dream, and I told myself in the car that if I wanted the man to take me seriously, I needed not act like a schoolgirl who was all too eager for attention.

Just as I was about to return the compliment, Frank announced, "Well, here we are, Alice. I hope you brought your dancing shoes. I do love a good dance." He parked the car near the one-story brick building, and we could see a long line of dancers waiting to enter the dance hall. "How about you and I stay inside the car a while, you know, visit until that line dies down a bit? I don't want you to wait outside in the cold with such a light coat."

My mother had always warned me about the good and bad intentions of men. No matter how good-looking Frank was, staying in a car alone with any man for long periods could lead to other activities in which I was unwilling to participate. If I wasn't already nervous, I was now. But I had to give Frank the benefit of the doubt.

"Frank?" I asked as I turned sideways and leaned comfortably against the door. "Why did you ask me to the dance? I mean, I heard you asked Dorothy before me. If you don't mind me asking, why me? Did Dorothy turn you down?" Of course, I doubted Dorothy had turned Frank down, but I was curious and couldn't shut my mouth.

Frank smiled and reached behind my seat to grab something in the back. He pulled out a small box and handed it to me. "I heard today was your eightieth birthday. I'd planned on asking you out sooner or later, but when I heard today was your birthday, well, I figured tonight was the perfect time to celebrate *you*."

"You knew it was my birthday?" I was more than shocked; I held the boxed gift as if it were a delicate baby bird.

"I know a lot about you," Frank confessed.

I cocked my head and asked suspiciously, "Like what?"

"Oh, well, let's see; from what I hear, you are a hard worker and just took the lead as the fastest part assembler in your division. You eat lunch with your friends in the break room instead of the cafeteria. And you usually eat a cheese and onion sandwich. But I think what made me take notice was hearing your laughter clear across a room. It is quite contagious, you know. When I hear it, I want to know the secret of how to make that happen again and again and again. Should I go on?"

I sat dumbfounded for half a minute. I didn't know what to say for the first time in my life.

Frank nodded to the gift in my hand. "Go ahead."

Gently and gingerly, I opened the nicely wrapped box. Once the lid was off, inside it lay a beautiful yellow corsage matching my dress.

"And yellow is your favorite color," he said in an almost whisper.

My throat became a dry sock, and I croaked, "*Oh,* my word. How do you know all this about me? And I'm sorry to say, but I don't know very much about you." Truth be told, I knew a lot about Frank but didn't want to let on. Like how he came from an overly strict religious family and how he was hired to work at the factory because of the connections his father had. My favorite part was learning that Frank loved to swim and how I might run into him at the lake one day.

"Let's just say I've secretly had my eye on you for a while now. You're not like all the others, Alice. You're different from the other girls, and I like that. As for you not knowing much about me, we have time to change that."

We talked for over an hour in that car. Frank didn't need to turn the heat on, as I was warmer than the sun shining high at noonday. Praise be, I was able to shut my mouth long enough to listen to him tell me about his childhood, his adventures as a teen, and what brought him to the area. But when we talked, it was as if we had known each other for years rather than mere minutes.

By the time we got out of the car and made our way inside the building, my feet were already dancing, floating, and ascending high above the ground.

With the dark glow of the room so crowded that you could barely see the floor, Frank reached out to take hold of my hand, so as not to lose me. "Ready?" he asked.

I was born ready for this exact moment.

"Yes," I answered.

When our hands touched, a sudden jolt of electricity coursed through my body—an indisputable connection.

Like magic.

I couldn't stop smiling. Who knew your cheeks could hurt from smiling too much? But even if I looked like a complete buffoon, grinning from ear to ear, I didn't care. I especially didn't care when I noticed that not one employee seemed absent. As couples danced less than a foot apart, like sardines, I welcomed the close proximity to Frank that was forced upon us.

Dancing was one thing we had in common. With both of us standing a foot taller than most, we outshone everyone around us. And when they played a slow song, everyone else seemed to disappear into thin air. We were the only two on the floor. We fit together perfectly—as if divinely made for each other. My mood only dipped when they called the last dance. I didn't want the night to end. Part of me worried that at any moment, like for Cinderella, my life would return to the drab existence I knew before meeting Frank Clark.

At the end of the night, when Frank walked me to my front door, he sounded concerned. "Alice, is everything all right?"

We stood before the door, and I brought my hand to my chest in surprise. "Oh. Why, yes. More than perfect. Why would you say that?"

"I just hope you had a good birthday."

"Frank, today was the best birthday I've ever had. I'm sorry if I seem down, but it's only because I don't want this wonderful night to end."

"Then I would very much like us to do this again."

My heart felt like it was bursting when he implied he would ask me out again. But I wanted to play it cool, so he wouldn't think me too eager. "I'll have to check my schedule," I said with a shrug. "You know, my card might be full."

He laughed. "I believe it, Alice Clark. I believe it. Happy birthday, Alice."

Most girls wouldn't kiss on a first date. It was more proper to have a man court you for a while before allowing the first kiss. But when Frank closed his eyes and leaned in, I didn't want to ruin the best night of my life. Plus, I thought it was sweet when he stopped halfway, waiting for me to decide whether I would close that agonizing gap between us.

He didn't have to wait long.

Without a doubt, I was falling for Frank Clark.

When our lips met, his untamed kiss could have knocked out any feeble or weak woman. But for once, I didn't want to be that kind of woman. Instead, I kissed that man back with all I had in me, enough so that it was him who looked shocked and ready to keel over. That winter in Canada may have been the coldest, and with us standing outside, one would have expected goosebumps from head to toe, but I had none of that. Our first kiss was like a hot, sweltering summer, full of promises that neither one of us was willing to break.

When Frank finally pulled away, the look on his face said it all. "If I call you tomorrow, is that too soon?"

I'm pretty sure my laughter woke the neighbors a clear mile away. "Is ten minutes too soon?"

You could say we *nearly* fell in love on my eighteenth birthday, but it was on our second date when a million dazzling lights sealed the deal.

Chapter 10

Alice 1944

Winter hit hard a little over two weeks after my birthday when Frank called requesting a second date. "The lake froze over, Alice. Be ready at dusk," he said.

I hung up, muttering to myself, *dusk?* What would we be doing out on the lake at dusk? I was usually the first to ask my father, whom the town had nicknamed "Dangerous Joe," since he was the only one daring enough to walk out to the middle of the lake each winter with a needle stick to make sure that, in fact, the lake was frozen deep enough to allow skating or playing hockey. But it seemed Frank might have done this task himself.

Either way, I was giddy as I dressed in a new skating outfit—a thick, navy blue, long-sleeved wool dress with a fur collar and a cinched-waisted skirt that flared out from the bottom whenever I spun. I'd had to save up for nearly a year for the outfit, but it was worth it since skating was all I ever did in the long winter months. I smiled in the mirror to see if I looked fashionable enough.

As my mother applied a homemade rose petal stain to my lips, she laughed. "Alice, I'm going to get this all smeared outside the lines if you don't stop smiling. If you don't wanna look like a clown, I suggest puckering up these lips."

"Momma, I can't help myself. Frank Clark never asks girls out on a second date." Even though we flirted at work on many occasions after our first date, I didn't know exactly how Frank felt about me.

"Well, of course he would ask you out again. You're not like any other girl. You are one of a kind, Alice. A little off the cob and corny, but I bet that's why he likes you so much."

"But I'm a giraffe, nearly as tall as him. I thought men preferred small, tiny women they could put in their pockets."

"Maybe he doesn't want to put you in his pocket. Maybe he likes cake and wants someone who could fetch the cake pans from off the highest shelves in the kitchen."

I was about to ask her if it was possible to already love someone after only one date when a knock at the door stopped me mid-sentence. I grabbed my mother's broad shoulders and shook her in excitement. "Momma, I'm gonna marry him. You wait and see."

She laughed and shook her head. "You don't even know him yet, Alice. Now, grab your hat and gloves and go answer the door before he thinks he got the wrong house."

I answered the door and found Frank leaning against the door frame with a newish-looking pair of leather skates dangling from fresh white laces around his neck. They were navy blue with a white tag inked with my name on it. My jaw hit the floor, and my breath caught in my chest. "But how?" I asked him in shock.

He winked and gave me a wicked smile that made him look sharp in his all-black winter clothes. "I talked to your friend Shirley at work, who may have mentioned you had a new navy outfit but no new skates to match."

"But that must've cost you a fortune," I said. "I couldn't possibly accept these."

"If I told you that I cashed in big playing poker, would you possibly consider taking them off my hands?"

"I don't know," I answered hesitantly, even though, in fact, I desperately wanted them. I hadn't had a new pair of skates for years, and my old ones were broken down and worn out.

Frank grabbed the laces of the skates and took them off his neck, nearly dropping the pair to the floor while groaning and wincing as if they weighed a ton. "These are heavy, Alice, and I don't think I can carry them all the way back to the store for a refund." At that, he smiled sheepishly.

I reluctantly took the skates from his hand and gave him a sly look. "Is this your way of saying I got big feet?"

He looked down at his big black boots, which looked like they were surely made for a giant and laughed. "My momma always said people with big feet were meant to go places. Maybe we will go places together?"

I wanted to say I'd go to Siberia if he wanted me to, but instead, I nodded, smiled, and shut the door behind me.

To skate on a Canadian lake, you need perfect weather conditions, meaning the ice has to have frozen smoothly, without too much wind or any snowfall. There's only a short window of opportunity before it's not skateable anymore, and that's why I often skated at our town's outdoor rink and arena. But it seemed Frank must have been the first to find that Ross Lake had frozen over. He pulled off the side of the road and parked at the start of a path through the woods to the lake.

"I don't think I have ever in my life skated in the dark before," I said, climbing out of the car when he opened the door for me. "We must be the only ones here tonight."

"That is true."

"Wait," I said, pulling on his firm arm. "You don't have some nefarious plan to murder me and then dump my body in the lake, now, do you?"

"That would be kind of hard to dump a body in a frozen lake, don't you think, Alice?"

"Well," I huffed, "you got me there. But did you at least bring a flashlight? How are we gonna see in the pitch-darkness out here?"

"You'll see."

"Then I'm assuming you skate well?"

"I try." He chuckled as he led me down the path, holding my hand while carrying our skates in his other hand. "My father is a struggling, traveling preacher. I grew up in a religious Mormon family with nine brothers and sisters, and, well, my family never could afford to give me a pair of skates. It wasn't until after I came to this town and was finally making my own money from the factory that I bought myself a used pair. I've only skated a handful of times since last winter."

"Does your father preach at the church here in town?"

"He does, but now that I'm an adult, you wouldn't see me there. I don't believe in all the stuff my father is trying to sell."

"Well, you wouldn't see me at church, either. Even though our family has a big white Bible in the living room, I don't recall my parents ever picking it up to read to us kids."

"Trust me, with all the book's inconsistencies, it's not worth reading. Plus, who wants to feel depressed after learning about all the sins that would send you to hell for eternity?" Frank helped me step over a fallen branch. "Anyway, I'll admit that I won't be joining the Flin Flon Bombers team any time soon."

"Oh, so no hockey for you?"

"Nope. I learned quickly that paper-thin blades on ice can be really challenging for those struggling with the art of balance. Also, since I am taller than the average Joe, I have much farther to fall. This predicament doesn't seem to help my confidence. Hence, why I was hoping you could teach me tonight. I heard you are an excellent skater, Alice."

"I have a few tricks up my sleeve to help you," I said, trailing behind him. "If I had known ahead of time that you feared falling, I would have grabbed some extra chair cushions from the house."

"Chair cushions?"

"Yeah. For you to stuff the back of your britches."

He laughed. "The fact that you care that much for my tush means a lot to me."

At the end of the trail, where the lake came fully into view, Frank stopped and moved aside to allow me space to stand beside him. I was about to ask again if he had brought a flashlight when I saw we would not need it.

"Frank!" I gasped.

Frank's voice came soft and low, as if he didn't want to break the spell I was clearly under. "At our last church, we didn't have electricity, so my father never threw away any used candles. I figured, rather than let these votives sit in boxes for the next twenty years, I might as well get some use out of them."

I shook my head as I took in the dancing glow of hundreds of flickering flames. Like magic, they were dotted around the icy circumference of the glassy smooth lake beneath the moonlight. "I feel like I'm in a fairytale," I said. "Someone pinch me."

I hadn't taken my eyes off the lake when I felt wool-gloved fingers gently pinch my cheek. "Glad you like it, Alice."

"Like?" I tore my gaze away from the beautiful ambiance on the lake and looked up at this bewildering man full of surprises. "I love it, Frank Clark. I absolutely love it."

He breathed a long plume of mist and cloud into the numbingly cold air before smiling. "Good."

I looked back at the lake. "But this must have taken you hours to light all these candles!"

"Did I mention I have nine siblings?"

"They must love you very much."

He laughed. "I told them I'd do their chores for a week if they helped secure me a future wife." My eyes flew open at the word wife, but Frank seemed not to notice when he sat down, took his gloves off, and began putting on his skates. "I know it's premature to mention marriage," he said, chuckling, "but also, in a sense, wouldn't you think that the whole point of courting someone is to see if there is potential for that?"

I cleared my throat before I found my voice. "Of course, you're right. There's always potential. But I know you meant that in a playful way."

He shrugged. "Maybe." He finished putting on his skates and stood, pointing at the rock behind him. "Here, sit down, and I'll help you put on your skates."

"Oh no, you don't have to do that, Frank. I'm perfectly capable. Plus, you've already done enough," I said, looking out again at the marvelous lake sparkling with little orange gems.

"But I want to. Plus, I don't want your hands getting cold when you take off your gloves to lace up."

I shrugged and did as Frank told me and sat down. "They're all yours," I said, wiggling my booted feet at him. When this man put so much care into pulling off my boots and then slipping my foot into the soft leather of my new shiny skates, I had to resist the urge to swoon and fall over into the bushes behind me. There was no denying that I was under his magical spell. "I feel like Cinderella," I said with a nervous, breathless laugh.

He scoffed. "I am no prince, unfortunately. I don't have much to offer anyone here in Flin Flon, making war parts for a war that may soon be over. That is why, one day, I plan to leave this place as soon as I can and find a better job. I want to provide my family with all the luxuries a prince should offer his princess. A woman like yourself deserves no less, Alice. All I'm good for right now is a bunch of stolen candles and some silly skates I bought after winning a card game. You could do better. So much better than myself."

When his warm hand delicately folded around my calf to help guide my second foot into the skate, it sent a thrill all over my body, making me lose all thought of anything else. I had the strongest of urges to pull his face to mine and kiss away his worrisome frown.

But instead of devouring his face, I gently laid a hand on his shoulder. "Frank," I said, "this girl right here doesn't need much to make her happy. I would never ask the world from you. I would never expect valueless and meaningless perils such as greed and money to steer me in one direction or the other. And I certainly don't think having riches is what makes someone deserving. I am just happy to be near someone as thoughtful as you."

"You are too kind," he said, almost not believing me.

"Really. Here and right now, on the ice and under the stars, with a man I can hardly believe chose me, well, it can't get any better than this." I clicked the heels of my skates together and smiled. "If the shoe fits, I'd say I found my prince."

Frank's head tilted a half-inch before he eyed me with a curious stare. "You really are a practical woman, aren't you, Alice? And here I thought I couldn't like you any more than I already do." He reached out and took my hands before hoisting me up to stand in front of him. "You know, there haven't been a lot of things in my life that I have been super excited about until recently," he said. "There's just something about you that intrigues me, Alice. I do hope that after tonight, and after I fall a million times, and you finally see what a terrible skater I am, I hope you still view me as worthy."

"Stop. Don't sell yourself too short. After all the work you put into this date, I'm sure you're great at everything."

It was an hour later when I declared the obvious. "You really are a terrible skater," I said, laughing so hard that I teetered and pitched forward myself, nearly falling onto his already fallen form splayed out on the ice. "I think I've counted twelve times that I had to save you but ten times that I couldn't catch you fast enough."

"Yes," he said, sitting up, completely breathless. "I'm certain every bone on my backside is bruised down to the marrow. Your kitchen cushions would have been nice right about now." It was hard to make out his facial expression, since we were smack in the middle of the lake and lacking the soft glow of the candles closer to the shore, but it seemed he didn't like me hovering and laughing over him so much when he pulled me down and on top of him. "I did warn you," he said, with his face mere inches from mine.

"That you did." I didn't mean for my voice to sound like that of a wanton woman—husky, provocative, and all too telling. But I did. And I wanted to kick myself.

"So, does this mean this will be our last date?" he asked.

"What?" I pulled my face back a foot to see him better. "All because you can't skate?"

"I have nearly no money to my name, nor a permanent or promising job, and now I can't even skate," he jested.

"Good thing you are good-looking enough that none of that matters to me," I quipped back. He squeezed the sides of my hips, sending me squealing into his arms again. With my body snug against his, I was still laughing when I said, "What I can't figure out is how you are going to top all these candles and the new skates you bought me."

"Are you saying a third date is possible?"

The hopefulness in his voice sent me soaring as high as Mount Logan, and I couldn't take it anymore. "I think a third, a fourth, a fifth, a sixth, and for the rest of my life, is possible." At that, I leaned in and kissed him good and hard. He deserved it, after all.

That night, out on the ice-covered lake, when the wavering flames finally flickered out hours later, I, too, found myself out of breath.

Out of breath and in love with Frank Clark.

Chapter 11

Sam 2005

"There was no third date after that, not when Frank asked me to be his girl, and I never wanted anyone else."

I clapped after hearing Alice's story. "Alice, what a beautiful fairytale."

"It was. That evening will always be my favorite and most cherished memory ever. I sometimes wish I could blink and find myself traveling back to that particular day, which brought a fullness, a sparkle, a burst of energy from the skies above, as if the heavens had entwined us together in love, purpose, and meaning. They say love lasts a lifetime, and for me, it did and always will. But for some, magic only endures for as long as you let it. That is, until something with more sparkle comes along and destroys even heaven's best intentions."

I tilted my head to the side. "What do you mean?"

Alice's eyes were hooded. "*Ah*, life, life, life. I don't want to ruin this wonderful celebration with sad tales. Life is too short. Maybe another time I will tell you where my life took a turn, but for now, how about we get some of that ice cream?"

I didn't push any further. I knew she would eventually tell me what provoked the sadness behind her eyes. Alice was like a wide-open book, unlike Jane, who had held secrets so bitterly close to her heart that when she finally opened herself to me, her heart appeared broken, battered, and bruised from decades of suppressed regrets.

"I'm on it," I said to Alice before walking to the kitchen. After digging around for candles and finding them in the back of a drawer, I came to the living room singing, "Happy Birthday."

She laughed, clapping her hands, and sang the last chorus with me. "Happy birthday to me, Happy birthday, dear Alice, Happy birthday to me!"

Frank was right; Alice's laugh was contagious. I kissed her cheek and then handed her the cone with one candle. "Okay, Alice, make a big wish!"

"Oh, I love this part," she said. The candle wax began to melt the ice cream as she took her time. You would have thought there were seventy-nine candles when Alice blew that one candle out. "There. That should do it," she said.

"What did you wish for?" I asked.

"Nothing for myself. You'll one day find that life is so much better when our prayers and wishes are not for ourselves. Some people have desires, dreams, and hopes bigger than our own, and they are the ones who need saving the most. Besides, seeing others find their happiness always brings me joy."

I thought about Alice's selfless words as we ate our ice cream in contented silence. She had a way of reminding me that so many have suffered worse than myself. I made a note to remember this any time I felt sorry for myself.

I noticed Alice's legs were puffy and swollen, and her slippers looked too snug for her big feet. I asked, "Have you ever considered getting a helper to help you around the house?" Deep down, I wished Alice would hire me to work for her, the way the state had paid me to care for Jane, my first employer. Working for Alice would be heaven compared to working at the restaurant from hell.

Alice practically spat out her ice cream. "Nonsense! I may be old, but I'm independent. This girl doesn't need any help," she said proudly. "Well, at least not *yet*. God has provided me with this strong body all these years, and I plan to continue being independent until He says otherwise."

"Alice, your determination is quite admirable," I said, quietly feeling a little bummed. I laughed nonetheless and offered my services for free. "I think it is great you want to be independent, but I don't mind a little light cleaning or picking up some groceries for you occasionally. I miss the times I took care of Jane, and it would bring me joy if I could help out in any way."

"Oh, no, no. I couldn't ask you to do that."

"You mentioned last time that your legs weren't in the best shape, so I don't mind. *Really*."

"Well, only if you find yourself already out and about at the store for yourself, then I don't mind. I don't want you to go out of your way."

"When did your legs start to trouble you?"

Alice slapped her thighs. "These dumb things? Only lately."

"May I suggest something that will help your legs and help you stay independent?"

"What's that?"

"A walking cane." I held up a hand when she gave me a guarded look. "I mean, you probably don't need it, but it would help stabilize you more when walking. Better to be on the safe side, don't you think?"

"You sound like my daughter, Maria."

"Well, she sounds smart. If you don't want to go to the doctor, a cane is the best way to prevent yourself from falling. That's where a cane or even a walker would come in handy."

"Well, I'll think about it," Alice huffed. "It's not a terrible idea, but I'll think on it."

I laughed. "Okay. But write me a grocery list, and I'll stop by with some groceries the next time I go, okay?"

"Well, I need nothing for a few weeks, just some senior chocolate shakes. You don't mind?"

"Not at all," I said. I knew the adage that helping others makes you forget about your own problems, so I wanted to do just that. Alice would become the perfect distraction from everything that weighed me down. She would be my life preserver.

"Alrighty, then. I'll write you a check, of course," she said. "Sure is sweet of you, Sammy girl. Wish I could pay you for your time, though."

"How about you pay me in stories? I need to get lost in your stories right about now."

Alice smiled. "That I could do! I got plenty of them."

I stood to leave, and my stomach dropped when I saw the time. I still needed to tell my parents about the lawsuit. I let that word *lawsuit* roll around my mind a few times and couldn't believe it pertained to me. "Alice, I hate to run, but I have to meet up with my parents." I kissed Alice on the cheek. "See you soon, and happy birthday!"

I walked into the house to find my father in the living room, the television on full blast while my mother vacuumed around him. "Dinner's in the oven," my father yelled.

"Sorry," I yelled back. My mother shut off the vacuum to hear me. "Sorry," I said again. "I ate already. I went to see Alice for her seventy-ninth birthday and brought her and me an early dinner."

"Oh, well, that was nice of you, Sam," my mother said.

I motioned my mother away from the vacuum and towards the couch. "Mom, could you please sit down? I need to talk to you both."

I sat across from my parents in my favorite reading chair, one that my mother had snagged at a garage sale—a two-person wooden loveseat that rocked back and forth. With its blue and floral cushions, the chair always gave me a calm, comforting, almost nostalgic feel. I imagined it came from the home of someone's grandmother, where she sat for decades, telling stories to her grandchildren and great-grandchildren. But tonight, the chair brought me no comfort. My stomach twisted in knots, and I had to cease rocking to stop the ice cream and Thai food from reaching the back of my throat.

I stalled and looked around the living room while collecting my thoughts. Most people's homes seem to have a specific style or décor, but ours was always a mix of mismatched items, no rhyme or reason. I never understood my mother's odd collections, either. She loved antique vases and bowls but also collected weird glass frog figurines and angels. She also loved to buy things that reminded her of home, back on the farm. If an item had a rugged cowboy-charm look, we had it. Like the rug beneath the coffee table, it looked like something from the set of a Western movie.

My mother broke the silence. "Samantha? You wanted to talk?"

For some reason, I noticed my parents' skin—almost flawless, with no wrinkles. They were still young-looking, both barely forty, but I was somehow sure this conversation would make them age overnight.

"Okay, so I have some bad news."

"*Oh, geez.* What now?" my father asked while muting the volume on the TV.

"Dean, let her talk. I'm sure it's nothing terrible."

"Boy, do I wish that were true," I said.

Before I continued, my sister Stephanie walked into the living room and plopped beside me. "What's up with the serious faces? Did someone die?"

Stephanie was four years younger, which meant we found little in common. We had actually loathed each other for a while, a few years before I became a better version of myself. We were finally on good terms, so, for once, I didn't mind her presence in the room.

My dad waved a hand in front of me. "Go on, Sam, don't keep us in suspense. Out with it."

"Yeah. So, you know my car accident?" They nodded yes. "Well, it seems the guy I hit wants to sue me."

My mother sat forward. "Samantha, is that what that envelope was about?"

"Yes. My lawyer said that in most legal cases, the settlement would probably be half of what the other party is asking."

Her eyes widened. "A lawyer? Samantha, how much?"

I swallowed and whispered, "One hundred and fifty thousand."

"What!?" they both yelled in unison.

Stephanie stood up with a face that looked like she had swallowed a bug. "No way. We're already poor." She looked at my parents. "You guys promised me braces."

It was true. They had planned on maxing out their visa to pay for her braces like they did mine. "Hold on," I said. "Listen, there's no point in freaking out until we know more. But either way, I promise you two won't need to remedy this for me. It's my doing, and I will take care of everything, including the money." I didn't know how I would pay for any of it, but I couldn't put any more pressure on my parents. They were already hanging on by a thread financially. My sister's face told me she was relieved to hear this, and I added, "Don't worry, Stephanie. You'll get your braces."

My mom rubbed her eyes as if trying to smooth out the worries behind them. "We are going to help you whatever the outcome, Sam. You're our daughter, for heaven's sake."

"With what money, Julie?" my father asked her.

"We will think about that later, *Dean*."

I brought out the letter for them to read while I paced back and forth in our small living room. I tried to answer every question my parents had for me calmly and collectedly, but nothing I offered reduced their fears.

"So, when do you meet the lawyers for your deposition?" my mother asked.

"They haven't called to let me know just yet. But Ms. Smart, the lawyer, said soon."

"Ms. Smart is your lawyer's name?" my father asked.

"Yes, Cecilia Smart," I replied.

He stood. "Wow. Okay then, let's hope she is smarter than *you*."

His words hurt me, but I knew he was right. I was not smart when I created this mess nor smart enough at school, so it seemed.

Two days later, my lawyer called to set up my deposition as I was leaving for work. She told me this fun event would take place in just a week. After I hung up, my stomach jumped into a failed somersault. With that bit of news, and knowing I would have to see Brad for the first time since his hiatus, a case of hives crept its way up my neck.

We had no liquor in our house, but it was times like this that I wished for a stiff drink to ease away my fears. However, I had learned my lesson when taking care of Jane and knew drinking would only cause more heartache. I couldn't go down that road again; not when I already felt like my life was spinning out of control. With the trajectory of my current choices, why plunge an asteroid into the mix?

Once in the car, I looked into the rear-view mirror and pointed a finger at my twin. "Nope. Never again. You are *not* weak," I said. "*You* are in control, Sam."

I slowly pulled into the parking lot at work and sat in my car longer than I should have. Only this place could make a person want to start drinking again. I stared at the building and contemplated turning around or, better yet, lighting the building on fire.

Who needs money, anyway?

Oh, yeah. I did.

I dragged myself inside and found Shelly waiting for me at the kiosk. "Brad's back," she said, sounding just how I felt.

"Yeah, I figured," I said. "I've been dreading this moment. Did you run into him yet?"

"Yes. He's giving me the silent treatment."

"But that's a good thing, right?"

"Yes. It's a dream come true, actually. However, I've noticed something odd in how the staff's acting. It's kinda weird."

"What do you mean?"

"So, I've been here for over an hour, and everyone seems to be giving off these weird vibes. My gut tells me it's not good. For instance, I swear Lisa rolled her eyes when I walked past her. For a minute, I thought maybe I just imagined it, but then later, after I said hello to our bartender, Len, he ignored me like he couldn't hear me over the blender. Even after I spoke louder, he just looked at me and rudely said, 'What?'

"I don't get it."

"Sam, I think word got out, and everyone knows I turned Brad in."

"*No.* That can't be. I thought you said Kristen wanted to keep this on the down-low?"

"You're right. Maybe it's all in my head, and everyone's just having a bad day."

"Yeah. That has to be it. Len is usually the nice one out of the group. For him to be rude to you is out of character."

"I'm just being paranoid, right?"

I looked at the tight tension around my friend's eyes and tried to calm her. "I'm sure it's nothing. Let's see how the rest of the night goes. I'll talk with Len and see if he's in a foul mood or something, okay?"

Shelly patted my hand. "Good idea. I'll check in with you after rush hour."

"Perfect."

After I set up my station and took the wine quiz, the hostess immediately sat a party of six in my section. Then she double-sat me with two more tables. The following two hours went by fast, which was usually how I liked it, but when the dinner shift started to die down, I hurried around, trying to figure out whether the staff knew about Brad's three-day time-out.

I went to the bar and fake-requested a side of limes. While Len handed me three on a small plate, I asked quickly, "How's your night going, Len? Going good?"

He looked at the list of drink orders that needed filling, and when I noticed his hand hovering over the next one in line—which happened to have Shelly's name on top—I watched him hesitate even longer.

"It's good," he said. "You busy out there?"

"It kinda died down just now."

I watched him take Shelly's ticket and put it in the back of the line, and my stomach dropped. Shelly was right.

Shit. Shit. Shit.

"You're busy, Len. I'll let you get back to you doing you. Thanks for the limes."

I ran into the back kitchen and pretended to clean my tray while asking the sous chef, Jim, who was also Brad's leading friend, how his night was going. "Hey, Jim. How's tonight going?"

Jim was plating a line of dishes behind the counter. "It's going. You need anything, Sam?" he asked nicely.

"No. Just saying hi."

Shelly walked in at the tail end of our conversation and asked him, "Jim, can I change table twelve's order? Scalloped potatoes instead of the green beans with that medium steak? They switched on me after I inputted their order."

Jim pointed his pen at the tickets hanging above his head. "Shelly, I've got a million orders here. If everyone came in here yelling at me to switch this and that, it would throw me off. Get your order straight the first time."

"Jim, I didn't mess up the order. The guest changed their mind."

"Why are you telling me this anyway? You know the rules. Change it on the computer first. Plus, that's an upcharge, anyway."

Shelly gave me a side-eyed look, as if stating her case that people were acting weird. She turned back to Jim and cleared her throat. "I know this, Jim, and I planned on changing it in the computer immediately. I just came in here to give you a heads-up first so you don't waste time plating it wrong. You know, save you the hassle of replating?"

Jim saw Brad walk in and waved Brad over. "Brad, Shelly here wants me to change an order before she manually enters the change on the computer. What do you want me to do?"

Shelly looked at me again, and I nodded in understanding. Jim was indeed acting like a jerk over a simple change to a side dish.

Brad didn't even question or look at Shelly. "Jim, do whatever she wants. I don't want there to be any problems. Just fix the order. She can change it later." Brad walked away looking like a kicked puppy, leaving Jim to scowl at Shelly for him.

I grabbed my tray and nodded for Shelly to meet me at our spot at the kiosk.

Shelly's jaw clenched as she punched her server ID into the computer. "See? What did I tell you? Jim has never questioned an order change before. He knows I will get around to changing the order manually. He was just so rude about it."

"No, I see what you are talking about. Also, FYI, I just saw Len take your drink order and put it behind everyone else's order. So don't count on getting any drinks any time soon."

It was painful to watch Shelly's chest heave up and down as she gripped the side of the computer for stabilization. "They all know," she said in a strained whisper. "They *ALL* know. He told the staff."

I hurt for Shelly. "You might be right. With Brad's pathetic behavior we witnessed in the kitchen just now, it's clear this man is playing the perfect victim. He wants everyone to sympathize with him." I laid my hand on top of hers. "*Oh, Shelly*. This is all so screwed up."

"Sam, can you watch my tables? I need to use the ladies' room."

"Sure, but later tonight, you should ask Kristen how the word got out. I'm sure it's all Brad, but you came to her in confidence, and this is *not* okay that everyone somehow knows."

Shelly bitterly swiped a single tear away. "Like that will do any good. Plus, I'm pretty sure this is all Brad's doing." She brushed past me and practically ran to the bathroom before I got in another word.

I was a horrible person. What kind of friend was I not to have come forward with my own story about Brad? If I had done that, possibly two things would have happened: one, Brad might have been given a harsher punishment, and two, people might have believed us over him because it wasn't just his word against one woman. I knew I needed to come forward for Shelly's sake, because this was just the beginning. I knew in my gut that things would only worsen for her if I continued to sit on the sidelines.

After checking on both our tables, I went to the bathroom to find Shelly. She was at the mirror, drying her face with a paper towel.

She continued looking at herself as she spoke to me. "I'm fine. I'm a big girl. I'll deal with it. After my ex, I'm used to bullies."

"Shelly, that you are, but look, I was thinking that tonight after my shift, I'm going to Kristen and tell her my side, too. That way, everyone will believe you because there are now two of us with the same sick story. And who knows, maybe others will come forward if we both do."

"You honestly think all of Brad's friends care that a few of us have the same story? Sam, he has too many loyal friends here. And Kristen? That woman is *way* into him. I mean, anyone can see that they have something going on. If you told her your side of the story, I guarantee he'd only get three more days of suspension. So what's the point? You'll only have people treat you like crap too, and I don't want that for you."

"Then let's take this to corporate or HR or something? We have to go to someone higher up, right?"

"Okay, let's pretend we do that. Let's say, hypothetically, Brad gets fired. That's great and all, but guess what? Nothing changes here. People would hate us for throwing out their good buddy. Sure, we might not have any more sexual harassment issues, but hatred feels just as hurtful as harassment. And everyone calling us liars will just eventually eat at us until we cave and they force us to leave."

"So, what are you saying? We don't do anything?"

"I'm saying, we have to suck it up. I have my kids to think about. I need this job, and so do you, Sam."

I hadn't even told Shelly about the lawsuit, so technically, I needed this job more than ever. But she had a point about sucking it up. Still, it didn't feel so good when sucking it up felt like we were sucking up a dirty sock through a pencil-thin straw.

"Okay. We stick it out. Together." I reached out and hugged Shelly. "But I don't like seeing people hurt you, Shelly."

"Look, I had a moment, that's all." She pulled away and grabbed my shoulders. "Hey, look at me. They can't break me, Sammy. But you? If they started treating you the way they're treating me now, well, it would be like watching a duckling getting crushed by a fast-moving vehicle. You have a tender heart, and I can't take that, Sam. Let's look at the bright side; I don't think Brad will harass us anymore."

We touched our heads together, and I sighed, "I love you."

"Love you too, kid."

With our secret silent agreement, we knew Brad had won. But Shelly was right; going any further was pointless. HR could fire Brad if we had both our voices heard, but even after Brad left, we would still suffer at the hands of Brad's cronies, and a person could only handle so much in a hostile workplace. There was one thing I knew for sure, though; if I saw one more person give Shelly any more crap, tender-hearted or not, I was going to rip someone's head off and serve it on a platter. It was the least I could do for Shelly. I owed her that much.

Chapter 12

Sam 2005

When it rains, it floods.

By December 5, two full weeks had come and gone like a category 5 hurricane. After working fourteen-hour workdays consisting of school and restaurant life and adding three more hours of study that went into the wee hours of dawn, I was looking and acting like a character from the *Twister* movie. I had no idea if I would do well or not on my upcoming anatomy test, but I was still praying for a life preserver—a miracle to save me from the storm.

To add to my stress, the next wind squall came when I gave a very stressful deposition to a room full of suits and ties. I felt like a minnow in a pool of sharks when the opposing lawyers attacked me at every turn when unsatisfied with my answers. I testified truthfully, but it seemed Randy Jergins's lawyers wanted to drain me of all my blood and money.

Then came the hail, when I stepped out of my turtle shell and told off a few staffers at work after catching them treating Shelly poorly again. It was out of character for me to put someone in their place, and it was as if I were a different species each time I had to stick my neck out for my friend. But none of it helped. My getting involved only made it worse. There was a complete divide, and Shelly and I found ourselves on the losing end.

From the outside, it seemed like Brad acted like a good little boy by keeping his distance from us completely. But it was clear he had been working an inside angle—orchestrating all his friends to do his dirty work for him. It started with little things; like before our shifts, staff members would dirty our already clean tables of fresh linen and polished wine glasses, making us last in line for table seating. Or during our shifts, our food and drink orders were not filled on time, resulting in fewer tips from irritable and dissatisfied customers.

The same happened at the end of a very long shift. After checking off our back-of-the-house cleaning list, our areas magically dirtied themselves, making it hard to get signed off to go home. These tiresome antics made it hard for Shelly to get home in time to relieve her sitter, and she nearly caved many times. And as if that wasn't enough, my friend and I became the butt of all jokes and easy targets for the bullies. Shelly and I lost track of how many times someone purposely bumped into us while carefully balancing a whole tray of food.

It would have been easier if they had just unfairly painted us as outcasts. At least outcasts merely get ignored. But we weren't so lucky. So, after two treacherous weeks of rain, wind, hail, and flooding tears, I needed the one person in the world who could bring enough sun to dry the sopping-wet blanket of worries weighing me down.

Liam.

But I hadn't seen him for what felt like centuries, and I was drowning without him, which is why I blamed the next disastrous event on the fact that I was not wholly myself.

Lightning struck when my parents kicked me out of the house.

It was stupid, really.

How I became homeless went down something like this: nothing good comes of leaving two women alone in the same room, afflicted with high stress, raging hormones, exhaustion, and hunger.

It happened after a long day in high school for Stephanie and me at college when we both stood angrily in the kitchen, scouring the cupboards for something to eat. It didn't help that my mother hadn't made it to the store for a while. Sure, there were a few staples, but my father always strived to keep everyone in their best shape, so our staples were nothing exciting enough to obliterate a woman's feelings. We were most often not allowed processed foods, or anything containing much sugar or fat. In elementary school, we considered it a treat to spend the night at a friend's house, where we could eat all their sugary cereals without a lecture or guilt trip from my father.

As my sister and I foraged through the kitchen, finding limited choices, I groaned, wishing that, just once, we had something that didn't taste like cardboard. I looked into the fridge, hoping for some cheese for a meager sandwich, but found none, only an empty wrapper. "Really?" I said, turning to my sister while holding up the wrapper in my hand. "Not only did you eat all the cheese, but you also put the empty wrapper back in the fridge?"

She glared at me, her mouth full. "Big deal."

If I had realized my sister had experienced a horrific day at school, where a girl twice her size threatened to beat her up because a guy was interested in my sister rather than said jealous girl, I would have taken a different tack with Stephanie than the one I chose next. And what can I say? Hurt people hurt. I had had my share of bullies the previous night at work, too, so I came in hot on my sister.

"God, it's like you have a peanut for a brain." I showed her how to take the wrapper to the garbage like I was training a toddler. "Watch and try to take notes here, Stephanie." I threw the wrapper into the trash ever-so-slowly. "See? See how it's done? That wasn't so hard now, was it?"

I'll say this: she started it.

My sister's eye twitched briefly just before she held up her entire sandwich and snapped, chucking it straight at my head. I had no time to duck and gasped as mustard, ketchup, and mayo splattered onto my hair and all over my white work shirt. My first thought was: *Who puts ketchup in their sandwich?* I turned around slowly, finding where the other part of the sandwich landed. The meat and bread clung to the cabinet door like a pad of sticky notes, and the insides of the sandwich lay splayed apart all over the countertop, like a crime scene.

I was known for being OCD—a clean freak to the extreme and often the only one who cleaned the house. So, it was my turn for the eye-twitching.

I swung around and yelled plenty of profanities before adding, "I have work in forty minutes, you moron! Look at my hair and shirt!"

Maybe it wasn't a good idea when I instinctively lunged forward with a butter knife, but it was all too satisfying when my sister's eyes popped open in terror before she ran in the opposite direction.

She was too slow, though.

I dropped the knife and grabbed my sister's hair, yanking her ponytail back hard. She screamed, but she somehow managed to turn around and give me a good slap to the left side of my cheek and eye. As we both gripped fistfuls of each other's hair, it ended as quickly as it started when my father arrived home surprisingly early.

"What the hell?" he yelled.

We instantly let go of each other's hair and stood awkwardly in silence as we tried to catch our breath.

"She started it!" I gasped out first.

Stephanie pointed an angry finger at me. "No, I didn't! She practically broke my neck by pulling my hair out, all the while threatening to kill me with a knife in her hand."

"You threw a freakin' sandwich at me for no reason. And it was a stupid butter knife. And please, like I would actually stab you with it, Stephanie," I said dryly.

"Enough!" my father blustered. "I don't care who started the damn fight. First, you two do not get to disrespect our home by trashing it. I saw the mess in the kitchen! Here I am, working my ass off while you two sit around wasting and throwing food around!" He looked at me first. "*You* are the oldest. Where is your common sense? You, above all, should know you don't ever lay hands on anyone. And a knife? That is an unthinkable act towards your sister."

"But—"

"No, buts, Sam. I told you last year that if there were any more violence between the two of you, you'd be out of the house. Are you drinking again?"

My mouth dropped. "No!"

"Whatever. It doesn't matter. I can't have you here acting like this. You are twenty years old, Samantha."

"Are you kidding me? It was a stupid butter knife, for crying out loud."

I could almost see his anger coiling beneath his skin, building steadily before the bite. "I don't give a shit! What I say goes. Go pack your bags. You're out of here."

"*Dad*, I was never going to stab her with the dumb butter knife."

"Doesn't matter. I won't tolerate this behavior. I don't need any more crap from any of you!"

"For real?"

My father's voice was grave, along with an expression that said he was thoroughly disgusted with me. "For real." He pointed a finger at my sister. "And *you*, don't think this is over for you. You're grounded." As he stormed off, the words trailed behind him: "And *dammit*, someone clean all that mess up NOW." The look on my sister's face said she, too, was shocked by my father's rash decision.

I shrugged and didn't say another word as I walked to my room. It was only when I sat down on the bed in a state of shock that a tear fell onto my lap. It had been a long while since my sister and I got physical, so I couldn't understand why my father suddenly wanted to kick me out. It made no sense, not when my parents weren't the best examples either. How did their volatile arguments for over twenty years get filed under an exemption? Sure, they didn't lay a hand on each other, but I wondered how the plates of food felt as they were being flown across the kitchen table, breaking into a million pieces onto the walls behind the heads of my sister and me.

The reality of finding myself homeless set in, and I hurried and called my mother on my cell while trying not to sound like I was breathing into a brown paper bag.

"Julie Carey with Systems Health. How may I help—"

"Mom," I cried.

"Samantha? What's wrong?"

I wiped my nose and almost threw up when the smell of ketchup from my hand hit me. It was wet, fresh and all over me. "Mom, Dad just kicked me out of the house."

"What?"

"Stephanie and I got into this big fight, and sure, I grabbed her hair first, but she threw a sandwich in my hair before I did anything. I have to be at work in less than twenty minutes now, and I don't have time to pack up to move out. And where am I supposed to go?" She was silent for too long, and I tried again. "Mom, say something. What should I do?"

Her muffled voice sounded like she was cupping the phone, as if in fear someone in her department would catch her in the act of taking a personal call. "Sam, I'm so sorry, but I'm at work and can't come home to figure this all out. Hurry and just put your father on the phone."

"No, I don't want to talk to him. He's dead serious, Mom. He said I had to leave."

"He is probably in a foul mood. He just called me an hour ago, saying he's been laid off. I don't think he would have thrown you out if he hadn't already felt under so much pressure at work."

"Oh," was all I could say. It seemed I wasn't the only one with problems, but I didn't have time to contemplate anything. The alarm clock on my dresser showed I had fifteen minutes before my shift began.

"Honey, listen. Go to work as planned. When I get home, I'll talk to him. I just need to get home and talk to him, Sam."

I took a deep breath and let out a long sigh. She had a slim chance, but still, there was a chance I wouldn't be homeless and living in my car. "Okay, Mom. I'll call you as soon as my shift is over."

I quickly changed into a clean work shirt and almost cried when I saw the wrinkled fabric. But there was no time to iron it. I wiped most of the condiments out of my hair in the bathroom, but I was left with a rancid ketchup smell that wouldn't dissipate. Even after rearranging my greasy hair into a bun and spraying it with some perfume before running out the door, I knew I looked and smelled like garbage.

Kristen, my boss, found me the moment I clocked in. "Sam. You are nearly fifteen minutes late," she hissed. "What is going on? You do realize that we are trying to run an establishment here. Look, I'm sorry, but I have to write you up for this. You know this is your second written notice?"

"Yes."

"One more, and we'll have to have a serious conversation about your future here."

I wanted to tell Kristen to shove it. A man sexually harasses his employees and only receives a three-day suspension, but if an employee is late three times, firing is the only option? The unfairness of it left a bitter taste in my mouth.

Kristen put her arm out to stop me before I went onto the floor. "*Uh,* Sam," she said, pointing to my shirt. "You are *beyond* wrinkled. Frumpy and dumpy isn't the look we are going for here."

I stared at Kristen. "I know. I had a serious hiccup today and had no time to remedy this."

She shook her head. "I can't put you on the floor looking like that. Go to my office and use my iron. And *hurry*. I'll have to have Shelly continue to serve your tables. This is unprofessional, Sam. And whatever perfume you are using, don't. Just don't."

I swallowed, feeling like trash. "Sure thing," I said.

After ironing my shirt, I found Shelly running around the tables like a madwoman. She looked relieved to see me. "*Oh, thank God,*" she said, handing me all the orders for my tables. "Sorry, it's been a wild go from the start."

"No. I'm sorry. It seems I am having a horrible week, Shelly. I can't apologize enough but thank you for taking care of my tables."

She winked. "It's okay, but you owe me."

It was in the middle of rush hour when I walked into the back just in time to overhear two male servers talking crap about Shelly yet again. "*Man-hater.* The woman can't take a joke. Too emotional, if you ask me. Brad doesn't deserve any of this crap. The poor guy looks broken."

"They should fire her for lying," the other said.

Tim glanced up and saw me before he cleared his throat. "Oh, Sammy. Hey!"

I glared at them before the other, Karl, tilted his head. "What's with the face?" he asked me.

He knew pretty well why I looked angry. "You don't like this face?" I asked sarcastically. I wasn't in the mood and swiftly approached the pair of idiots. "Look. Don't take sides until you know the whole story. Just because Brad's your special buddy shouldn't mean a damn thing. Don't believe everything your friend feeds you. It's all poison."

I turned around to walk away but changed my mind. "Actually, you know what?" I said, spinning around. "Shelly has more balls than you two put together for telling the truth about your pathetic waste of a friend. And I can vouch for her when I say that *he* is the one they should have fired. So, I'd watch what you say, fellas. I'm real tempted to do something to prove you both wrong."

The pair stood in silence for mere seconds before the tall one laughed. "You girls will always stick together no matter what, huh?"

"And you boys will always use your small wieners instead of your brains, huh? Grow up already," I said before storming off.

By the night's end, I finally had a break to talk to Shelly. We were sitting in an empty booth folding linens when I desperately wanted to confide in her about my conversation with Tim and Karl talking shit about her. I also needed someone to talk to about my dilemma at school, my lawsuit, and now my father kicking me out, but I stopped short before dumping on her. Laying out all my problems didn't seem right when I knew she had so much on her plate already. I didn't want to ruin her night. Instead, I asked, "When do you think we can move on from this suffocating place, Shelly?"

She puffed out bitterly, "I'd leave in a heartbeat if I knew of another place hiring that paid just as well in tips."

"Maybe we should start looking now? You never know. This may be bad timing, but I hate this place so much. I need something to look forward to that doesn't make me want to throw myself off Mount Rainier."

"Believe me, I'd love to look, but I'm stuck for now. I don't even have a minute to myself, let alone try and look for a new job. I live and breathe here, and when I get home, I need to spend what little time I have focusing on the kids. I barely get to see them because they are in school all day, and I work evenings. But I get it; this place can suck the life out of you."

"Shelly, I have to believe we are not stuck here forever."

"Nothing is forever. We will figure this all out."

"Then, at least promise me we will go together when we leave. I couldn't live knowing I left you here to rot alone."

"When the time comes—and who knows, it might be sooner than later—but I promise we will go together. Soul sisters for life, Sammy girl."

I drove home, unsure if I even had a home. All I wanted to do was call Liam, but I was too embarrassed to tell him about my latest turmoil. My mother waited by the front door as I pulled into the driveway, looking at me like she had lost the argument with my father.

"Sam. He's just so stressed about work right now. He can't deal with any more pressure," she said as I approached her. I didn't want to hear the platitudes or her excuses for my father, but she continued anyway. "It's not forever, just for a while, sweetie."

I was exhausted and laughed half-heartedly, thinking about how Shelly had said the same exact words: *Nothing is forever*. "Sure. If you say so, Mom." I looked across the lawn at the door to the house feeling unwelcomed and unwanted, which wasn't new. "I just think it's funny."

"What's funny?" she asked.

"How you guys fight all the time, and no one else ever gets kicked out. This isn't really about the stupid butter knife, you know. He has never really liked me."

"You shouldn't think that about your father. He loves you. But you're right about one thing; it isn't about the butter knife, Samantha. He is going through a tough time at work and is unhappy with himself."

When *isn't* he going through a tough time, I wanted to say. When is he *ever* happy, I wanted to ask her but didn't. It was exhausting having to walk on eggshells, never knowing my father's mercurial moods. But God forbid that we Carey women ever had any feelings, emotions, struggles, or bad days that were bigger than his.

"Sam, I know your father kicking you out seems harsh, but again, your father loves you very much," she said, sticking up for him like she always did.

Did he, though? I wanted to ask. Did he really *really* love me? If love was working eight hours a day putting food on the table and providing a roof over your family's head, then sure, I knew he loved me. But love had shown me a different meaning when I found out very early on, as far back as the second grade, that my father wasn't like the other dads. After play dates, sleepovers, and birthday parties at my friends' homes, I had learned that not all fathers wanted their children unseen and unheard.

I had become immune to how often my mother gave the excuse that my father was tired, how he had a very stressful job, and because he had grown up in a home without love or discipline, he was habitually insecure. That last excuse, and possibly the sole reason for our disconnect from ever having a normal, loving father-daughter relationship, had left me feeling jilted for my whole existence. But I had adapted.

Or did I?

I tried to remember if my father had ever attended any of my school functions, piano recitals, or sports games, even if baseball only lasted that one season in the fifth grade, but none came to mind. Nor did he ever ask me how I was doing or if I had school troubles or even say to me that he was proud of me for working so hard to get good grades my whole life. As for affection, my mother seemed the only one on the receiving end of that. As for us kids, affection came only when my mother nudged him onto us, and told him to hug us, as if he needed reminding that he had once fathered two children at some point, way back when. But hugs were never voluntary. Luckily, my mother tried extra hard to make up for all that we lacked from our father by pouring a plethora of hugs and kisses onto us.

All in all, I thought I was used to the feeling of not being wanted by my father. Now that I was older and saw our dysfunctional family through a more mature lens, you might think I had accepted that the love I wanted or needed from my father was something I couldn't get from him. I had given up on that dream. A loving relationship could not happen, not when all his talks were of how we could eat better and stay thin, how his job took too much out of him, how job strikes threatened, how the government was running everyone into the ground, and how my parents' many debts were going unpaid. With all his anxiety, fears, and insecurities always at the forefront, there was no room for love or happiness. My father's *un*happiness loomed over us as if every day it was a hopeless doomsday.

Perhaps that's why I always worried about my future. I didn't want to become like my parents who, as much as they tried every day to work on their marriage, they were often despondent and seemed miserable.

"Did you hear me, Samantha?"

"Sorry, what?" I asked my mother, still standing outside my car.

"I said, he is just so unhappy with himself. Depression is a real thing."

"Depression?"

You would think that would explain so much, since my father had deep-seated anxiety that none of us could ever quite understand or grasp. Instead, because I had endured his "moods" since birth, his chastising and anger became like a second layer of skin. I simply got used to it.

But *depression*? I tried to remember when I had last seen my father really smile. And then I remembered those rare moments, like when a good song came on the radio, that he would grab my mom and slow dance with her. And there was that one time when I was little when he let me stand on his feet as he danced with me in the kitchen. Or that time when he surprised my sister and me with a Nintendo, where he sat down and actually really played it with us for that whole Christmas morning. And sure, we went on occasional trips to the ocean or hiked the trails around Mount Rainier, but if there were more happier times, I couldn't recall past those very few snippets.

Maybe the problem wasn't so much of me trying to remember the good times, not when there were too many bad times overshadowing the good. I no longer bothered counting or comparing when the happiness scale became so unbalanced. But still, depression or not, I had to remind myself that it could be worse. At least I didn't have a father who beat me like Alice's father. And I wouldn't say my father verbally beat us, either. Sure, his outbursts and disappointment in all of us, along with his rising anxiety, pushed him over the edge at times. The way he hurled loud words and salty insults could scare just about anyone into submission, but I was never scared, which only seemed to agitate him further. If anything, his unwarranted explosions only angered me. My indifference towards him and my coolly unaffected outward appearance towards his ill-tempered outbursts affected him more than it did me.

And so, it was no secret that we disliked each other. Having a father who seemed not to care or love me in the way I needed, only made me dislike him even more. He often said I was disrespectful, but it may have been my indifference to mind control that seemed to do him in. Did my eye-rolling or shaking my head while walking away from an argument mean I was being disrespectful? Sure. Was it disrespectful when I tilted of my head or narrowed my eyes every time he spoke to my mother in a derogatory, demeaning way? I suppose. But it was because I had already lost much respect for someone who seemed to care so little about me or my mother and sister. If he didn't care, why should I?

Was this why we didn't like each other very much? Yes, I was good at reminding him of his bad behavior just by giving him the side-eye or the way I set my jaw, and the way I stood unmoving, like he had no effect on me. I'd lost respect and trust because of how he treated us and because he seemed not to love anyone but himself. By now, at almost twenty-one years of age, I think he knew how I felt just from the look I gave him. And so, I didn't believe it was depression that made him kick me out, as my mother had suggested. I believed he wanted me out because his pride and ego had been so damaged from my reciprocating and mirroring back to him exactly what he gave me from the beginning.

Which felt like nothing most the time.

But still, I couldn't understand why we were the way we were, except in the simplest terms that suddenly dawned on me; he often demanded respect just because his blood ran through me, but I believed I could only give respect after I felt his love wash over me. So, depression or not, and for all the lack and dysfunction my father dished out, did I really expect him to care for me? No. No, I didn't, which is why I was shocked to feel so hurt when he kicked me out. It had seemed he had done it without a second thought.

I swallowed back this revelation of hurt and looked over at my mother, wanting to confide this theory to her. But something stopped me. I realized I could never have said any of this to her, him or anyone. We were beyond fixing. We were broken. End of story.

Great.

I had daddy issues.

"I'm fine, Mom," I said, trying to shrug off the way my heart methodically panged against my chest. "Don't worry about me. It is what it is. Maybe it's time, and maybe it's best for everyone that I leave."

My mother's head and shoulders dropped so low to her chest that I bit the inside of my cheek to stop myself from crying. "But I don't want you to leave, Sam. Just know that," she said, finally looking up at me.

"I know." I swallowed. "I feel that love from you, Mom, and I'm going to miss you."

"I'll miss you more." Mom gently touched my arm. "I called your Aunty. She said you could stay with her until this all blows over, unless you want to go to a friend's house for a while instead?"

I pulled my arm away, momentarily angry that she had allowed my father the final say. But even if she didn't have the guts to stick up for me, I couldn't really be mad at her when it seemed I wasn't capable of sticking up for myself, either. "Mom, I don't want to bother my friends. I'll just stay with Aunty."

My mother trailed behind me as I bitterly went inside the house to pack. "Sam, I'm so mad at your father. But I'm also so damn mad at you two girls for not having more control over your emotions. I don't know where you both get this kind of violent behavior."

Exhausted, I sat down hard on my bed and asked, "Seriously? Mom, you had a ton of siblings. You're telling me none of you fought or hit each other?"

"Well, sure. My brothers were the worst. They always had fistfights, but it was never in front of my parents. But as for us girls, we *never* hit each other. Never could I imagine hitting one of my sisters."

Guilt washed over me. "I am sorry the fight happened; honestly, I am, Mom. It just got out of hand so fast today. And if anyone is disappointed, I'm disappointed that I lost control. It's like whenever my mistakes pile up like this, the harder it is for me to find the better version of myself, to make good choices."

I firmly closed my lips to stop my chin from quivering, but my emotions were stronger than my will. "This isn't an excuse," I said, angrily wiping the tears off my cheeks, "but I feel as if my life is like a sandcastle crumbling into pieces with each wave crashing into me. I never get to see Liam anymore, I'm failing my anatomy class, and even if I study my butt off, I still probably won't get into the dental hygiene program because you have to have a 4.0. The thought that I've wasted all my hard-earned money on these classes makes me sick to my stomach."

She sighed. "And now the lawsuit."

"Exactly. I'm so stressed about the uncertainty of it all and I'm scared. Where would I even get that kind of money, Mom? Should I rob a bank?"

"That sounds like a great idea," my mother said, trying to lighten the mood.

"No, really, jail sounds *nice* right about now, like a mini-vacay from all my responsibilities. And don't get me started on my job."

"Wait. What's wrong with work?"

I had never told my mother about my work issues for two reasons: One, she was in the middle of perimenopausal symptoms and had been losing hair, not only from that but from all the stress with my father and from enduring so much at her demanding job. The second reason: I feared she would tell my father about my perverted boss. With his temper, he'd probably show up at my work and demand justice by beating the living crap out of Brad. Just like the time when a boy in junior high started a dirty rumor about me, and my father showed up after school to find him. With a crowd of three hundred students in the courtyard, I was mortified when my father lifted the boy up by his collar and threatened to destroy him if my name ever escaped his lips again.

But wait. Was that a form of love? When my father stuck up for me? Or was it that he felt he'd been disrespected by someone tainting the family name? Maybe both. I would have to give my father credit for that one. But still, it was better that I continued to keep what was happening at work to myself. So, instead, I told my mother a partial truth. "Well, for one, Mom, work is sucking the life out of me."

"Sorry to be the bearer of bad news, but most jobs suck, Sam." My mother tucked a fallen strand of hair behind my ear. "I know life's been piling up on you lately, and I hate to see you this way, but Sammy, we *all* have trials to overcome, and unfortunately, you are not the only one going through hurdles and uncertain obstacles. I do feel bad, though. As a mother, it's hard to see your children struggle. Either way, it sounds like everything has hit you pretty hard lately."

"Yeah, and all at once." My voice cracked, along with the dam holding back an ocean of tears. "I just want to know when I can catch a break, Mom. When does it get easier?"

"I ask that same question all the time." Her next words came with a note of sympathy. "I get it, Sam, I do. But God never promised an easy life. We should strive to be grateful—grateful we even *have* a life. Some are not so lucky. Just remember, there is always a way out, but no one ever said the way out would be easy."

Easy? What did that even look like, I wondered.

"All we can try to do for now is be there for each other more," she continued. "And pray for each other and ask God to show us the way when everything seems hopeless."

What I couldn't understand was how, ever since the day I was born, my mother had been praying for God to lead her complicated marriage in the right direction. I never quite understood why my mother threw God into the mix as an actual option for fixing your problems. Just pray, and somehow a path will magically appear and remove all your problems and worries? It didn't look like praying ever helped her, but I sure wished it was that easy.

I looked at my mother and a wave of remorse washed over me when I looked into her eyes, which revealed just how tired she really was. She was the hardest working person I knew, working all day and coming home to do all the grocery shopping, cooking, cleaning, bills, and yard work. Even though I volunteered to help her clean—and I was often the only one to offer—it wasn't enough. And now, with my actions, I had added more worries and problems onto her plate. "I'm sorry, Mom. I'm sorry I made everything worse."

"None of us are perfect, Sam. We will figure this out. Just remember, it's true what they say: 'This won't last forever.'"

"I know. It just feels like I'm inside a never-ending tormenting loop without a way out. I want this ride to stop and let me off already, you know?"

She patted my leg, stood up, and choked back a sudden sob. "I understand. Sometimes, I wish I could just get up and jump off this ride, too. But I don't want *this* ride with *you* to end. Just know that my heart aches without my baby home with me. I love you."

Whether I believed that prayers worked, her last three words to me were what I believed to be true. "I love you, too, Mom."

She walked to the door and turned to face me with the saddest expression I had ever seen. "I'll give you some privacy and some time so you can pack, okay?"

"Sure, Mom. I'll be okay," I said, trying to ease her pain and worries as well.

After packing, I finally caved and called Liam to tell him all that had transpired. Just hearing his voice on the other end released the floodgates yet again. I was lost, feeling directionless, with no idea where home was, and I needed Liam more than ever. He told me over the phone that he felt terrible and wanted to see me and that I needed to call him as soon as I arrived at my aunt's. But as I followed behind my mother's car to my aunt's, all my unanswered questions weighed me down like a ton of bricks.

How long would I stay with Aunty?

Should I look for an apartment?

But with what money?

Should I quit college and use that money for rent instead?

Should I get a second job to help pay for my lawsuit?"

Stuck in uncertainty and hopelessness, I jumped when my cell chimed. I waited until I was at a stop light to answer. "Liam? I can't talk. I'm driving."

"Sam, I spoke to my parents."

I nearly started crying again. I didn't want anyone to judge me or my dysfunctional family. "Why did you do that, Liam? Why did you tell them? What will they think now?"

"They don't think anything of it. Sure, they are sad for you all, but they love you and would do anything for you. They said you should come here and stay with us instead of going to your aunt's house to live. You need to be here with me, where you belong."

I choked back a sob. "But I feel so stupid."

"You are *not* stupid. No one is perfect. I love you—flaws and all. I want you here with me, all right?"

I couldn't argue with Liam when my entire body ached for him to hold me. It had been weeks since I had seen him, and I knew if I went one more night without him while all the junk piled on, threatening to bury me alive, I wouldn't last—whatever that meant. "You sure I can stay with you?" I asked.

"Indefinitely."

Liam would always be my home. That was another thing I was absolutely sure of. "I'm on my way," I said, drying my eyes. For once, a path had appeared, the dark clouds had parted, and Heaven's doors opened just when I needed rescuing from the storm.

Chapter 13

Sam 2005

My first night at the Becker home wasn't an easy transition. Mainly because, after my mother spoke to Liam's parents, they all agreed it would be best that Liam and I didn't share a bed. I couldn't believe my ears. It was the twenty-first century, not the fifteenth century, and I was twenty, not fifteen. But I didn't argue. Not when I was without a leg to stand on and homeless to boot. Beggars can't be choosers, I figured.

But still, even after Liam spent an hour consoling me and tucking me in, making sure I was comfortable enough, I woke around two in the morning feeling sorry for myself. Unable to sleep, tossing and turning in an unfamiliar bed alone, all the while wishing I had brought a glass of water down with me before bedtime, I couldn't take it anymore.

I tossed the covers off and threw on my pajamas before making my way upstairs and into the kitchen. I didn't want to turn on the lights or wake anyone, and because I had been there so many times to visit Liam and his parents, I was able to feel my way around to find the correct cupboard with glasses. When my fingertips felt a plastic cup, I pulled it down, but not before its bottom caught on the lip of the shelf. It slipped out of my hands, hit the floor, and bounced around, making a loud racket.

"Shit," I said, crawling on all fours, trying to locate the damn thing. And I felt very much like that damn cup—lost, in the dark, alone and empty. I missed home. I missed my mother kissing me goodnight, I missed my own bed, and I missed my pillow.

"Why did I not grab my pillow?" I said, choking those words out.

A familiar prickling feeling behind my eyes came when tears threatened to fall. Even with Liam in his room just down the hall, not even twenty feet from where I was crawling around, I very much wished I could crawl into bed with him. But I couldn't. He had a big game the following day and needed his sleep. He was anxious as it was, wanting so badly for basketball scouts to be at his game and to see he was an asset and had the potential to play for a bigger school. So I didn't sneak into his room. I couldn't screw up his chances just because *I* was a total screwup.

I finally found the cup and cursed some more when I tried to fill it at the faucet in the dark and felt water soaking over the cuffs of my pajamas. The lights suddenly flicked on overhead, and I turned to see Liam's father, James, standing in the doorway.

"It's easier to see if you turn the lights on," he said, chuckling.

"Sorry," I said while hurrying to wipe my face of any evidence that I had been crying. "I ... I couldn't sleep, and I didn't want to wake anyone, but it looks like I failed miserably at that." *Just like I fail at everything else*, I muttered under my breath.

Liam's father didn't seem mad that I woke him; instead, there was a softness behind his eyes, like always. "It's fine, Sam, really. We can't see the kitchen lights on from our bedroom. And you don't have to worry about waking Liam. Once he is asleep, he's dead to the world."

I smiled. "Okay."

"You said you can't sleep, though?"

"No," I said, unable to keep my chin from quivering like an idiot. "But I'm fine."

"You don't look fine. Here," he said, walking over to the kitchen island and pulling out a chair for me. "Come sit. Let's talk. Sometimes, when things are pressing on my wife's mind, it helps to talk before sleeping."

As much as I liked James, who always ensured I felt comfortable in his home, I didn't want to talk to Liam's father. I didn't want him to see me in this vulnerable state. He always seemed to have his life perfectly together, and I must have looked weak to him, standing there with red, swollen eyes and my hair in disarray from all the tossing and turning. But I sat anyway so as not to seem rude. I mean, unlike my father, the man *was* letting me stay in his home without any questions or worries that I might actually stab him in his sleep with a butter knife.

James took a seat at the opposite end of the island and fiddled with the cribbage board that they often played games on during family meals. They never played it with me, ever since the day I told them it wasn't my favorite game, maybe because I had the worst time counting up the points without using my fingers. Instead, we always played rummy or wisp.

"I'm sorry you're having troubles at home, Sam," he said, finally cutting through the silence. "This must be hard, with tonight being your first night away from home."

I swallowed down the lump in my throat and awkwardly rubbed the cup's outer layer and design, feeling the plastic grooves and ridges beneath my fingers. "I'll be okay," I said, not fully believing the words out of my mouth.

"You know, there was a time in my life, back when I was sixteen, living on the farm in North Dakota with my six brothers and sisters. I wished so hard that I had a place of my own. I'll never forget, though, when I finally got a place on my own, when I moved all the way out here to Washington to work for my cousin—it was only then that I missed home. Without all the noise from the hustle and bustle of my siblings and my parents and the farm animals bleating, mooing, and clucking, well, I realized how very much I really missed home. But with each passing day, it got a little better. It helped that Liam's mother followed me out here a few months later."

I looked sheepishly down at my hands. "It does help to know that Liam is right here under the same roof with me. I was even tempted to wake him up, but I knew he had a big day tomorrow."

"That he does. We are really excited about his big game. We wish you didn't have to work so you could come and cheer him on with us."

"Me too. I feel terrible having missed so many of his games because of work." I angled my head ever so slightly, critiquing the man before me. "You love watching your son play."

My question was more of a statement, but Liam's father sat up straight to answer me anyway. "Are you kidding? It has been the highlight of my life watching that kid play basketball. Besides you, basketball is his passion. And he is really good, too. And I'm not just saying that because he's my kid, either," he said, smiling. "To finally see Liam's dreams come to fruition after watching him play his heart out, ever since he was in the second grade—well, it's been an honor. I really believe he has a shot at playing for a bigger university." He laughed. "I just realized something, but I have never missed a game of his. To see how far he has come as a player, I really believe those scouts are going to notice him."

The way James's eyes twinkled when he spoke about his son and how he smiled ear to ear, as if Liam was the center of his world, somehow made me feel smaller, insignificant, and worthless. No one needed to know I had daddy issues, nor did I want to speak ill of my father by comparing Liam's dad with mine. I kept how I truly felt to myself because I didn't want James or anyone, not even Liam, to judge my father too harshly. Despite all my issues with my father, I still loved him. But deep down, I wished I'd experienced an iota of what Liam had with his father. Through actions, they clearly loved each other beyond just speaking those three little words.

My heart swelled the moment it dawned on me. There was a huge chance that Liam would one day become the world's greatest dad, with the example of a doting father like James. I wiped a tear from the corner of my eye and asked James, "Do you ever regret moving out here? You know, moving away from your family?"

"There were times I missed my family back home, but no, I don't regret anything. Not when I made a new home and a new life here by starting my own family. You'll find that when you and Liam are one day married with children, they will become your main focus, and all the problems you face now will hopefully fade away, just a distant memory."

"I hope so," I said.

"Trust me. It may feel like your world is crashing down on you, but during and just after a fight, wounds are fresh, and tempers are high. Give it time."

I made a feeble attempt to laugh. "Our family needs a lot of time, it seems."

I wanted to ask James why his family didn't argue, scream, or yell at each other like mine did, and it almost seemed like Liam's father saw the gears turning in my mind when he said, "But no family is without mistakes or faults. On the outside, a family may seem perfect, but behind closed doors, it very well may be another story." He picked up a crumpled napkin left by someone after dinner and began to fold it carefully. "Families are complicated. Like our family, for instance."

I tilted my head in confusion. Liam had never mentioned they had family problems or alluded to anything amiss. They honestly looked like the perfect family.

"It was around the time when Liam was born that I was working a twelve- to sixteen-hour day just to keep our new business afloat. I remember after a long day of never-ending emails, running crews, and bidding proposals, along with all the stress of learning how to become a new owner while struggling to make ends meet, I thought, hey, a hard-working man deserves a few hours at the bar with the boys. More often than not, it would be so late by the time I came home that both Liam and my wife were fast asleep. I pretty much missed out on watching my son grow up between the ages of birth and three years old."

"Really?"

He looked up at me. "Yep. Until my wife put her foot down." he laughed. "We had our fair share of disagreements and quarrels before I finally saw the light and realized I could lose what mattered the most. After that wake-up call, I strive my hardest every day to do the right thing. But it is true; as a father who is working so hard to make sure that his family is provided for, well, sometimes it isn't good enough. And sometimes, we don't immediately see the damage we've caused."

Or ever, I wanted to say.

"But just know, Sam, behind all the stress and all the arguments that your family seems to be struggling with, your parents love you very much. Your family will get over this one day. You'll be all right."

I really hoped so. I didn't have to fake a smile when I looked up at James. I genuinely felt better. "Thanks for the talk, James. I needed to hear that tonight."

"Well, good, then. But do you know what helps with the restlessness and sleeplessness?"

"No. What?" I asked.

"A little game of rummy," he said sheepishly.

Liam was so much like his father—never could say no to a card game. I laughed, "Okay. But just one game, James."

Chapter 14

Sam 2005

Say it three times.

Sunshine and roses. Sunshine and roses. Sunshine and roses.

Some say bad luck comes in threes. But that mentality only suggests that the person saying it is thinking negatively. I wanted to reflect differently on how luck would dish itself out. No more wallowing. It was time to take a more positive viewpoint. I needed to believe that my luck was about to change and that my future could only shine brighter from here on out. So, sunshine and roses it would be.

You could say that, by December 12th, Liam had everything to do with my new outlook on life. In just a few short weeks of living with his family, I was feeling calm and accepting about everything I feared. He was my life raft. His presence alone helped me deal with all the stress I had been harboring, and I realized it was no wonder my ticking timebomb had exploded onto my sister. I owed her an apology, but I also owed Liam for bringing me back to life and piecing this Humpty Dumpty back together again. He was not just my sunshine and roses but my anchor in a storm.

"I love you so much," I said, kissing his forearm, which was splayed under my neck as we spooned on the couch, watching a romantic comedy, *Jerry Maguire*.

He playfully nudged his nose against the soft spot behind my ear. "Love you more. I must say, you seem different today. I'm glad you switched shifts with someone. I like spending an entire Sunday with you. I like hearing you laugh again."

I snuggled my back closer to his body for warmth, making the hairs on his legs brush up against my clean-shaven ones. I sighed in relief. "It helps that you are with me. You make everything better."

Liam's chest puffed out against my back. "Yeah. I have that healing charm about me. Maybe I should go into business? Like, charge for snuggles to all the women in crisis?"

I snorted. "Over my dead body."

"You're right. Charging a woman in crisis doesn't seem right. Free snuggles it is."

I flipped around, bringing our faces nose to nose. "Do you have a death wish?"

He laughed. "Nope. Just this genius plan to get you to turn around so I can do this."

The tender kiss lasted not long enough. We heard slippered feet shuffling down the hall, and I quickly turned around to face the big screen. I returned to my previous position only after Liam's mother greeted us with good-morning kisses, grabbed her cup of morning coffee, and left the room.

My forehead rested on his. "I've had ten minutes to rethink."

"Think what?" he asked.

"No one should suffer alone; everyone needs someone to lean on. So, I decided that if any woman in crisis comes to you, instead of ignoring her as I would rather you did, maybe just give her this advice: Nothing stays bad forever, and fearing your future is a waste of energy. Positive thinking over negative. It's something I learned in my Psychology class just recently."

"Well, your way of thinking seems to be working."

"Guess some college courses do pay off."

Liam tilted his head to the side of mine. "I was doing some of my own positive thinking. Part of me wants to be selfish and keep you here all to myself today, but maybe you should take an hour or two and have lunch with your friends for once?"

"Sick of me already?" I asked.

"Hell no. I mean, it is true we finally have time to see each other, even if it is just in passing between school and work, but I was thinking lunch with your friends would do your soul some good."

"Aww, look at you, caring for my well-being. I had planned to tackle a few hours of studying for my upcoming final. But I think at this point, realizing the full gravity of my dire situation of possibly not passing, maybe I should live a little. I could squeeze a few hours in for my friends. I do miss everyone, Alice included. That poor woman must think I've died. I'll stop at the store and grab her some staples she always needs. Thanks for the suggestion."

"You are so welcome. I would do anything to keep you smiling like this."

I cocked my head and wiggled my eyebrows. "Anything?"

"Anything."

"Then kiss me again."

He gave me a delicious kiss before he pulled away. "You know what is better than a kiss?"

Liam threw the blanket off of us. "We bake chocolate chip cookies for breakfast."

I laughed. "I thought nothing could beat a kiss, but you had me at chocolate."

With all the laughter coming from the back of the Trellis Café, it wasn't that hard to find Emily and Heidi. I smiled wide. "Girls, order me the strongest tea and a bucket of scones with extra jelly and whip, please." I twirled around, flipping my long, curly hair away from my face. "This girl right here is letting loose!"

Heidi clapped her hands, making the black bob around her face wiggle. "We get Fun Sam today? Are you sure we shouldn't leave the café and just go to a bar instead?"

"Did *you* just get back from a bar?" I joked, looking at Heidi's outfit. Except for the oversized red puffer jacket and combat boots, she looked like Betty Boop's Wild Night Out in her tight black dress with fishnet stockings. There was a big hole in the stockings above her knee, which I knew she probably tore herself.

Emily cocked a head of strawberry blond curls at Heidi's statement. "I can't go to a bar. I don't have a fake I.D."

I plopped myself down onto a soft cushion. "I'm sure Heidi could get you a fake I.D., but it doesn't matter. I'm not interested in going to a bar, even *if* I'm turning twenty-one soon. Just being here with you two makes me feel good again. Liam was right. I've missed you girls."

"You look different, and I bet it's all that shacking up with Liam, isn't it?" Heidi asked me, as her painted-on dark eyebrows wiggled up and down inquisitively. "You two lovebirds doin' the nasty? Because, whatever happy pill you're on, it sure looks good on you."

"Sorry. No nasty here," I said. "But can't a girl just be happy for once?"

Emily asked, "Wait, don't you guys sleep in separate bedrooms? Do I have that right? Him upstairs and you downstairs?"

"Yeah. Our parents were strong in their opinions that we were going to sleep in separate rooms. I'm fine with that, anyway. Having Liam in my bed is all too tempting. But it doesn't stop Liam from sneaking in occasionally." I winked and gave them a mischievous smirk. "We gotta have a few night snuggles to keep the nightmares away, you know."

"Sneaky kids," Heidi snickered.

I took a swig of my water before shaking my head. "It does sound ridiculous, though, that we have separate bedrooms. I mean, we are both grown-ass adults. I *am* in total control of myself, so there is nothing to worry about. But I think our parents each wanted to prove they had better morals than the other, which is stupid because I'm sure they were doing worse at our age."

We ordered our food before I remembered something funny. "Speaking of sneaky, I have to tell you something." I leaned forward and whispered, "This story proves why we need to get our own place. So, Liam's parents went to bed one night—well, *so we thought*. All the while, here's Liam sneaking into my room for another kiss goodnight and a round of snuggles."

"Oh, give me a break," Heidi quipped. "*Snuggles*?"

"All right, maybe there was some heavy petting, but no one's pregnant, so calm yourself," I said, rolling my eyes. "Now, can I finish this story? Because you are going to die laughing. It goes a little something like this ... "

"Liam, what are you doing in here?" I had said, nearly asleep. "You tucked me in ten minutes ago."

"I know," he said, sitting on the side of my bed. "But, now that my parents are in bed, I thought you'd want to wake up for this." He turned on the lamp next to my bed before pulling from behind his back, a giant plate of chocolate cake.

My eyes widened. "Is that—"

"Yep," he smiled. "Straight from Alberto's on Fifth Street."

"Are you seriously trying to get me fat? We already ate popcorn and M&Ms during the movie."

With eyes that sparkled in challenge, Liam grinned before slowly pulling the plate back behind his back. "*Oh*, so ... so you don't want the cake?"

I glared at him, sitting up, fully aware I had zero control when it came to Alberto's moist, deep, dark, seven-layered chocolate cake. "YOU! Hold it right there and bring that damn cake back to me."

He laughed and placed the cake on top of my blanket-covered stomach. "I thought so. Also, I realized something today, Sam. Popcorn doesn't have much play in them. But cake with a smooth, buttery frosting, now that is something we can play with." I didn't know what he was talking about and grabbed the fork on the side of the plate, but he slapped my hand away. "Nope. I have other plans." He dipped his forefinger deeply into the thick layer of icing and said, "Open wide, but not too wide," he said, bringing it to my lips.

I rolled my eyes. "Boy, I don't know if I want to choke or hug you."

"Both sound good to me. Now, do as I ask."

"And if I don't?"

"I'll scream and tell my parents you are trying to take advantage of me."

"What?" I laughed. "*You're* the one in *my* bedroom. I think they'll know who is taking advantage of who."

"You're ruining this. No more talking," he growled, shoving his finger into my mouth, which I didn't mind at all. I played his game by slowly applying pressure around his finger and bit down lightly before scraping my teeth down it as I sucked all the icing off. "Ouch," he whined.

"Oh, that hurts?" I played back.

Liam's eyes of honey, gold, and green darkened when he squinted at me in a threatening manner. "Okay. *My* turn."

My heart raced a bit, knowing that playing games with someone bigger than me always meant I'd lose. I swallowed when Liam threw the covers off my chest and lifted my pajama top over my head and onto the floor. "What is it with us and desserts?" I asked him, laughing.

Liam dipped his finger into the frosting again, but instead of putting it into my mouth, he placed a thick amount over my neck before trailing it down to my intermammary cleft—cleavage. "I learned quickly that since food is one way to melt your heart, it's *desserts* that seem to melt all the *other* parts of you that I love so much."

I forgot about eating cake when he brought his hot mouth over the top of my neck and onto my chilled skin. "Oh, my word," I moaned while gripping the sheets tightly in my fisting hands.

"And then?" Heidi asked me.

"Well, I wish I could say what happened next was that we ate that damn cake in all the possible ways one would if they were in a cake-eating contest, but no, that is not what happened."

"Well, what the hell happened?" she asked again.

"We heard the upstairs bathroom toilet flush," I said.

Heidi leaned forward, sitting at the edge of her chair now. "So?"

"So, Liam looked up at me, wide-eyed in fright, frozen, with chocolate frosting all around his mouth, and when we heard the creaking of footsteps coming down the stairs, he tossed the plate of cake on top of my nightstand, threw my shirt back over my head, and covered me up with the blanket, all before grabbing an anatomy book at the end of my bed."

"Oh crap," Emily said.

"Exactly," I said. "Anyway, do you know how hard it was for me to keep a straight face as Liam read a random anatomy page to me without knowing how to pronounce the words? And the worst part was how I wanted to tell him he still had chocolate all over his face, but I couldn't because that's when Liam's mom, Susan, knocked on the door and came in. I tell you guys, the scene she walked into was picturesque—like a father reading to his child a bedtime story, and I was all like, 'Oh, hey, Susan. We're just getting some late-night studying done. Liam's quizzing me for my test tomorrow.' I looked at Emily. "I mean, it wasn't a total lie; he *was* teaching me some anatomy lessons," I said, worming my eyebrows up and down.

Heidi looked thoroughly crushed and disappointed. "So, no sex or cake?"

"Nope. And how could I, when I got cake-blocked by his mom? The best part was when she pointed at Liam's mouth and asked him what all the brown stuff was. He quickly wiped his mouth with the back of his hand while nodding to the cake on the nightstand. 'Cake,' he squeaked out."

Emily's mouth hung wide open with a straw dangling from her lip. "Tell me she didn't believe you?"

"I think she believed us, because Susan walked over to him and wiped the corner of his mouth, saying, 'You are one messy eater. Now, you two don't stay up too late, because you both have class tomorrow.'"

Emily burst into laughter while Heidi looked at me unfazed. "Okay, so not only is that story PG-rated, but it is also the worst ending to a story ever. Unless ... " she eyed me suspiciously, "unless something happened with the cake *after* she left?"

I laughed, "Sorry, but if you want an R-rated version, I suggest you find your own boyfriend. You can't live your fantasies through me, Heidi."

"Hey, that's not fair," she pouted. "And FYI, I *am* looking, but it's slim pickings out there. With you and your stupid cake-eating boyfriend, what's left? Besides, not everyone can find a literal sugar daddy like you, Sam." She took a swig of her drink before slamming it down and then glared at Emily. "Hell, why don't you ask Emily about the date she tried to set me up on last week?"

"A date?" I asked Emily, who gave me a weak smile.

Heidi pointed an accusing finger at her. "This one here made me think I might have hit the jackpot after she says I will love this guy who is super hot and has a huge snake."

Emily threw her hands up. "How was I supposed to know you took that last part figuratively and not literally? I thought, with you being a vet assistant, you'd like that last part."

"Well, it would have been nice to know exactly what you meant, because I had to sit through an entire dinner with a guy who talked about his ginormous *pet* python at home. I actually got up and left when he pulled out his newest pet addition."

"Wait, like, he brought a real pet snake on the date?" I asked, mortified.

"Trust me," she said, "I would have stayed to finish my pasta if it was the *other* kind of snake in his pocket. But no. It was an actual look-alike garter snake that he named Baby Gilbert." When Emily and I couldn't stop laughing, Heidi slapped her knee and mimicked us mockingly, "*HA HA*, so funny, right? You guys have no idea what it's like dating right now."

I smoothed a hand over the laugh lines on my face to give my best serious expression. "So, what kind of guy are you looking for exactly?" I asked.

"Obviously not the cold-blooded kind," Emily joked.

Heidi pretended not to hear her. "I don't ask for much. I just want someone who makes me breakfast in bed and makes me laugh. Is that so hard to ask?"

"So you want someone funny?" I couldn't help myself and added, "Like, *hisssssterically* funny?"

"You two are so immature. Enough with the snake jokes. Moving on, please." She looked at me. "On a serious note, what's happening with that jerk trying to sue you?"

My stomach dropped. "I'd rather not talk about it."

"How bad is it?" Emily asked.

"After my deposition, the lawyers tried to settle on a number. We offered an amount, but his lawyers said no." I twisted my napkin in front of me, wishing we could return to talking about pet snakes. "So now, the jerk plans on taking me to court."

"I'm sorry, Sam," Heidi and Emily both said.

"The thing is, I truly believe he's lying about how badly he was injured. I saw him right after I hit him, and there's no way he needs that much money for his pain and suffering."

"What's this guy's name anyway? You said he was about our age. Do we know him?" Emily asked.

"I've never seen him before the accident, so I don't think he went to our high school or to our college. Anyway, his name is Randy Jergins."

Heidi choked on the spoonful of tomato soup she had just sipped. "Randy Jergins?"

"You know someone with that name?" I asked.

She set her spoon down. "I freakin' know a Randy Jergins that's about our age."

I leaned forward. "Wait. Skinny guy, dark curly hair, drives a black car?"

Heidi slapped the table so loudly that it startled the table next to us. "With a license plate that reads 'three ways for fun'?"

"Holy freakin' crap, Heidi, YES, that's him! How do you know this guy?"

"Oh, boy," Heidi said, shaking her head. "He's terrible. *Really* bad. He lives down the road on my street. You probably don't remember him going to our high school because he was only there for less than a semester. He had to transfer to an alternative school for nearly choking out another kid." She leaned in closer to me. "Just a low-life kinda guy. Smokes weed a ton, doesn't even have a real job, unless you count selling pot on the side and sometimes tinkering in his dad's garage."

I interrupted Heidi. "Do you actually *know* him?"

"Well, no. But our family is in the loop about everything that goes on in our neighborhood. We are tight with most of our neighbors, except for the Jergins family. And Sam, you're gonna freak when I tell you the best part."

"There's a best part?"

"Yep. I can't tell you how many times my dad's heard of them having yet 'another car accident.' They are always driving different cars, never the same one for more than a year. For a while, we just thought Randy's dad was fixing and selling cars, because he runs a small autobody shop inside his garage, but if my vague recollection is correct, I heard something about the Jergins family being 'sue-happy.' It's a strong possibility that this is how they make their money." Heidi pointed a finger at me in warning. "Shit. I think you are being scammed, Sam."

I slowly eased my back into the chair and blinked several times. "I honestly can't believe what I'm hearing." After a few seconds, I sat forward. "Heidi, if I can prove they're a fraud, it might save me from owing thousands and thousands of dollars."

"I hope so."

"Wow. This is nuts," Emily said. "What are you going to do, Sam?"

"First thing tomorrow, I'm calling my lawyer and giving her this precious tidbit. I pray to God that this information can be useful in court."

"When is the trial?" Heidi asked.

"My court date is set a day after my birthday, one month and a day from now."

"I hope you get this guy," Heidi said.

"Me too."

The news Heidi gave me put a little pep in my step as I made my way to the grocery store to buy a few items that Alice always needed. I couldn't hide the satisfied grin that spread across my face as I strolled down each aisle, thinking about how crazy it was that this new information had come to me just at the right time. Maybe for once, just maybe, things were looking up for Samantha Carey.

I walked down the aisle for the senior chocolate Ensure shakes and paused to check out the walking canes for sale. Alice had said she would 'think' about owning one, but if I knew anything about seniors, it was that they were stubborn and didn't like change. The cane was pricey, but I thought, what's another thirty dollars added to my hundred and fifty-thousand-dollar debt? I placed the pink cane in my cart and hoped Alice wouldn't see the suggestion as overstepping on my part. I'd have to tell her the cane was a gift; that way, she couldn't return it.

The bakery section was next. A little apple fritter celebration treat seemed appropriate in light of the recent news. I also grabbed a pretty indoor plant for Liam's parents to thank them for offering me their home and hospitality. Once I paid for the items, I headed to Alice's.

Alice didn't hear me enter when I found her in the kitchen chopping vegetables. I didn't want to startle her, especially since she held a knife in her hand, so I alerted her by banging on the wall in the hallway to cause a vibration. Only when she paused to look up did I move forward and wave a bag of groceries in my hand.

"Samantha!" She beamed.

I yelled, "Brought you some staples!"

Her eyes immediately took in the pink cane I held in my left hand. "What in the world is that thing for?"

"This is a gift for you."

"Now, why'd you go and do that?" she said, not looking too happy.

"Cuz, I love you," I said, batting my eyes. I held the cane up. "How about I leave this by your chair in the living room? If you choose to use it, then excellent. If not, no worries. It's only there 'just in case.'"

Alice gave me a dubious look. "I told you I didn't want you to spend money on me. I'll pay you for it."

"No, no, Alice. Really, it's just a small gift."

"Fine, you silly girl. But in return, you gotta eat some soup with me, which should be ready in an hour or two. You got time to wait for it to cook?"

"Sure, I'll be hungry again in an hour or two." I held up the bag of donuts. "Will this go with the soup?"

"Donuts with borscht soup? Why not?"

I asked, "What is borscht soup, anyway?"

"Borscht is my absolute favorite. It's a Ukrainian dish. I have a wonderful Ukrainian friend who gave me the recipe years ago. It is made with only vegetables—beets, beans, cabbage, potatoes, carrots, onions, and garlic. Then, add a little chicken broth, and voila—the most delicious and healthy meal."

"Can I help you chop vegetables?

"Have at it," Alice said. She slid over a cutting board and handed me a knife and a hearty beet the size of a large softball. "Here, go ahead and peel the outside of the beet before cutting it into smaller pieces."

"I don't think I have ever made anything with beets before."

"What? They are the best. You can even eat them like a dessert, you know. Cut them into pieces, boil, drain, and mash them with butter, salt, and honey. It makes my mouth water just thinking about it."

I laughed, "Alice, the beet lover."

"Well, I'm not a picky person. I'll eat just about anything. I lived on rice and beans for a portion of my life, when I lived in Mexico, so beets are a treat." Alice began chopping the onions. "So, dear, what's been happening?"

"I haven't told you yet. I didn't want you to think wrong of me, but I got kicked out of my house, and I'm living with Liam. I know your faith is strong, and you probably disagree with my new living arrangements, you know, not being married yet."

Alice wiped her eyes. "This isn't me crying about your living arrangements; it's only these pesky onions. But if I'm so strong in my faith as you say, then you should know I wouldn't ever judge you, dear. One of God's most important standards is, 'Thou shall not judge.'"

How could I forget? Alice wouldn't be one to hold anything against me. "Of course," I said. "Sorry. I just always worry about what people think."

"Well, it isn't their right to think anything about what you do. But tell me, child, if you don't mind, why did you get kicked out of your home?"

"I'm not happy about my actions, but my sister and I got into a heated argument that turned a tad physical—some hair-pulling and face-slapping." I didn't mention the butter knife to Alice.

"Kicking you out seems a bit rash."

"Yeah."

"I'm sure your father has his regrets, but I bet in his mind, he's just doing what he thinks is best. Of course, parents aren't perfect, either. No one is."

"True. Was being a parent hard for you?"

"I had troubles with all four of my kids. Each one was a little different. But I did the best I could with each one. Many mistakes along the way, but then again, who doesn't make mistakes?"

I laughed. "I can tell you, Alice, I've made quite a few mistakes lately. My car accident, for one. Also, I didn't help a friend at work when I should have, and of course, the fight with my sister." I handed Alice the chopped beets and then looked down at my hands, which were stained red.

Alice nodded to my hands. "Forgot to mention that happens. Beet stains are like mistakes; with time and after a few clean washes, you'll be new and have learned a lesson."

"What's the lesson?"

"If you don't want to make a mess, wear gloves next time, silly."

I laughed as Alice poured three cans of broth into the large pot and added a few spices before pointing to the veggies. "Okay," she said, "so now that we've chopped all the vegetables, let's put them into this pot and let it simmer for a good two hours."

"That's it?"

"That's all she wrote. Now, wash your hands and put your coat on."

"You want to go for a walk?" I asked.

"Sure. I figure, why not try out that cane you got me? Who knows, maybe walking with stability might be fun again."

We made our way outside into the cold, brisk December day before I asked, "Alice, will you finish where you left off with your story about meeting Frank?"

"Only if you're ready for an earful, with all the good, bad, and ugly. As I said, we all make mistakes, and no one is perfect. But, for some, the hardest life lessons aren't about our mistakes, but about learning how to let go of all our regrets."

"Like Jane?"

"Just like Jane."

Chapter 15

Alice 1945-1947

I know a lot about making mistakes.

Six months after I met Frank, we discovered I was pregnant. And because we weren't married, Frank asked me to keep quiet about the pregnancy. He was too ashamed and scared to tell his bishop father. He didn't want him to know he had soiled his precious white-gloved hands. So, reluctantly and cowardly, I allowed Frank to hatch a plan. We would say goodbye to everyone we loved and leave our hometown to have the baby without anyone ever finding out. I was so in love with Frank that I would have followed the man to the moon if he asked.

At first, I was scared, but with World War II pretty much over, we were anxious and ready to experience new opportunities. We chose to start our new secret lives in America, specifically in Detroit. We were not yet citizens of the United States, so Frank applied for a work visa. Back in those days, if they granted residency to the husband, wives were protected under the law as long as they stayed married. So, we secretly hurried to the altar and married.

We found jobs fast. Until I was ready to have our baby, my husband worked as a shoe salesman, and I worked across the street selling nylons in a cute boutique. I remember Frank saying we should have a contest to see who made the most sales.

What my new husband failed to remember was that before, when the war was still on, nylon products were rationed. Nylon was in such high demand by the military for parachutes that women found themselves out of luck when trying to find a pair. So, by the time the war ended, there wasn't a woman in the country who didn't desperately want to buy a pair. In fact, once the restrictions were lifted, there was a nylon riot in Pittsburgh! Forty thousand women lined up a mile long to get their hands on them. I won that bet with Frank. I only wish there were other bets I had won, too.

After the nylon frenzy died down, we found that selling shoes didn't allow us to save up much. We lived paycheck to paycheck. But luckily, the fashion world was steady enough, and Frank and I made do with what little we had. I didn't care that we weren't rich. Money was never important to me, not when my happiness was walking home each day, thinking about how marvelous it was to have a living human being growing inside me. I was creating life, just like my mother, her mother, and my grandmother's mother.

But Frank had other plans.

"Alice," Frank said one day after I came home from work, "I need you to sit down and listen to what I have to say. It's important."

I plopped my heavy form onto an old hand-me-down mint-colored sofa we'd found at a thrift store and sighed. At eight months pregnant, I was always happy to sit down. I grunted to lift my feet onto the stool in front of me. They hurt terribly from standing all day selling nylons. When Frank didn't say anything and only stared at me, I followed his gaze to my swollen feet—my flesh protesting through the too-tight, bare-back pumps I wore. I asked while rubbing my enormous belly, "What? Do I look that bad?" I was sure the baby would be fat and healthy—any parent's hope.

Frank looked worried and uncertain, as if he was testing his footfalls over a lake covered in thin ice. He finally said, "You know I love you, and I wouldn't ask this of you unless it was a dire situation."

His tone sounded alarming, and my mind diverted from the thoughts I'd had about him possibly feeling guilty that he couldn't afford to buy me wider shoes, even with his employee discount.

"What is it, Frank?"

Frank raked his hands through his thick hair before letting out a long, exasperated breath. "Alice, I can't go through with this."

"Through with what?"

He pointed to my stomach. "You know, with having the baby. How are we going to take care of it?" He whispered as if worried the neighbors could hear him, "We're barely making enough for the two of us to eat."

I thought for sure he must be joking. "Don't be silly. We will make do. You're thinking irrationally. You're just getting cold feet, is all."

He shook his head all too fast. "No, no. It has nothing to do with cold feet, and I am completely thinking logically here. The rent is coming up, and I did the math. It's plain and simple. We can't afford to have this baby."

A cold chill ran up my back, and I rubbed my belly feverishly. "Tell me you're only kidding, Frank Clark."

"This isn't a joke, Alice." Frank stood and paced the room while waving his hands wildly about in the air. "What kind of life would this child have, with two parents working full time? We barely have enough food on the table. Then, there will be diapers and formula, and what about medical care? We can't afford that right now. And don't get me started on childcare. You would have to quit your job and stay home while I look for a job that pays double what I make now."

"Frank. Please stop this nonsense. We will figure this out."

Frank jerked around and faced me with a hardened stare. "There is no stopping the rationality of this long-overdue conversation, Alice. This isn't nonsense. What's nonsense is thinking we could have this baby in the first place."

I grunted and pushed myself to stand before crossing my arms like a defiant child. "I don't want to hear another word. I mean, Frank, what did you expect? People have babies all the time and make it work. If we can't afford this child, then why did you bring me to America, out here alone, without our family's help?"

"You know why."

I threw my hands up. "This ego of yours. Put it aside so we can return home to our families. Our parents could help us. We can do this, with a little help."

"We can't go back home, Alice." He sat down hard on the sofa. "I can't face them."

My husband hung his head so low that I rushed over to him and held him, all the while hoping he would listen to reason. "We can face them together."

"No. You don't understand," he said, pleading. "I can't go home. Our families would figure out that the baby was conceived *before* we got married. They aren't stupid; we would be a disgrace, a laughingstock."

I didn't understand why my husband needed to save face. I only knew that he was scared, and I had to help him see the light. "Sure, the news would initially shock them, but they would get over it. Such is life. Frank, you're acting like a buffoon, allowing your pride to take precedence over what's right. If we can't have the baby here alone, then it's decided—we *must* go back home for help until we get back on our feet and save up a little."

Frank shied away from my touch, stood, and wiped his hand down his face in frustration. "Alice. I don't want to say this, and it hurts to even say these words, but I've made up my mind. I *can't* have this baby, and I won't. We need to do the right thing and give it up for adoption."

My eyes prickled with tears. "I will do no such thing."

Frank held his ground and pointed to my belly. "We have to give this baby a fighting chance, Alice. Stop thinking of yourself. This baby needs a family that can afford to take care of it. They will love this baby more than we can."

Tears of anger came crashing forward, and I wiped them away bitterly. "I will love my baby just fine! Love is not defined by the worldly goods we give them. A baby needs their birth parents' love. How could you ask such a thing? I won't do what you ask of me, Frank; I won't."

"But Alice, love is also a selfless act. I *know* what the right thing to do is. And if you don't realize what is best for the child, then I don't know what else to say, except if you keep this baby, then you will have to love this child on your own. Without me."

I took a faltering step back as if his words physically pushed me. "You would abandon me? Abandon *us*?"

Frank walked to the front door and opened it. "It physically kills me to do this. But it's this baby or me. You choose."

And at that, Frank left the apartment.

The shock of Frank's decision left me frantic.

My heart split in two.

I could barely breathe after hearing Frank's ultimatum. To choose my baby over a man I was madly in love with was like deciding whether to live without a beating heart. Yes, his actions made me loathe him, but my heart still belonged to him in every possible way. And yet, being left with such a decision physically made me sick. I could barely contemplate what to do next.

If I decided to return home alone with my child, I'd be a single mother, and Frank could never forgive me for making him look like a fool in his hometown. I would lose him forever. But staying in America and raising a baby alone was an even more frightening thought, and as much as I hated Frank's way of thinking, he had a point. It was nearly impossible to care for a baby with a lack of decent financial stability. I didn't want to admit the truth. We couldn't afford even one pair of shoes for ourselves.

I tried to imagine what our life would look like—our future—when we were so impoverished. How one day our child, perhaps a boy, would eventually attend primary school. Instead of games and laughter on the playground, I saw other privileged children sneering and laughing in cruel, torturous ways that left my little one in tears for lacking what others took for granted. I couldn't help but ask myself, would our baby understand as I wiped the sad tears from his little face, explaining how those meaningless and unkind words didn't hold a candle to the thing that mattered the most: our love for him?

Was love enough? Was I selfish for wanting to keep my child? Could a child's life of want and need negatively affect him, causing embarrassment and resentment? Or would my child understand that a mother's love was worth far more than the pull of material things in this world? Such a demand was almost too much to bear. And it didn't come as a surprise when I went into early labor.

On February 15, 1946, I gave birth to Joyce Ethel Clark.

Dark, wet whorls of matted hair clung to her tiny head, while curious dark blue eyes stared back into mine, as if daring me to choose her over him. Maybe some young mothers could look away, but I didn't dare. I memorized every finger and toe, every fine, delicate detail of her perfect little body—skin silky like cream, a button nose, and pursed lips making soft, mewled cries like those of a kitten.

How could I ever forget her?

"It's a selfless act of love," he said, trying desperately to console the inconsolable.

I couldn't bear to look at his face as mine became wet with anguished tears, mimicking my daughter's tears. Her face was contorted in confusion, wondering why I couldn't give her what she needed.

Milk?

Security?

A mother's love?

Already a blurred question.

The nurse took her from me all too soon, and, like a frayed seam, my heart split apart as I watched my child's arms fling wide—searching and needing the warmth of her mother's arms, arms that lay limp against the bloodied bedsheets.

It was the hardest decision I'd ever had to make.

A mistake that would never be mended.

I was inconsolable for what seemed like months. My body ached for relief—to once again hold my baby girl. The doctor had warned Frank that my emotional state could leave irreparable damage, and he was right. Even if I wanted to talk to Frank about the ache in my heart, I couldn't. I was too absorbed in my pain to wonder if he felt any guilt himself. All my thoughts were of my baby.

Where was she?

Was she okay?

Did she cry out for me?

The void in my heart became unimaginable pain that soon turned into resentment. I detested my husband for what he had made me do. I was already having a hard time forgiving Frank for making me choose, but for many years, I also hated myself for giving in to his gut-wrenching request. The resentment I held toward us both became my constant. They say time heals, but still, to this day, my heart waits to be made whole again. I have a baby girl out there in the world, and I will never have the chance to tell her how sorry I am.

But life tends to go on, regardless of heartache. Work helped numb the pain as we stayed in Detroit a year more to sell shoes and nylons. Frank began working extremely long hours when the shoe business finally boomed, and keeping up with the new fashions became all the rage.

During the war, many women worked in factories and had to wear long pants with rounded, closed-toed shoes for safety, but by 1946, they were tired of pants. Fashionable dresses and more feminine shoewear came back in style. Frank couldn't keep up with all the ruffled pumps flying off the shelves, and it became a theme when Frank stayed late at work most evenings. But I didn't mind. I was still angry at him.

As for me, they'd just come out with a new seamless style of stocking that didn't wrinkle or run as severely as the silk kind, so selling nylons kept me busy, too. But not busy enough to steer my mind away from wondering.

Every woman who came into that store could have been my child's substitute mother. I wondered if it was this mother or that mother who gave enough kisses to my little girl. I wondered if, maybe, instead of shopping for nylons, they should be home with my baby to ensure she had everything she needed.

It was worse when I saw toddlers out in public.

Could that one be mine?

Could I ask to hold her to make sure?

Could I have a second chance?

Eventually, it became all too depressing. We both needed to escape the guilt and shame we felt, so it wasn't long after that we chose to move to sunny Los Angeles, California. The new city offered warmer weather and, with little to no snow, California happened to be a prime location for selling fashionwear. We could make a decent living for once, which would help if we ever wanted to start a real family. We lived near the famous Ambassador Hotel, where lots of actors resided at the time, and Frank felt living so close to all the action was exciting, which he hoped would help me not think so much about the daughter I had given up.

How stupid, though.

I would think of my baby girl every single day for the rest of my life.

Making the move to Los Angeles sure helped us a little more financially, especially for Frank. Even though I couldn't find a job in the nylon business again, I did okay selling purses. But it was Frank selling shoes in Hollywood that made all the difference. Hollywood's fashion industry was booming, keeping us alive and enabling us to make ends meet. When the calf-length skirt that Christian Dior created came out, and the iconic dress pushed for the pointed-toe look, Frank was busy selling those shoes in various styles all day and every day. Not only did women love their shoes, but they loved Frank. With his good looks, he sold many, many pairs.

And boy were we grateful for the extra cash Frank was making because not even a year after giving up our baby girl, and a few months after my twentieth birthday, I found myself pregnant again. But this time around, we had reason to celebrate. My husband had no reason why I couldn't keep this baby. Frank was making just enough money for me to stay home and care for a child. So, it was settled.

We finally celebrated my pregnancy one night when Frank said he wanted to take me out for late-night drinks to meet some of his new friends and the dates they were all bringing. Even though I was only four months pregnant, I had only one dress that didn't fit snugly across my stomach. Frank looked at me with eyebrows drawn inward and glowered.

"What?" I asked, my hand hovering over my belly. "It's the only thing I have to wear that looks decent."

"Well, it just won't do, Alice. It's a nice place that we're going to."

I crossed my arms. "And what do you expect me to do? Steal the neighbor's clothes?"

He smiled mischievously and said, "What a great idea. Put on your shoes, Alice. I know of a place."

"What are we doing at your workplace?" I asked him ten minutes later, when we pulled into the shoe store where he worked.

He opened my door and helped me out of the car. "We gotta enter through the back door. We can't be seen from the front," he whispered.

"I don't understand, Frank."

"Just wait and see." After he walked us around the building and led me to the back door, he pulled out a ring of keys and then unlocked it. Frank always had the keys with him, since he was the closer for the shoe store each night, but I shook my head after we walked in and stood in the dark for a long moment before our eyes adjusted to the pitch-black. He whispered again, even though nobody was there, "We can't turn any lights on. We don't want to alert anyone that we're here. Besides, we're just gonna borrow a pair of shoes. I'll bring them back tomorrow when I return to work."

"But I thought," I said, looking around the tall metal racks of stacked boxes of shoes that lined the walls, "I thought you were bringing me somewhere to get a dress or something."

Frank disappeared behind the mini rows of shoes, but I could still hear his voice from ten rows back. "Alice, if there is one thing I know about fashion, it's that shoes come before the dress. I know exactly what I'm looking for, too. And these shoes that just came in from Paris are beautiful, just like you."

It felt nice he paid me the compliment when I hadn't felt so pretty lately, looking like an over-stuffed pin cushion. "But won't you get in trouble when I ruin the bottom of the shoes, Frank? I mean, I can't just float about the room so they don't get scuffed and scratched up."

Frank walked toward me, holding a fancy red box. "Don't worry. I'll just have Tony from our shoe repair department put on some new outer soles. He won't question me when I tell him that a customer returned them after finding a defect." Frank set the shoe box down, took my hands in his, and squeezed. "Alice, I want you to look like an angel, even if it is just for one night. I promise you, you won't need to worry. Let me take care of this."

"Okay," I said warily as he pushed me onto a bench nearby.

"Wait." Frank walked several feet behind me before flipping on a tiny light near one of the office desks in the back corner of the room. "There," he said, returning. "I can't be fully blind doing this. Now, let me see if the shoe fits again, shall we?"

I giggled when his fingers ran across the bottom of my nylon foot. "I don't know if it's the thrill of you sneaking me in here or touching my feet in the dark like that, but maybe we could stay in here a while longer," I hinted.

He took hold of my foot and laughed. "If it wasn't so late and I hadn't already told the boys we would meet them and their girls at eight, I would stay here with you in a heartbeat, doll." He slipped a gorgeous gold and sparkled shoe on me, or should I say, wrangled my foot into the shoe like I was a bull and he the bull rider. "Oh," he said, sounding a bit shocked. "The shoes are too tight."

"Well, seriously, Frank. What did you think would happen to a woman when she grows a baby inside her?"

He sat back on his heels and looked up at me in bewilderment. "Well, I don't know. Last time, I didn't seem to notice your feet. I guess I thought it was only your belly that grew."

"Well, it doesn't. My feet are swollen now, so go get me another pair, you silly man."

Frank came back with one size bigger. "All right. Let's try these," he said. He slipped my foot perfectly into the glittery evening pumps, which seemed made for a golden goddess. They had a rounded front with a small toe opening and a strap attached with a buckle on the side, just above the heel. He sighed, "Phew. That was our last size up." I didn't know whether to laugh or slap him for implying that there were no shoes bigger than the ones I already had on, but he stood before I said anything. "Now I'm gonna grab myself a pair of shoes too. Sit tight."

When Frank returned with a box of shoes for himself, I asked, "Okay, now what? Cause I still don't have a dress to go with these fancy shoes."

"Well, little do you know, Missy. That connecting door right over there," he said, pointing to the side wall of the building, "that door leads into the town's newest store, Frederick's of Hollywood. And, it so happens that I have a key."

My mouth dropped open. "Frank, just one of those dresses in that store happens to be the price of our electrical bill."

"And?" He pointed to my shoes. "Those shoes you have on cost the same, if not more." He kissed my forehead. "Only the best for my girl. Now, come on. We don't have a lot of time to dillydally."

After he unlocked the door, he had to push pretty hard. The door seemed not to have been opened in years. We tiptoed around the tiled floors and in between racks and racks of clothes as if scared there might be a guard on duty of some sort. But there wasn't. "Okay," he said, "I didn't think this through, but we're gonna need a flashlight."

"Well, don't look at me," I whispered. "I didn't bring one. You didn't even tell me the plan until we got here."

"I know, I know. But it's just that I haven't been to this store, so I don't even know where to find a gold-colored dress. And I still need a suit, too. Hold on," he said, walking back from where we'd come. "I have to go back into my manager's office real quick." When Frank came back, he was out of breath. "We're gonna have to be super quick, so how about I flash my lights on a rack, and if we don't see the color we want, we're gonna quickly move to the next rack. Are you ready?"

"I guess so."

"Okay. Let's go."

Frank found a suit immediately before we looked for my dress, but you should've seen us. We were like Bonnie and Clyde in the dark of night, robbing the store of its finest treasures. It was the fifth rack when I said too loudly and pointed my finger. "Frank! There's a gold one right there." He shushed me, and since my back hurt from all the ducking around beside the racks, I stood at my full height before rubbing my back. "I don't know why we must be quiet," I said. "No one is in here."

He grabbed my arm, pulling me back down to a crouching position. "I know no one is here, but if someone sees us through the front windows, with us walking around in the dark looking all suspicious-like, it's just not gonna be good. I can't risk losing my job or going to jail, Alice."

"You're right. I'm sorry."

"Good, now grab that dress, and let's go."

"Wait, Frank. Quickly look at the tag on the dress. What size does it say?" He aimed the flashlight at the back of the dress and at the tag. After he told me the size, I vigorously shook my head. "Sorry, there's no way I'm fitting into that, Frank. I couldn't fit into that even if I were still in the third grade."

He sorted through the next five dresses before finding my size all the way at the end of the line. "Here," he said, handing me the dress. "Try it on real quick."

I slowly stood erect before taking a sneak peek outside the windows just to make sure no one was there as I undressed. When a couple of figures walked past the store, I panicked and stopped undressing mid-zip. "I'm sure it fits. Let's just go. I cannot go to jail, either, Frank. Could you imagine me giving birth in jail? Our baby born in jail, Frank?"

"All right. Take it off, and let's go home and try it on. I'm sure it fits, too," he said, sounding slightly worried.

It did not fit.

Back at home, and while I stood in front of the mirror attached to our small closet door, my breasts looked unholy as they pooled out and over the low V-neck of that dress, like two full moons at a Sunday morning church service. And because I was so tall, the dress ended practically at my knees when it was meant to go over them.

"But look at those shoes, Alice," he soothed after seeing the scowl on my face.

I looked down at the shoes but then quickly back at my chest. "I look like a hooker, Frank. A pregnant hooker to boot."

"No, you don't, Alice." He pulled me into his arms. "You're the most beautiful woman I have ever seen. You are going to make all the men envious that I have you on my arm."

I stepped away from his embrace and smoothed a hand over my borrowed silk and gold crisscross-wrapped dress with oversized padded shoulders and pockets. I gave myself a quick look over before turning to face my husband and smiled. "It is a beautiful dress, Frank. And these shoes are gorgeous." I kissed his cheek. "Thank you for risking jail for me. I do feel really, really pretty."

"Someday, Alice, I will have enough money to buy you a closet full of these dresses and shoes. I don't want you to ever worry about not fitting in. Not ever."

I wanted to tell my husband that I had never worried about not fitting in, as long as he loved me and our baby, but I didn't have time to get the words out when he looked down at his watch and whisked me out the front door, saying, "Showtime."

That night, with all his friends and their girlfriends sitting and laughing around the table, my husband's eyes beamed like two crystal gems whenever he looked me over with approval. It made me happy how he admired me so much, but there was a strange feeling in my gut. I had thought he knew that money was never more important to me than our happiness. And for the rest of the night, I couldn't get it out of my head, the way Frank said he didn't want me to 'worry about not fitting in'. It made me wonder if perhaps it was *him* who felt like he didn't fit in.

Chapter 16

Alice 1947-1955

We welcomed our beautiful baby boy, little David, close to my twenty-first birthday in November 1947. I shouldn't say he was so little. He was over ten pounds. There were times I'd look down at his tiny face to see if he held any resemblance to the baby girl Frank had forced me to leave behind. But, being a new mommy, I didn't have much time to dwell on the past during the day. I found motherhood suited me. It was at night, when all was quiet, that my thoughts would linger longingly on my baby girl.

After little David, my hips stayed wide, making it easier to welcome the following two children, spaced two years apart. First came Greg, then Maria, each born at the Hollywood Presbyterian Hospital. Our children were our pride and joy, but raising three children wasn't easy, and it often took a toll on both of us financially, mentally, and physically. As a housewife and mother, most of my life at home consisted of cooking, cleaning, and raising our babies. It was most tiring, and at one point, when all three children were still wearing cloth diapers, I wished we could afford diaper services.

Just thinking about how long it took me to clean the diapers makes me feel panicked. First, I had to swish the diaper in the toilet to get most of the solids out. Then, scrub with bleach and soap. Next was the boiling and sanitizing process, and the final step was to rinse and dry on the clothesline outside. I was most definitely losing my mind from exhaustion. Sometimes, I felt like if I saw one more dirty diaper, I'd have to run away to that glitzy hotel down the road. It seemed like the only way to save my sanity. But I somehow found a way to push forward and survive the daily chaos.

By 1953, when the children were two, four, and six, Frank and I started to have marital issues. No one had told us raising children would be so hard.

We argued a lot back then—about little things and some more significant things too. But mostly, we couldn't see eye to eye. It wasn't hard to see a profound change in Frank. He seemed to have lost his joy, and most of the time, he seemed distant—not present with the kids and me. I often wondered if Hollywood was too much of a reminder of everything we *didn't* have. I could see how, when those pretty, elite women came into the shoe store each day, he caught a glimpse of their glamorous and fanciful lives. There was nothing glamorous about selling shoes, running a household, and raising three little children.

Or maybe it was all too depressing for my husband to come home each night to a rundown nobody of a wife when beautiful, wealthy women surrounded him every day as he fitted their perfectly pedicured feet with shoes that cost more than our rent. Perhaps if he had come home once in a while to relieve me of my duties, then maybe I would have had the chance to present myself more attractively, but most days, I didn't have a second to myself, let alone time to take a shower. Dressing nice, putting on makeup, or doing my hair was unheard of, because I simply did not have the luxury of time to pamper myself. So when I sensed an unsettled restlessness in Frank, as though the direction of our lives was not one that he imagined or dreamed of, it scared me.

One day, Frank came home in the middle of the afternoon with such energy—energy I hadn't seen in him for a long time. "Alice, where are you?" he shouted from the living room. "Things are about to change!"

He sounded out of breath from the other room, as if he had been running. He seemed to bounce off the walls when he found me in the laundry room. "There you are. Alice, I have fantastic news." He took the knickers out of my hands as I was mid-fold and threw them aside. "Well, it's mostly good news, but some bad. What do you want to hear first?"

I grabbed the knickers back and continued folding to avoid reaching up to fix my messy hair and making him notice that I had yet to change out of my robe. "Tell me the bad first."

"All right. I quit my job. I'm done, Alice, finally done for good."

I stood frozen, holding a toddler's sock in my hand.

He continued, "No more having to put shoes on fat, sweaty, smelly feet. No more getting up and down on my knees and fetching this and that size for Miss Entitled. Nope, I'm done with all that. I honestly did it!"

"What? Have you lost your godforsaken mind? Frank, *NO*."

"Hold on. Before you blow a gasket, this will change our financials, and our lives, for good. Will you put down the dang clothes and look at me?"

"What?" I said and folded my arms instead.

"I was offered a sales job selling insurance. It starts tomorrow. That's the good news!"

"Wait, how did this all come about so suddenly?"

"I happened to befriend this rich lady who is a regular at the shoe store. One day, as I fitted her for a new pair of heels, she said, 'I have to be honest with you, Mr. Clark. I've known you for a while now, and it's clear you have the knack and talent to sell just about anything.'"

"Go on," I said.

"Alice, she told me I am a natural salesman and said she happened to be looking for someone to train to help her run her successful business. So I asked around, and she is the sole owner of a highly prominent life insurance company in town."

"That sounds so—"

"It sounds so what? Too good to be true? Or a dream come true?"

"No, it sounds oddly ... convenient."

"I don't know what you mean by that. All I know is that it's worth a shot, Alice. So, of course, I told her I was interested." When I didn't say anything, Frank grabbed my shoulders. "Why the face, Alice? This is good news."

"Whatever happened to discussing things together? And what exactly will you be doing for this woman?"

"I'm sorry I didn't tell you. I wanted it to be a surprise. But as for what I'll be doing, I suppose I will need to run door-to-door selling life insurance for a while. And if I prove myself, I'll be in the office running all the accounts I acquired during the trial stages. Life insurance is a lucrative career, Alice. This is BIG."

"Wow. I can't believe it," I said, dumbfounded.

"Well, believe it." His smile was wide as he picked me up and spun me around. "I love you so much, Alice. This is the break I've been waiting for!"

Frank was right; he was forever done at the shoe store and never returned. But what we didn't know was that his new life insurance job would forever change our lives—his for the good and mine for the worse.

In 1955, after working two years at his new job, we discovered I was pregnant again at age twenty-nine. I didn't take the news well since I was already tired from raising three kids, but with Frank bringing in a better income, the career change gave us hope that anything was possible. Unfortunately, I soon realized I would be raising the children by myself. With the new job, Frank began working long hours after what was already a ten-hour shift. You could say that staying home with three kids without a break was wearing me out, and the fourth child hadn't even arrived yet.

Maybe I was jealous of Frank's new adventures and that he got to work all day without three children barking at his heels. But I had to question him when he came home from yet another late night out. I grilled him the moment he walked into our bedroom. "Frank, it's almost midnight! Where have you been?"

When I turned on the bedside lamp to reveal his face, he squinted and covered his glassy eyes to block out the light. He sat down heavily beside me. "Alice," he said, slurring my name, with what smelled like his favorite Canadian whisky on his breath. "You know I've got to wine and dine all these potential clients. Sometimes, these meetings run longer than expected."

"But midnight, Frank?"

"I'll try to make it home earlier, dear."

"You said that last time *and* the time before that. What I don't like is all the drinking you're doing. Who's driving you home?"

"I'm perfectly capable of driving myself, "Frank said while struggling to remove his shoes and socks.

I sat up and helped him yank his sock off. "Clearly not. I don't like any of this."

Frank's eyes seemed to focus on my worn-out face. "You like the money I've been making, don't you?"

"Excuse me? Frank, it's not a huge difference like you said it would be."

"That's because I'm still working hard to build up my clientele. It's not gonna happen overnight. Just be patient." He threw his blazer onto the floor. "What is it with you? Always nagging me. Nothing is ever good enough."

"Oh, Frank," I said, irritated. "Shut up and go to bed."

That was just one fight of many that soon followed. By the time I was eight months pregnant, Frank was coming home late nearly every night, entertaining clients and drinking himself silly. As husband and wife, you would have thought we lived on two separate planets. He left me in my most vulnerable state.

I was despondent, depressed, tired, and feeling like a speck of dust with the whole wide world crushing down on me. I questioned what was happening to us. I wasn't the religious type back then, but, left without direction, I questioned over and over what life was about anyway. What was my purpose, where did we come from, and if there was a God, where was He when I needed Him the most?' I desperately needed someone to lean on, because Frank was useless.

After another exhausting argument with Frank one evening, I stood outside our home, alone, to find peace and quiet. I lifted my wet eyes into the night sky, wishing for a speck of clarity. For the first time in my life, I said a prayer out loud, to anyone or anything who could hear my pleading cries.

"Dear God, I don't know who you are, but they say you're the God up in heaven." That's how it started.

Even though I didn't hear his voice after my long prayer, an image came from the back of my mind. Growing up in Canada, my father had this giant white Bible on the hall table that we never used nor opened. But he once told me it was supposed to have all the answers. In that desperate moment, standing outside in the dark, I knew the white Bible was the answer. I knew I had to go out and find myself the book of answers.

The next day, I bought a miniature Bible for $1.25 and read it daily. I needed something to ease my mind of my endless worries. Any day, I was about to give birth, and I wasn't even sure if Frank would be there at the hospital to welcome our fourth child. That Bible was the only thing that satisfied and comforted me during a bleak and desolate time. Sure, I still held worries in the back pocket of my mind, but after reading the stories of centuries of people who suffered just like me, that book showed me I wasn't alone. Just knowing someone above was in my corner gave me hope.

But by the time I was nine months pregnant, I was spent and beyond myself with exhaustion. Not even the Bible helped. The words alone were not enough. One night, right before bed, I had just read a quote: "Come to me, all who labor and are heavy laden, I will give you rest." I thought about that and laughed. "Wow, Lord, ain't that the truth? Here I am, heavily labored and needing rest! But where are you? I need you!" After reading that verse, I lay awake past midnight, unable to sleep. But what happened next forever changed my life.

I was lying facing the couch, with my back to the living room, when I felt a firm hand on my shoulder. I was angry and tired, and I said, "Frank, is that you? What do you want." I hadn't heard him come in, nor had I heard the children's doors open.

There was no answer.

Because I was so tired and heavy with the child, I didn't bother to roll over to see who it was. The hand touched my shoulder again, yet it was firmer this time. I said loudly and quite impatiently, "Frank, is that you? Leave me be. I need my sleep."

Still no answer.

"Frank, if that's you that keeps touching me, answer me already."

When there was no answer, chills ran down my spine.

By the third time that hand touched my shoulder, my heart raced with a knowing feeling. I squeezed my eyes shut and whispered, "God, I've been reading your word, and you said you are the way and the light. So, if that is you, please don't touch me again, because the hairs on my arm are standing on end."

When I finally turned around, I was shocked to find no one there. But even so, that night, I fell asleep smiling for the first time in a long time, knowing that whatever happened in my life, good or bad, I was never truly alone. Someone above must love me. And even if it was my imagination, how can one ever truly be alone when the moon lights our paths, the stars guide us home, the sun warms and feeds us, and when the wind caresses your skin with a whisper: "You are not alone."

So, on that unexplainable night, I became a believer. Whoever created all the beauty in the world came to me the moment I needed comfort the most. And I would especially need comfort and guidance for what came next in my life, after birthing our last son, Johnny.

Chapter 17

Alice 1955-1962

From 1955 to 1962, I worked like a dog raising our four children. It was already hard enough raising three kids with *two* parents, but now there were four, and I had raised them all single-handedly while my husband continued to stay out late, wasting our money on drinking and entertaining his fancy new clients. With so many mouths to feed, and with the first FDA-approved birth control pill on the market, this mother of four should have been the first in line to sign up. But there was no point, not when Frank and I never saw each other. And, with what little extra money his lady boss promised Frank, he now spent it on his new lifestyle, including fashionable suits, hats, and Italian shoes, all to impress his important clients.

I eventually had enough of the lies my husband kept feeding me. Waiting for the coffee to percolate early one December morning, in 1961 just before Frank left for work, I contemplated how much more I could take. We had endured months of bickering before Frank decided to avoid it all by nearly ignoring me. I was invisible. Unseen. Or worse, I was treated like a nameless house servant with little say in our future.

Frank didn't acknowledge me as I stood in the kitchen—my permanent domestic spot. The floor's wear and tear came from the soles of my feet and the soul of a hard-working mother, so much so that I'd worn down the floral design on the linoleum. But Frank wouldn't know about any of that. He was too busy becoming someone important.

I barely heard what our newly elected president, John F. Kennedy, said on television, not when a second notice about unpaid utilities lay on the kitchen counter next to the coffee pot. I picked one up, with its bold, red letters screaming at me. "Frank," I yelled from the small kitchen wall opening into the living room, "Why are we late again on paying the garbage bill?" When he didn't reply, I asked, "What will we do with all the trash bags sitting outside in the back?"

"Alice, one more week isn't going to hurt," he said while looking for something underneath the coffee table.

I set the papers on the counter and poured some cream into a chipped cup. "But the neighbors will start to complain again, Frank."

"I'll pay the bill soon. Stop worrying." His head was under a chair next, muffling his voice.

"Things are a little tight this month. You know that." When Frank finally stood, he continued to look around the room with a perplexed expression. "Where did they go?"

I stared at the man from behind the kitchen counter. Our measly Christmas tree flickered in lights of white and silver tinsel, showing me the glow of my husband's face—freshly shaved and smooth like a newborn's, with hair still wet and slicked back from the long shower he had the privilege of taking. I could smell his spiced, smoky cedar-and-sage cologne from where I stood across the room.

It was hard not to admire how sharp my husband looked, wearing a new pair of shiny leather shoes, a tailored suit, and a matching blue-trimmed hat. He looked like a Hollywood dream. But my admiration waned when I glanced into the stainless coffee pot, which mirrored my less-than-desirable reflection. I had let myself go, I thought. I looked no better than a worthless, messy old housemaid.

"Where did what go?" I asked.

"Dammit! My keys, Alice. Where did the keys go?" Frank grumbled.

I slammed the coffee pot down. "I don't know where your keys are. What I'm more worried about are these unpaid bills. Maybe if you'd stop splurging on those new suits, hats, and shoes, we could afford to pay our bills on time for once."

Frank looked down at his watch in frustration. "Alice. We've been through this before. If I don't look the part, I won't fit in at this insurance company. This lifestyle comes with the territory. You know the saying, 'Dress to impress.' These potential clients of mine will eventually pay off."

"You've been saying that same line forever. Shouldn't your clients already be happy when you take them to lunch and dinner and buy them those expensive drinks at the bar every night?"

What I really wanted to ask him was when the day would come when he wanted to take me out, his wife. When would I become someone he wanted to impress? But I didn't ask such a thing.

"Well, I could have had a car by now, Frank," I said. "Instead, I'm stuck locked up here, day in and day out. I don't even know what streets are new in town."

"Here we go again," Frank said, waving his hand in the air like I was a fly he needed to swat away. "You just don't understand the insurance life. I'm doing my best." He turned around and faced me while pointing up to the ceiling. "You got a roof over your head, correct? Clothes on your back? And the kids are fed? Can't you, for once, be happy that I am taking care of us the best I can right now?"

For a moment, I had no words, as my chest just heaved up and down. "Happy?" I finally said. "*Happiness* has not been a theme in our lives for a long time, Frank." My husband gave me a nervous look before conveniently moving over to the couch to search for his keys. My words were clear and precise, "We haven't been happy since Johnny's birth. And, tell me, how can I, or any wife, for that matter, be happy with you gambling away your paychecks?"

Frank froze, mid-step, with his back to me.

He didn't know I knew about his gambling.

I continued, "I've known for months. It is no secret. Suzy's husband saw you at the casino more than a few times. The cat is out of the bag." I laughed bitterly. "For God's sake, Frank. Why? Gambling is so wasteful. When will it all stop? When is it enough? And when do you put this family first?"

Frank spun around. "All right. So a man works till his fingers bleed but can't enjoy a little of his hard-earned money? You make me sound like the devil."

"Yeah, well, you don't see me enjoying any of my hard work. I take care of *your* children day in and day out, with little to no help. So, when do I get something for myself, Frank? When do I get a break? It must be nice to have a career to fall back on. It must be nice after work, night after night, to sit and relax with other adults while I run around like a chicken with its head cut off, serving our children's needs. I don't think you'll ever appreciate all that I do, not when it is only your needs you ever see."

Frank stood with an open mouth while gripping his chest. "How can you say words that cut me so deep? I am home most weekends, am I not? And on some Sundays, you leave Johnny home with me while the rest of you go to church. I do help. I am doing my best. And trust me, I'm always thinking of you and the kids. It's you who seems to think it's never enough."

It seemed Frank saw me as a nagging wife who constantly inconvenienced him, but I didn't cave. "I'm sorry if you feel nothing is good enough for me, Frank. I didn't think wanting a husband to come home occasionally to spend quality time with his family was unheard of. But even when you are home, you are not present. Your mind is elsewhere. And counting the few hours on Sunday with your son isn't enough. I doubt you even know what extracurricular activities the rest of the kids take. Instead, you stay out late and drink more than you should. You wine and dine with people that you *think* are your friends. You buy yourself an entire wardrobe fit for a king. And now you're gambling? The question is, Frank, why aren't *we* good enough for you?"

We both jumped at the sound of keys jingling and turned to find little Johnny standing by the hall tree and bench. He smiled wide, with bright blue eyes. "Silly Daddy, your keys are right here. I found them for you."

My heart sank to the pit of my stomach. Who knew how much of the argument our son had heard? But with Johnny, his father could do no wrong. Our six-year-old would depict the scene before him with the smooth strokes of a paintbrush. The truth of it was that this was a failing marriage made with the angry strokes of a palette knife that cut far too deep.

Frank bent down and gently took the keys from little John's hand. "Wow, son. I don't know what I'd do without you. And here I thought I'd be late for work." Frank ruffled his son's thick brown curls. "Daddy's got to go, buddy. So you be good for your mother, all right?"

Johnny nodded with a big grin that always meant trouble for me later. Out of all my children, Johnny was *more* than a handful. He was always exhausting me. Part of me thought he was acting out and being naughty because he craved his father's attention. But Frank didn't see this. He didn't see that a young boy needed his father.

It hurt more than the argument had when my husband walked out the front door without even a goodbye or a glance in my direction. And yet, as much as his actions hurt me, and it seemed we would never resolve our issues, I loved him something fierce. Flaws and all. I wanted more than anything to be with the man who had once looked at me with adoring eyes. I missed being held and loved. I missed the man who once said I was the air he needed to breathe.

And maybe that morning, I was just like Johnny—acting out and needing Frank's attention—when I quickly tightened my robe and ran outside before Frank closed the car door.

"Frank! Wait!" I yelled.

Frank put one foot out of the car door. "What is it, Alice? I'm going to be late. Can't we talk about this later?"

I knew later would never come. With the panicked thought that I was about to lose him, I had to do something.

"I love you, can't you see that, Frank? I'm not trying to nag you. It's just that ... I only want us to be happy—like we once were. Don't you think something has to change?"

Frank took a heavy breath. "Alice, I—"

"I used to be able to reach you, but you're so closed off. You've changed. Why?"

"I don't know," he said, looking down into his hands.

"This may sound odd, but maybe you don't love yourself enough, Frank?"

He looked up with a bewildered expression. "What? What kind of statement is that?"

I was hesitant. "It's just that, well ... I was reading the Bible and—"

"*Oh*, here we go with more of this Bible crap."

It wasn't new that Frank disliked my religious turn. He often looked down on me for it. He couldn't relate to how much I needed to believe in something bigger than us—something that gave me hope that what we did in life was for some greater purpose.

"Let me explain before you get so negative, Frank. You don't have to be a Bible freak to hear good advice. I went to church, and the pastor said we need to love ourselves first before we can love others. I see you constantly trying hard to be this important figure at work. It's like you are trying to prove your self-worth, when you don't need to prove anything to us. I love you; we love you, and God loves you for just being you. So, maybe there is something deeper that makes you feel that you aren't good enough. Maybe you can't give your best to us because you don't love yourself as you should."

Frank shook his head. "You know I hate when you throw *your* God in my face. It's all just a bunch of Bible-thumping mumbo-jumbo. Has it ever occurred to you that what you are reading sounds very cult-like? Can you not fathom how, out of all the wars we have had in this world, more people have died because of your religious myths and ideology than any other reason?"

It seemed we were at war, each fighting and pushing the other towards opposite dreams, goals, and values, and I was losing the battle day by day. But still, I tried. "But, Frank, what I am saying isn't necessarily religious."

"So you say, but the implication is the same. You make it worse when you act out this stunt each time. Like you are better than me. I never signed up to have a holy-roller for a wife, so just quit it already." Frank turned on the engine. "Thank you very much, but now I am going to be late for work, Alice."

When Frank slammed the door shut, and all my hope for amicable changes vanished into thin air, I'm ashamed to say that I took my frustrations out on an innocent party. With all my despondent thoughts on one chaotic loop, you could say I wasn't myself that day when I entered the house feeling defeated. Again, I was unseen and unheard by my husband *and* my children. Without a father ever home to discipline them, my voice had become like a broken siren to them. Not even the cat listened to my pleas to stay off the counter. And so when the cat jumped onto the counter for the umpteenth time, with dirty paws tracking its mess all over everything I had just cleaned, I knocked the poor thing down a little too hard, and he hit his head on the corner of the dining table.

As the cat had a mini seizure, I couldn't help but wonder why my life was falling apart. I quickly sat down on the floor, picked up the cat, and rocked him in my arms, crying, "I'm sorry! It's not your fault, sweet boy."

The cat lived but was never right in the head after that. We no longer called him by his name; instead, the children called him Ding-a-ling. Truth be told, I wished someone had knocked me over the head. I would have liked to forget a few things, like that next evening when my husband came home and told me it was over.

It was only six at night when Frank walked in the front door. I was shocked, as he usually didn't come home until after eleven p.m. But, how stupid of me to think how he must have heard my pleas earlier. How silly to think that maybe my words had penetrated his head, and here he was home early to want to attempt change—choosing *us* over *them*. I even ran to the bathroom to quickly arrange my hair and put a bit of makeup on.

Optimistically, I looked into the mirror, took a deep breath, and said to myself, "Alice, we're gonna get him back!"

I could hear Frank shooing the kids to their rooms from the living room. "Kids, your mother and I need to talk. Please give us some privacy," he said.

The beating of my heart accelerated in hopes of hearing the words I had wanted. Words like, "I'm sorry, and I love you, Alice, and I made a mistake in not wanting to be here with you all."

Oh, how silly I was to hope that such fairytales existed.

When I came out of our bathroom, Frank wasn't in the living room. I found him still dressed in his work clothes—an immaculate suit, tie, and fedora hat tipped oddly off-center as he sat on our bed, next to two open and empty suitcases. He didn't look at me when I walked into the room. Instead, he quietly stared out the bedroom window to the backyard, where the grass was dead and unmowed.

My heart dropped as I noted his long side profile, etched with a look of defeat.

"Frank?" I said, almost too scared to ask. Still, a tiny door in my mind suggested the suitcases were for us to pack and go somewhere—a long overdue trip for him and me to salvage all that we had lost. "Why are the suitcases out? Are we going somewhere?" I asked stupidly. His body slumped forward, and his head fell into his hands, and I ran to his side. "What is it? Tell me what's wrong."

He stifled a cry. "I ... oh, Alice. I just can't anymore." He looked up at me, standing there like a fool. "We aren't happy, Alice. This isn't working out. I can't do this anymore. I'm so sorry. I ... I'm leaving."

I shook my head and took a step back. "Leaving?"

"I ... I filed for a divorce today."

The room rolled, nearly taking my feet out, as if a wave had crashed into me. I couldn't breathe. "No." I pointed a finger at him, taking a few steps back. "No, no. Don't you dare say that. You don't say that kind of thing unless you mean it."

"Alice, I—"

My hands felt empty, and I grabbed at the bottom of my shirt, twisting and squeezing it, the way my heart felt. My voice came out higher than I wanted.

"Sure, things have been bad between us for a while, but we can fix it. We just have to try harder. Marriage takes work."

"Who are we kidding, Alice? We can't change. I am who I am, and you are you."

I dropped my shirt from my hands and fell between his knees. "Yes, yes, we can change. Let's go and see a marriage counselor. They have free ones at the church. We can—"

"No! Stop with this nonsense," he said, pushing me away. "I am not going to church. You can't change me." Frank stood up and said, his words clipped: "I don't like this 'woman of God' you've become, and I don't like how you make me feel all the time." He turned to the bed and threw his clothes into the suitcases. "When I come home, I feel guilty that somehow I am not who you want me to be. I've done my best, but it's still not good enough."

"Frank, we just have to try harder. If you want something bad enough, anything is possible. I know we can make this work."

"*I* can't make this work."

"But you ... you don't just stop loving someone. Love doesn't stop just when things aren't perfect."

The packing altogether stopped, and instead, he stared ahead at the dully painted, pewter-colored wall behind me. I had never quite got around to decorating this room with pictures of the kids or the one photo with all of us at the beach in a happier time. That long-delayed task seemed so insignificant compared with trying to run a household, raise our children, and keep my head above water.

It was a minute before Frank whispered, "And what if I don't want it bad enough, Alice?" When his eyes met mine, they were empty. "I am tired, Alice. I'm *so* tired of this tango. I'm not the man I used to be; you aren't the woman I married. We've changed. We've grown apart. Surely you see this? This isn't healthy."

I stood then. "So you're just going to pack up and leave us all behind? Everything? Years of building a life together, and you want to just leave?"

It was as if something in Frank's mind clicked, and he turned back to the closet in haste, grabbing his suits and ties as if being in the same room with me any longer would kill him. "I don't see it any other way. I'm sorry it has to be this way," he said, tossing his clothes into the suitcase.

My mind searched for the words to stop him. "Frank. Stop! Look at me." But he couldn't. And he didn't. I threw myself between him and his suitcase and begged, "Tell me this isn't happening. Tell me you still love me, even if a little?"

"Please don't make this any harder, Alice. I've made up my mind."

He had always been the one to decide everything. He was always the one who paved the way to where and what we would do as husband and wife and as a family. I had done everything he had asked of me, so why? I beat my fists against his chest. "You can't do this to us! What did *I* do that was so bad? What did I do to make you not love me anymore besides give away our firstborn, raise your four children, cook, clean, and endure everything for the sake of this marriage?"

"Alice!" Frank said, grabbing my wrists. "*Stop.*" His eyes were sad which only made it worse. "I will always love you for *all* of those reasons, but the love *I* need and what *you* need no longer exists."

"Please, Frank!" I cried. "Don't do this to me. And what about the kids? They will be devastated. Don't you care? Maybe just think about it some more, for their sake."

Frank wiped his brow. "You think I haven't thought this through?"

As he reached around me, shifted his suitcase to the side, and continued to pack beside me, I roughly wiped the tears off my cheeks before facing his side profile. "You know what? Ever since you got this stupid insurance job, you've changed. So what kind of life do you want, Frank? *Huh*? Tell me, please! Is it no kids? Less responsibility? A trophy wife whose boobs don't sag to the floor? How about a bigger house? Dinner out every night with a bunch of schmoozers? If that is what you want, then I guess you are right; I can't give you any of those things."

For a moment, time stood still before it all hit me. And maybe I knew it all along. I took a step back from him and whispered the one question that tasted sour in my mouth. "It's not me you want but *her*, isn't it?"

Frank threw his heated eyes down at me. "You don't know what you are talking about."

"I don't?" I pushed hard at his shoulder. "Your boss has had her eyes on you from the moment she walked into that shoe store and put her foot into your hands. And now, at her insurance company, she's molded you into exactly who she wants you to be—a dummy who abandons his family just because his life at home isn't glamorous!"

"Alice—"

"No! You and all your fancy clothes—a Hollywood wanna-be! Did she tell you to dress like that?" I said, flipping the top of his hat up. "Look at you! She's pruned you into something unrecognizable. Beneath all these fine silk and velvet layers lies a man whose heart is bare of principles or grit. You wouldn't recognize what is truly good if it slapped you in the face. You are a coward, Frank, simple as that. A coward."

Frank swallowed. "Then I am a coward, Alice. It is true I can't be the man you want me to be. I have tried, I did. But I know I'm no longer cut out for this life with you. I can't dance this dance with you anymore. I can't handle it anymore."

"You can't handle it?" I scoffed. "Your choice of words sure is a way to sugarcoat it, but what you truly mean is that you simply don't love me anymore."

The way his eyes dropped to the floor and how his mouth opened and closed without words indicated I was right. Bitterly and truthfully right. Even though Frank couldn't admit it, I knew he was smitten with his boss. He was choosing her over me. I ran to the bedroom door and swung it open wide, even though doing so killed the very fiber in my being. "Then go! We don't need you, Frank Clark!"

It was an absolute lie. I needed the man more than he would ever know. I needed him like a home needed a foundation to stand on. I needed him like a tree needed its roots securely buried deep into the ground, and I needed my Frank like the earth needed rain to quench its desperate thirst. Who was I without him? Could I survive? Could I be a single mother of four? Would I crumble? Would I ever be the same without the love of my life?

While I stood in the doorway, I swallowed my pride and pleaded with my eyes for him to fight, to prove there was still hope, but my world crumbled when he only shook his head in defeat and clicked the suitcases closed. He picked them up before he faced me. "Alice, I will always love you. I am sorry, but we lost ourselves long ago. Tell the kids for me that I am sorry. Forgive me," he said as he gently nudged me to the side and left without another word.

I stood in the doorway for a long time, still hearing the click of those suitcases closing. Nothing can describe that sense of feeling so small and insignificant, while his words clattered inside my head like rain pounding on a metal roof.

I can't do this dance with you anymore.

I wondered how the love of my life could just give up on us. How could a father leave his children? Was this what our firstborn felt when I deserted her? Is this what she felt when I walked away? In that moment, I understood the meaning of mistakes and regret, and how abandonment can affect you for a lifetime. It is and continues to be the hardest lesson I have ever had to learn.

Chapter 18

Sam 2005

With the sun hiding behind a large cloud, Alice and I sat on a park bench, looking at the tall, leafless maples that scattered across the landscape. I touched her shoulder. "I am so sorry, Alice."

"Thank you," she said, wiping her cheek with her coat sleeve.

"I can tell you loved Frank unconditionally. Maybe you still do?"

The tip of Alice's winter boot nudged at a lone rock resting on the dew-frosted earth below her. A black crow above us cawed a greeting to its companion beside it on a bare branch before they flew away together. "Maybe I am a firm believer that love lasts forever. Even though Frank broke my heart and the children's, I never stopped loving him. So yes, I will always love him. In fact, I never remarried because, in some weird way, my heart still belonged to that man."

"You never found love again?"

"No. There was only one love of my life."

"You are truly a hopeless romantic."

"Possibly."

"Whatever happened to Frank, if you don't mind me asking?"

"When he was sixty, he had a heart attack." She gave a sad laugh. "He was a chain-smoker who ate too much ice cream. When we lived together, he always had a small pint of chocolate mint hidden in our freezer. And when he moved out—I never saw it for myself, but the kids once told me—he and his wife had an entire freezer full of ice cream, big tubs like you'd see at Baskin-Robbins."

"Then he did end up marrying her? His rich boss? The insurance lady?"

"Of course. And I was right all along. I'd had my suspicions, but love is often blind. I just couldn't bear to believe it."

"What did you do after the divorce?"

"As many women do after divorcing, I found work to support my children. I didn't receive anything substantial from the divorce because we had nothing of equity to split, and since we didn't own our home or even a car, I took the first job I could find. I went door to door selling Fuller Brush products to pay for rent and put food on the table. Conveniently, after we split, Frank's career took off. In my opinion, his lady boss made sure he didn't make much money until *after* we divorced. She was smart, and I was too naive."

"But didn't he have to pay for spousal support?"

"Here's the kicker; Frank's money was *all* hers. That woman was wickedly clever. I still don't know how the law works, but somehow, she only married him after the courts granted me one hundred and fifty dollars a month. Me and the kids lived like beggars. After living on rice and beans for so long, I finally found the courage to call his wife one day, nearly begging for her to have a heart, explaining to her that Frank's kids needed more financial support. I will never forget her words: 'Go hang yourself in the street,' she said before hanging up on me. After that, I never called their home again."

"She sounds like the devil," I said in disgust. "Did the kids like her?"

"At first, the kids would go to her house to see their father every other weekend, but two months in, he suddenly became too busy for visits. I'm sure that was all her doing, too. She had her son from a previous marriage, so there was no room in her heart for *my* kids."

"How very sad."

"And little Johnny," Alice said, shaking her head, "he took it the hardest. The day I told him his daddy left us, little Johnny packed his suitcase and ran away, saying, 'If Daddy's leavin', so am I!' He was only six years old, and because he didn't have anywhere to go, he returned home after two hours. I will never forget him walking through the front door with his head hung low, saying, 'I'm hungry, Momma.'"

"Bless his little heart," I said. "You and your kids didn't deserve any of that, Alice."

"Such is life, I suppose. 'Life Life Life,' is what I like to say when we have zero control over the wrongs done to us."

"Well, for what it's worth, *you* are the true catch. Frank was the idiot."

"Yes. A dummy he was, that man. He was feeble-minded when it came to responsibilities, and I should have realized that the day he asked me to give up our baby girl." Alice tightened the thick yellow wool scarf around her neck before slowly coming to a stand. "It's getting cold sitting here. My legs are stiff. Let's say we get back to the house. I'm sure our soup is ready."

"I almost forgot about the soup. Unfortunately, I'll have to eat and run. I promised a movie with Liam."

The way Alice's face fell led me to believe she perhaps didn't want to be alone, especially after reliving her past. I remembered Jane's crestfallen moods right after she talked to me about her past loves and heartbreak. She was always fragile after a session of stories. "You know what, Alice? Come to think of it, I think Liam has basketball practice. I can stay and hang out a while longer." Liam didn't have basketball, but I knew he would understand.

"Really? And you don't have work tonight?"

"No work. Being that it is so close to the holidays, and with everyone scrambling to buy their kids presents, I knew my friend Shelly at work could use the extra shift. So, I gave her mine."

"That would be wonderful. We can have a girls' day here, and then maybe for tonight,"—Alice looked at me with excitement—"I don't suppose, since you don't have work, would you be interested in attending a Victorian Christmas fair with me? I was invited to walk around and sing with the choir as part of the ambiance for the patrons. I wasn't planning to go, since Maria couldn't take me, but it might be fun for us. And you could invite Liam too! That is, if he gets done with basketball in time."

"I would love to take you and hear you sing tonight, Alice. I've never been to a Victorian Christmas."

"Then it's settled."

There was no snow on the evening of Tuesday, December 14, but it seemed Christmas came early. Once Alice and I stepped through the golden gates of the big Western Washington Fairgrounds, every tree and bush looked snow-covered and inordinately brightly lit. A display of Christmas lights circled around the fair's enormous, iconic water fountain. Along with Santa's reindeer, which you could feed for a small price, there was a lively nativity scene to our right, involving zoo animals that you could pet. To our left was a pavilion holding what I assumed was their holiday craft and gift venue, and down the middle was an endless line of food trucks selling festive food that made my mouth water after just one sniff. Finally, past the food trucks and past the ice-skating rink, there was a handful of rides, including a Ferris wheel that turned slowly, front and center.

"I don't see Santa," I said to Alice as we entered the large pavilion, with rows and rows of vendors selling Christmas market-themed crafts.

She pointed to the far back, at a lively, decorated Christmas section that was roped off, with a line of at least fifty parents wrangling their impatient children. "Santa is always sitting comfortably inside the elf cottage past the North Pole, you know, just in case it rains."

Alice was dressed in a floor-length skirt of thick, dark green wool and a lacy, button-neck cream blouse, topped by a heavy red shawl. "You sure look sharp, Alice," I said.

"You think?" she said, fanning out her skirt with a matching lacy gloved hand. "Oh, wait. I forgot the best part." From her large purse, she grabbed a simple red wool hat with a buckle, placed it on her head, and tied the ribbons under her chin with a big bow. "This old girl cleans up nice, huh?"

With her long, silver-white hair pulled elegantly into a bun at the nape of her neck, she looked beautiful. I whistled appreciatively and said, "Wow. I feel like I'm back in the Victorian era." Alice didn't have a lick of makeup on, but she didn't need it. She looked like she could command the attention of anyone in the room. I looked down at my outfit—nothing special, just simple jeans and an old black and white striped sweater. "Should I have dressed up for this?" I asked her. "I've been to the Puyallup Fair every September, but I have never been to their Victorian Christmas festival."

"What you have on is fine. I'm singing in the choir, so the event provided us with these outfits to play the role of Christmas carolers." She looked at her watch. "We better go. It takes a while to warm up these pipes," she said, massaging her throat.

"What part do you sing, Alice?" I asked as we walked through the crowd.

"I'm a soprano, through and through. Whitney Houston's got nothing on me."

I laughed. "I can't wait to hear you sing. I'm sure you sing like the angel you are."

She waved to a group of carolers before turning to me. "You're welcome to follow behind me as we sing carols around the fairgrounds. My shift is typically two hours, but with these legs, I might be only able to do an hour of walking. Maybe I'll be able to go longer with the cane you got me, but we will see. How about I meet you back here at this very spot later to touch base?"

"That sounds good. I will definitely follow you around until Liam shows up."

I followed ten feet behind Alice, singing along with her church choir for a good twenty minutes before stopping to grab a cup of hot chocolate when my hands felt cold. After warming my throat with the chocolate goodness, it was easy to catch up and find Alice in the crowd. I was sure Alice's soprano was competing against Mariah Carey for that all-time high note. As we all walked near the nativity scene with all the animals, I felt someone pinch my butt. I smiled and turned around, thinking I'd find Liam, but it wasn't him.

"Brad? What the—"

He chuckled, "You think you're the only one to get the night off?"

I flashed him a gruesome smile before nodding to the pigs gated in their pens behind him. "You visiting your relatives or something?"

"Funny." I was about to tell him off and that I didn't appreciate him putting his hands on me, but he shocked me once again when he threw a heavy arm around my shoulders. He leaned in close to my ear. "You know, if my kid weren't here, I'd say you and me could keep warm under the hay back there," he said, pointing to an empty stable behind the pigs. "I have a feeling you're an animal in bed."

I didn't even know Brad had a kid, or which one was his out of the thirty petting the animals in the barn, but it didn't matter. I yanked his arm off my shoulder and took a huge step back from him. "Look here, I said, don't—"

I didn't get to finish my sentence, not when a tall form dressed in a black coat and a black beanie hat swooped between me and Brad. Only when I saw those long, slender hands on Brad's chest, pushing Brad a good few feet away from me, did I realize whose hands they were. "Am I missing something here?" Liam asked. I wasn't sure if Liam was talking to me or Brad or both of us, but he only looked at Brad when he spoke again. "Do you normally put your hands on someone else's property?"

Brad lifted his hands in defense. "Oh, I'm sorry. Is she yours?" Brad said, knowing quite well that this was the boyfriend I had spoken about often. "Cuz, Sammy here has never mentioned any boyfriends." He snickered.

I cut in front of Liam. "The hell I didn't mention a boyfriend."

Liam looked at me. "Who is this clown that has his hands all over you, Sam? And yes, I saw the whole thing when I was coming through the gate."

"Liam, this is my boss, Brad," I said scathingly, looking at Brad with pure loathing. "And Brad, this is my boyfriend, Liam, whom I have mentioned to you several times, so cut the act already."

At the mention of Brad's name, Liam practically pushed me aside and went for Brad's throat. "So, you're the asshole at work, harassing my girlfriend?"

I heard a child's voice behind me say, "Dad?" and turned to see a mini-Brad looking scared.

I reached up and grabbed Liam's shoulders to try to pull him away from Brad. "*Liam.*" Liam turned to face me, eyes looking half-crazed mad, and I tried to reason with him as I whispered, "His kid is right here, Liam. Please don't." Liam's hands were still tightly clamped around Brad's neck when he looked behind me and then down at a child no older than five. Liam looked back at me, hesitating as if he wasn't sure he could control himself. I tried again. "Liam. Let go of Brad. Please?"

Liam's glare suggested he was angry at me for even requesting such a thing, but he must have come to his senses. His clenched jaw relaxed, and he gave the little boy a reassuring smile before gently patting Brad's chest and then smoothing out Brad's bunched-up collar. Liam's façade of a laugh didn't fool me, though. "I was teaching your father here," Liam growled, glaring at Brad, "how a tiger will attack his prey." He looked back at the kid. "Do you like tigers, kid? Or do you like rats?" he said, turning back to Brad with narrowed eyes.

"I like tigers," the little boy responded enthusiastically, clearly no longer noticing something amiss between the adults.

I grabbed Liam's hand to pull him away before Brad said anything stupid. "Let's go."

We were only ten feet away before Brad taunted, "Bye-bye, Sammy." I turned to see his smug smile as he cheerfully added, "See you at work!"

Liam pulled away from my grip on his arm, making me drop my cup of hot cocoa, and then turned around and took a stride forward to finish what Brad started. But I pulled and tugged him back again. "Liam," I hissed. "He's just goading you. Ignore him." If it weren't for Brad's kid, I would have let Liam finish the job, but instead, I pulled at Liam to follow me, to distance us as far as I could from Brad.

We walked all the way to the rides and near the Ferris wheel before I finally stopped and faced him. Part of me admired him for wanting to fight my battles, but part of me was mad that he wanted to fight my battles. Either way, it felt like a no-win situation.

"What?" he said in anger as I stood there, unable to figure out what to say exactly. I watched his face contort in all kinds of emotions, practically syncing to the glowing rainbow of colors reflecting off the Ferris wheel lights: red for anger, yellow for protectiveness, green for disgust, blue for sad, purple for rage. I touched his shoulder, but he flinched away from me. "So that was Brad?"

"Yes. But I was about to tell him off before you got there. I had it under control."

Liam half-laughed in a mocking way that I didn't quite appreciate. "You didn't *have* anything under control, Samantha. The minute he put his hands on your ass was when you should have slapped him across the damn face."

"Well, I—"

"But no, instead, you allowed him to put his arm across your shoulders *after* he pinched your ass."

"Wait, are you saying—like, I was somehow liking his attention or something?"

"No, that is not what I'm saying, because clearly, you would never go for a creep like him. What I'm saying is, stand up for yourself, Samantha. I already told you to talk to your boss about him, but because you're too chickenshit to do anything about it, look where you still are. He's got you under his thumb, thinking you're a naïve child."

I looked around uncomfortably, well aware that we were causing a scene with Liam's voice booming so loudly at me. I couldn't remember ever seeing him this angry. "Can you lower your voice, please?" I asked quietly. "I also don't want Alice to see us making a scene. And I was going to handle it, Liam," I said. His hooded eyes suggested he didn't believe me, so I tried again. "Liam. Trust me. I swear I was about to deal with him. Maybe I wasn't going to slap him per se, but I was definitely going to stick up for myself and tell him off. Can you trust me that I was at least going to do that?"

"No. I don't trust your judgment right now. You don't get it. Your words wouldn't have any effect on a narcissist like him. Look at how well that worked out for Shelly when she told him off. Anything good come from that?"

I shoved my hands deep into the pockets of my coat before looking up at the Ferris wheel full of happy people enjoying their drama-free night. "No. Nothing came of anyone telling Brad off."

"Exactly. What that guy needs is a lesson. He needed his ass beat."

I tilted my head down a notch, revealing the whites of my eyes. "*Oh*, because physical violence is supposed to just solve everything, huh?"

"Says the girl that almost stabbed her sister with a knife?"

My mouth dropped open, and I pushed at Liam's chest. "It was a butter knife!" I looked around at the faces who stopped to look in our direction, and I quickly faked a smile with a shaky, pathetic laugh. "I mean, can you believe this place, Liam? Who doesn't have butter knives to cut our food?" I said, trying to persuade the passersby that we weren't fighting.

Liam gave me a dry laugh. "You don't *have* any food to cut, Sam."

I couldn't tell if he was trying to make a passive joke, but I still glared at him and crossed my arms. "Seriously, though. Were you really gonna beat his ass in front of his own kid?"

"No, and I didn't, okay?" Liam rubbed the back of his neck and didn't meet my eyes. "I'm just mad that I couldn't follow through with the task because I really, *really* wanted to tear him into shreds." He looked at me then. "I should have broken all his fingers just for touching you."

"Well, get in line. More than half the women at my restaurant want to murder him."

We stood there in silence for a long moment, watching the Ferris wheel go round and round, before Liam reached over and grabbed my cold hands in his. "You're shaking. Come here."

I pulled away. "No, I don't want to."

"Yes, you do," he said, trying again.

"No, I don't."

"Stubborn."

"Stupid."

We both took in a long breath of cold air before exhaling a bunch of sorries.

"I'm sorry I haven't taken care of the situation at work yet, but I will, Liam. I promise. Sooner than later. And whatever the outcome at work, whether Brad is a jerk to me afterward, or he has everyone gang up on me, or I have to quit my job, I promise I will do something about it. All right?"

"Fine. And I guess I'm sorry I got mad at you when technically it's not your fault. That guy is a creep, and you don't deserve this kind of crap from him."

"Well, I'm sorry I didn't let you throttle the idiot."

"I'm sorry you didn't let me." Liam took my hands in his again, and I finally succumbed. He brought my cold hands to his lips before blowing a long breath of warmth over the tops of them. "I was really looking forward to having a fun night with you. Is it ruined?" he asked. "Did this hot head of mine deflate the mood tonight?"

I looked to my right at the food truck selling mini shepherd's pies, next to the ticket stand for rides and games. "Maybe a meat pie, a ride on the Ferris wheel, and a picture with Santa could redeem you," I said, shrugging.

He laughed. "Done. Your wish is my command."

We were on top of the Ferris wheel, swallowing the last bite of a beef pie, when Liam set the empty container onto the floor of our cabin. When he swiftly pulled me up and over to sit on top of his lap to face him, I nearly screamed with panic. "What are you doing? Are you nuts? This is dangerous, and I could fall out."

Liam squeezed his arms tightly around me. "Like I would let anything bad happen to you." His voice rumbled low, "Now shut up and kiss me."

I almost did what he asked but quickly splayed my hand over his puckered and impatient mouth. "Not so fast. Just so you know, you can't rescue me from all the bad things that happen to me. Sooner or later, you have to let me try to fix things on my own. I might not be good at having the right answers for everything, but I'll figure it out. I'm not totally incapable, you know. I'm a big girl."

"I know you're a big girl. But is it such a crime that I want to save you?"

"No, but I also would like to know that you have a little faith in my capabilities as a woman. And also, I'm not your *property*," I said, reflecting back on Liam's words when he spoke to Brad: 'Do you normally put your hands on someone else's property?' The furrows on Liam's brow suggested he didn't understand my meaning, and I tried my best to explain. "Liam, my heart is forever yours. I don't mind you backing me up and supporting me when I need it, but I don't ever want you to think you own me or decide for me."

"I honestly don't know why I implied you were my property. I know I don't own you, Sam. But trust me, when I say that you are mine, I only mean that you are mine to protect. I would stop anyone or anything that risked harming or ever losing you."

I thought about his words and how I would do the same if anything ever threatened to him or us. "I guess I can live with that. And I'll hold you to your word on that."

"Good. And you should."

My mind went to Alice's story and how Frank deserted her and the kids. "Also, the minute I don't feel that you have my back, don't think for a minute I don't have the option to trade you in for someone better," I joked.

He laughed, "Duly noted. Now, shall we seal the deal with that kiss?" he asked pleadingly.

"I suppose," I said before finally bringing my lips to his. I was food-drunk-kissing on top of the world and groaned when our cabin came to a stop at the bottom, ready for us to exit. "I wish we could have stayed up there forever. Far, far away from the real world below."

As we stepped out into the crowd, Liam took hold of my hands and gave me an apologetic look. "It was pretty nice up there, far away from all our problems down here, huh? How about one day I build us a castle far above the clouds, so you feel like you are forever on a Ferris wheel?" He stopped and kissed my knuckles before tightly wrapping them in his. "Would you like that?"

I thought of Alice's story again and how she had told Frank she didn't need frivolous things, not when she knew love was more than enough. I stood on my tippy toes and leaned in real close to Liam. "I don't need such elaborate things. I only need you to promise me a forever and always."

He kissed the tip of my cold nose and smiled. "When it comes to spoiling you, I'll do whatever I darn well please, but yes, I promise you forever and always."

"Good." I smiled back.

We were almost to the pavilion when I looked at my watch. "Crap. I'm five minutes late meeting Alice to take her home. I didn't even get to do half the things I wanted to do here with you."

"I'll take you next year."

"Promise? Because I have never had my picture taken with Santa."

"What? You know, I could dress up like him if you want. My parents have a whole Santa suit, with boots, glasses, a beard, and everything."

"Of course your family would have such things." I laughed. "And although you would make a devilishly handsome Santa, I sort of wanna meet the real deal. I'm not looking for a Santa that would grope me when I sat on his lap," I said, winking up at him.

"I'm offended. Just so you know, I would take that job very seriously."

"Sure," I said, rolling my eyes.

We found Alice sitting at a round food table, drinking something hot from a foam cup, and sitting next to a beautifully tan-skinned woman of some ethnicity I couldn't quite pin down. She had long, lush, wavy black hair and looked to be in her early sixties. Alice waved us over. "Come, Samantha. Liam. Meet my dear choir friend from church. Malaya here is Filipino and was born and raised in the Philippines."

While Liam gave Alice a hug, I reached my hand out to greet Alice's friend. Malaya smiled at me warmly and gripped both my hands in hers. She clicked her tongue to the roof of her mouth and shook her head. "Wow. Pretty, pretty girl. Tell me. This name, Samanta? Does it have meaning?"

I liked how Malaya's staccato, choppy accented speech came out thick and how she said my name without the TH sound—replacing it with just a T instead. I smiled. "I'm told Samantha means 'God has heard' or 'flower'," I said. "What about the name Malaya?" I asked. "Malaya is a beautiful name. I have never heard it before. Does it have a meaning?"

Malaya's smile faded, and her shoulders drooped slightly. She let go of my hands and clasped her fingers around her coffee cup as if needing to draw warmth from it. "In my mother's tongue, the Tagalog language, it means freedom."

"Well, that is lovely," I said. "But you don't think so?"

She gave me a one-grunted sigh before shaking her head fervently. Her brows furrowed deeply before she spoke in a soft whisper, "My birth name, the one my father gave me, was meant for someone else. Because freedom was something I never have till I came here to the States."

"Oh," I said. "I'm so sorry. That doesn't sound very good."

Alice's mouth formed a grim, thin line before she spoke, "Malaya's sorrowful story is one for the books. If you thought mine or Jane's life stories were bad, Malaya's beats anyone's."

"When did you come here to America?" I asked her.

"Sadly, not till I am adult."

"I'm sorry to hear that."

"It okay." There was a moment's pause before the woman looked up at me. "Alice, she tell me you love to hear stories?"

"I do. I think there is much to learn from all the women who came before me."

"Well, someday, I tell you my story, Sammy?"

You'd miss the telltale signs at first if you didn't look closely, but as I studied this woman's face and looked deeply into her golden-brown eyes, behind the wall that hid the secrets of her heart, I caught a glimpse of the deep wounds that haunted her. I gave Malaya a sympathetic smile, knowing it was important to allow a person to tell their story. I was beginning to learn that women often heal better after they open their hearts and minds and reveal all the things this world took from them. "I would love to hear your stories, Malaya. I'd be honored," I said, and I meant it.

She smiled as if pleased we were going to be friends before she took a gander over at Liam, who stood stoic, quiet, and listening. She sat up a little straighter, and her face suddenly lit up, like a wilting flower given fresh water. She wiggled her eyebrows at him. "He cute. Very, very handsome. The gold in his eyes reminds me of someone I once knew." He blushed, actually blushed, before she looked back at me in question. "You caught a good one? Yes?"

I laughed, loving how Liam's cheeks continued to redden. "I think I caught a good one. But there is still time to see if he is 'the one.'"

Liam shook his head and smiled before reaching out a hand to greet Malaya. "Thank you for the kind words. Very nice to meet you, Malaya. I'm Liam."

She winked at us and clapped her hands in excitement. "*Oooh*, you two will have pretty babies someday. I just know it!"

Alice swatted at Malaya's words in the air before she looked at me and Liam. "You two don't want to waste any more of your time listening to us two hens yapping, so how about you two go see Santa before we talk about having any babies," she said, rolling her eyes at her friend.

At the mention of babies, it was my turn to feel my face warm to whatever shade Liam's face was. I asked Alice, "But didn't you say you needed a ride home after an hour of singing?"

"Good news. Malaya has offered to take me home tonight. So, I think you should stay and have fun with your sweetheart, Liam."

"Are you sure, Alice?"

"I'm sure. I had a lovely time spending the day with you. Now go get in line and see that Santa you've wanted to see. But just so you know, he's not real. His name is Jeffrey, and he goes to our church."

Liam laughed. "There goes her hopes and dreams, Alice. Sam was hoping she could tell Santa what she wants this year."

"And what do you wish for?" Alice asked.

"Yeah, what are you going to ask Santa for?" Liam asked me.

"Um, besides the gift of eating chocolate cake every day without ever getting fat?"

Alice nodded in agreement. "Yes. Every woman's dream. I like that."

"Oh. Now I want chocolate cake to go with this coffee," Malaya said, laughing.

Liam shook his head. "No. Really. What will you ask?"

"If I share it with any of you, it might not come true. So, I guess only Geoffrey will ever know." I kissed Alice's cheek. "I had fun spending the day with you, too, Alice. I will see you soon?"

"Hopefully sooner than later. I'd like to know how you did on that big test you mentioned. And isn't your birthday in a few days?"

"Yep. I'll be twenty-one."

Alice sighed. "Oh, to be young again. It's the time in one's life for new beginnings."

Chapter 19

Sam 2005

I never much cared for birthdays, not when mine fell so close before Christmas. Wearing a long over-sized cream sweater that passed for a dress and high coffee-colored boots only to show a tiny bit of thigh, Liam sat me in a cozy booth at a fancy restaurant, saying that twenty-first birthdays require celebrating and that I had no choice but to let him take me out. "I love that your birthday is only six days away from Christmas," he said with a giddy grin. Clearly, he was more excited than I was. "I was torn between buying you two gifts," he gushed, "so I bought both, one for your birthday and the other for your Christmas gift."

"You didn't have to get me anything."

"*Pshh*. I'll do whatever I want. Now open."

With his face freshly shaved and wearing black jeans and a caramel sweater that matched his soft, thick hair, I wasn't lying when I said, "You are the only present I need, Liam." But when he placed a small rectangular velvet box before me, I felt a tinge of panic. I tried to hide my worry. I was never a fan of jewelry. I had even told Liam this on several occasions, but it seemed he didn't believe me. Surely, he knew books or even food was a better way to my heart than some tacky jewelry I'd just end up losing. I forced a smile as I reluctantly opened the soft top and then almost immediately laughed. "What is this?" I asked, pulling out a single pink key attached to a simple silver chain necklace.

"The key means three things. First, since you need your privacy, when we get home, you'll find that the door to your bedroom downstairs has a new lock. This key fits into that."

"That is very thoughtful. Thank you."

"Also, I know you think you'll only be staying with us for a short while, but I'm hoping you might stay with me until we find our own place. Even if you work it all out with your parents, well, now that I have you, I guess I simply don't want to let you go. Not now. Not ever." His green and gold eyes peered deeply into mine. "Say you'll stay with me forever?"

I didn't have to think twice about it. Even though I missed my mother's incomparable love, staying with Liam and his parents was a new feeling altogether. It was different. I had never felt more comfortable and at ease. I belonged. "Yes. I will stay with you," I said. "Forever and wherever you go."

He smiled big. "Good. Then it's settled. And now, secondly, and more importantly, someday, there *will* be a ring in a box instead of a key. But until then, this key symbolizes that you will *always* have the key to my heart."

Liam batted his eyes at his cleverness, and I kissed him. "And you will always have my heart too, Liam. And three?" I asked him eagerly.

"And third, this key means I promise one day that our dreams of owning a home together will happen. I can't wait to start our lives with cozy heater blankets and a white little dog named Chewy."

I hugged the key to my heart and shook my head. "How did I get so lucky? *You* are amazing, you know that? This is a perfect, thoughtful gift, Liam."

"Good, because you're a tough one to shop for. You don't like clothes, and you don't like jewelry, so I'm glad you like the key."

"Yes. I love the symbolism of the whole gesture."

"And the best part is that we won't worry about my parents walking in on us anymore."

"That will be nice." I blushed. "I never did finish eating that cake you got me."

"I know. That's why, if you look under the box, there is a small note."

Flipping the box over and reading the tiniest note attached there, I burst out laughing. "An IOU for chocolate cake?"

"Yep. We need an uninterrupted re-do of that one night."

I kissed him again, but a good and hearty kiss this time. "I love you more than cake."

"I doubt it."

"Okay, it's a close tie."

"I'll take that."

I took a sip of my water. "You know I love your parents. They've been super kind and gracious during all this."

"I kind of like them too, and they adore you, by the way. They mean it when they say you can stay as long as you want." Liam ran a finger around the rim of his water glass. "You know, being a single child, it can get lonely at home sometimes, so this year, with you living with us, it's going to be so much fun. Christmas, especially."

I placed the key and chain over my head and around my neck before picking up the menu. "I'm excited, too. And even if I end up working a lot, since it's the restaurant's busiest time, I'll still get to see you Christmas morning. By the way, your mom and dad sure go nuts for Christmas. I've never known people to put up *two* giant Christmas trees. And I think I counted over forty-three Santas all over the house?"

"Yeah. As you know, Christmas time is our favorite time of year."

"*I can tell.*" I looked down at the menu in my hand, with the name *A's* across the front. "You know, my only other wish for my birthday was that my grades reflected the name of this restaurant, but now, I just don't care anymore. As long as I have you to feed me cake, all my problems seem to have just vanished."

"I'm sorry you didn't get the grade you needed. You worked so hard. You sure you can't do anything about your grade in that class?"

"No. That last test I just took was *huge*. Even though I studied my butt off, I secretly knew I couldn't achieve an A. It was a long shot. Maybe if I had quit my job, I would have had more time to study, but 'such is life,' as Alice would say. I will survive this."

He took my hand in his. "*We* will survive this together."

I looked at the man I loved so much that I felt my heart squeeze, almost in discomfort. "Together, for always."

"Still, it sucks about school. So, what's your plan now?" Liam asked.

"Well, since I can't afford to change my career choice, I'll have to drop this one class in order to keep my perfect GPA. But I won't drop it until the end, because I still need to learn as much as possible for when I retake the class next year. I also need to look for another job that doesn't suck the life out of me, one that doesn't stay open so late and allows me more time to study. It means less money, but it's doable. I think. But I'll be fine."

"And it would beat working for a perv."

When Liam gave me a sideways look, I set the menu down. "Don't give me that look. I know you want me to turn my boss in, but I can't quite yet. First, let me find another job before I blow this guy to smithereens, okay?"

"All right. I'm not happy about you procrastinating, but I support you."

"Thank you. Also, I don't think I told you but thank you for helping me study these last few weeks. You are the best study partner ever." I kissed his cheek. "I guess I'll keep you."

Liam tapped my nose. "Yes, I *am* a keeper, especially since now I hold all the knowledge about human anatomy."

"Is that so? What exactly do you remember from those flashcards? Because I doubt it was *anything* unless it had some sexual innuendo attached to it," I said, rolling my eyes.

"*Oh, stop*. I know that the rectus femoris is part of the quadriceps."

"See, you only remember rectus femoris because 'rectus' sounds like rectum?"

"Okay, you got me. But let's move on to more important things. What kind of drink are you ordering for your twenty-first birthday? A Long Island? A pina colada? A mimosa?"

"Since when do you know the names of drinks? You never drink."

"Just because I choose not to drink until I'm twenty-one doesn't mean I'm a complete moron." Liam shrugged. "Okay, maybe those drinks are the only ones I know because my mom orders them when we're on vacation."

"Well, I'm not a fan. And since I don't like the taste of any of it, I think I'll pass and just order a hot chocolate."

"But it might be bad luck not to order a drink on your twenty-first birthday. Besides, it's not like you're going to become an alcoholic for having just one drink."

"I know *that*. It's just, why waste the money on a drink that tastes like tar?"

The waitress came over and introduced herself, and Liam took charge. "What is a sophisticated drink for someone turning twenty-one today?" he asked, smiling at me.

The older woman followed his gaze to me and beamed. "Well, happy birthday."

"Thank you."

"A gin and tonic is somewhat sophisticated. But may I see your I.D. for that birthday drink?" she asked me.

Liam's excitement mounted as he waited for me to hand over my credentials. I couldn't understand the big to-do with ordering my first legal drink, but I handed over my card for his sake. "Okay, I guess I'm ordering a drink."

"Be right back with that special drink," the waitress said.

Liam laughed when I kept shaking my head. "You hate this, don't you," he said.

"I hate the attention on me, but I don't hate you being here with me." I snuggled up close to him. "I'm going to order the biggest bowl of pesto pasta they have, with extra sun-dried tomatoes."

"Same, minus the tomatoes. Or maybe I'll order the carbonara. Speaking of not liking attention, are you all set for the court appearance tomorrow? And what did you decide to wear?"

"I don't think I will ever be ready for a courtroom full of jury members. Just saying that out loud sounds too bizarre. But as for clothes, no matter what I wear, I think I'm going to feel naked in front of all those people judging me."

"I wish you'd let me come and support you."

"I know, but you have an important basketball practice after classes. Your coach won't play you if you miss it. Besides, who knows how long this trial will last? It could be days. So why sit through all that?"

"I just can't believe they set your court date tomorrow, five days before Christmas."

"Right?" I said. "And how am I supposed to enjoy the holidays if their decision comes swiftly, and I lose this case? Merry Christmas! You're a hundred and fifty thousand dollars in debt!"

"Did your lawyer have any final thoughts? Like any clue with which direction the case would go?"

"She said the information Heidi gave me about Randy Jergins has changed their strategy in court."

"Hopefully, in your favor."

"Agree, but my lawyer can't just go off what my friend assumes. They have to base the case on concrete facts. I'm just praying they have thoroughly investigated Randy."

"Either way, I hope you find something to wear. I don't like the thought of you standing naked in front of all those people."

I scratched my chin. "Well, indecent exposure could get me at least a week in jail. Even though jail time sounds better than going to work during the holidays, Christmas time is our busiest, and I need the money right now. I'll be so busy working that I may not see you for a week solid."

Liam sat up straight. "Speaking of Christmas, you need to make me a list for Santa."

"My wish is simple: win my case tomorrow."

The waitress returned with my drink. "Thank you," I said.

We ordered our food, and after the waitress left, Liam patiently waited for me to take my first sip. "Well, go ahead."

"Fine," I said. "Cheers to me." I clinked my drink to his water glass before taking a small sip.

When my face puckered, Liam sucked in air between his teeth and cringed. "That bad?" Since he was underage, he discreetly lifted my glass and took a tiny sip to see if I was telling the truth. "You're right," he said, disgustedly setting the drink down. "Let's order you something else. How about champagne or a pina colada?"

"You are the sweetest, but no. My water is fabulous. But hey, we did it; we ordered my first legal drink! *Woo-hoo!*"

"We did. And although it was an epic fail, we still have dessert to look forward to. Chocolate lava cake or apple crisp?" he asked.

"I can't choose. They both sound divine. You pick."

"Both it is, then."

"Now you're speaking my language. But the only bad thing about all this pasta and dessert is that I'll look super bloated when I walk naked into court tomorrow."

Liam pouted. "So, no dessert?"

"Don't be stupid. I never say no to dessert, even if it makes me look nine months pregnant."

"Perfect. Plus, looking pregnant might make the jury go easy on you."

"True."

Liam must have noticed me tensing up and asked, "What's going on in that head of yours?"

"I know clothes should be the least of my worries, but I just realized I really don't have anything formal to wear to court tomorrow." I looked at him. "Give me a second," I said, pulling out my cell phone. "I have to raid someone's closet tonight."

After dinner, and ten pounds heavier, Liam drove me to Shelly's. I jumped out of the car. "Thank you," I said, kissing his cheek. "This will only take me a few minutes."

I had just opened the gate in Shelly's white picket fence when her door flew open, revealing my friend wearing a fluffy pink bathrobe, with three small kiddos clinging to her legs behind her. "Happy birthday, Sam!" She looked to her kids then. "Well, go on then. Sing to Sam what you practiced."

After they sang the sweetest off-key "Happy Birthday" to me in their tiny, innocent voices, I gave them each a high-five. "Wow. Amazing. Just beautiful. Best birthday gift ever! Now I wish my birthday was every day instead of once a year."

Shelly's eldest, wearing only Spiderman underwear, looked at me horrified. "But that would mean you would die in eighty days!"

"Wow. Your momma said you were good at math. What grade are you? Second?"

I looked at Shelly, and she bit her lip. "He's in first. He's my curious one and recently asked me when people die. I just said we all die at one hundred."

I laughed, looking down at him, and ruffled his hair to calm him. "Well, good thing then my birthday only comes once a year. No one is dying any time soon, kid. Now, who wants to help me find a dress to wear?" I followed Shelly's screaming kids into her bedroom, where instead of them all helping me pick a dress, they jumped on the bed to show me their many acrobatic talents. "You have your hands full here, Shelly," I said, smiling.

"Girl, you have no idea. Don't go having kids any time soon, unless you don't mind losing your hearing," she said over all the screaming, which intensified when someone fell off the bed.

Because Liam was waiting for me in the car, Shelly quickly helped me choose a dress in a small floral print that landed just above my knees. I thought the dress might be a good sign, as Alice's favorite color was yellow. I stood in front of the mirror, tugging at the hem. "At least Liam will be happy to know I won't be showing up to court naked," I said.

"Yeah, you don't want to do that."

I turned around to look at the back, with its open scoop just above my shoulder blades. "I don't know. I still feel bare." I faced Shelly. "Does this dress make me look like a good person? Am I a good person?" I knew my clothes would not be the sole factor in the jury's decision. I prayed that if I won my case, I would indeed be a good girl, making no more mistakes from here on out.

"Look, you made a mistake, Sam, but that doesn't mean you are a bad person."

"Maybe, but I feel sick about this." As if on cue, my stomach made a gurgling sound. "Liam doesn't know it, but he just wasted forty dollars on me tonight."

"What do you mean?"

While changing back into my clothes, I explained, "After dessert and thinking about what's going to happen tomorrow, I couldn't help it. I went to the bathroom and threw up everything."

"Oh, Sam."

"And it's just my luck that every single person I know either has work or school tomorrow, so I'm literally all alone in court."

"I wish I could be there for you, Sam. If I didn't have to pay outrageous daycare prices, I would call out of work tomorrow."

"Oh, I know you would come to support me in a heartbeat; it's just that being in uncharted waters, I'm afraid I will sink. I'm scared."

"I know this is scary, but all of this will be over before you know it. Worst-case scenario, being in debt isn't the end of the world. Look at me; I'm a divorced mother of three, barely making it, and if I died tomorrow, I could honestly say I died happy." Her kids were in the middle of a pillow war when she looked at them with a motherly love that I had yet to understand. "Money can't buy you happiness, Sam," she said. "As long as you have people who love you and you have your health, what's to worry?"

It took me a moment to absorb her words, but she was right. Even if I worked the rest of my life to pay off my debts, money wouldn't be my main focus. Happiness comes from being with the people you love. "Thank you, friend. I needed this little pep talk."

"Good. You are—"

"Sam!" Shelly's second youngest screamed, interrupting us. He was almost four and still had what looked like a red Kool-Aid stain above his top lip. "You wanna hear my armpit fart?"

Shelly turned to face me again and grabbed me by the shoulders. "Now, before you leave, say it three times, like I have to do every single day; IT WILL BE OKAY." She rallied her kids around me. "Let's all help Sammy say it together!"

Even after I left Shelly's house with those four words beating their way into my mind, and even as I fell asleep that night, holding a single pink key to my heart, I said it over and over again: "It's going to be okay. It's going to be okay. It's going to be okay."

Chapter 20

Sam 2005

I would have chosen ten root canals over one day in court.

At seven forty-five a.m., my lawyer, Ms. Smart, led us to the courtroom. She knew I was nervous and attempted to make small talk. "Your dress was the perfect choice, Ms. Carey," she said. "I think the jury will be pleased with what they see."

"I hope you're right." But I wasn't so sure. I worried the jury would see right through me—a twenty-one-year-old who couldn't seem to get her crap together.

As we walked down the long halls of the old courthouse in Tacoma, Washington, I cringed at the loud clickety-clack my low-pump heels made against the cold stone floor, a sound that reverberated off the walls in a distracting echo. I was so worried about wearing a respectable dress that I had completely forgotten how much I hated heels. I tried to walk quietly on my tippy-toes to avoid drawing glances, but that left me feeling pigeon-toed.

On entering the large courtroom, since it was the dead of winter, I immediately regretted not wearing something warmer. A cold chill ran up my spine when I spotted the so-called victim, Randy Jergins. He sat seated at a front table with his lawyer leaning over, whispering something into his ear. When Mr. Jergins turned in my direction, I did a double-take. Everything about him looked different.

I don't know why I assumed Randy Jergins would be showing up looking scruffy, dressed in holey black clothes, and wearing a messy mop of hair like I had remembered when I first met him. Instead, he wore clean khakis with a blue, well-pressed button-up shirt and shoes that looked straight off the Nordstrom rack. And with his hair smoothly combed back and away from his eyes, Randy almost looked like he worked in a sophisticated Seattle office. Besides his clothes, his face surprised me the most. Instead of the agitated face he wore for me right after the accident, he now displayed to the courtroom a pained and worried expression that gave him an almost innocent, boyish look.

For a minute, I questioned if he was the same person I'd crashed into. *Is he really worried and in pain, or is he just faking it?* "The jury is going to side with him," I said in a panic to Ms. Smart.

She showed me to our seats and pulled out a chair for me. "Try to look calm and collected. It's going to be okay."

Once seated, my chair squeaked and groaned when I swiveled around to assess the room with a nervous glance. The stenographer was in front, preparing her station, and behind us, only a handful of people sat relaxed in their seats. Still, the nerve-wracking feeling was building up, and I immediately began chewing the inside of my cheek, which was already raw.

Ms. Smart sensed my fear and squeezed my arm in reassurance. "Nobody comes to these boring trials. These people are most likely here waiting their turn or taking notes on the ins and outs of courtroom procedures. Please relax."

I turned around, nodding towards the front. "Why is there a police officer here?"

"Don't worry about the bailiff. He's here to keep order and to kick out anyone who becomes a distraction." She began to open her files. "In a bit, the jury will enter and take their seats, and then the judge will follow. Be sure to rise each time the judge enters and leaves, as it is a sign of respect. Once, a lady was sent to jail for a hundred days when she refused to stand." My eyes widened, and Ms. Smart shook her head. "Sorry. I'm not sure why I told you that. I just always find that story interesting. I'm sure you won't do anything distracting."

"Like take off all my clothes?" Ms. Smart's head angled in question, and I quickly waved a nervous hand in the air. "Just kidding. I won't be causing a scene."

"Look, Samantha. You are nervous. That's normal. Just remember what I told you; relax and don't speak out of turn. And when you are called to the front to testify, give clear yes-and-no answers. No *uh-huhs* or *yeps*."

"Gotcha," I said.

Just as the side doors opened and the bailiff announced, 'All rise,' my heart dropped a few notches below my knees. "It's going to be okay. It's going to be okay. It's going to be okay," I whispered under my breath.

The judge walked in and positioned himself comfortably in his oversized leather chair. Strangely, his appearance comforted me. His wispy silver hair and kind blue eyes gave off grandpa vibes that I hoped perhaps reflected his true nature.

Ms. Smart whispered, "Another reminder, in case you forgot: you are the defendant, Sam, and Mr. Jergins is the plaintiff. It can be confusing when we start."

"Okay."

The judge politely asked if the counselors were ready to proceed. After agreeing, the jury came in and took their seats, and things took off fairly quickly.

First to take the stand was Randy's doctor. He was in his late sixties with a pudgy middle and wore thick bifocals that sat snugly on top of a robust nose. He nervously scratched his ear, which seemed as large as his hands, as he waited for Randy's lawyer to question him.

Randy's lawyer stood and tried to reattach the bottom button on his cheap-looking suit before he spoke. He had difficulty with this task, as he was middle-aged and overweight, like the doctor. Finally, once he had buttoned himself in, he approached the witness. "Doctor, thank you for coming today. We know your time is valuable, so I will get right to it. When did you first see your patient, Mr. Jergins?"

"Mr. Jergins came to us the day *after* his accident, on November first of this year."

"Can you describe Mr. Jergins's condition that day?"

"Yes. Mr. Jergins complained of severe neck pain and a migraine. We ask all our clients to rate their pain levels: One is the least pain, and ten is the worst. Mr. Jergins complained that his neck pain was at a level nine, and his migraine was almost a ten."

"Did you order X-rays the same day?"

"Yes, we did, as well as an MRI."

"Doctor, may I ask you, the jury, and the courtroom to turn your eyes to the screen on the wall? We have enlarged the MRI you provided so everyone can have a better look." A large medical scan took center stage, and the lawyer asked, "Can you verify that these images are from Mr. Jergins?"

The doctor nodded. "Yes. This is Randy Jergins's spinal cord."

"And Doctor, what is the extent of the damage here that we are looking at?"

"I will try to explain in simple layman's terms. The spinal cord is made up of stacked bones called vertebrae. In between these bones lie spinal discs, which act as a cushion to provide shock absorption for the neck. Each disc has a jelly-like substance surrounded by a hard outer ring. The circled area is the damaged area—specifically discs C2 and C3. You can see that the force of the accident has caused a slight protrusion between these two discs. We call this injury a herniated disc. Herniated discs occur when the soft inner core of the spinal disc protrudes through the outer ring."

"Thank you for explaining. May I ask what symptoms a person may have with a herniated disc?"

The doctor explained all the possible symptoms and then stated that Randy had exhibited pretty much all of the symptoms mentioned. I glanced at the reactions on the faces of the jury, and I saw how they sympathized. *I am so screwed.*

"Doctor, what post-care did you advise Mr. Jergins for this type of injury?"

"This type of damage we see tends to be linked to other structural damage in the surrounding areas, like the spine's soft tissues, muscles, ligaments, and nerves. We see this type of injury all the time with people who suffer from whiplash. So, we immediately advised and fitted Mr. Jergins with a neck brace to prevent further damage. We also prescribed him pain and anti-inflammatory medications, as well as advised him to alternate heat and ice to the neck every forty minutes. We told Mr. Jergins to discontinue all physical activities for two weeks and begin physical therapy a week later to help improve his mobility."

"In your opinion, how is Mr. Jergins's treatment working?"

"We have seen some improvement, but it's slow going. Everyone's body heals differently. But if my client finds no relief after twelve weeks of treatment, we may need to advise the use of steroid injections and surgery as a last resort."

"Thank you. Extremely insightful. One last question. Would you say this type of injury can result in permanent and/or chronic pain?"

"About twenty-five percent of patients will experience permanent or chronic pain lasting years—if not a lifetime. Unfortunately, it is often hard to predict the future, and it could take years to know."

"Thank you for your expertise, Doctor. No further questions."

The judge asked, "Is the defense ready for cross-examination?"

My lawyer stood. "Yes, Your Honor, I'd like to bring forward exculpatory evidence. Please see exhibit A." Ms. Smart handed out the essential documents she had carefully prepared. I held my breath in hopes that what happened next would stick.

Ms. Smart faced Randy's doctor. "Doctor, in your hand is an X-ray and an MRI scan conducted by Timothy Spencer Crean. These images were ordered approximately two months *before* your offices took similar images of Mr. Jergins's injuries. Did your client divulge any past or previous accidents, and did Mr. Jergins disclose that he had seen another doctor just a few months before seeing you?"

The doctor's bushy eyebrows knitted in confusion. "No, Mr. Jergins did not divulge this. I did not know of any previous accidents." The doctor swallowed and quickly added, "I want to clarify that my staff and I take extensive measures when reviewing our client's medical histories. But we would not know any of this if the patient was not forthcoming with such vital information."

"So, you had no idea of Mr. Jergins's medical history or about a previous accident?"

"No. And, if we were made aware, we would have made the appropriate inquiries to communicate with any previous doctors before assessing and advising any further treatments."

"If you don't mind, Doctor, with your expertise, could you explain the damage you see in this older MRI that was ordered by his previous doctor, dated two months prior to your MRI?"

"Well, I need a moment to look over these before evaluating."

The judge nodded. "Doctor, please take your time. Then, when ready, please answer the question."

After five minutes, the doctor cleared his throat. "All right. I have made an assessment. The MRI before me shows comparable results, and the damage to the spinal cord is extremely similar to our images." The doctor looked baffled. "I would say that they may even be identical."

Ms. Smart asked, "With this new, substantive evidence presented to you, and with the new enlightened assessment, would you agree, Doctor, that it is *impossible* to determine if Mr. Jergins's injuries occurred from this trial's specific accident and not from a previous accident?"

Randy's lawyer objected, and a series of arguments followed. It was like watching an hour-long game of ping-pong. I wanted to look at Randy's face to see what he thought of our discovery, but I was too scared to take a gander.

The jury remained attuned to every word my lawyer spoke, and by ten-thirty, the judge called for a fifteen-minute bathroom break. He advised the jury to refrain from communicating with anyone other than themselves when out in the halls and ordered them not to seek any information on their own. I didn't waste any time and quickly went to the bathroom.

When I came out, Ms. Smart awaited me by the bathroom entrance. "Ready for round two?"

I loudly exhaled. "Ready."

We took our time walking back to the courtroom before she asked, "How are you holding up? That got pretty intense in there."

"I'm okay. That was good, right—the surprise evidence we brought?"

"It's good we looked deeper into his past medical records by discovering a previous car accident with a similar injury, but it was no surprise. We think the plaintiff's lawyers may have known ahead of time about our plans."

"How?"

"Randy's lawyers are entitled to a copy of all the records we subpoenaed before trial. So, they could have put two and two together when we ordered past medical inquiries."

"Oh."

"So, we just have to see what they come up with to deter the jury from seeing the obvious."

We found our seats again, and my hands began to sweat when I learned that Randy was next to testify. The room was silent as he took the stand. I wondered if his hand burned against that Bible as he swore the oath.

Randy's lawyer began, "I want to take you back to the accident, Mr. Jergins. In your own words, can you describe what you remember?"

"Yeah, it all happened pretty fast. My friend and I stopped to take a left, and as we waited for cars to pass, we heard this loud screeching noise, like wheels skidding on asphalt. Then, *bam*—my entire body felt the whiplash. The records show that the seat I was sitting in actually came off from the floor, and that is why I had such bad neck pain afterward."

After Randy talked for ten minutes about how much he hurt and how the pain had affected his daily life long after the accident, his lawyer asked, "I'd like to return to the moment, right before the impact. Was your blinker on?"

"Yes."

"And can you remember how many seconds you heard the tires screech before impact?"

"Well, it was raining when it happened, so it sounded like it was coming too fast for the brakes to work. I think the tires screeched for only two seconds or less."

I stopped listening briefly as my brain wrapped around what Randy had said. I grabbed a piece of paper before me and quickly scribbled a note for my lawyer. Ms. Smart looked up from the message and nodded in understanding before she scribbled back, 'When it's your turn to testify, yes, bring this up.'"

When Randy's lawyer finished, Ms. Smart stood to cross-examine him. "Mr. Jergins, you stated you had to quit work after the accident. What kind of work do you do?"

"I work for an autobody shop. Working underneath or over the top of the vehicles is very hard on my body."

"I understand. And, before the accident occurred, were you wearing a seatbelt?"

"Yes."

"Did the airbags deploy?"

"No, but they should have."

"Did you remain in your vehicle or get out of the car?"

"I got out for a moment. Honestly, I was a little in shock from it all."

Ms. Smart asked, "Did you have any problems driving home after the accident?"

"My neck hurt."

"Did the car drive normally, or were there any hiccups on the way home?"

"I drove the car home fine."

"Mr. Jergins. The autobody shop where you took your vehicle stated it was totaled. So how could you drive it home if it was totaled?"

"The engine worked fine. But the cost of the back-end repairs was more than my car was worth."

"Was the back end the only damage to your vehicle?"

"No. The driver's seat broke off from the floorboard, which is why my body whipped forward so forcefully. But that was the only damage to the inside of the car."

"Mr. Jergins, I have in front of me the name of the autobody shop where you took your vehicle for assessment and estimates. I indeed see where it states that the accident ripped the seat off the floor, and the seat came forward almost two inches from its original position. Does this sound right?"

"Yes."

"But you stated you drove the vehicle home without any problems?"

"Yes, but I didn't notice the seat moved then because I was a little shocked by it all. I just wanted to get home and ice my neck."

"The establishment you took your vehicle to is called Dino's Autobody? Is this the same place you work?"

"Yes."

"Why did you choose this establishment to take your vehicle to?"

Randy's lawyer stood and objected, "Question is irrelevant. Where my client chooses to go for estimates and repairs is his choice."

The judge ruled, "Sustained."

Ms. Smart said, "Sorry, let me rephrase that. May I ask what your relationship is with the owner of this establishment?"

"Objection!"

"Overruled," the judge called out. "Let's see where this goes. Ms. Smart, you may continue. Mr. Jergins, please answer the question."

I gripped the edge of my seat and watched as Randy shifted in his chair. He cleared his throat as if he had an irritating itch. "The owner is my father. I trust him over anyone."

I wanted to stand, clap, whoop, and holler. Instead, my gaze shifted to the jury, whose expressions changed from puzzled to comprehending. Would they piece it together? Of course, there was no way my lawyer could flat-out proclaim the scams Randy and his family did to make extra cash. It was all hearsay. But she could hint at the fact they could not be trusted.

"Your Honor," she said, "the evidence from Dino's Autobody exhibits bias. The plaintiff's father could have easily lied about the actual damages to the driver's seat in order to make it seem the accident was worse than it was. I submit that it cannot be considered credible."

While this led to another twenty-minute argument among the lawyers, I tuned it out. Instead, I focused on preparing myself for the questions they would soon ask me.

I tuned in again when the judge announced that all documents from Dino's Autobody were inadmissible and that the jury could not make their decision based on evidence from that specific establishment or its owner—another big win for me.

Before I knew it, it was my turn. My legs felt wobbly as I took the stand and swore the oath. "I do," I answered.

Ms. Smart was first up, asking me simple questions before moving on to more important ones. "Ms. Carey, by your best estimate, how long was your foot on the brake before your vehicle struck the vehicle in front of you?"

"Longer than two seconds," I said dryly. I tried not to get too excited when Ms. Smart nodded for me to continue, and I knew this was my cue. "It didn't happen as quickly as Mr. Jergins says because, on that day, it was sunny and warmer outside than normal—no rain whatsoever. I had worn a skirt and sweater on my way to college that morning. I needed no rain gear. I also know there was no rain because afterward, as I drove to work, the sun was in my eyes; in fact, I remember that I had to pull the visor down. I broke a nail doing it. Also, I noticed a burnt smell after the accident because my tires skidded for quite some time when I slammed on my brakes. I'm no expert, but I don't think the smell of burnt tires would be present if the roads were wet from rain."

"This is important information. Thank you. How about your speed? How fast were you driving before the accident occurred?"

"When Mr. Jergins initially pulled out in front of me, I slowed down to the speed limit, which was thirty-five. And when I noticed too late that he had completely stopped, I slammed on my brakes before slowing down significantly."

"Were you injured, and did you seek any medical attention?"

"No doctor visits. I just had a minor bump on my head. I took a Tylenol and went to work that evening."

"Did you exit the car to see if Mr. Jergins or the passenger was hurt?"

"Yes. I asked the other guy inside the car if he was okay, and he said yes. Then Mr. Jergins got out of his car and walked around to survey the damage to his car. He seemed more upset that his car was damaged than about any pain he may have felt. However, he did rub his neck a little and said that me wrecking his car would cost me."

"Thank you, Ms. Carey. No further questions at this time."

Randy's beady eyes never left mine after his lawyer stood to cross-examine me. It was unnerving, but I tried not to show my fear. As his lawyer walked towards me, he held his shoulders back and looked smug. There was a hint of intimidation in his expression, but his exaggerated posture only pushed his thick middle out further.

"Ms. Carey," he said, emphasizing the 's' in Ms. "It seems my client and yourself have a minor difference in opinion about the weather that day. But how do you know for certain you were able to slow your vehicle down so quickly? Did you look at the speedometer just before crashing into Mr. Jergins?"

"Well, no."

"So, you don't know for certain how much your driving speed had slowed at that point?

"No, but I'm certain I was braking for over two seconds. The skid certainly seemed longer."

"Did you or anyone take pictures of these skid marks?"

"No."

"And you said my client rubbed his neck in pain when he exited the vehicle?"

"Yes, a little."

"Ms. Carey. Have you ever heard of people suffering from shock after an accident?"

"No. This is my first accident."

"I've been in law for a long time, and in our world, we see this thing called 'shock' happen to a lot of injured victims after a severe accident. Some of the symptoms include dizziness, confusion, anxiety, and—"

"Objection," Ms. Smart argued. "Mr. Navak is not a professional expert on shock syndrome."

The judge declared, "Mr. Novak, this is your only warning. Watch yourself."

"I apologize, Your Honor. But, Ms. Carey, did you state earlier that Mr. Jergins was more agitated about his car than his injuries?"

"I ... I don't remember if I said that exactly."

"May I ask the court reporter to pull up the transcript from earlier?"

It took the stenographer a moment to find my exact words. "I have Ms. Carey saying, 'He seemed more upset that his car was damaged than about any pain he felt.'"

"Now do you remember, Ms. Carey?"

"Yes."

"Do you know if Mr. Jergins showed any signs of shock when he exited his vehicle?"

"No."

"Then, do you know for certain if my client was merely upset about his car or might simply have been in shock and therefore not yet aware of the severity of his injuries?"

"No. I don't know for certain."

"No further questions."

The judge allowed my lawyer to ask additional questions—a re-direct.

"Ms. Carey. Just to be clear, your airbag did not deploy?"

"No."

"You didn't feel any physical after-effects from this accident, correct?"

"Nothing but a small bump and headache."

"Last question. You haven't missed a day of work because of this accident?"

"No."

"No further questions."

I was relieved to be asked to step down.

With the testimony over, the judge moved the trial on to closing arguments, with Randy's lawyer speaking first. I tried not to roll my eyes as he recapped the emotional journey of a young kid who had his whole life before him, but for whom simple day-to-day activities had now become a struggle. Then, his lawyer went into full detail about how Randy was still in emotional shock the next day, which explained why he forgot to disclose his previous medical history to his current doctor. And last, Randy's lawyer argued that most people would take their vehicles to someone they trusted rather than to some random mechanic if given a choice.

Ultimately, Randy's lawyer did a surprisingly good job of trying to convince the jury.

Next came my lawyer. "Let's look at the facts. Can you honestly prove without a doubt that the cause of the plaintiff's injuries is the fault of my client? There is clear evidence of a near-identical preexisting injury just two months prior that Mr. Jergins failed to disclose. And why is that? Why did Mr. Jergins keep important information hidden? Could it be for the same reason the plaintiff did not reveal that the mechanic who reported an exorbitant cost for back-end repairs also happened to be his father? Have you ever heard of a twenty-five-mile-an-hour rear-end that knocked the entire front seat off the bolted floorboard? This is biased evidence at best. Maybe even a scam."

I had to refrain from clapping and shouting out, "Preach, girl, preach!"

Ms. Smart continued, "And there is no evidence proving Mr. Jergins's father paid him wages for actual work performed, no paper trail that would back up his claim for lost income. We can only assume. The plaintiff claims, conveniently, that his wages were paid in cash. So, you tell me, could it be that this young man is smarter than we think and believes that our justice system is a ticket to easy money via a frivolous lawsuit? When you return to the deliberation room, please look carefully at the facts before you decide the defendant's fate. My client, Ms. Carey, should not be burdened with a one hundred and fifty thousand dollar claim for damages that could have been caused by a previous accident. I rest my case."

"Thank you," the judge announced. "At this time, each side has had equal time in closing arguments, but the plaintiff is entitled to final thoughts. Please proceed, Mr. Novak."

"Thank you, Your Honor. Counsel, ladies and gentlemen of the jury, let us look at the hard facts again. The police report states that Ms. Carey is at fault for my client's accident on November 1st. This life-changing accident has caused immense pain for Mr. Jergins, which he will most likely suffer from for years, if not for a lifetime. Earlier, we showed you a long list of past, current, and future expenses for medical, rehabilitation, lost wages, pain, and suffering. So ask yourselves this: is it too far-fetched to ask that my client, Mr. Jergins, be awarded something closer to five hundred thousand dollars? Because our numbers show this to be accurate. But Mr. Jergins is not asking for that; he only asks for a minimal sum of one hundred and fifty thousand dollars. Thank you."

The judge sent the jury to the deliberation room, and since it was almost noon, my lawyer suggested the McDonald's across the street while we waited.

Too nervous to eat, I picked at the cold fries before me. "Ms. Smart," I asked, "what do you think will happen?"

She swallowed a bite of her fish sandwich. "I think it went well. The jury has a lot of information to mull over. I'm hoping they make the right decision."

"How long will it take for them to come to that decision?"

"That I don't know."

I took a sip of my Coke. "Do you like your job, Ms. Smart?"

"It took a lot of education to get here, but I enjoy defending people, most days. You mentioned you were in college. Remind me again what you are studying?"

I explained my struggles with managing a full-time job, having little time to study, and how one challenging college course jeopardized my future.

"I completely sympathize," she responded. "When I realized how many years it would take and how much money it would cost, I decided the best way to get my legal training was to join the Air Force. It provided all my needs to get there. Best thing I ever did."

"You went into the military to become a lawyer? How does that even work? I remember seeing recruiters at our high school during our career fair, but I never considered it an option or particularly beneficial."

For the next hour, my lawyer explained how serving in the Air Force had helped her with her long-term goals. "So, it was a win-win for me. You might benefit, as I did. You should check it out."

"Thanks. I'll have to consider that as an option. Sounds almost too good to be true."

Ms. Smart's phone rang. "Sam, I have to take this. Excuse me a minute," she said as she walked away.

I couldn't help but wonder if the Air Force might be the answer to my problems, too. One, if the jury condemned me to that kind of debt, I could pay for some of it with the money I would earn in the military. Two, they would pay for my college, and three, the Air Force would allow me the time to study without so many distractions. But one frightening question etched itself in the back of my mind: if I were to be stationed far away, how could I live without Liam for four long years?

I came back to reality when Ms. Smart returned to the table. "Ms. Carey? That was the courthouse. The jury has made a decision. We need to get back."

"But it's only been two hours. What do you think this means?"

"I couldn't tell you for certain, but let's go and find out."

It seemed colder in the courtroom than earlier. My jaw clenched, and my body tensed as I contemplated whether to keep my coat on as we waited for the jury to enter. When the jury came in and found their seats, I held my breath.

The judge asked, "Has the jury come to a decision?"

A man rose, holding a piece of paper *and* my fate in his hands. "Yes, Your Honor."

"Good. Then please read the verdict."

"We, the jury, award the plaintiff, Randy Jergins, the following: For vehicle damage and repairs, eight thousand dollars. For past and future lost earnings, four thousand dollars. For current and future medical expenses, ten thousand dollars. And, for all current pain and suffering, ten thousand dollars. Thus, the total amount awarded to the plaintiff is thirty-two thousand dollars."

Relief flooded me as the pent-up air left my body. I could breathe again. Ms. Smart patted my back. "Congratulations. This is a huge win for us." I could have done cartwheels across the room. I wanted to cry happy tears, knowing my insurance covered the total amount and I would owe nothing.

As I drove home to Liam's with my car heater and radio on full blast, I belted out Gwen Stefani's "Hollaback Girl," all the while thinking of the look on Randy Jergins's face, falling in disgust at my win.

People hear you talking like that,
getting everybody fired up
So I'm ready to attack, gonna lead the pack
Gonna get a touchdown, gonna take you out

Pulling into the driveway of Liam's family home, I hatched a mean plan and hastened to hide my grin when I walked through the front door.

Liam immediately stood up from the couch and rushed over to me. "You're back! Why didn't you call me on your way home? Any news?"

I dropped my purse on the floor and suppressed my happiness to take on the look of a deflated balloon. Forcing a frown, I sadly confessed a lie. "I didn't call you because I needed to tell you in person."

"*Crap.* Is it bad?" he asked, squeezing my hands in his.

I nodded.

"*Oh, Sam,*" Liam whispered painfully before pulling me to him.

No longer able to contain myself, I pulled away from him and laughed. "I'm not going into debt! The jury only awarded that liar thirty-two thousand dollars!"

Liam closed his eyes, exhaled, and dropped his head back, "*Oh, thank God!*" With the biggest smile, he picked me up and spun me around the room. A little squeal escaped my lips as we fell onto the soft carpet. He bent forward, congratulating me with a deep, dramatic kiss that left my toes tingling. "Promise me you won't ever trick me like that ever again," he said.

With my fears finally behind me, I felt light as a feather. I wrapped my arms around his broad shoulders, thanking my lucky stars for this clean break. "Okay, no more scares," I promised.

I believed those words I spoke to Liam to be true. I did. But sometimes promises don't anticipate change, and often, new fears come with change, too.

Chapter 21

Sam 2005

Christmas immediately followed the trial. You'd think this would be a time to celebrate my newfound freedom from debt, but as with all the holidays, work took priority. Having to work a double shift on Christmas Eve and Christmas Day, I'd miss celebrating with Liam *and* my family. My mother was not thrilled when I called to tell her the news.

"Sam, it's just not the same without you here. I miss you terribly. Couldn't they find someone else to fill in for you?"

"I miss you too, Mom! And I wish I could be with you on Christmas, but even Shelly, with three kids, didn't get the holiday off. This is the restaurant life I signed up for. Remember when I missed Easter? You guys survived, and we celebrated the next day. No biggie."

"I know. I suppose we can celebrate Monday night. It's just weird. I'll never get used to it."

"Well, there is nothing I can do about my schedule. But, trust me, I wish there was."

"Let's talk gifts," she said, changing the subject. "I just wrapped your and your sister's presents. I hope you didn't buy anything for your father and me. You need to save up your money."

"Too late. I already got you all a few presents. Plus, I think I can splurge a little now that I know I don't owe a bunch of money to that sue-happy idiot. Heidi actually saw him the other day, riding his dirt bike over some manmade hill track behind his house, so it doesn't seem he was too hurt after all."

"Unbelievable what people will do to make a quick buck. So, tell me again? You won't owe anything whatsoever to that guy?"

"Nope. Zilch. Well, except for me having to pay a five-hundred-dollar deductible. But yeah, I owe nothing else."

"That is just the best Christmas gift ever, Sam. But you know what an even better gift would be?"

"No. What?"

"That you'd say you'll come back home to live with us?" My mother was silent for a moment before I heard her voice waver. "It's been long enough. Everyone here has had time to calm down, and we are ready to move forward. Your dad has a lead on a new job in Seattle, so he seems in better spirits. He doesn't mind you moving back home."

Doesn't mind? Not, 'he misses you, Sam', or 'he wants his daughter to come home'? Not wanting to hurt my mother's feelings, I hesitated before answering sympathetically, "Oh, Mom, I don't know. I'll have to think about it." The truth was, even if I missed my mother, I didn't want to go home just yet. There was still much hurt and negativity that I couldn't handle. For one, there was no fighting at Liam's, and two, I felt at ease for once.

Plus, maybe by moving out, maybe my father and I could start fresh? For once, we had nothing to disagree on, and if I wasn't living at home, neither of us could disappoint the other. Who knew? Maybe one day, we could be friends if he saw me as a person and not a child? I liked this trajectory of thought; however, I hated the nagging feeling that I could be overstaying my welcome at Liam's. His parents said they loved having me, but part of me wondered if they maybe wanted their normal back without a permanent guest.

But dang, I missed my mother, too.

I sighed heavily. "Mom, do you ever feel like you don't belong anywhere?"

"What do you mean?"

"Like, I'm at the stage in my life where I want my own space, but I'm stuck in this weird place, like an in-between world where I don't belong at home or with anyone else except Liam."

"Sure. I can relate, honey. Those feeling are only natural. Remember when I told you I got pregnant with your older sister at fourteen?"

"How could I ever forget that," I said. "I'm still in shock that you kept that a secret from all of us for so many years."

Only two years ago, I had the opportunity to meet my long-lost older sister, Tina, after discovering that my mother had kept a deep hidden secret from all of us. She found Tina through an adoption registry, where we all learned that my sister, who was twenty-one at the time, lived far away. It had been a surreal experience meeting a second sibling who looked like the spitting image of my mother. Tina was now twenty-three, and I corresponded with her monthly through letters and made a mental note that I needed to write her back soon.

"Sam, you know the shame of that secret made me too scared to tell anyone. And I am sorry I waited so long to tell you about having another sister."

"It's okay, Mom. You had your reasons. I am just glad we found her. Anyway, you were saying something about not belonging?"

"Yes, so here I was, fourteen and pregnant. At the time, my parents were going through their divorce and made me decide whether I wanted to live with one of my older siblings or an aunt who lived two hundred miles away. I tried living with both for a while, but nowhere ever felt like home."

"That's so sad, Mom."

"It was a lonely time for me. In a perfect world, I imagined being able to raise my sweet little girl in my own place, the two of us against the world. But of course, I was too young and naive and had no money or support."

"I'm sorry your parents forced you to give up your baby."

"Even if it was over twenty years later, I'm just happy I found her. But to answer your question about belonging, the first time I really felt I belonged was when I had you and moved in with your father. I had a purpose, I had a plan, and I was loved."

"I suppose someday I will have that with Liam. I'm just impatient."

"You have always been impatient."

I laughed. "You're right." I paused for a moment, wondering why this story brought familiarity. And then it hit me. "Mom. You just gave me an idea. Your story about giving up your baby reminds me of Alice." I retold her Alice's story about the one mistake that had haunted her forever, just like it did my mother. "I guess what I am getting at is that if Alice gave her baby up almost sixty years ago, is it too much of a stretch to think that Alice could find her daughter, as you did with Tina?"

"From what I have learned, Sam, nothing is too far out of reach."

I bit my bottom lip. "I'd like to believe that. But now that I'm thinking about it, Mom, maybe I shouldn't bring this possibility to Alice. Giving her false hope about something that *may* be unrealistic seems cruel."

"True. How about you let me do a little research first? Without making it obvious, ask Alice for some important details, like date, name, and birthplace.

You never know. Until then, that feeling you mentioned, of not feeling whole or belonging—just know that someday all the pieces to the puzzle will fit, and you won't feel that emptiness anymore, Sam."

"I hope."

"Patience and hope go hand-in-hand. Remember that. And speaking of patience, I will patiently await your call after work to wish you a Merry Christmas Eve, my daughter."

"You got it, Mom. Love you."

I pulled up to work twenty minutes early to swap gifts with Shelly. Dressed in my standard black slacks and white button-up, I added some holiday cheer with a fashionable glittery-red necktie and a pair of green sparkly earrings shaped like Christmas trees.

"Sam, wait up!" yelled Shelly as she closed her car door a few stalls down. She wore similar festive attire but in opposite colors—a green necktie with red and white candy cane striped earrings. Shelly wiggled her eyebrows up and down with an enticing grin while shaking a beautifully wrapped box. "Are you excited?"

As a puff of cloud billowed from my nostrils, I shivered and threw my arms around my body. "I am, but are we opening gifts outside?"

"Why not? Santa is out there right now, delivering gifts."

"If you say so."

Shelly blew warm air into her hands. "Okay, you're right, it's too cold. Let's go inside."

"Good idea," I said, relieved.

We raced into the building laughing. "Perfect," I said, sitting down when we found the break room empty. "We have the place to ourselves."

"You want to open yours first?" Shelly asked as she removed her coat.

"Okay."

I carefully unwrapped my gift and had to comment, "Shelly, you took a lot of time wrapping this, and such pretty wrapping paper."

"I was up till three in the morning wrapping the kids' gifts, so I'm surprised it looks that good. I think I wrapped with one eye open."

I held up a soft red scarf, candy canes, an apple-cinnamon-scented candle, and a new book by Jude Deveraux. "I love all of this. Thank you so much."

"You mentioned she was one of your favorite authors."

"She is! And since my college is on Christmas break, I'll finally get to read something for enjoyment rather than torture!" I handed Shelly my gift to her. "Okay, now, ignore the wrapping job. I suck at it."

When Shelly pulled out her gifts one by one, she laughed. "Oh, *this* is too funny," she said, holding matching red mittens, chocolate, a pine-scented candle, and a large book. "Great minds think alike." She held up her book and examined it. "Sam, this book is seriously thick."

"The thicker the better. It's about eight hundred pages, but I swear you won't be able to put it down. Ken Follet is another favorite of mine. I think you will like it."

"*Pillars of the Earth*?"

"It's a story of life and humanity set in the 12th century, telling the dramatic tale of an entire village's struggles building the world's greatest historical cathedral ever. If you like anarchy, betrayals, secrets, lies, and good vs. evil, this book is it."

"Sounds intriguing." Shelly looked at her watch. "Crap. My station still needs prepping."

"Go. I don't work for another ten. I'll clean all this up and put the gifts with our purses."

"Deal."

After Shelly hurried off to her station, and I finished putting a bow inside her bag, I heard a scratchy voice behind me. It belonged to the Grinch himself. "Ho, Ho, Ho, Sam."

I slowly turned around and gave him a flat smile. "Merry Christmas Eve to you too, Brad."

"What's all this?" Brad said, waving his hand towards the presents. "Gifts for little ol' me?"

"Sorry. Plum out of coal, I'm afraid. Maybe next year?"

Brad slid the red bow off my gift box and played with it like a cat would with string. "So, what did your boyfriend get you?"

"I wouldn't know yet. I'm working the holiday shift, so we'll only open gifts on Monday."

"Well, then, what did you buy him? Something with lace, I hope?"

I was a trapped mouse in a corner with nowhere to run. But if I could just answer him this one question, maybe he would let me go and leave me be. "I bought Liam a small gold chain necklace with a basketball in the middle." The gift to Liam was a splurge, but I wanted to show him how much I adored him for all his support during the school stress and my nightmare of a trial.

"Seems a waste of money, if you ask me," Brad said, holding up the red bow and stroking the silk's tail end. "You could have worn nothing but this bow around your neck. Trust me; guys don't care about gifts. With your little hot body, it's a gift in itself."

Something shifted within me, and my heart pounded. But not the kind of pounding that suggested this man somehow still had power over me. He did not frighten me. Not anymore. The feeling was oddly quite the opposite. I wasn't scared of this pathetic excuse for a man hovering over me like a gorilla in heat. Instead, my heart pounded with the thrill of realizing that I was finally ready to stick up for myself. For once, I didn't care what the repercussions were, either. Because I had had enough. I was ready. I was finally ready to do what I should have done from the very beginning.

After shoving our purses and gifts into a locker, I finally faced the man who had harassed me for nearly two years. "Thanks so much for that suggestion, Brad."

"You are so welcome."

"Nope. You missed the sarcastic tone in my voice, *Boss*, so let me try it this way. Thanks *so much* for ruining Christmas for me. Not only will I be scarred for life knowing that you imagine certain images about me and my boyfriend in that little head of yours, but now, when Liam opens his gift, the present I got him loses its value. It loses its specialness because I will have your disgusting suggestion stuck in my head forever. You *really are* an asshole."

I threw on my apron and viciously tied the strings around my waist. "And I get that you are a complete moron who assumes everything you say is a compliment, but for your information, I could do without all of it. Because if you haven't figured it out yet, you gross me the hell out, Brad. I gag a little every time something stupid comes out of your disgusting mouth. Now excuse me while I try and go to work without you ruining the rest of my evening," I said, pushing past him.

He always had to have the last word, so I wasn't surprised to hear his words trailing behind me. "Holy shit. Shelly has rubbed off on you. God, you girls are too damn sensitive. But that's all fine and dandy. And yeah, my suggestion was a compliment, but whatever."

I was on a high for seven long hours. Not only did I find Brad's avoidance and silence a blessing, but working the holidays had its perks. Customers were always in a joyful mood to give; some even gave bigger tips, feeling guilty that we were stuck serving them rather than at home with our families. And with only two hours left, I had already counted three hundred and ninety dollars. It was turning into a forty-five-dollar-an-hour night, not even including wages yet. Of course, after the holidays, my tips would drop significantly.

While running a customer's credit card at the kiosk, I couldn't help but do some quick math on what it would cost me to live alone. I jotted down an estimate of expenses for college tuition, car, gas, food, rent, and utilities and came up just shy of $2000 a month. If I had a roommate, I could make it work with even a little extra to save up for emergencies.

"Earth to Sam!" Shelly said while snapping her fingers in front of me.

I looked up. "Sorry. Did you say something?" I grabbed what I wrote on the paper and asked, "Walk me to the kitchen?"

"Sure."

Throughout our shift, I desperately wanted to tell Shelly how I had stuck up for myself with Brad. But there was no time. "So, what were you saying?" I asked.

"Just that I'm glad this is almost over. My kids said they would wait for me until I got home, which doesn't help me any. Now I will have to wait another hour or two until they fall asleep before putting out all of the gifts from Santa."

"You are going to be tired come morning."

"For sure."

I motioned to Shelly to hold on a second as I dropped my customer's credit card slip off at their table. "Happy holidays, folks. I hope the rest of your evening is magical." They smiled and thanked me before I continued to walk with Shelly to the back kitchen.

"So, where were you just a second ago?" Shelly asked. "You were in La La Land, back near the kiosk."

"Yeah. I'm looking for a roommate. You interested?"

"Are you kidding? Sam, you would *not* want me and my three hellions living with you. Don't misunderstand me; I love my kids, but count your blessings, Sam. You are not encumbered by motherhood like me. You'd be scarred for life—never wanting children of your own—if you lived with us."

"*Pshh*. Nonsense. I love you and your kids."

"Well, we love you right back, and although it is tempting to shack up with you, I can't because ..." she cleared her throat, "I started dating again."

I pivoted and grabbed Shelly's arm just before entering through the kitchen doors. "Say what? This is great news! When did this happen?"

Shelly shrugged. "Two weeks ago. I wasn't sure if the guy was a keeper. That's why I haven't said anything to you yet. After my divorce, I figured no decent man existed. Anyway, I think this one is different." Shelly peered over my shoulder and through the tiny window above the kitchen door. "I'll have to tell you more about him later? I think I see my food ready."

I blinked several times. "Yes, please."

We walked into a chaotic kitchen, with cooks yelling and sweating all over the food, kitchen staff hustling to replenish stock, and servers running in and out with hot plates of stacked food that lined all along the window. Our boss had even hired two extra food preppers with names I had not yet learned because I was too busy.

I walked up to the crowded window to see if my orders were ready. "God, I hope we don't run out of prime rib," I told Shelly. I started to turn around to fetch the au jus to accompany the meat, but someone slammed into my chest head-on before I could complete the turn.

I gasped as I felt the brown liquid began to seep through my white blouse. And not half a foot away, my eyes locked onto the culprit.

Brad.

His face mirrored my disbelief as he stuttered, "I ... I did NOT mean to do that. I swear, Sam."

I couldn't find my voice. I stood frozen in shock, unable to move as the torrential downpour of an entire commercial-sized two-quart storage container of homemade A-1 sauce doused over and through the front of my blouse, cool and thick as a mud bath.

A burst of laughter filled the room before someone yelled, "Find towels and clean up the floor before someone slips!"

I glanced over at Shelly's shocked expression. Her hand hovered over her mouth, as lost for words as I was.

Brad continued, "Honest to God, I didn't see you there, Sam. I swear it was an accident." I wanted to believe him, but I was skeptical, given my earlier snub. I could easily see him acting out his revenge as he had with Shelly a month earlier.

Someone handed Brad a towel. "Way to go, Boss!"

Brad immediately started wiping the sauce off my shirt's front, but Shelly smacked his hand away. "I'll take it from here, *Brad*."

"Of course. You get the top, and I'll get the bottom," he said, crouching down to clean my shoes, which were also covered.

Jasper, one of the servers, patted my back. "It looks like someone took the runniest shit all over you, Sam. I don't think that's coming out."

"No crap," I said.

Brad looked up while wiping my shoes. "I'll buy you a new shirt and tie."

"It's fine. I'm sure it was an accident."

Or was it, I wondered.

Shelly gave up on wiping my shirt. "Oh, girl, we still have two more hours. You can't go out on the floor looking like this."

Kristen, my boss, came to my aid. "It's a good thing I have a spare shirt in my office. As for the tie, you can do without it, this once. Hurry and change while I run and check on your tables for you."

"Thanks," I said.

As I hurried to change in Kristen's office, I could only think about one thing. Whether or not Brad meant to dump a bucket of slop on me, it was time I found a new job. *Any* job. I couldn't stay dealing with his bullshit any longer. Leaving had to be my top priority.

Chapter 22

Sam 2005

Christmas had come and gone. With previous weeks consisting of finals, the trial, and working the holidays, guilt ate at me. I had not seen Alice in quite some time. It was dark outside when I pulled into her driveway, but at least I could see the walkway thanks to the white powder of icy snow that covered the path leading to her door. I took extra precautions not to slip as I carried gifts and a hot bag holding our Mexican dinner from Puerto Vallarta. It was one of my favorite restaurants in downtown Puyallup.

I found Alice sitting in her usual spot in front of the TV with a small metal orange-lit orb positioned at her feet. The amount of heat it gave warmed the small room enough to dry out my eyelids within seconds. I blinked several times to gather whatever moisture remained in my eyes before looking around the room. The place seemed the same except for a small two-foot tree with tiny red and green ornaments on her coffee table. It was the first time I saw anything so decorative in her home.

Alice looked up from reading her bible with a surprised look when she saw me. "*Oh, my word.* I thought you died, girl! I worried you forgot about me."

"I know! It felt like ages for me, too. So much was going on, Alice, and I wanted to call you but figured you probably wouldn't hear the phone ring."

"Well, good news. I got a new hearing-impaired phone—one for the hard of hearing." Alice picked up beside her a black phone and its whole housing unit. "See here?" The red light will blink—alerting me if I have a call. And the speaker at the end of the receiver is extra loud for me to hear people, but even if I can't hear some days, I can read the captions on this little screen," she said, pointing to a small grey screen displayed on the phone's base.

I set my bags down and checked out her new equipment that was the size of a large book. "No kidding. This is great."

"Yeah. My daughter got it for me for Christmas."

"Technology is sure coming around. I love it, Alice!"

"Sam, did you bring your cell phone?"

"*Um* ... yes?"

"Good. Go ahead and give me a ring."

"Like, right now?" I asked in confusion.

"Yes. Let's give this baby a whirl."

I laughed. "Okay." I found her number labeled on top of her phone and dialed it.

When the large red light flashed sporadically, Alice beamed, as if she won a prize. She picked up the handset. "Hello?" she answered.

I smiled. "Hello, Alice. It's me, Samantha."

She read the captions of what I said before answering, "Isn't this neat? Now, we don't have to yell back and forth. Instead, we can visit right here in the living room using our phones."

I lifted an eyebrow. "Wait, do you want to stay on the phone with me for the whole visit?"

"Yep!"

Alice probably didn't realize that my cell phone cost me in minutes unlike her landline, but what were a few bucks when she seemed so happy with her new toy. Plus, I had to give it to her—it was a clever idea, and it beat having to yell the whole time.

After we ate our meals and finished opening gifts, I asked Alice over the phone, "Alice, if I told you something, would you promise not to laugh?"

"Sure. What's on your mind, love?"

"Well ... I haven't told anyone just yet, and this may sound like a stupid idea, but I don't think I have any other options."

"Go on."

"I recently went to a recruiting office, specifically The Air Force. After they had discussed with me all my options, I've decided I want to sign up."

"Now, why would you think that was a stupid idea?"

"Maybe because it seems like a last resort kind of thing. Which, I guess, for me, it is."

"Nonsense. Joining the military and serving your country is a splendid idea. But if you don't mind me asking, why am I the first to know? Are you scared to tell Liam and your parents?"

"A little."

"Well, sure, it may be a little shocking for them at first, but I'm sure they will support whatever decision you make. I know first-hand because my second oldest, Greg, came to me one day and announced his enlistment with the army. In fact, that is how I came to reside in Washington State. When the military relocated him to Fort Lewis, me and the kids followed him here. And let me tell you. If my family stayed in L.A. any longer, I'm positive all of us would be dead."

Chapter 23

Alice 1967-1968

Almost five years after my divorce, in 1967, my daughter, Maria, found she was pregnant at sixteen. I couldn't stop her from moving out and marrying her twenty-one-year-old boyfriend, Carlos, who had duped her into believing he would take good care of her. I warned her that Carlos was not only too old for her but also that no decent man would prey upon a young woman like her. But she was brainwashed. And although I was right, a mother never wants to be right about such things.

A while after she'd moved out to live with Carlos, I saw bruises on her arms and face. We were at the pregnancy clinic when I discovered, to my horror, what he had done to my sweet Maria. But she denied it all, saying the bruises came from clumsiness, like running into an open cupboard or tripping on a rug. Myself, the nurse, and the doctor all knew it was a lie, but what could we do? Force her to come home when she was no longer in my care? She was legally a married woman.

But Maria wasn't the only one I was worried about. Without a father to guide him, my youngest son, Johnny, got himself involved with the worst of people in Los Angeles and became the neighborhood misfit by the time he was fourteen. It was clear he felt abandoned by his father, who pranced around Hollywood with his wealthy wife in their big house and their fancy pool, while his children barely ate and lived in a tiny apartment that had only two bedrooms for all five of us. I'd like to say Johnny's trouble started the day he got involved with the wrong crowd, but I'd be lying. Johnny's trouble started the day Frank moved out.

At age nine, Johnny stole his first car and got his head stuck in the steering wheel. At age ten, I found him smoking cigarettes and lighting sheds on fire. At age eleven, he was drinking and dabbling with drugs. And at twelve, my boy survived his second overdose. It was no surprise when, at thirteen, Johnny was the youngest kid initiated into one of the many gangs that preyed on our streets like vultures.

Through all those difficult years, it didn't matter how much I loved or disciplined that child; my son was fighting a war within himself. I believe he acted out, hoping that one day, his father would come around to care enough about the shenanigans he got into, but sadly, Frank never cared enough to save Johnny from himself. And it seemed none of us could save him.

Even with their father absent, even if my discipline didn't work, I tried to be a good example to my children. I packed all my kids' lunches, took them every day to school, helped them with their homework, joined the PTA, and became a den mother for my middle boy's Cub Scout group while managing to go door-to-door selling Fuller Brush products.

But still, none of what I did helped Johnny see how much he was loved.

Thinking back to when it all began to slide sideways, I wondered what I could have done differently. At the beginning, as a desperate mother whose nine-year-old child rebelled against doing what was right, I knew that Johnny needed more structure than the average child in school. He needed to recognize that falling short of goodness only hindered his path to happiness and that, even though he didn't have an earthly father to show him love, there was still a God big enough to love us all.

That's why I did what I thought was best: I got a group of moms together to take our children to a missionary school called Going Fellowship.

But I quickly learned that even a Christian school couldn't help my boy.

Even my own daughter—who was golden in Johnny's eyes—even she could not keep insurmountable pain from tearing at my sweet boy's heart.

Maria was twelve and Johnny nine on that hot, smoldering summer evening in Los Angeles in 1964 when we all truly saw the beginnings of my son's downward spiral and how no one could save him. We had all not eaten a thing yet, which we were used to.

"Who's home?" Maria asked me after turning down the volume on the television. With her dark brown waves held high in a ponytail that accentuated her still-rounded cheeks, her light blue eyes looked toward the sound of pots and pans clanging loudly in the kitchen of the rundown apartment we five shared. Her two older brothers wouldn't be home for a while, working their jobs at the local convenience store just around the corner. So the noise had to be from Johnny sneaking in through the back door.

"I'll go see," I said when the noise increased unnaturally.

The backs of my knees felt sticky with sweat when I stood up from folding the laundry and walked into the dark kitchen. The unshaded ground-floor apartment felt like a hot box when the summer sun hit us from all sides, which was why every window was covered in dark black curtains to keep the heat out. With the measly one hundred and fifty dollars Frank gave us in child support, I could barely afford rent, utilities, clothes, or food, let alone air conditioning, with the lousy commissions I got selling door-to-door. But it was something we all dreamed about.

"Johnny?" I saw him standing over the stove, which *never* seemed to work when we needed it to. I had complained to the landlord to fix it so many times that we just gave up. I can't begin to tell you how many times dinner was peanut butter sandwiches without the jelly.

"What!" he barked back.

Whatever my son was cooking in the pan was now smoking, filling the tiny kitchen with a gray cloud as the smell of burnt fish hit me. He turned to the garbage can beside him and bitterly threw away what looked like a small carp he had caught at Echo Park Lake down the road. He had often tried to provide us all with a little fish protein in the months when my sales weren't enough or when his brothers' paychecks barely stretched to pay the utilities.

I pulled back the black curtain and lifted the peeling and cracked painted window before fanning the room. When we could breathe again without choking, my crestfallen son was standing hunched over the sink in defeat. His dark, unruly hair hung past his ears and into his eyes, and I made a mental note to try to cut it on my next day off. "Dang, this stove. I'll call the landlord again," I said, feeling terrible as he stared at the blackened fish skin left in the pan.

He swiveled around to face me, his cheeks dirty and reddened from too much sun while fishing among the reeds in the mud. His hands were fisted at his sides, and his nostrils flared. His eyes were slitted, which was sad to see since they were a big, wide ocean of beauty to look at when he wasn't angry. "What's the point of calling that no-good fat cow?" my son spit out. "He doesn't give a shit about any of us."

I was too tired to discipline him for using a curse word. Plus, a mother knows when her child's heated words reflect something deeper, more profound. His outburst wasn't really about the landlord. As always, it was about his father's abandonment.

I let my shoulders slump like his when I opened the cupboard beside him that held our scanty provisions. There was a can of green beans, a pickled jar of beets, a box of powdered potatoes, a can of corn, and a slumping bag of rice that could maybe feed two people. I didn't bother to open the fridge. I knew the milk was out, and as tempting as it was to eat the remaining half stick of butter, I wanted to save it for the potatoes, which tasted like chalk without it. "Do you want me to make you a peanut butter sandwich?" I asked him. "Or some mashed potatoes?"

He crossed his skinny arms and leaned back against the sink. "No. I'm not hungry anymore," he said, which was a lie when I heard his tummy grumble in protest.

I turned toward the fishing rod, leaning against the door, and grabbed it. "How hard can fishing be? Let me go see if I can catch us a fish," I said. "Plus, some fresh air will do me good." Even though my feet were swollen from a long day of walking door-to-door on unforgiving, boiling pavement, I couldn't see Johnny beaten like this. He was always proud of catching us what little fish he could from that murky lake, and it made him feel good to contribute until his useless father's check came in the mail.

Johnny took the rod from my hands and shoved it back into the corner. "No. I'll go back to the lake. I just," he said, his voice hitching, "I just need to go to the bathroom first." At that, he pushed past me, but not before I saw his chin quiver. I wanted to comfort my son, but he stormed off before I could say anything. Besides, I was beginning to learn that sometimes it was better to let him cool off until he was good and ready to talk.

After I turned the water off and washed out the pan, I heard Maria in the living room trying to console him. The two were best buds; I was convinced either would jump off a mountain to save the other if need be. "I'm just saying, last week, you stole that car and got your head stuck in the steering wheel. You're lucky the cops chose to drop you off here rather than take you to jail. And this week, I heard the neighbor boy crying, saying you hit him," she said.

"Albert? He is a whiny baby. He deserved it."

"Well, I'm just worried about you, is all. And let's not forget, Mom says the Christian school you go to wants to kick you out if you don't behave."

"I don't care if they kick me out. To hell with them."

"Well, I care. What's changed?"

There was a long stretch of nothing before Johnny released a stifled sob. "Everything. Everything has changed. Dad never calls or says he wants to come and get me to go to his house anymore, and Mom is always crying, and you are always too busy with your friends. And now, my brothers both got to get a job, but I'm too little to work, they said. I just wish everything would go back to the way it was."

I peeked my head past the kitchen doorframe and saw Maria rubbing her brother's back. "*Oh, John*, I don't think it ever will go back to the way it was. And I know change is hard, but isn't there something that makes you happy? What about school and friends?"

"I hate school. I'm behind on arithmetic, and my teacher keeps picking on me to stand up in the middle of the class when I don't know the answer."

"Tell her in private you don't like to feel embarrassed in front of your peers."

"I did, but she just sends me to the corner."

Maria gave him a questioning look. "Did you sass her or something? And don't lie."

"Well, when she said she was teaching me to try harder and that she doesn't need a child to tell her how to teach, I told her she should try harder to do something with that ugly face of hers."

Maria dropped her head sideways and gave him a blank look. "Well, there's your problem. You can't run your mouth and expect good things to happen. But what about friends? Don't they make you happy?"

"Kenny is my only friend, but he doesn't go to the school that Ma forced me to go to. And all the other kids at my stupid school make fun of the holes in my shoes and say my clothes stink."

I cringed hearing that last part and lifted the hem of my shirt to take a quick sniff. I couldn't tell for sure, past the sweat from all-day walking, but it seemed the hand washing wasn't doing the job well enough. I'd have to scrub harder since I couldn't afford a laundromat. Nor could I afford to fix the teasing my son was experiencing.

"Well, you don't listen to them kids," Maria said. "They don't know anything."

There was a bit of silence before Johnny asked, "Do you think the reason Dad won't come and see me is because I don't get good grades?"

Maria blew out a long sigh. "No. I just think he has a busy life."

"You mean a busy life with his *new* family," Johnny grunted.

"Look. I know it's hard. It's hard for me, too. But you are not alone."

"I'm alone now that everyone is gone all day, busy making money while I can only catch a single lousy fish."

Maria bumped her shoulder with his. "How about you and me go do something fun tomorrow?"

"Really? But without David and Greg, right? Because I don't like them," Johnny confessed.

Maria laughed. "You don't like your brothers because you're too far apart in age, but I like them."

"You like them more than me?".

"I don't have favorites," she said, tousling his hair, "but you will always be the fun brother." He looked down and smiled, as if happy for the compliment and attention. "Also, speaking of favorites, one day John, you'll meet a girl, like David did, and you won't be lonely anymore. You'll be happy and content."

"*Ew*. No way. Girls smell weird."

"Well, I guess you aren't ready yet for girls, but for now, now that I know you feel lonely, how about we ditch David and Greg tomorrow."

"You promise?"

"I promise."

"You wanna go fishing with me right now?" he asked excitedly. "The stove just burnt our dinner, and I'm starving."

"Sure. But I'll come only if you let me reel in the fish."

"Deal."

Maria stood and hugged her brother to her, his head coming to just below her chin. I reflected that it wouldn't be long before Johnny had another growth spurt and would jump past his sister's height. "By the way," she said, "what are the fish biting? Because I'm not looking for worms in the dry dirt."

"Boloney."

She pulled her head back and looked at him oddly. "Lunch meat? But we don't have any lunch meat."

"I know. I stole it from the neighbor boy's lunch."

She shook her head and laughed. "What are we going to do with you."

And that was the truth. What were we to do, when Johnny continued to find trouble? I'd like to say that between Maria, me, and her brothers, all trying to show Johhny our unconditional love, we found a way to mend him, but we were just never enough for his broken heart. A boy needs his father. Even if I had all the time and money in the world for my son, his father's attention was the one thing I couldn't give him.

Fast forward, and after my youngest son's behavior worsened over the years, I was at my wit's end, still trying to heal the deep wounds Frank had created. When I met a nurse named Nellie at the Angelus Temple, a church in L.A., and told her all my woes and troubles with having a thirteen-year-old wannabe gang member and a sixteen-year-old pregnant daughter, well, Nurse Nellie offered us a surprising solution. She asked us to join her and her brother on a missionary trip to Mexicali. The thought of living in Mexico seemed terrifying until John came home late one evening higher than a kite. That was the last straw. His eyes were bugging out of his head, and he was screaming, "Make it stop, Ma!"

I cried so hard that night as I helplessly held my son in my arms, seeing him close to death. Many hours later, in the hospital, after they pumped his stomach and he sobered up, he finally confessed to why he had taken so many drugs at once. "I'm sorry, Momma. I'm sorry. I'll find some way to pay you back for the hospital bill."

"Why do you keep doing this to yourself?" I pleaded. "You are killing me and yourself!"

"Momma, I just wanted it all to go away."

"You wanted what to go away?"

"The pain in here," he said, pointing to his chest.

I kneeled beside the hospital bed and took hold of his hands, which were now almost as big as mine. He had long, shaggy hair, but his baby face, much like his voice, which kept cracking, had somehow morphed him into half-man/half-child. He looked like he had just been hit by a truck, with his eyes red and swollen with dark circles under them from crying all night. I realized just how much the drugs had affected him. "You have pain in your chest?" I asked, nervous that we weren't out of the woods yet. "Should I call the doctor in?"

"No. I mean ... I wanted to block out all the pain stabbing my heart. That's why I took the drugs."

I wanted to kill Frank for having this effect on our son. If only Frank had showed an ounce of interest in our boy, maybe Johnny wouldn't be struggling so terribly. "Your father—"

"It's not about him. I hate him."

"Then what is the pain about?"

"Guilt."

"I don't understand."

"I didn't tell you or anyone, but it's my fault Kenny died."

"What?!" I said in shock. I shook my head, not comprehending. Kenny had been Johhny's best friend since the second grade. I didn't even know he had died or when. "Baby. My God, what are you talking about?"

My son held in a sob before he entirely broke down. He could barely speak.

"We were ... we were walking past a gas station, and I thought sniffing gasoline straight from the hose would be funny. Some say it gives you a quick high." The pain in Johnny's eyes was almost too much to bear. "Momma," he cried out, "it happened so fast. Kenny took the first sniff and then ... and then he just dropped to the ground beside me. I called for someone to help us, but nobody did. I was holding his head, yelling for him to wake up and stop messing with me, but then his face turned blue. He turned blue, Momma! I ... I got scared and ran away before anyone came out of the gas station. But he is dead, Momma! Dead because of me!"

My hand hovered over my mouth, and I cried out, "My God! *No*. Are ... are you certain he is gone?"

"Yes," he squeaked out. "I called his house yesterday. His sister answered the phone crying and said the gas station clerk found him dead on the ground. They couldn't save him, Momma. That's ... that's when I took the drugs. I wanted to—"

"To what? Kill yourself, too?" I practically screamed.

"I don't know. I don't know!" he said, sobbing into his hands. "I'm so sorry."

After hearing rumors that Johnny had joined a gang and now this, that his best friend was dead, and my son played a part in his death, it took me only seconds to decide. "You'll be the next to die if you continue down this path of destruction. It's my job, as your mother, to protect you *and* Maria and her baby. So it's settled. We *have* to leave Los Angeles before it's too late."

I didn't hesitate to call his pregnant sister and beg her to come live with us in Mexico. Luckily, it didn't take much to convince Maria, not after a few months of living with her abusive husband. who daily made her feel as if she were facing an opponent in a boxing ring. She was against the ropes and without gloves, so it was no wonder when she jumped at the chance to escape that monster. She, too, had to try to save her child.

Living in Mexicali seemed like the right decision for us all. For once, our focus quickly turned to the needs of others, which, for a while, helped both my children forget their own troubles back home. My kids began to see how much they had taken life for granted. Me and Maria didn't know a lick of Spanish, but Johnny did from the gang life. He was able to help us teach the word of God the best we could. And together, we helped feed and clothe impoverished people and even offered medical care. Many of the children we met in Mexico suffered from malnutrition. We saw first-hand how not getting enough vitamins made their teeth rot.

As for myself, the experience I had as a new missionary servant was incredibly valuable. The journey showed me my life's calling. What I was doing seemed precisely where God had wanted me to be. For once, I understood the meaning of life. For once, I knew my purpose was to love and serve others with a joyful heart. And with this new experience, an unexplainable peace came over me. By helping those who wanted and needed my help, I finally belonged.

So, it crushed me when, after just a few months, my children began saying they wanted to go back home to live with their brother Greg.

I understood that living in a foreign country made them feel out of their comfort zone, but I refused to let them leave. I told them they couldn't go because Los Angeles was unsafe and full of evil influences. But none of that sunk in. The kids went behind my back and contacted their father. They begged him for the money to help them travel home.

Of course, with Frank having such a phobia about anything religious, when he learned I'd taken them out of school and forced them into the life of a missionary, he secretly sent them one-way tickets home, to spite me. How funny that after all these years, when we had gone without so much as an extra five dollars from him for our struggles, this was the one time he chose to help his kids. He had no clue that what he did was risking their very lives.

As much as Frank was ignorant of our children's danger in L.A., I hate to admit that he made a good point. He said that since Maria was seven months pregnant, giving birth in the States was safer for her and the baby. Either way, it had become quite clear—my children would not listen to or obey me, and I no longer had any control. I could only pray for them.

Before they left, however, I did the only thing I could and called my second eldest, eighteen-year-old Greg.

"Greg, the children are coming home. Please take care of them," I begged. "And remember, Maria's husband is not to be trusted, so I hope she can remain hidden while living with you."

"I don't think Carlos knows where I live, Mom. But I'll take extra precautions. If it helps, I can ask David if we can borrow his gun?"

"Please don't say that. You know how I feel about guns. Now, as for Johnny, please watch who he hangs out with. I don't want him pulled back into that trap again with those gang members. And just so you know, he is still fragile with the loss of his friend, so be a good ear when he needs it?"

"I will try, Mom. I will. But I have to tell you something. When you left for Mexico, I did a thing. I enlisted in the Army. I just finished boot camp two days ago."

"Greg, why didn't you tell me? This is wonderful news."

"I didn't want to worry you. You have enough to worry about, Mom."

"*Now, stop that.* I know a lot is happening, but I want you to always come to me with anything you have to say. I'm proud of you, Greg. I think that's great for you. But how could you monitor the kids if you're serving?"

"Well, that's the thing; I might be unable to watch them if they relocate me."

"*Oh, dear.*"

"You could always try calling David to help?"

"Maybe," I said hesitantly. We both knew my eldest, David, wouldn't be much help. He worked practically day and night, trying to make his father proud at the insurance company. As much as I hadn't wanted my children to pick sides after the divorce, David was the one I felt I had truly lost. It broke my heart, but again, I had lost my influence over the direction of all my children's lives.

Greg interrupted my thoughts. "But hey, let's not worry about that for a while. The good news is, I'll make enough money to take care of all of us now."

I cried into the phone. "My sweet boy, I don't know what I'd do without you. You've always provided and contributed to this family."

Greg was a real blessing in more ways than he could ever imagine. But neither of us could control the future.

Chapter 24

Alice 1968-1970

While I stayed in Mexicali, Greg updated me regularly on the children's activities. My daughter gave birth to Laurel Michelle Mendoza. She had her father's olive skin and brown eyes, but her delicate features were all her mother's. I cherished the many pictures Maria sent me, but I often felt guilty for missing such tender milestones. As for Johnny, I was proud when he started attending junior high with the best intentions. Even if he struggled with attendance and keeping up his grades, there was no news on anything gang-related, which was a blessing.

Although I was torn between the mission and wanting to be near my family, I felt God was calling me to serve, and I wanted to finish what I started. Eighteen blessed months went by without a hiccup until Greg called to warn me that he had been transferred out of state. The Army was sending him to Fort Lewis in Washington State. My son said he would continue to pay rent for the kids to stay in his old apartment in L.A., but it was still frightening to know that Maria and Johnny would have to fend for themselves. I had a nagging feeling that I should head home soon before it all fell apart.

I was feeling torn about this decision, but the decision to return home was easier after we experienced a car accident involving the pastor, his wife and children, and four of us missionaries. Our crew had been crammed into a small, worn-out Ford truck to deliver clothing to a village. The driver lost control, and we veered off the road, flipped, and rolled multiple times before landing in a deep ditch. When the dust settled, it was indeed a miracle that we had only trivial bruising, plus the pastor's broken arm. If angels hadn't been watching over us, we should have all been dead. We thanked Heaven above for sparing our lives; however, because the vehicle was totaled, our group could no longer get around to the villages transporting goods. And, since we already lived a meager life with little to no money for ourselves, I thought it was a sign to return home.

And boy, I am glad I did.

Call it a mother's intuition, but I was right. After the car accident, the second and third catastrophes came in quick succession. Not long after returning to Greg's apartment in L.A., I discovered that Johnny was again involved with gangs when he came home with a bloody face, beaten to a pulp by whoever wanted to kill him. And to make matters worse, my daughter's husband had learned where we all lived. It wasn't long before Carlos came around, demanding to see Maria and his eighteen-month-old baby.

At first, Carlos was kind to her and the baby, but that didn't last long. Maria wanted to believe her husband could change, but she was young and naïve.

"Maria," I told her, the same day that Johnny was lying on the couch, icing his face, "your husband will never change. Carlos is psychotic. He is violent, unforgiving, explosive, and unpredictable."

My grandbaby screamed excitedly as her mother tickled her sides, unaware of the fear we all harbored. "So, what do I do?" Maria asked. Like Johnny, she was sporting a black eye and a split lip after trying to block drunk Carlos from coming into the apartment the night before.

My family was a mess.

An absolute mess.

"I'm not sure what to do," I admitted. "Going to the police didn't help us. The restraining order on Carlos is no good. I know he'll come back at any moment."

Maria nodded in agreement. "He will. We all know it." We were all silent for a long time, weighing what little options we had before she asked, "What about Dad? Do you think he could help us?"

Johnny made an obnoxious, guttural laugh, but I waved him quiet. "I tried that tactic already," I said. "I called your father and begged him to take you and Johnny in for just a little while, but his witch of a wife refuses to help us." I looked down at my daughter on the floor, who tried not to show her despair so as not to frighten her child. "You're right, Maria. It's only a matter of time before Carlos comes back. And we're out of options." I glanced around the room, already feeling trapped, but my idea was the only solution. "We have to take whatever measures we can to keep you both safe. And not only you and Laurel, but your brother, too. I suspect whoever beat him up will come looking for him here and try to finish him off."

Johnny, now fourteen years old, sat up. "No. I'll leave. I don't want to bring more trouble here to you all."

"Oh, shut up," I said, so thoroughly angry with him. "It's too late. You should have thought about that before."

That day, before we locked and barricaded the doors and nailed shut all the windows, we went to the neighbors and made sure they knew to call the police if they saw Carlos or any suspicious cars show up. By the time we were done, it was late, and we were almost too tired and sweaty to allow the fear to grip us unconscious,

"Maria, how about I put Laurel down to sleep for you? We can clean up the dishes tomorrow."

Lately, Maria had been more exhausted than usual and moody to boot. My daughter looked ready to drop, and her face showed relief. "You sure, Mom?"

With the heat of summer crashing into our boarded-up apartment, we were boiling. Dishes could wait. I held out my hands and took Laurel from her. "I'm sure," I said.

"Okay. I'm going to go lie down. I don't feel good."

With sweat dripping down my back, I entered the living room with Laurel on my hip, looking for her favorite blanket. Johnny had been tight-lipped about the assault on him for days, and I decided it was time to confront him. "Where were you when this happened, anyway? Who exactly did that to your face?" I demanded.

"Do we have to do this right now, Mom?"

"When are you going to learn?" I asked him. "It's no good, you running around with God knows who, doing whatever it is you're doing. You're going to get yourself killed! I'm begging you. Stop all this." The baby cried, and I shifted her to the other hip. "Can't you, for once, do the right thing?"

"Mom ... *please* not now, okay? And you don't understand."

I found and grabbed the thin pink blanket from the floor and spat, "Make me understand." When he said nothing, I swallowed the lump in my throat. "Boy, you are always going to do things without thinking of others, aren't you?"

At this, he looked crushed. "I *do* think of you guys. That's why, whatever money I get, I always give it to you, Maria, *and* the baby. I keep nothing for myself."

I cocked my head at that. "Well, as thoughtful as that gesture is, how are you obtaining this money? What good is any money if it's coming from the devil's purse?"

He ignored me, walked into the kitchen, and asked, "So, what's for dinner?"

I knew it then. Johnny would never say it, but at that moment, I understood that he had joined the gang to help his struggling family the only way he knew how—selling drugs, stealing, or whatever it was that they did. And now, even if I was begging him to stop, I'm sure getting out of a gang wasn't easy. And maybe that was the reason he had been beaten up.

They wouldn't let him leave.

They owned him.

My heart ached.

"You, Mister, are unbelievable," was all I could say. "While I put the baby to sleep, I suggest you get to bed too. Tomorrow, we will all figure out a way to get us out of this, once and for all."

Maria always slept with me, with the crib snugged adjacent to our queen bed. After I put my sweet grandbaby to bed, Marie and I lay splayed out on top of the thin sheets with the fan on full blast. By 11 o'clock, the whirling noise of the fan finally lulled us all into a fitful night of sleep.

But our nightmares would soon turn into a reality.

It felt like we had only dozed off for a few minutes when a loud thump woke me. I turned the lamp on beside the bed and nudged Maria. "Did you hear that?"

She remained motionless but mumbled, "No, Mom. Go back to sleep. It's probably the raccoons again."

I figured she was probably right. Johnny often placed the garbage cans outside without the lids. I thought about going outside to check, but I was too tired and fell back asleep. I heard a soft rustling noise at the foot of my bed not five minutes later. I opened one eye just in time to see a dark figure move past my feet. I thought maybe Johnny had come in to check on the baby. He loved that little girl. But when Laurel made a fussy grunt, I turned my head towards the crib and whispered, "John, leave her be. She's perfectly fine. Go to bed."

My eyes began to adjust to the dark as the dark figure at the foot of our bed stood tall—too tall to be Johnny. Cold fear ran through my body, and I bolted upright to turn the bedside lamp on. There, by the crib, stood Carlos, holding my half-asleep grandbaby.

I gasped, "What in God's—"

Maria turned over, half asleep, and moaned, "Mom?"

"Don't move, Alice," Carlos warned. The whites of his eyes were no longer visible. They glowed glassy and red-hot, as if he was drunk or high or both. "Stay right where you are," he threatened.

Maria sat up, alert, at hearing her husband's slurred, raspy voice. "Carlos? What are you doing?" Her eyes widened when she saw him holding the baby. "Carlos. Please. Please give me Laurel."

"You think you can hide?" He gave his wife a sloppy sneer. "You think your family can protect you, Maria? And Johnny joining that shitty gang, thinking he had numbers on his side to deter me?"

"No. No," my daughter said in a high-pitched, pacifying tone. "I wasn't hiding. I just needed a break, that's all."

"Now, Carlos," I tried to intervene. "You have no right barging into this home. Give us the baby right now, and I won't call the cops."

Laurel awoke with a startled cry once she realized she was not in her mother's arms. But Carlos didn't care. "I have every right to be with my wife," Carlos yelled. "My child needs her father. Look at her," he said, shaking the baby. "My kid is flipping out because she doesn't even know her own father!" He kicked the end of the bed. "Maria, grab your things, and let's go *now*!"

My heart raced at the thought of Maria and Laurel leaving with him. "Maria," I cried out when she pulled the sheet off her legs.

"It's okay, Mom," she said, her eyes never leaving her child. "Carlos, I'll come with you if you just give the baby to my mother."

Just then, Johnny walked into the bedroom. "What's all the yell—"

No one moved the moment Carlos revealed the knife. He pointed it at John. "Boy, don't come in here unless you want me to slice you in pieces. Get out!"

I cried, "Please stop this, Carlos!" I turned toward my son. "*Go*. Listen to Carlos. *Go!*"

I hoped Johnny was smart enough to leave the room without a fight. And I hoped he was smart enough to call for help. But I mostly prayed he didn't do anything stupid to escalate the situation further. Gang life had taught him that saving your pride always comes first, which often overruled common sense and smart choices.

When the baby screamed louder, as if begging us to take her from the monster, I tried again. "Please, Carlos," I said. When my son finally left the room, I begged, "Please give me the baby. She's scared. Can't you see that?"

Maria frantically nodded. "Yes, please, just hand her over to my mother. I'll do whatever you want. I'll come with you. Look, I'm getting up to dress now."

Laurel's wails were wild as she stretched her arms out for her mother to hold her, but Carlos shook his head. "No! I'm not stupid. Look at you; all you want is this stupid baby. But what about me, *huh*? Am I not important?" When little Laurel let out a high-pitched scream because no one would comfort her, Carl tightly squeezed her to his body and growled in frustration, "Shut this stupid kid up! I can't hear my own goddamn thoughts!"

"Stop, Carlos!" Maria cried out.

All the screaming only seemed to provoke the man even more, and when he shook the baby so hard that her head jerked back and forth, Maria and I lunged out of bed. "Stop! No, Carlos, you're hurting her," we yelled.

"Back up! Stay back," Carlos said, pointing the knife at his daughter. "Both of you, get back into bed. *Now!*"

We were quick to do what he asked, but as Carlos slowly backed out of the bedroom, taking the baby with him, I silently prayed to God to intervene. I knew we couldn't let Carlos take that baby out of the house. But I also knew he would end all of us if we tried to stop him. Once he was out of the room, I counted five whole beats, and only then did we run through the bedroom door.

We barely made it into the dark living room before hearing Carlos roar with what sounded like pain. I quickly ran and turned on the hall light to find my son and Carlos fighting it out while Laurel lay crying on the floor next to her father's feet. With all the drugs or alcohol in his system, it seemed Carlos didn't fully feel the large knife stuck deep into his right shoulder. He grabbed the hilt of the knife's handle with his good hand and pulled the jagged blade out of his wounded arm just before ramming the handle's end hard against my son's head.

"Johnny!" I screamed, running toward my son as he dropped unconscious to the floor.

Maria nearly reached her baby, but Carlos was too fast and kicked her away. "No! Don't touch her, you slut! She probably isn't even mine, is she?" A demonic look crossed over his face just before he snatched the baby up by one delicate foot and dangled her upside down like a rag doll. "I hate you, Maria! And I hate this baby!"

"No!" we screamed in unison.

"This is all you care about, isn't it?" he screeched. "How could you choose *this* over me?"

Maria fell to her knees and threw her arms above her head, palms splayed out to stop him. "*God*, Carlos, Please stop! *Please*. I'll leave her here. I'll leave the baby and go with you right now. Let's do it; let's go *right now*," she begged.

Carlos's laugh mirrored his black heart. "Oh, sure. But then you'll just find another way to leave me. You'll just keep hiding. I'm not that stupid, Maria."

As he gripped Laurel's leg in one hand, I watched the dripping of blood run down his arm with the other hand that held the six-inch knife. I *had* to think of a way to distract him.

Maria pleaded again, "I promise I won't leave you. I'll do whatever you want. I swear!"

I looked back and forth from Carlos's crazed eyes to my daughter's face, wet with wild tears. My heart was torn as my beautiful grandbaby cried out in pain, still hanging upside down.

Carlos continued to shake the baby in anger, his laugh hysterical now. "What is it with you women? You have a baby, and somehow, there's no more room to love your husband? These babies have this much hold over you?"

Maria cried again, "That's not true. I love you. I love you so much. I had to leave, Carlos, because I was scared. But, if you just put the knife down and don't harm the baby anymore, then I will leave with you. This very moment."

"You remember our vows, Maria? For better or worse? Well, you left me like I was nobody—as if I meant nothing to you."

Carlos turned and pointed the sharp end of the knife toward Maria, and I jumped on instinct, stepping in front of her. "No!"

"Alice, move!" Carlos bellowed.

"No," I cried. "Hurt me," I pleaded, "hurt me, if you want to hurt anyone!"

"That's the thing, Alice. I want to hurt you *all*."

When we heard sirens in the distance, relief flooded over me, but only for a brief moment.

Because, in the next second, everything changed.

I couldn't get to the baby fast enough when Carlos panicked and dropped her headfirst onto the hard tile floor. As he rushed out the back door in a mad rush to escape the cops, I screamed, rushed forward, and fell to my knees in front of the baby.

It was every mother's nightmare.

I watched in turmoil as Maria crawled toward her daughter's frail body, I quickly reached out a hand to stop her. "Don't. Her neck could be broken, Maria," I said. That didn't stop Maria from cupping her hands over the top of her daughter's tiny head and kissing the child's tears, still fresh on her innocent face. As for me, I did the only thing I could.

I prayed.

On TV, you always see family in a hospital waiting room praying for a miracle, but I never thought that would be us. We were stars in a horror movie of our own, and I wanted anything for it to be untrue. After the police took our statements, I knelt in the waiting room and prayed the baby would live and have a normal life; I prayed Johnny would not have suffered brain damage, and I prayed that God would give Maria the strength to overcome all the trauma she had just experienced. And I especially prayed that, one day, our family could live without fear and find the peace we all desperately desired.

Who knows why some prayers work and some don't? All I can say is that I was beyond thankful when, two hours later, Johnny emerged from the ER wearing only a small head bandage. His X-rays showed he had a minor skull fracture, but overall, he would be all right. However, it was his pride that had been hurt the most. He was devastated, knowing he had not been able to prevent harm to sweet little Laurel. He felt like, as the man of the house, he had let us all down. But the best news came when, ten hours later, the doctors confirmed Laurel would survive. It was indeed a miracle. Nevertheless, while they kept our sweet girl in the hospital for three more days, I didn't waste any time calling my second eldest.

After I broke down and told Greg everything that had happened, his response was another miracle, the answer to all our prayers. "Mom, listen to me. Pack up everything as soon as possible and drive to Washington to live near the military base. Carlos will never find us out here. And you won't have to worry about Johnny. From what I can tell, there aren't any gangs here."

Greg was right. We had to get out of L.A. and for good this time. We left for Washington State the day they released us from the hospital, and we never looked back.

Chapter 25

Sam 2006

"Oh, Alice," I said, "that is the scariest thing ever. I can't believe you all went through that. What a terrible man Carlos was."

"Yes, that was a terrifying and challenging time in our lives. And, if it wasn't for the army transferring Greg to Washington, who knows what would have become of all of us? We probably would be dead, like I said."

"So, in a sense, the military saved you? Wow. And Carlos never found you? You didn't have to worry?"

"Oh, I suppose he would have eventually found us if it wasn't that he'd been sentenced to fifty years in prison."

"What? How?"

"Believe it or not, it wasn't our police report that did him in. We got word that Carlos had murdered someone on the streets, someone who owed him money. Him going to prison was a blessing; it allowed us never to have to worry again."

"Thank God," I said. "So, what happened to your family after?"

"Washington was and still is good to us. It helped that there were little to no drugs or gangs where we lived to entice my son. And then, because Johnny could focus more on school rather than getting himself into trouble, Johnny was sixteen when he fell in love with an angel. She helped him turn his life around, and he eventually found his way to church. Maria eventually remarried and had more children. Little Laurel grew up with zero signs of injuries and had no recollection of that terrible night, thank God. Greg continued serving in the army and started his own family. As for me, I lived with Maria, took care of all her children, cooked, cleaned, and never left her side."

"Wow. Everyone did well, then?"

"Yes."

"And you never married again or met anyone, Alice?"

"No. When you've gone through hell and back, you finally realize that your children are your world. My focus was on them, so I never remarried. Plus, as much as I hated what Frank did to me, I would always love only one man. I don't think it would have been fair to a second husband if I still secretly prayed Frank would recognize his mistakes and someday return to me. Besides, the Lord above was all I needed."

"I am so glad about the way it turned out."

"Me too. And that is why we owe all of our success to Greg and his joining the army. It was the best decision for our whole family, saving all our lives. So, Sam, whatever you decide with the military, your family will understand. If not, at first, they will when they see you have made something of yourself. Maybe this career move will take you places, like it took our family. Either way, you need to pray about this decision. Only God knows what is best for you."

I thanked Alice for her story and headed home to talk to my parents. It would be an interesting conversation, to say the least. But if the military helped Alice, surely it could help me.

When I pulled up to my house, it was seven p.m. and already dark. With the engine off, I stalled and sat in the car, gathering my thoughts. The lights inside our small Rambler gave off a soft, warm glow—almost like a welcome-home kind of feeling—but for some reason, I felt like a stranger after not living with them for months. Even though I had sporadically seen my family around Christmas time, we avoided the elephant in the room. There was an unspoken agreement to ignore the past and pretend all was normal, but with still unresolved issues, I felt awkward knocking on our front door.

Stephanie answered the door wearing a new short bob. Although her blond hair, cropped behind her ears, gave her a boyish look, the new 'do complemented her big blue eyes. "Look what the cat dragged in," she said with a smirk.

I didn't take that negatively; the old cliché had become something of a joke in our family, ever since I got caught sneaking out and our pet cat had ratted me out. I accepted my sister's olive branch. "Hey," I said. "Love the new 'do."

She cupped the bottom of her bob and shrugged. "Thanks. I needed a change."

"How's life been treating you?" I asked, stepping over the threshold.

"It's been just peachy. You coming home to stay?"

"Not sure."

"Well, it's been nice with all the peace and quiet, but not nearly as entertaining."

"What? Mom and Dad not filling that void?"

"Oh, you mean with all their fighting? Well, there's always that." She laughed. "Never a dull moment here."

I dropped my purse by the front door. "By the way, where are they?"

"In the kitchen."

I gave her a weak smile. "Sorry for chasing you with a knife."

She eyed me suspiciously before giving me a half-smirk. "Sorry I threw my sandwich at you."

"Sorry I pulled your hair."

"Sorry I pulled yours harder."

I laughed before taking a deep breath. "So, I have some big news to discuss. You're welcome to stay and listen in."

"Preggo, are we?"

"Heck no," I scoffed. "That would be a nightmare."

I followed Steph to the kitchen as she announced, "Sammy's here."

At the kitchen sink, my mother turned around, holding up soapy rubber-gloved hands. "Sam!" She clapped her hands, making soapy suds pop in the air around her face.

"Hey, Mom," I said, walking over to hug her. I stopped to see her at her workplace a few times but had not had a meaningful conversation with my father until now. I was still bitter at how quick he had been to throw me out. And, going deeper, I was mad that, for as long as I could remember, he had looked at me as if I was a disappointment, that he had never really wanted me to begin with. But still, I tried for my mother's sake. "Hey, Dad."

My father remained at the counter, covering leftovers on a plate with plastic wrap. "You hungry?" he asked me. "I can heat this back up for you." I knew offering me food was his way of letting me know he didn't want to re-hash anything. He wanted to move on from any ill will. This was nothing new. Our family was very good at hiding our messes under the rug. And sometimes, I preferred it that way. It was better than going around and around in circles and never getting to the root of the issues.

"No, thanks," I said. "I ate dinner with Alice tonight."

"Oh, tell me, how is she?" my mother asked, removing her gloves.

"She's doing great. She told me a lot about her life, along with some good advice, which is kinda why I am here. Can we all sit at the kitchen table and talk?" The curious looks around the room were valid, as I never had anything important to say. However, once we were all seated, I pondered how often we had actually sat together at that table, except for Easter, Thanksgiving, and Christmas.

"So, I'm just gonna spit it out," I said.

My father's lips formed a thin line before he blurted, "You're pregnant."

"What? *No*. What is it with everyone always assuming the worst in me? No, I wanted to tell you guys I've decided to join the Air Force."

The room was silent for far too long before my mother, Julie, finally spoke, looking bewildered. "Really? The Air Force? But why, Samantha?" Her voice carried both confusion and sadness, and I felt a little bad for not prepping her better.

For ten minutes, I expressed all the reasons for my decision. But even though I gave them a compelling argument, they were not happy. My mother interjected, "But Sam, I know this might seem like a great way to further your education, but you could be deployed to Iraq and get bombed or shot down."

My father had an altogether different response, "I don't think you've fully thought this through. You could be harassed or, worse, raped."

"Dean!" my mother gasped.

He looked at her. "What, Julie? This is the harsh reality of life." He looked at me point-blank. "Sam, tell us how you think you will defend yourself in an environment full of testosterone."

"I ... I think—"

"No. That's the problem. You won't have time to think. You're setting yourself up, and we all know you won't be able to ward off any man twice your size."

My father's words put ugly images in my head, and I wondered if what he said really was valid for women in the armed forces.

"Dean. Stop. You're scaring her."

"Julie, I'm not trying to scare anyone. But let's be real. These are real problems she will face. Every day, women in the armed forces are victims of this kind of thing."

"Sam. Your father is being too blunt," she said, giving him a biting look, "but he has a point." She squeezed my leg as if to emphasize her own point. "Unfortunately, women are only ten percent of the armed forces, so with ninety percent of the military consisting of men, well, it's something you should consider. I wouldn't go so far as to say the word *rape*, but as you are a beautiful young woman, harassment would be almost guaranteed."

I rubbed my eyebrows with my thumb and forefinger to try and ease the tension behind my eyes. "Guys. Look, so maybe I didn't think of these issues, but I will now. Either way,"—I looked at my mother, as she would be the one I needed to convince—"I will be fine. The Air Force is unlikely to put *me*, a soon-to-be hygienist, anywhere near a combat zone. And Dad, if it makes you feel any better, I'll take a self-defense class, okay?"

My father shook his head and loudly exhaled before speaking. "It's your life. But I can't imagine why you'd choose a career where you will always have to look over your shoulder."

"Dad, I'm used to all that. I already live that life at the restaurant where I work. The kitchen boss is a complete creep. And I'm doing this so I can finally train as a dental hygienist. I'll be in an office, not out on the battlefield."

"That's not true," my mother said flatly. "Military life usually means a lot of moving around. They could station a dental hygienist anywhere in the United States, even in another country."

"My recruiter said I had a good chance staying local, Mom. I trust him." My sister Stephanie was sitting quietly, and I wondered what she thought. "Stephanie, do you think this is a stupid idea?"

She shrugged. "No. If this is what you think is best, then more power to you."

I smiled. "Thanks." My gaze met my mother's, and I slid my hand over the top of hers. "Mom, I think going this route would give me a head start. I want you to be proud of me. Let me do this. Please?"

Her smile did not match the concerned look in her eyes. "I *am* proud of you—always have been. I just worry. I am your mother, and mothers worry." She was quiet for a while before her shoulders sagged. "But if this is truly what you think is best, then I support you. I may not like it, but I will always support you."

I let out a long sigh of relief. "Thank you."

She looked at my father. "Dean? Our daughter is asking for our blessing."

The look on my father's face said he was still skeptical, but he gave me a half-shrug. "Of course, I hope never to be proven right, but this is your life," my father said. "You are old enough to make your own choices. Maybe the military will be good for you."

It was the best I'd get from my parents, and even if it wasn't the grandest of gestures, I had their support.

But the biggest test would be convincing Liam.

By the time I walked into his house, it was close to ten. Liam's parents were sitting in their comfortable leather recliners, watching a comedy. "Samantha!" his father called out.

I hugged them each before going to the dining room, where Liam was working on something. He focused intently on a piece of paper marked with what looked like a bunch of x's and o's before he saw me peeking over his shoulder. "Hey," he said, looking up.

"Hey, yourself. Whatcha doin'?" I asked.

"Going over the new scrimmages that our coach emailed to us players. He wants it memorized before the new semester starts next week."

"Speaking of school, can I talk to you downstairs?"

He set his pencil down and wiggled his eyebrows up and down playfully. "*Oh*, school, *huh*?"

"Something like that."

He stood, grabbed my hand, and led me downstairs. Once inside the guest room I now occupied, I smoothed out the stylish bedspread printed in oversized burgundy, gold, and burnt-orange flowers and asked Liam to sit. I sat silently at the end of the bed while sliding my toes up and down through the thick carpet tufts, leaving long, indented lines.

Liam squeezed my leg. "Guess this is serious. What's up?"

The air felt stifling, making it hard to breathe. "You know I love you, right?"

"Well, yeah. And I love you, too." He tilted his head and gave me a quizzical look.

"Before I begin,"—I swallowed hard—"I just want you to know that I am doing this for us, for our future together."

"Okay, now my heart's jumping. You're making me nervous."

"Sorry. So, I have been thinking about this for a long time and have decided to join the Air Force. I can sign the papers as soon as tomorrow, and after that, I have a month before basic military training starts. And, sure, I'll have to train for two months in San Antonio, Texas, but two months of boot camp isn't anything."

Liam tilted his head in thought as if the magnitude of my decision seemed incomprehensible to him. Then he laughed, "Is this a joke?"

"No." His words hurt me. Did he think I was a joke? Did he think I couldn't do this? Did he think me incapable? I tried to ignore my negative thoughts and explained. "Anyway, once boot camp is over, I can choose which department to work in. The recruiter told me I could earn wages *while* assisting in an office with other dental hygienists and learn from them while going to school for an associate's degree. It's perfect. Money, school, a job; it fixes everything."

His eyes slowly widened, realizing I wasn't joking. "But ... but where would you live?"

"They pay for my housing on site. It's not too far from here. And when I am not working, I'm just a quick forty minutes away. And I would have the weekends off, too. No more working the holidays."

Liam sat quietly as if soaking in my words before giving me an anxious look. "Is there a chance you could be deployed elsewhere, like out of state? Remember Kevin Gowin from school? He joined the Air Force two years ago and was just deployed to Afghanistan. That could be you."

"Like I told my parents, my recruiter said that deployment for a hygienist was only a *very* slim possibility. I'll probably stay local."

Liam lay back on my pillows and crossed his arms. "*Right.*"

"Liam, I doubt they would send a dental hygienist assistant out of the country. Look, I know this is out of the blue, but this is a way for me to make money *and* get a free education. It's a win-win."

Liam sat back upright. "A win-win?"

"Yeah, this opportunity kills two birds at once."

He shook his head. "If they send you away, it would be more like killing three birds at once—counting me into that scenario."

"Liam, I— "

"How long have you known this was what you wanted to do?"

I bit the inside of my cheek. "I didn't want to say anything until I knew for sure."

"How long?"

I swallowed. "A few weeks?"

"And you're just now telling me this?"

I flinched at his heated words. "I know I should have included you, but I guess I was too scared you wouldn't understand. I was afraid you'd talk me out of it. Plus, I needed to research all my options before deciding."

"Okay, I understand why the military appeals to you, but I don't know why you wouldn't want to include me in our future together. Most people make plans like that *together*."

He was right, and I felt guilty. I scooted closer to him and reached a hand over his knee. "Honestly, two weeks ago, I was just curious when I inquired, and I didn't think anything would ever come of it. But last week, after talking to the recruiter multiple times on the phone, I knew it was for me. It's only been a couple of days since I decided."

"Whatever. And I don't want to sound like a baby, but what about me? What does this mean for us, Sam? Could we do long distance if you leave for another state or out of the country?"

The pain in Liam's question made me feel like crap, but he was right; he should have been the first person I discussed things with. We planned to get married in three years, so at this point in our relationship, we needed to prove we were in it together. But deep down, I knew the reason I had procrastinated so long before telling him was that I couldn't guarantee they wouldn't send me away.

"In a perfect world, Liam, I'd stay here with you. But where would I end up? There has been so much on my mind lately, with college, bills, and my crappy job. You know this. Also, I want to save up enough money so we can eventually get a place of our own, without the confines of our parents. Liam, the Air Force will give us this opportunity. Can't you see I'm doing it for both of us? Plus, I doubt they will transfer me out of state."

"So you say."

"Hey, may I remind you that if a big-time college scout wants you to play basketball for their school, you could move anywhere in the country? I know you were hoping for SPU, since it's closer to home, but there is nothing guaranteeing that you won't need to leave the state. So, what would I do if that happened? We've never talked about it, but I'm sure you assumed I would wait for you here, right?"

"Or come with me."

"You know I can't afford those fancy colleges."

"No. But you could find a local community college near mine."

"It's not that easy," I said.

When Liam laid back down and stared at the ceiling, I laid down too. I rolled over to study his profile while he spoke. "At least with my plan," he said, "you could technically have followed me. But whatever. Like I said, I get the appeal of the military, but you must know nothing is guaranteed. They could easily transfer you the minute boot camp is over, and I can't follow you if that happens. Not with a basketball scholarship dictating where I had to go." He turned to face me. "Can you be certain you'll be able to stay in the state?"

I rolled onto my back, imagining the stars above and beyond the ceiling. Stars are up there on any given night, but they're indiscernible if obstacles are in the way. You couldn't see anything if walls or clouds were in the way. "No. I can't know anything for certain," I finally said.

He rolled over to his side and rested his head in his palm before asking, "So, what if you have to leave for three or more years?"

I smoothed a finger over his right eyebrow, where the short, honey-brown hairs lay in disarray. "First, you're thinking super negatively. I can't imagine them deploying a hygienist overseas or out of state. *But* ... if they did send me away, will you wait for me?"

He huffed out one breath before replying, "Such a silly question. You know I would wait for you." He ran his thumb over my jawline. "Maybe I'm just worried that with you being around all those men, someone will come in and take my place. I'm afraid you'll forget me."

"Now who's being silly? I'm not going to find anyone else. I'm yours, forever and always."

I meant the words I spoke with every cell in my body, but I could tell by Liam's frown lines he wasn't sure he believed me. It was understandable—this scary and unforeseen future, especially if I had to go far away. Part of me already regretted this decision, but I was a girl who, once committed to an idea, stuck to it like glue. Plus, it felt like the only realistic option for a girl like me.

That night, as Liam fell asleep beside me, all the worries about my decision came to the surface. Could a future so colorful suddenly become bleak, dark, and gray without my person beside me? Could I really see myself surviving without Liam? I didn't know for sure, but I couldn't think like that. Instead, under the low glow of the lamp beside my bed, I lay awake, memorizing his beautiful face. No matter what obstacles came our way, I'd prove my love to him. No matter where I was stationed, Liam was stuck with me for eternity.

The next day, I knew I had much to do if I wanted to enjoy my last week of winter break with Liam. I still had to work evenings at the restaurant, but by dropping out of school, at least my days belonged to him. I looked down at the list in front of me.

1. Call the college and get a refund for upcoming tuition.

2. Call work and give two weeks' notice.

3. Talk to friends about new plans.

4. Sign recruitment papers.

5. Begin workouts to prepare my body for boot camp.

Item one was manageable, and it was nice to have that tuition money back in my bank account. Item number two was even easier. I called work to speak to my boss, Kristen, about leaving, and she barely sounded fazed that she would be losing me. I knew restaurants always had a revolving door of employees, and I suppose I was no exception.

I couldn't tell Shelly my plans yet, but I made a mental note to tell her in person at work.

As for my other friends, I called Heidi and Emily on three-way. "So, what do you guys think of my new plan?" I asked after laying it all out.

Of course, Emily only had words of encouragement. "Wow. This is huge. Good for you, Sam."

On the other hand, Heidi's tongue was sharp and straightforward, like an arrow to my heart. "Are you crazy? Sam, you're nuts. This is the worst idea ever."

Heidi, always blunt, never held back. That's why I liked her so much. But at that moment, I wished she'd mask her true feelings. "Wow," I said. "Thanks for the vote of confidence, Heidi. It's not like I don't already have a ton of anxiety or anything."

"I'm sorry," she said, "but seriously? This can't be your only way out. Look, maybe there's still time to get out of this. Maybe we all could help you come up with a plan."

"No. I don't want to get out of it. Anyway, I sign the papers in a few hours."

"You haven't signed yet? Then good, there's still time."

Emily interrupted. "Heidi, shut up for once. If this is what Sam wants, why make it worse?"

Heidi groaned. "But the military? *Our* Sam in the military, Emily? I'm sorry, but I'm calling it. This isn't you, Sam."

"It's the Air Force, Heidi. Not the Marines," I said. "Besides, the benefits outweigh everything else I've got going on; I'm failing school, my job sucks, and I need to save up for a place to live for Liam and me."

I could almost see Emily smile through the phone. "It's not nuts, Sam. On the contrary, I think what you are doing is commendable. What you are doing takes guts."

"Thanks, Em."

"So you feel this is your only option?" Heidi asked.

"Truthfully, I am still going through all the emotions and haven't fully grasped it all yet, but I'm sure once I'm in it and I am accomplishing my goals, then yeah, I'll probably feel it was the best decision."

Heidi pounced: "See? Sam, if you haven't fully grasped the situation, maybe you're not ready. Sounds like you almost don't know if this is what you want to do."

"Well, gosh, it doesn't help that every single person I've told thinks this is a bad idea."

"*I* don't think it's a terrible idea, Sam," Emily pointed out.

"Well, minus you, Emily. And Alice, too. She thinks it's a grand idea. But most everyone disagrees, and now I'm starting to doubt myself." I plopped down onto the kitchen chair and rubbed my scalp with my fingertips.

"Sam," Emily said, "Why do you even listen to anyone else? This is your life. What were your thoughts before everyone chimed in?"

I paused for a moment. "Well, I thought it was perfect for me. It would solve all my problems. Of course, the only downside is missing Liam and my friends and family if I end up being transferred somewhere far away, but I'm trying not to think about that. I have a good feeling about this."

"Then keep that feeling going. Block out all the negative opinions."

Heidi let out a drawn-out sigh, "Sam, I'm sorry. Don't listen to me. What do I know? But damn, girl. We are going to miss you."

"Heidi, boot camp is only for two months, but afterward, when I get back, it sounds like there is a good chance I'll be stationed close to home. So I'm not leaving anyone."

"Fine, but listen," Heidi warned. "If I can give any advice, it would be that you toughen up. It's for your own good. Because the military is hard, especially for a girl."

"I know. I'm going to have Liam help me get into shape."

"Well, if you need someone to yell at you," Heidi said, laughing, "I'm your girl."

"I know you are. Thanks, you guys."

I hung up the phone and looked up at the clock, ready to mark off item number four. I gave Liam a big kiss. "Hey. I'm off to the recruiter's office." I knew I had to go immediately before someone else told me I was making a mistake.

"You sure you don't want me to come with you to sign the papers?"

"No. I have to do this on my own."

Liam nodded in understanding, but his eyes said differently. *Don't go. Stay,* they seemed to say. I looked away and quickly left the house before I could change my mind.

In less than twenty minutes, I stood in front of the Air Force's two-story brick recruiting office. I took a long pause before opening the door.

Here's to your new future, Sam, I told myself.

"Hi. I'm Samantha Carey, here to see Mr. Keith Thompson?" I told the receptionist.

Mr. Thompson poked his head out from his office, "Oh, good, you're here. And please, call me Keith, remember?"

"Hi," I said, suddenly feeling like I was having an out-of-body experience.

I had spoken to Keith on the phone many times before finally making a decision, but his high-pitched voice didn't match his face. He looked nothing like how he sounded on the phone. The man towered over me, at six feet, four inches tall, with chest muscles that barely fit inside his uniform, and I wondered if the military had made him bulk up or if he loved working out just for the fun of it. His black hair was cropped short at the top, but the sides were baby-smooth as if just waxed. He looked almost cute if it weren't for his chin that jutted out unnaturally, giving him an unproportioned look that clashed with his dark brown, beady eyes.

He greeted me with his usual bubbly self and shook my hand. "Samantha, you ready to do this?"

I sat across from him and stopped myself from picking at my chipped nail polish. "I think so."

"This should be quick and easy," Keith said. "That way, you can continue enjoying your day. Any fun plans for later?"

"Unfortunately, no. I'm going to work right after I sign."

"I bet you're looking forward to quitting your little waitressing job, hey?"

"We are more known as servers, but yes. I already gave my two-week notice."

"Excellent." Keith handed me a pen and pushed a thick pile of papers to me. "All right. I won't read word for word. Instead, I'll briefly review each section with you. Sound all right?"

"Sure. Let's do this." There wasn't a lot of paperwork; less than an inch thick. I couldn't imagine this taking more than a half-hour.

We had made it three-fourths of the way through the pile before Keith explained the next section, "This is the section I discussed with you before. Once you finish boot camp, you will be given a list of job descriptions to choose from."

"Like assisting in a dental office, like we discussed?" I asked. "Because as long as that is on the list for me to gain experience in what I hope to go to school for, then great. I'm in."

"Oh, yeah. Of course. That shouldn't be a problem."

"Great."

Ten minutes later, we were finished.

I put my pen down, and Keith announced, loud and proud, "Well, guess this makes it official." He stood and held out his hand. "Welcome to the Air Force, Samantha Carey."

Chapter 26

Sam 2006

I returned to Liam's to dress for my night shift at the restaurant and *again* had to kiss him goodbye.

"It went well?"

"Yeah. I was surprised it went super fast. Anyway, the next step is a two-day assessment test in Seattle. I take that next week. And then, I attend their two-month boot camp in one month."

"I wish you didn't have to work tonight," he groaned, standing by the door, holding my purse. When I tried to grab it, he didn't let it go. He was already acting like a mother hen whose baby would one day fly the coop.

I nudged him aside to look into the mirror in the hall and contemplated whether I had time to fix my hair. "Look on the bright side," I said, braiding my hair out of my face. "Now that I have checked each item off my to-do list, and we both have a winter break, I'm all yours for the next six days. Well ... minus having to work evenings for two more weeks. But seriously, I can't remember a day I didn't have to work or go to school. I've worked since I was fifteen. It's going to be weird doing nothing at all."

Liam turned me around to face him. "Then, we will make our time together really count." He flicked my finished braid off my shoulder and rested his head in its place. "I want to be with you every moment until you leave."

I fluffed his hair. "We will make it count. When you start school next week, I'm only gone for two days to take that assessment test. But for the most part, I'm all yours for six whole days."

"I can't believe an assessment test takes two days."

"I thought the same thing. I guess one day is a physical test to show our strengths and abilities, and the other day is dedicated to an aptitude test. I am not looking forward to either one. I feel like I may need to prepare for the physical, but as for the aptitude test, well, there isn't much I can do to prepare for that. What is currently in my noggin will have to do."

"Where do you go for the assessment test again?"

"They put us up in a hotel near SeaTac."

"Interesting."

"Yeah."

Liam lifted his head off my shoulder, his eyes wide in excitement. "We should plan something fun before you *go go*."

"Like what?" I asked.

"I know I've only skied once in my life, but the college is hosting a two-night ski trip to Crystal Mountain for students interested. I thought of you when I saw the sign posted around campus. If you like, I'll purchase some tickets for us."

"But you don't like to ski. After I took you for your first time, you told me it was stupid."

"I didn't particularly love it, no. And yes, I admit I have no balance, and falling on my ass all day isn't fun, but you like to ski, so let's do it."

I turned to face him. "You would take me even if it isn't fun for you?"

"Anything I do with you is fun," Liam said as he tugged at my long braid. "We could be doing nothing at all, and I'd be happy as long as I'm with you."

"Well, gosh, that may be the most romantic thing you've ever said." I kissed his cheek and asked, "Should we invite all our friends, too? Or do you want just us two?"

"The more, the merrier. You should invite Matt too. I know you both love to ski. You mentioned you felt bad not having seen him in forever. It will be like a *bon voyage* with all your friends before leaving for boot camp."

"That sounds like a great time. I'll call him."

The excitement that had been in his eyes moments before seemed to vanish. He shook his head. "*Boot camp.* Those two words sound so weird and foreign."

"I know," I said. I didn't want to leave on a sappy note before work, so I quickly asked, "But hey, can I ask you a favor?"

"What? Are you going to ask me to stop worrying? Because I can't—"

"No. No. That's not it. I know you can't help but worry. I was actually going to ask you if you could train me for boot camp—you know, for the physical aspect. My body is so out of shape. The last time I ran more than thirty seconds was for fifth grade track."

Liam smirked. "Oh, well, since you asked me nicely," he squeezed my body close to his, with the light in his eyes suddenly returning, "I think I can help you with that. But I need something in return for my services."

"Here we go again." I rolled my eyes and asked hesitantly. "And what would you need in return?"

"How about every hour I train you, I get a kiss."

"I think I can work something out. But first, we will have to see if you're any good as a trainer, for that kind of payout." I looked at the clock. "*Crap*. Gotta go. Sorry."

Liam handed me my purse, slapped my butt, and roughly pushed me out the door. "Now get to work before I make you give me twenty!"

"*Great*. I've created a sergeant monster," I said without looking back.

It was the first time I had ever arrived at work feeling excited. Knowing I only had two more weeks to work at the place I absolutely loathed, I soared like a balloon floating high above the clouds, and no one could burst my bubble, not even Bad Rap.

Shelly greeted me in the break room with an unpleasant scowl. "The staff is talking about you quitting and that you are joining the Air Force or something? Tell me they are screwing with me again."

My bubble burst.

"*Crap*. Kristen wasn't supposed to tell anyone! I'm so sorry. I wanted to tell you in person. *Damn* that woman." Shelly looked hurt, and I hurried to remedy it. "You are my favorite person here, and you don't deserve to hear the news this way. I'm sorry Kristen ruined that. *God*, she is so annoying."

"It's fine," Shelly said, sliding heavily into a chair by the wall. "I think I'm more upset that I'll be stuck here alone without you." She crossed her arms with an accentuated pout to prove her point. "I literally thought everyone was making that all up."

I straddled a chair facing her and rested my chin on it. "I'm sad, too. I'll miss you like crazy."

"But the military? What gives?" I explained everything to her, and she nodded. "I guess that makes sense. But the thought of leaving you here alone makes me sick."

We sat silently for a sad moment before a lightbulb went on in my head. I sat upright. "Wait. Unless—"

"Unless you change your mind and stay with me?"

"Sorry, girl, no way. I'm done living in a suffocating coffin. What if we can find you another job so you're not stuck with these bloodsuckers?" I wanted Shelly to have what I had—a new beginning, a fresh start. "Boot camp is a month away, so if you would like, and since you said you never have time to look for a new job, how about I run around and turn in your resumes for you? I'll drive all around to these fancy restaurants until one bites. I mean, you never know until we try, right?"

"Really?" Shelly asked. "Truth be told, I turned in a few resumes a couple of months ago, but no one called me in for an interview."

"Well, let's try again. Let me do it for you. Let me save you from this place of doom. And actually, there's this new restaurant that Liam took me to for my twenty-first birthday. Maybe they're hiring? It was an expensive dinner, so at least you know the tips should be decent. And, the place was clean, and the food was delicious."

"All right. Deal. I'll print off a few resumes and get them to you. Are you working tomorrow?"

"Yes, unfortunately. Honestly, I could have quit without giving Kristen a two-week notice and said, 'Screw this place!'"

"Why didn't you? I would have."

"I wanted the extra cash. But mostly, I wanted to spend more time with you before I left."

"You know, Sam, if I'm being honest, I am still a little shocked about you joining the military."

"Welcome to the club. You're not alone in that arena."

"Well, I think it's a great idea, for what it's worth. The world is your oyster."

"Thanks, Shelly."

We both stood and made our way to the kitchen before Shelly giggled. "Remember that cute guy I told you I'm seeing?"

"Yeah," I said, swinging the door open for her to walk through.

"He's in the army. Even though the pay isn't the best, his benefits are amazing. He loves it."

I looked at her sideways and squinted as I detected the sweetness in her voice. "Shelly, are you holding out on me? Are you and this guy serious?"

Her eyes lit up. "I don't know. Maybe?" she said, practically jumping on her toes. "I'll tell you about him when you come over to grab my resumes."

"Deal!"

"Oh, I forgot to tell you. Brad is wine-testing the servers for the evening's dinner shift."

I rolled my eyes. "Tell me again why I bothered giving a two-week notice?"

"To spend more time with little ol' me?" she said, batting her eyelashes.

"And worth it," I said before running off to find Brad.

I found Brad in the back corner of an empty section, quizzing another server, and waited to approach him until they were finished. "Hey. I'm ready for my quiz, Brad."

"Look who it is. Or should we all start by calling you Lieutenant Carey?" He laughed.

"No, I don't think I get any title just yet. It's probably just Ms. Carey."

"Well, *Ms.* Carey, I think what you are doing is crazy talk. Can you even *do* ten pushups with those little arms of yours?" he said, squeezing my left arm.

"First, I didn't ask your opinion," I said, pulling my arm away from his touch. "And second, what I can do physically is none of your business." Physically, I wanted to punch him in the throat, but I didn't. "Can you just quiz me already?"

"*Whoa*, already a tough girl, *huh*?"

Knowing I no longer needed this job, I tossed all caution to the wind and fired a blatant glare. "Wines, please? And sometime today?"

"All right, but instead of wines, let's try an easy cocktail."

"Sure. Whatever."

"How about you try to list out the ingredients for what's in a …" Brad took his time coming up with a drink that most likely wouldn't be on the list, just hoping for me to fail. He snickered, "Okay, got it. What's in a 'Bend Over Shirley'?"

"What the hell?" I snapped.

"The drink is perfect. Get it? Bend Over Shirley because that is what you'll be known for in the military, you know, with all those meatheads fishing for tail." Brad laughed at his cleverness and snorted when he got too much air.

"Just shut up. You are a complete jackass, Brad," I said, turning on my heel. "I'm done quizzing. I'll be on the floor if you need me."

Shelly jumped out from a corner and gave me a slow clap. "You handled that pretty well. You sure you can deal with him for another two more weeks?"

"At this point, I hope he does something stupid. I have nothing to lose."

The next day proved to be chilly in the Pacific Northwest. I wasn't thrilled when Liam woke me early in the morning to announce he wanted to take me on a jog before starting training. I rolled over in bed onto my stomach while holding a pillow over the back of my head, muffling my voice: "Can we *please* start tomorrow?"

"Nope. Up and at 'em." A cold draft invaded my warm space as Liam ripped the heavy comforter off me and barked, "I've only got this week to help you, Sam, and then you are on your own. So get up, and let's go, sleepyhead."

He slapped my backside, and I yelped and rolled over. "Ouch." He stood with his arms crossed, daring me to argue, so I tried a different tactic. "Come cuddle with me first," I purred, trying to prolong the inevitable.

"No. I know what you're doing, and *no*. Get up or else."

"Or else what?"

"You want to find out?" he said with a glare.

"*Okay, fine. Geez*, Mr. Serious."

"Better get used to people yelling and bossing you around, Sam."

He had a point.

My bare feet hit the floor, and I asked, "Do we get to eat first?"

"No. I need to push you hard today; if you eat beforehand, you might throw up. I am trying to help you avoid that."

I narrowed my eyes, and I gave him a lousy smile. "So very thoughtful of you."

I dressed in black leggings and a thermal top but decided it wasn't warm enough. I added a pair of thick sweatpants and a sweatshirt, zipped myself into an enormous plush jacket for extra warmth, and finally topped it with a black beanie hat before grabbing snow gloves. "All right, all set," I said.

Liam shook his head. "You look like that little brother from *The Christmas Story*. How are you going to run with all that on?"

"The goal? Like a sloth wearing a winter coat—very slowly."

"You're gonna be hot; just warning you."

"*Psh.* I think I know my body, but warning noted."

We opened the front door to an onslaught of thick fog that hung low in front of our faces. Even though the snow had melted a week prior, the landscape barely looked visible, except for a surge of clouds exhaled from our mouths. "My nose is already turning red," I said. "I'm glad I'm wearing these extra layers." I looked over at Liam as he shivered from a lack of clothing. "Maybe you should grab a thicker coat," I suggested.

"*Nah.* We're going to warm up real quick." He pointed towards the driveway. "Let's start over there with some stretches first."

The ground was white with frost, stiff, and frigid beneath my feet as I stretched my arms over my head a few times, and I shivered while trying hard to avoid slipping on a thin sheet of crystals that made the earth slick. "Okay, now what?" I asked when finished.

"Now bend forward and touch your toes." I bent down, grunting, as my fingertips strained a whole foot away from my feet, which made Liam laugh. "Wait. You can't touch your toes?"

The blood rushed to my ears as I tried again. "*Hardy har har.* No. I've never been *that* flexible. Maybe I could reach further if it wasn't for this thick coat."

"We will need to practice stretching each morning to improve your muscle tone and range of motion. Just saying."

"Obviously," I said, irritated with myself.

"*Okie dokie*, let's go," Liam barked.

For a while, the only sounds were the rhythmic patter of our feet meeting the crisp ground as I followed Liam down a path leading into the dense forest behind his home. After ten minutes of running, my chest was beginning to burn, and I couldn't help but slow my jogging to a sluggish, foot-dragging pace. I wasn't about to admit to Liam that I was already sweating under all the layers I wore.

Far ahead, Liam called, "Come on, don't tell me you're tired already."

I lied. "Nope. I just need to tie my shoe," I said, stopping to pretend to fuss with my shoelaces. When he rounded the corner ahead, and I knew he couldn't see me, I tore my coat off and tied its massive bulk around my waist instead. I finally yelled out, "Got it tied. I'm coming!"

I tried sprinting to catch up, but not even ten seconds later, I had to stop altogether to catch my breath again. "*Mother of God*," I said, bending down with my head between my knees. If I couldn't run ten minutes without dying, how could I manage two months of boot camp? I pushed myself to continue, but my worries increased with each agonizing step forward.

This girl was in trouble.

I found Liam leaning casually against a tall pine while he cleaned invisible dirt from under his nails. He didn't say anything, but I knew what he was thinking. I wanted to wipe that smug smirk right off his face. "What?" I snapped.

He waved a suggestive hand toward my middle, where I had tied my coat, and asked, "Do you want me to carry your coat for you?"

"Shut up," I said. "Let's go, brat."

As we continued running, I tried to focus on anything *but* all the ways my body failed me. I gazed up at the enormous trees looming above me. The fog visually cut off their tops, and they looked almost headless. "This forest is a little ghostly, yet peaceful, don't you think?" I asked, just before I slammed into Liam's back, unaware he had stopped. "Sorry," I said. "Why are we stopping?"

Liam pointed ahead and to his right. "See that over there?" I followed his gaze past a cluster of smaller trees, where a massive, beautiful, leafless oak stood rooted. It was adorned with an old treehouse perched amid its sprawling limbs. "That's been there for as long as I can remember," he said. "My friends and I used to come out here and play when we were little."

We walked over to the treehouse, and just as Liam began to climb up its rickety wooden ladder, I swung out a protective arm, stopping him. "Wait. Are you sure it's safe?"

He ignored me and continued climbing up the eight weathered planks. "Whoever built this knew what he was doing; it's pretty solid." Once Liam reached the top, he held his hand down for me. "Come on up." When I hesitated to join him, Liam goaded me, "You're not scared of heights, are you?"

"Not the least," I said, rolling my eyes before starting the climb. "Just looks old, is all."

"I promise it's fine. Plus, I'm sure the camp you will be going to will make you climb something taller than this. This is good practice."

At the top, I grabbed Liam's hand, and he pulled me up. "Thanks," I said. It surprised me how we both could stand tall inside the bones of the treehouse without needing to duck our heads and that it was wide enough for at least four individuals. "Wow. Pretty spacious in here," I said while admiring the view below.

"Right? We could see some of the valley below if there wasn't so much fog. The sunrises here are pretty epic."

"Wait, did you bring me up here to take advantage of me?" I said, giving him a playful hip bump.

"If I wanted to take advantage of you, I'd have done it at the house when you first woke up, while my parents were at work. The thought crossed my mind *then*."

"Darn it." I laughed. "Have you ever brought other girls up here to see the sunrises?"

"Nope. Just you. Guess you're special."

"*Aww*, shucks."

"Hey, since we're up here, let's continue your training."

I tried to hide my disappointment. "Way up here?"

"Yeah. Like you said, it's spacious enough."

I just needed a diversion. "Or, we could make out? You know, make some memories to tell our grandchildren one day?"

His eyes narrowed, not at all fooled by my innocent expression. "You are insufferable. Stop stalling already and drop and give me twenty!"

I unwrapped my coat from around my waist and handed it to him. "Fine," I grumbled.

"Fine?" he threatened.

"I mean, yes, *sir*!"

I found a large knot in the weathered wood plank beneath me, a focal point that helped me get through the first round of pushups. But by the twelfth pushup, my arms tired and began to tremble. While Liam counted, I had to fess up. "This is hard," I blew out heavily on my way up.

"Come on, Sam. You got this."

Despite the cold, sweat began to pool beneath my boobs, and I immediately regretted wearing the many layers of clothing. Halfway up from the fourteenth pushup and hovering six inches above the floor, I finally cursed out loud as I inched lower and lower until my nose touched that knot in the floor. I collapsed to the ground and moaned, "I'm gonna die at this stupid camp, aren't I?"

Liam sat beside me. "Sam. If you do this for a month straight, you'll eventually build stamina. But, I won't sugarcoat it; you should have started training months ago."

"But I don't have months." I pushed a strand of matted hair away from my sweaty face and pouted. "I'm screwed."

"Stop thinking like that. You're stronger than you think. You can't give up, okay? Let's keep going. Just push through, all right?"

"Fine," I said.

"Good. Now try giving me fifty situps."

Determined to prove I was this 'strong' woman Liam claimed me to be, I closed my eyes in search of a happy place. I thought about a vacation on a beach with a book in hand while my other hand held an enormous bagel coated with cream cheese. I imagined Liam standing behind my lounge chair, massaging my head as my feet buried themselves into the soft, warm sand that felt like butter between my toes. I pictured an ocean of waves crashing to shore as Liam fed me a plate of chocolate-glazed donuts.

"Almost there, Sam."

It burned so bad. No longer in my happy place, I groaned in pain. "I think I'm going to die. It feels like Freddy Krueger is inside my stomach, trying to claw his way out. MAKE. IT. STOP." On the thirtieth situp, a muscle under my ribs seemed ready to split. "Holy hell, it hurts," I cried out again. I tried two more situps before stopping and grabbing hold of my left side. "I can't. I think I pulled something."

Liam didn't have to say it, but his tone said everything. "Okay. No biggy. It's all good. Let's move along to something else?" He sounded worried, making that two of us, but I nodded, grateful he didn't push me to do more. "Since you're already on your back, Sam, let's do hip thrusts to work the butt muscles."

"Your favorite?" I joked.

"Yep." Liam placed his hands on top of my feet. "Now, keep your feet planted flat on the ground while you lift your hips as far as they can go."

"How many do I do?" I asked.

"Let's try for whatever your body allows today."

"Probably not much, apparently," I said, already grunting.

Following Liam's count, I breathed in and out steadily. At the count of thirty-five, just when my legs wanted to cave from pain and exhaustion, Liam held his hand under my rear to help me stay up. "Good. Now, hold that position at the top, and I'll count down to zero," he told me.

When he got to zero, I gasped and dropped flat to the floor in utter submission. "For the love of Pete."

"You'll get there," Liam said.

"No, I won't. I am a weakling. I'm useless and pathetic." I hated that my voice sounded whiny, especially considering that it was me that got me in this predicament. "God, what was I thinking? I can't do this bootcamp thing."

"Don't be so hard on yourself. We just started training."

I flung an arm over my eyes and sighed. "They're going to eat me alive. I know it. And then what? What if I don't get in because I'm useless?"

"Stop that. I don't know what the instructors will have you do, but there is no reason to get yourself all stressed out. You just have to do your best, little by little, day by day. It was like this for me when I had to start basketball training after a long summer break. It takes time."

I felt Liam lie beside me, and I glanced over at him. "Time is something I don't have. And even if I had time, at this point in my life, I'm not confident in anything I do. I have no clue what will stick and what won't or what works and what I will fail at. Hell, even with this little military plan of mine, I still don't know where I'm going in life."

He crossed his hands under his head for a pillow and looked up at the ceiling of the treehouse. "I know you've been feeling a bit lost lately, with everything hitting you all at once, but I'm not sure I totally understand." He looked over at me then. "Wherever you end up in life, don't all roads lead to me? I mean, isn't that reassuring enough?" The way Liam said this came out playful, yet I noted a hint of insecurity.

But did all roads lead to Liam? My gut said yes, and technically, knowing all my roads lead to him should have made me feel reassured and good about myself.

But it didn't.

So, why?

Do I know myself apart from Liam? Do I have the confidence to see the real me and that, no matter the road and where it led me, could I be happy alone? And then it hit me. Maybe it wasn't enough that I had a good man at my side. Maybe because I didn't know who I was just yet, I ultimately wanted a path that made me feel enough for myself.

I thought of Alice and Jane's tragic stories and how each woman had lost themselves when certain roads led them astray. Roads that led them to men they *thought* were their forevers. But maybe if Alice and Jane had known themselves, like truly knowing their worth *before* falling in love, maybe things would have gone better for them. There was something to be said for being a confident woman who knew who she was and where she was headed in life.

Wasn't there?

"Yes and no," I told Liam. "Yes, it is reassuring to know that you will always be there as my person, but who am I *without* Liam? That's the question."

A single brittle alder leaf was lying on the plank beside his head, and I reached over to pick it up by its stem so it didn't crumble. I examined it, turning the delicate, dead brown thing in my hand. A beetle must have gotten to it before it fell, because it was nearly see-through, missing most of its skin, leaving it naked and bare, skeletonized, holey, and veiny like a spider's web. "I sorta feel like this leaf sometimes," I finally said.

"What do you mean?"

"Ready to crumble to dust. Or Swiss cheese—holey and missing in parts. Like, I'm not enough whole or fully me yet." I twisted the stem in my fingers, rotating the leaf round and round. "If I'm being honest, with or without you, I'm not sure who *me* really is yet. And that's scary. I have this worry: what if I never find her, or what my place is in this great big world?" I looked at Liam. "What if the weather beats her down for the rest of her life, leaving her to wither and age, and because she is buried and missing in parts, she is forever lost?"

Liam took the stem from my hand, held the fragile leaf above his face, and eyed it carefully. "I don't know. I think, even with all its messy and broken holes, she is still beautiful."

"But beauty doesn't mean anything when you're dead inside."

"Okay, sure, this leaf appears dead, but don't you think there is beauty in death? I mean, aren't we all dying a little bit every single day? And yet, the thing is, like you, like this leaf, we're not totally gone yet, or even lost. When I look good and hard at this leaf, I see that she has been through a lot. When you fill in the gaps and holes you call life, this leaf has a story."

With my head still flat on the ground, I looked up at the ceiling, considering this, as if the bones of this old treehouse could offer some wisdom. "So, you're saying life adventures, good or bad or holey, are the roads and paths? They are the stories that make a person who they are?"

"Exactly." Using his elbow as a kickstand, he rested his head sideways in his hand before looking at me, still holding the leaf in his other hand. "And maybe," he said, hovering the leaf over my left eye, so I could see through and past its fine mesh and into his eyes filled with love, "maybe with a little time, you'll see what *I* see in you."

"What do you see exactly?"

"What don't I see? I look at how you were with Jane and now with Alice, and you are kind, caring, and generous. I see that you are a deep and thoughtful individual who, as much as she plans for better intentions and yet fails, she still doesn't give up. You are funny, loyal, faithful, and so much more, Sam. You are simply *you*. Painfully messy, beautiful you."

I wanted to believe I was everything he said. I wanted to believe I was enough.

"But the thing is, Sam, your story isn't over. You will continue to find out who you are over the course of, let's hope, another eighty years. So, like this leaf, we can admire it for a long time if we preserve it well."

"Eighty years, huh?" I laughed. "Do you think if we continue down this road, we can make it to the end together?"

He spoke without hesitation. "Yes. And even into the next world together."

"How did I get so lucky, finding you?"

Liam moved the leaf away from my face and set it down behind me. "Do you need a hug? Will that make you feel better?"

"Yes," I said, feeling more whole and less lacking. "I think a hug could fix everything."

When he wrapped his arms around me, I inhaled all his goodness mixed with the surrounding scents of pine, fir, hemlock, and spruce. He smelled heavenly, making me suddenly miss him, even though he was right there with me. I don't know why it hit me then, in that moment and not before signing the papers, but the gravity of my choices finally sank in, and I felt the weight of what was coming. My time with Liam was short and even shorter if I would have to move far away from him, and I didn't know if I could survive without his familiar scent. He was the only person able to make me feel light as a feather and whole and round as the earth, the moon, the sun.

Had I made the wrong choice by setting up the possibility of leaving him? Had I raised a threat to our bond? Might we unravel if pulled too far apart? I shivered in the cold with that one question mark in my mind. What could become of us if I left? Even if I had the confidence to know I was enough for myself, it absolutely scared me to think of being without him.

Wanting my mind to stop running wild with negative thoughts, I softly brought my lips to his, hoping to obliterate my worries. As always, his kiss washed away my doubts and replaced them with dreams of just the two of us, nothing and no one standing in our way.

I took a quick intake of cold air when his chilled hands found their way under the fabric of my shirt, and without breaking the connection of kisses, I removed my gloves to return the favor. When I ran my fingertips over his hot skin, his breathing became ragged, his heart beating hard. I wanted to stay there forever, my hands roaming across his perfectly formed abs—which proved that hard work paid off. But then, my heart faltered for a second.

There it was again, that nagging stitch in my side, reminding me that everything in my life always seemed to go wrong, so why wouldn't the worst happen again? And it *would* be just my luck that the military sent me far away, far from the one person I needed most.

"Liam?" I whispered while trying to swallow the stinging ache that was creeping up my throat.

He kissed and tasted the side of my neck. "Yes?"

"I'm realizing the truth of it all. Just now. And I'm so sorry."

He paused and looked at me as if I was depriving him of a delicious dream. "Sorry for what, gorgeous?"

I couldn't meet his eyes. "For being naive that they wouldn't send me far away from you. I don't know if I can handle being without you … if it comes to that." I looked up to a pair of forgiving eyes that I didn't quite deserve. "I messed up. I'm sorry. I don't know why I thought my decision would come without risks."

He was quiet for a moment before his eyes moved down to the necklace I wore, with the key he gave me—the key to his heart, in a sense. He slowly rubbed the key between his thumb and forefinger. "I can't believe you thought otherwise. I'm already dying inside knowing there's a risk."

I took off his beanie hat, ran my hand through his hair, and said the only thing I could think of. It didn't make up for my decision to just up and leave him by joining the military, risking everything I held dear to my heart, but it was all I could offer. "I love you, Liam."

His face was unreadable for a moment until it wasn't. He sighed with what seemed like acceptance, "I love you too."

"Are you mad?"

He took a long pause before taking my hands out from under his shirt. "Not mad. Just sad."

We sat quietly, still, in the moment, our hands warmed by the other's while listening to the birds wake and sing their morning love songs. A few heartbeats later, the romantic moment seemed lost when he handed me my coat. "Let's finish up and walk home, okay? I don't want to push you too hard today."

"Okay, sure," I said, feeling guilty. I picked up the leaf behind me for safekeeping, hoping that maybe it would bring me good luck for the next month, for when I left for boot camp and for whatever our future held for us.

Liam stood, hauling me up with him, but instead of helping me climb down the ladder, he turned around and pulled me to him in an unexpected, almost tight, desperate hold. He didn't let go of me for the longest time, and I felt that hug in a different way.

It felt uncertain.

It felt scary.

It felt like a silent goodbye.

"You want to take a hot shower first?" Liam asked, back at the house.

"No. You go ahead. I take forever."

While Liam showered, and after I placed the holey leaf by my bedside, I plopped down onto the bed and began the long process of removing the many layers of thick clothing that were sticking to my body. In the coolness of the room, and as I sat naked too long in my thoughts, I almost regretted not showering first. I started to shake as goosebumps overtook my body. It didn't help that the shivering worsened the soreness in my tensed muscles.

It felt like forever, like Liam would never be done showering, especially when I heard his voice singing a catchy tune that softly carried its way from the shower to me. He was definitely taking his time. His singing usually put a smile on my face, as he was tone-deaf and never could sing on key, but as I replayed our conversation in the treehouse, I couldn't ignore the melancholy settling into my bones. I wondered if it would be enough, living a long distance away, to hear that voice only through a telephone. Could it replace all the other things I loved about him—his sweet smile, tell-tale looks that only I knew, tender touches, and kisses that melted my heart?

Could I live without his kisses?

The truth was, after all the training that day, only one muscle hurt the most.

My heart.

Tired of waiting for Liam to finish showering, tired of wondering what our future would look like, and tired of the crushing, guilty pain in my chest, I made my way to the bathroom.

I needed healing from the inside out.

For months, my life had been spinning out of control, so what more could I let slip from my grasp? Was my control even worth holding onto?

When I quietly stepped inside the steaming hot shower and tightly hugged my shivering, cold body to the back of Liam's hot and wet one, he jumped in response. "Well, *hello* there, gorgeous. What do you think *you're* doing in here?"

My tears hid amid the droplets that bounced off the back of his wet hair, but when he turned around and saw my crestfallen expression, he gently lifted my chin. "*Hey, you*," he said with worry.

"Hey yourself." I stifled a sob.

Not needing to ask how or what my thoughts were, Liam offered me a sad smile in understanding. He knew me. He *saw* me. And he felt the pain of my selfish choices just as much as I did. But it was a little too late to go back and fix the mess I made. Instead, in the silence of the four-by-three-foot porcelain walls, he lathered his hands with lavender soap and gently washed my aches and pains from head to toe.

After he shut the water off, and after he dried us, and lifted me effortlessly onto the bed, there were no words spoken. Our minds synced intuitively, the way a tree knows precisely when to offer the earth its dying leaves. The subliminal message was clear:

Love all of me now.

There comes a point in every decision when you let go of the uncertainty and just be. Whatever willpower, self-control, goal-setting, and following through ever meant, it didn't matter at that moment, not when needs and wants blurred into one, and regrets were made for tomorrow.

Chapter 27

Sam 2006

The following week flew by fast. Each morning, as Liam attempted to train my feeble body into the Wonder Woman I was not, we had to laugh at the ridiculousness of the situation rather than cry at what seemed to be my inevitable failure. It was clear that when I took the assessment test the following day, the Air Force would realize that my physical abilities would never help them win a war. But it was their fault they had signed me in the first place, knowing the only reason I wanted to join was to become a dental hygienist. And Liam made a good point. It didn't seem practical to send a hygienist into battle with a tartar scraper as my weapon of choice.

After my last cold morning of training with Liam, I ran around town all afternoon, dropping Shelly's resumes off at various establishments, at least those with four- to five-star ratings. Tips were crucial for a single mother with three littles. It was like dropping a fishing line into an ocean of restaurants, but Shelly just needed one to bite, one person to take a chance on her. I hated leaving her to defend herself amongst the slimy bottom-dwellers if no one hired her.

After dropping off the last resume, I ran home and packed my bags for Seattle.

"Wow. Are you planning on staying in Seattle longer than two days?" Liam asked, pointing a finger at my giant bag.

I dropped the heavy load next to the front door so I wouldn't wake anyone when I left early the next day. "I didn't know what to pack."

Liam and his parents sat at the table, playing cards. "Sam," Susan asked while pulling out a chair for me to join them. "Do you want me to pack you some brain food for your trip? James just made some delicious smoked salmon."

"That is sweet," I said, "but the Air Force said they would provide all our meals and snacks. I'll probably be too nervous to eat, anyway."

Liam's father dealt me in for the next round of cards and shook his head. "I can understand being nervous. Performing in front of others isn't my cup of tea. My fear is public speaking. I could never eat the day leading up to any speech I had to give to my peers."

Liam laughed. "I think you passed that gene on to me, Dad. Speaking in front of people is my worst nightmare."

"Opposite for me," I said. "I'd rather speak in front of people than take written tests. I clam up and forget everything I memorized. I guess the assessment test is pretty straightforward, like the SATs, which is worse than speaking to an audience, in my opinion."

Susan picked up a card in the pile and nudged me. "Sam, don't you worry. I'm sure you'll do just fine. Liam said you both have been working hard on the physical aspects. That should relieve some stress."

I almost choked when Liam suppressed a naughty smile, affirming what our physical training led to that first day.

"Yes," I said, drinking my water, "Liam has been *super* helpful in training me, but I still need to build more strength. I'm trying not to dwell on the fact that I need more time when I've just run out of time."

Liam threw his cards onto the table and yelled, "I'm out, suckers."

I rolled my eyes and tossed my cards into the pile. "How are you this lucky all the time? I don't get it."

James gathered up the cards. "I say the same thing, Sam. 'Lucky' should have been his middle name."

"As soon as he turns twenty-one, he should buy a lotto ticket," said his mother. "But the question is, how would you two spend a million dollars?"

"How would I spend my fictional million?" I asked. "I'd buy a yacht and travel the world with whoever wanted to join me and Liam."

Liam smiled. "With my million bucks, I'd ask Sam to stay and not leave me, and we would live happily ever after."

I smiled at him bittersweetly before kissing him on the cheek. "Happily-ever-after? You are so Disney-cute right now."

Liam's mother dealt a new round of cards and asked, "Jokes aside, Samantha, if you had the means to stay home and *not* join the Air Force, would you?"

The question threw me off a little. "Well, of course. If given a choice, I would stay here with Liam. But it isn't in the cards for me. I don't have that kind of luck."

"I know how much it means for you to make a future for yourself," she said, "but you know, Liam will likely, sooner than later, work for his father's business after college. You wouldn't have to worry so much, you know, financially." She patted my hand on the table when I didn't know how to respond. "I don't mean to make you feel uncomfortable; I just know you two are mad for each other. Anyone can see this."

Liam shook his head, "*Mom.*"

"What? All I'm saying is that Liam only has two more years of college, and money shouldn't be something to stress over so much. You both plan on getting married soon, and we just want you both to be happy. Leaving to join the military, well, it seems such a sad decision for the both of you."

I could tell that it was hard for Liam's mother to bring up the issue. I also knew the intention behind her words. She meant well with wanting her son happy, but at the same time, I felt like a charity case. "I know you guys want us to be happy, and I love that you care so much, but I have to do this for *me*. I don't think I would ever be okay with having your family be responsible for me financially. That's kinda weird."

"I figured you would say that. But I had to try," Susan said.

I nodded. "I understand."

"As a mother," she continued, "you just want to see your kids happy. And Sam, you have become like a daughter to us, so you *are* family. Someday, what is ours is yours."

"*Mom*, let it be. She gets it. You love her. I love her. But she's made up her mind."

I smiled. "But thank you, Susan. To hear you say such kind things means a lot to me. In this situation, I'm just trying to look at the positive. Four years will go by fast, and the recruiter said I'd most likely be stationed right here in Washington. Plus, I already signed a legal contract with the military, so there's no backing out now."

I couldn't sleep.

Anxiety over the next day's testing volleyed back and forth in my brain like a game of ping-pong. And after a while, new worries started bouncing around as well. I was so sure leaving and starting this new adventure was exactly what I needed to gain a more promising future, but if I had learned anything about guilt, regrets, and making bad choices, it was that there was a good possibility I had messed it all up again. I wanted a happily-ever-after for myself and Liam, but now I wondered if joining the military had ruined the ending to our story.

At the testing facility the next day, I found myself drained from lack of sleep, not a good beginning. I looked around the conference room, which smelled like stale, burnt coffee, to see if any of the other thirty recruits had eyes as heavy as mine. But the only thing that looked tired was the run-down hotel, with its low ceiling, outdated wallpaper, and dingy carpets featuring purple and green swirls.

As the instructors discussed what we should expect for the tests, I was disappointed to see that there weren't many women; in fact, I spotted only one other girl. After the twenty-minute welcome spiel, I met Laura, who was assigned as my roommate for the overnight stay. We had been given only a half-hour to drop our belongings off in our rooms and get to know each other, so we hurried to find our sleeping quarters.

I laughed as I opened the door to our room. "Nice. It looks like the rest of the building."

Laura wore simple blue jeans and a long-sleeved black sweater, like me, except her dark brown hair was pulled back into a sharp bun, whereas mine was pulled back into a loose ponytail. She threw her bag on top of her twin bed. "No extravagant expenses paid on our behalf, I guess."

"Right? I was hoping to make good use of their spa after our testing. What do you think?"

"Yeah, I'm thinking there is no spa." She laughed.

Laura was slightly shorter and a year older than me, but we oddly shared many physical similarities—hair and eye color, body shape, even shoe size. We immediately hit it off. The only difference was that Laura had a generous degree of confidence, which I slightly envied. We talked about trivial things before making our way back downstairs.

"You don't seem nervous about enlisting," I commented. "Why is that?"

"My brother joined two years ago, so I know something about what's expected. Plus, he seems to like the enlistment job they assigned him, which reassures me a little."

"So, you're joining because your brother did?"

She shook her head. "Not just that. My brother joined for the same reason I am; my family can't afford to send me to college, and the Air Force helps pay for it."

"Yeah, me too. When my recruiter said I could actually get paid to work in the career of my choice while they paid for my college, well, it was a no-brainer."

"What will you study?"

"Dental. You?"

Laura replied, "Nursing. OB/GYN specifically."

I was about to ask Laura more when we were interrupted by an instructor outside the conference room. "Ladies, we are about to begin testing. Please find your seats."

I winked at Laura. "Hey, good luck on the test."

The five-hour Vocational Aptitude Test consisted of arithmetic reasoning with critical real-world problems, word knowledge, comprehension, and basic math knowledge and formulas. Unfortunately, my anxiety kicked in when I got to both math sections, but I did my best and pushed through. It was a relief when the timer screamed, alerting us that the first half of the test was over. The recruiters picked up our papers and invited us to move to another room, where lunch awaited.

Laura gave me a look indicating she didn't think lunch would be anything special, but to our surprise, they had a beautiful buffet-style lunch laid out for us. Her eyes widened. "Wow. I guess they're trying to make up for such crappy accommodations?"

"Probably. But I'd eat anything at this point. I'm starving. I couldn't get breakfast down this morning. My nerves were shot."

We loaded up our plates and found a corner table. As the only women at our table, it felt like high school—the two of us outcasts versus all the men who outnumbered us. I swallowed a bite of pineapple. "You think the food will be this good at boot camp?"

Laura took a sip of her drink and laughed. "No. They don't put that much effort into the food at camp. My brother says you barely have time to enjoy it; you shovel it down your throat before the next difficult drill."

"Do you know how intense the drills are? Like, is it throwing-up-each-day intense?"

"Sadly, more days than not," she said.

"Oh, great."

One of the training officers approached our table and introduced himself as Jim. He was in his late thirties, paper-thin, like he desperately needed to eat a burger. It didn't help that his hair—a very short buzz cut—gave him a *Schindler's List* look. "Mind if I join you two?" he asked.

"Sure."

He placed his plate of food on the table. "You know, at boot camp, you'll likely see more women. It fluctuates occasionally with the number of women joining quarterly. I am glad you two are here. We need a more diverse recruitment."

After he chatted about how hard our testing was and what to expect for tomorrow's physical, I had to confess to Jim, "I'm a little nervous about the physical tomorrow. I've only been training my body briefly and am nowhere near what I had hoped for."

"Tomorrow is a piece of cake," Jim said. "It's nothing like the PFT, Physical Fitness Test, that you must pass to graduate boot camp."

"I'm sorry. The PFT isn't what we are doing tomorrow?"

"Didn't your recruiter explain this to you? Tomorrow's physical is just the doctor testing you for unknown medical issues. We need to know if you are medically capable of finishing boot camp."

I scratched my head. "He mentioned a physical test, but I assumed that would be situps, pushups, and running. Sorry, I was under the impression the test tomorrow was serious."

"Nope."

I couldn't help but exhale hard in relief. "Thank God. So I do have more time to train?"

"Yes, you have a little more time left to get into shape before boot camp. Tomorrow, you will only need to undergo a blood and urine test and hearing, eye, and range of motion testing. It's pretty standard for the MEPS."

I felt stupid but asked, "What does MEPS stand for?"

"Military Entrance Processing Station."

"Well, this makes me feel much better."

"Samantha." Laura smiled. "You look amazing. I'm sure you'll do just fine."

"*Ha.* Looks are deceiving. This girl needs *all* the help she can get."

Laura and I were first in line for the next morning's physical. The doctors were kind and quickly examined us separately, and we both finished the whole process in less than two hours.

"Well, that was easy," I said, grabbing my bags.

"Totally. I guess this means we can go?"

"I think so." I went to hug her goodbye but realized that men in the military probably never hugged. Instead, I stuck my hand out. "Laura, it was super nice to meet you. I'm happy I wasn't the only female here."

"Same. Let's pray we can be roommates at boot camp?"

"Yes, that would be amazing," I said. "Also, when I get home, I'm going to call my recruiter and ask if your nurses' training facility is anywhere near the dental facility. Wouldn't it be wonderful if we worked closely together after camp?"

"Well, that all depends on two things. How well we tested on yesterday's placement test will determine whether they will accept us into those career programs. And two, sometimes they don't even have those career positions open after boot camp. There's a huge chance you'll be put on a waitlist until your specific job training position opens."

I shook my head. "What? I am so confused."

"Yeah, unfortunately, job requests are not guaranteed."

My heart began to thump. "Holy hell. My recruiter told me none of this. He said that right after camp, I could immediately sign up for the dental hygiene training program and then eventually work in that program as my career choice after finishing college."

"That's military recruiters for you. They can be a little dishonest. They get paid on commission, so sometimes they say whatever it is you want to hear just to get you to sign."

I swallowed. "No kidding."

"Unfortunately, that's what happened to my brother. At least with me, I learned from his mistakes and knew what to expect. I read all the fine print before signing. But don't get me wrong—there is a possibility you'd get the career of your choice, but, like my brother, he initially wanted to train for something entirely different, only to find out there were no openings. So, he had to settle for something else. This is standard practice, as it states in the fine print of the enlistment papers we signed."

"I wasn't given any papers."

"Really?"

"No. I wasn't given a copy to read beforehand. And I never asked for a copy of my signed papers because I assumed, with him working for the government, what he said and promised verbally was the truth."

"Yikes. If I were you, I'd ask them to send you a copy of your signed contract immediately. You should have received something beforehand. Also, remember, if you don't get the job you want right away, you have to pick another. But don't worry, they'll add you to a waitlist for your desired job."

There was a sudden burning sensation in my skull as if my neurons were misfiring signals to something vital to my survival. "How ... how long is this waitlist?"

"My brother waited for over a year, and after no word, he finally gave up and had to pick a different career altogether."

I tried not to sound manic as a rush of blood pounded in my ears. "Over a year?" My knees buckled, and I suddenly felt like I had just finished boot camp. "So essentially, I could be stuck with a job I hate for a few years, possibly a desk job, or worse, a janitor or a cook, all the while waiting for God knows how long before the career I wanted opens up?"

"Unfortunately, yes."

I couldn't breathe; my brain was going into hyperactive mode. "Why wouldn't my recruiter give me a contract to read, or any of this vital information, before signing?"

"I'm not sure. I'm sorry, Samantha. It is hard enough knowing that, once you sign, the government owns you for four years. So, extending that to five or six years, just to wait for the career you want, well, that's a tough pill to swallow."

I couldn't look Laura in the eyes. How could I, when it was obvious I didn't know what exactly I was getting myself into? "Thank you for all this important information, Laura. I think I may need to contact my recruiter right away."

Or buy a rope to hang myself, I thought.

Chapter 28

Sam 2006

As I drove home mad—mad at myself—I asked myself two critical questions: Why didn't I think to ask to read the fine print before I gave my life away? Did I really think nothing could go wrong when nearly everything in my life seemed to go sideways?

Idiot.

Idiot.

Idiot, Sam!

When the recruiter did not answer my call, which went straight to voicemail, it dawned on me that it was a Sunday. No one was in the office. I tried to hide the rising panic in my voice as I left a message asking the recruiter to call me as soon as possible.

The road before me seemed to blur as I chewed the inside of my cheek. Even though Laura had said not to fret, I couldn't quell the unsettled feeling deep in my bones. I had only counted on being in the Air Force for four years, and the thought that they could own me longer than that made me sick. And worse was the possibility of hating whatever job they gave me and getting nowhere and nothing in return.

And I wanted so badly to go somewhere. I wanted to prove myself as someone who did what she set out to do. I wanted to feel proud that I had done something for myself, and I believed that success would come to anyone who tried hard enough. But how could any of that happen if my desired job never became available? What would all this prove? The scenario I had landed myself in only proved I was a person who could be duped into thinking that dreams were easily attained by a girl like me. *A stupid, stupid girl like me.*

Battling an urge to fling myself out of the moving vehicle, I rolled down the window to get some fresh air, allowing winter's biting wind to slap some sense into me.

Positive thinking, Sam.

Sunshine and roses. Sunshine and roses.

You're okay.

Your future is secure.

One day at a time.

No one ever died from joining the military.

Unless they send you to war, you idiot.

My thoughts were interrupted when my cell rang. I glanced at the number on my phone and slumped into my seat, realizing it wasn't my recruiter. It was Shelly. I tried to avoid giving her the impression I was having a complete meltdown. "Hey, Shelly," I answered. "What's up?"

"Sam, hi. I need a huge favor. I know you took off work tonight for your thing in Seattle, but, by chance, would you be home by four p.m. tonight?"

"Funny you should ask. I just finished testing. I'm on my way home right now. Why?"

She squealed in delight. "I just got a call for an interview. One of the restaurants where you turned my resume in just called me!"

"What? Already?" Even if my world had just been flipped upside down, I was happy Shelly's world might soon land her on her feet. "Wow. I just turned in those resumes. That is wonderful news," I said.

"Yeah, I'm shocked too. But the problem is that this new restaurant wants to interview me today at four. Only that's when my shift at work starts. So I'm in a bit of a jam."

"I'll take your shift," I said, glad to have anything to distract me from the reality. "I'm driving home right now from Seattle and should be home in forty minutes. I owe you anyway, for all you've done for me at work."

"You are a doll, Sam. Fingers crossed, I get this job?"

"You will. I just know it. Besides, your days of Bradzilla terrorizing you have to end at some point."

"You said it. Just yesterday, Brad gave me a bunch of crap for not aligning the condiment jars specifically along the backboard."

"You're kidding. Since when does he care about that stuff?"

"My sentiments exactly. He hates me."

I laughed. "He hates all women, especially if they don't give him what he wants."

"Right? Okay, Sam, I got to find something to wear for this interview. Don't forget, my shift is at four fifteen."

"You got it. I'll be there. And good luck, Shelly."

With my Sunday evening plans altered, I quickly ran to Liam's to change into my work clothes and snagged a protein bar to eat in the car. I didn't even have time to tell Liam about my recent painful discovery, but then again, I thought it best to keep that news to myself for now. There was no point in everyone panicking until I learned exactly what the Air Force's stipulations were.

I was clocking in at the kiosk when Brad found me. "Hey. Just FYI, Kristen is out of town, and corporate has brought us some stupid substitute for the weekend."

"Oh?" I said, not caring.

"Yeah. I liked the last substitute just fine, but this guy they brought in thinks he is some fancy corporate know-it-all. I don't know why they need him to oversee this place when I can easily run it myself. It doesn't take a genius." Brad tipped his head toward the offices. "Guy thinks he owns this place already, too."

I couldn't understand why Brad was so bent out of shape, but I played along. "Well, he can't be that bad."

"We'll see."

It dawned on me that Brad might have been struggling with having another male in seniority over him, and I couldn't help but tease him, mostly because I was not in the best of moods. "You know, bro-bonding is important, Brad. You should tell him one of your special jokes. That would seal the deal. Who knows, the two of you could be buddy-buddy by the night's end."

"Yeah? NO. The guy's a douche. Too uptight. Prim and proper is not my style."

"So you're saying he's not the kinda guy to appreciate your dirty jokes, huh?"

"Nope. I save all those jokes just for you, Sammy."

I glared at him. "Oh, *geez*, thanks, but don't."

Not even a minute later, I watched Brad grab another female server's attention and start his rant all over again. I had not even met this substitute manager that Brad seemed so thrown off by, but of course, curiosity forced me to seek him out, to find out what all the fuss was about.

When I couldn't find this mystery man in the back offices, I made my way to the front of the house, where I found an extremely tall, brawny figure standing by the hostess section. He wore a fitted grey suit with a muscular, toned body beneath what looked like expensive fabric. He was bending over the podium, concentrating on something. At first, I saw only a head of thick, curly, reddish-brown hair, but as I moved closer, his beautiful side profile proved just as pleasant to the eye.

The hostess, Alyssa, standing at his side, was being extra chatty before she finally noticed me behind them. "Oh, Sam, this is Mr. Hudland. Mr. Hudland is taking Kristen's position until she's back."

Mr. Hudland turned to face me and quickly thrust out a large hand. "Sam, is it?"

His wide, straight-toothed smile created two dimples on his smooth cheeks, and I swallowed just before shaking his strong hand. "It's Samantha, but most of my friends call me Sam for short. But either is fine."

The man's nicely trimmed goatee gave him an almost rugged look, but as a pair of green eyes stared kindly back at me, they made him impossible not to like.

Poor Brad. Our substitute clearly challenged Brad's insecurity complex, and that was the problem.

Mr. Hudland gave me a wicked smile that I imagined would give Brad an aneurysm. "Then I will call you Sam, for short. I would like to consider myself everyone's friend."

But not Brad's, I almost said out loud. "Are you Irish by chance, Mr. Hudland?" I asked.

"The red hair gave it away, I suppose?" He laughed.

"Well, partly. My great-grandmother's side is fully Irish; her maiden name was Hudland. So I was just curious."

"Yes. You caught me; I'm Irish through and through. Perhaps we are related in some way along the many genetic lines."

"Maybe?" I laughed.

I glanced to my right, just in time to see Brad seething as he leaned against the corner of the kitchen door with his arms crossed. I was right; Brad was super jealous of the new guy. I was also sure that by the end of the night, all the girls at work would find themselves captivated by Mr. Hudland. This, of course, would probably torture Brad's ego enough to send him crying into a corner like the little baby he was.

"How long have you worked for us here, Sam?" Mr. Handsome asked.

I had been enjoying imagining a weeping Brad in a corner so much that I almost forgot the gorgeous man before me. "Oh, I've been here for almost two years, straight out of high school. But I just recently put in my two weeks' notice. So technically, I only have one more week left here."

"Oh? I'm sad to hear you will be leaving us. I'm sure you made a wonderful server here."

"Thanks. I'll miss a few people here and some not so much."

He gave a deep laugh. "If you don't mind me asking, what are your future plans now?"

"I'm joining the Air Force. Boot camp is nearly three weeks away."

"No kidding. My little brother is in the Air Force. He met his wife there, and her older sister is now *my* wife."

"Oh, wow." I leaned in and quietly added, "But to be perfectly honest, I am really nervous about it all." I wanted to add, *especially since finding out that I may have screwed myself.*

"I can understand. There's always an element of mystery when you seek out new adventures. It's natural to be anxious. But I wouldn't worry. You seem like a bright young lady who has the world on a hook." He looked at his watch. "You probably have to prepare your tables before the masses arrive, but hey, after your shift, come find me. Let's talk more. My brother had some interesting tales about boot camp, and I may be able to help you prepare for it by giving you some pointers."

"Yes. That would be awesome. Thank you."

I thought about Mr. Handsome as I went about prepping my tables. He was kind and professional and *nothing* like Brad. He made Brad look like a dirty handtowel—a hand-me-down manager, so to speak. And I highly doubted Mr. Hudland was any kind of pervert. So, I polished the wine glasses with a critical eye, paying extra attention to detail, just in case Mr. Handsome found himself in my area to inspect my preparedness. It's funny the lengths you will go to impress a manager you respect—something neither Brad nor Kristen would ever understand.

Two hours into my shift, I noticed I had missed a call from Shelly. I took my phone back to the break room and called her. When she answered, I asked, "Hey, sorry I missed your call. I have less than a minute to talk. Is everything all right?"

"I'm good. I was calling to see if you needed me to return to work to take over. I finished my interview early."

"I'm fine staying. I got this. You go and enjoy the rest of your evening with the kids. Unless you want to come back because you need the money or something?"

"I *do* need the money, but starting tomorrow, I'll be earning my tips from another restaurant."

"*What?*"

"Sam, they hired me on the spot. I start training tomorrow!"

"That is the best news ever. Wait, so, you start work tomorrow? Like *now*? Without giving a two-week notice?"

"Yep. I'm quitting. They don't deserve a two-week notice. But I'm coming in later tonight to say farewell and good riddance."

"It's pointless. Kristen is away, and corporate brought in a sub. Only Brad remains."

"I know. I spoke to the sub when I called to take the night off. I still need to come and give a formal letter in writing. Plus, I need to grab a few things from my locker."

"Then, good. You can meet Mr. Hudland in person. He's super nice." With a heavy heart, it dawned on me. "Shelly, this means I'm stuck here with Brad for another week by myself without you."

"I'm sorry," she said.

"No, it's okay. I'm just so over it all, you know?" I thought about why I was staying in the first place and realized the few hundred bucks I'd make wasn't worth it if Shelly left me alone to defend myself against Brad. And I was so sick of Brad. The thought of having to deal with another one of his come-ons made me want to scratch my skin raw. I felt horrible for all the women that would come after Shelly and me; all the women stuck dealing with his bullshit as long as he worked there. And then it hit me: an exhilarating and culminating thought that could destroy Brad for good.

"Shelly? Find me at work before you talk to Mr. Hudland and quit, okay? I have an idea."

For the rest of my shift, my mind raced with thoughts about how to pull off my plan. Adrenalin and anticipation surged through my veins, and since I wasn't concentrating on the task at hand, my serving suffered, which left my customers to suffer as well. I forgot the condiments for one table, I completely missed ringing in a drink order, and my last mistake ended with a customer returning their entire dinner because I had forgotten to inform the cook that they'd requested no garlic butter on top of their steak. All in all, I didn't care too much. The moment Shelly and I had been waiting for was nearly here.

Back in the kitchen, as I stood at the assembly line waiting for the chef to remake an entire new steak, Brad grabbed the wasted plate from my hand. "What the hell, Sam? This is a thirty-five-dollar steak that we have to throw away now. How hard is it to listen to your guests and enter an order correctly?"

He was right, but I didn't care. I shrugged, showing my indifference. "*Oops. I guess shit happens.*" I pushed the envelope further. "Are you going to suspend me for three days?"

Brad's face scrunched into a scowl. "Listen, Samantha. I know you have less than a week left here, but your full effort is still needed. Unless, that is, you want to leave now? If not, you need to respect those with seniority."

My heart raced, and for the first time, I didn't shy away. "Last time I heard, respect is something earned. So, I'm all out of respect at this moment."

Brad tilted his head sideways, as if seeing me with two heads. "Do we have a problem here, Sam?" he asked. "Because we *really* don't need you here. I can have Kristen terminate you now if you'd like. I mean, why wait?" Brad's eyebrows stood high in a challenging stare while his mouth formed a thin line, waiting for me to respond.

I boldly stepped forward and whispered in his ear, "Kristen isn't here to back you up, Brad. But maybe we should sit down with Mr. Hudland instead? I'd love to share with him a handful of insights that prove *your* lack of respect towards *all* female employees here."

Brad's arrogant expression slowly died down to a questioning sneer. When he realized I wasn't kidding, he casually waved his hand in the air. "The Air Force can have you—*good riddance,*" he said before exiting the kitchen.

I stood with a silly smirk on my face as the cook gave me an odd once-over. "What?" I asked innocently.

The cook shrugged. "Nothing. Nothing at all."

My intuition was correct. Mr. Hudland's presence at the restaurant was making Brad very uneasy, which intrigued me. It was nice to watch Brad squirm for once. His behavior confirmed that he either despised or feared Mr. Hudland, or maybe both, which meant Mr. Hudland could potentially become an ally when I took my revenge. But I wondered how much this new manager knew about Brad. Did he or corporate know about Brad's suspension? Would my words be swept under the rug, as they were after Shelly's testimony?

When all my customers left, I finished closing out my meager receipts and hurried to find Shelly waiting for me alone in the break room. A quick three minutes later, we agreed on what needed to happen.

It was now or never.

Arm in arm, we left the break room and walked towards Kristen's office, which Mr. Hudland now occupied. Shelly lightly knocked on the door before popping her head in. "Is this a good time, Mr. Hudland?"

"Oh, you must be the Shelly I spoke to earlier. I thought you took the night off."

I could see through the crack in the door as he rose behind the desk and waved her in.

"I did, but—" Shelly looked over her shoulder to find me missing and motioned me to enter the room.

I gave a nervous wave as I entered. "Hello, Mr. Hudland."

"Hey there, Sam. You come to talk about the Air Force?"

"Well, not necessarily," I groaned.

Shelly interrupted. "We're afraid we have some bad news. Both of us felt you were someone we could talk to, as the topic we are about to discuss is a little touchy. We know it's already late at night, but is this a good time to talk?"

"Yes, I can talk now." He pointed to the papers on his desk. "I can finish all this tomorrow. Please take a seat. I'm all ears. But I do hope the news isn't too terrible?"

We took our seats, and Shelly started first, "Yes, well, I know I said I needed the night off for personal reasons, and it was personal. But, full disclosure, I took the night off because I had an interview with another restaurant."

"*Oh, wow.* Okay. So I'm assuming the interview went well, and maybe the bad news is that you are leaving us for good?"

"We both are," Shelly and I said in unison.

The look on Mr. Hudson's face was one of confusion, and I felt terrible that he would be the one to have to deal with our absence on his three-day subbing gig.

I tried to explain it in the most straightforward terms. "Sadly, tonight will be the last night for both of us. Shelly isn't giving her two weeks' notice, and I'm not finishing my last week here. Before I joined the Air Force, Shelly and I had been desperately looking for a way out of here. Working here has been, *uh,* ... let me find the right word—"

"Miserable," Shelly inserted. "Sir. It's been a nightmare working here."

I bit the inside of my cheek as Shelly took over the conversation. "You probably already know a little about my issue with our kitchen manager, Brad. I'm sure Kristen had to inform HR and whoever else about his behavior."

When Mr. Hudland cocked his head to the side, Shelly asked, "You don't know about Brad's suspension on sexual harassment?"

Mr. Hudland looked us dead on. "Absolutely not."

"Oh. Well, that's odd. I'll fill you in, then. I reported Brad to management a while back, and he only got a slap on the wrist, with a three-day suspension."

"Which was a disappointment," I added. "Because what no one knows is that it's not just Shelly who had this problem with Brad's sexual advances. Me and a handful of other female employees, have had to deal with the same thing. Brad is rude, crude, and a disgusting huge pervert, and quite frankly, a bully when he doesn't get his way."

"This is true," Shelly said. "And because of Brad's long list of distasteful actions, he is the sole reason we are at the point of no return, you could say."

"Yeah, we're both burnt out, to say the least," I added.

Mr. Hudland blinked several times before shaking his head. "I'm ... I'm so sorry. I didn't know any of this. I don't know what to say. This news is a little ..."

"Shocking?" Shelly suggested.

"Yes. Extremely. Again, I knew nothing about this."

"You might not know anything because Kristen has an oddly close relationship with Brad, which makes me assume she never told anyone about me reporting him. She is most likely looking out for his best interests rather than the employees' well-being."

When Mr. Hudland sat silently for too long, I worried we had made a bad call informing him. I mean, a person doesn't really know someone's heart in a day of meeting them. But then he put on his glasses and sat upright. "All right. Here is what's going to happen. We will start a new report right now, which will be reviewed by all, meaning HR and corporate. I promise we will closely examine these claims. I don't stand for such behavior in this industry, and I want you to tell me everything." When he grabbed a blank paper and a pen, Mr. Hudland's face almost matched his hair color. "Please. Start from the beginning, and don't leave anything out," he said.

While Mr. Hudland looked like he was going to break the pen he held, Shelly and I both spent the next thirty minutes explaining in detail all of Brad's transgressions.

And we left nothing out.

It wasn't easy repeating all the nasty things Brad had said and done to us over the years, but we could also tell it wasn't easy for Mr. Hudland to hear. He stood and paced the room after we finished. "This is absolutely unacceptable," he finally blurted. Shelly's eyes widened like saucers, matching mine, when he nearly slammed his pen onto the table. "I want the two of you to know I understand why you both want to leave, and I don't blame you. I am disgusted. And you say this has been going on for nearly two years?"

"Yes," we both said.

Mr. Hudland sat heavily in his chair and slowly dragged his hand over his face. "Can I ask if there is any way you both would want to stay? That is ... if we corrected and changed the situation's outcome?"

"You mean, like, fire Brad?" Shelly asked.

"I'd have to bring these accusations to the board first, but essentially, yes. I can't imagine why they wouldn't vote to terminate him."

I wrinkled my nose up and looked at Shelly as she hesitantly shook her head, confirming my own sentiments. "Unfortunately, no," I said. "I think both of us are ready for something new. There is too much bad blood here, meaning that most men here are Brad's friends, plus Kristen."

"It's an uncomfortable working environment here," Shelly added.

"Yeah, this place gives off negative vibes now. But thank you for the offer, Mr. Hudland. This means a lot to us."

"Well, as much as I am sorry to see you both leave, know that I will do everything in my power to ensure this information is documented, filed, and passed along to my superiors. And I can say with certainty that Brad will no longer be harassing any female in this establishment ever again. You have my word." Mr. Hudland picked up the framed picture of Kristen and her dog on her desk and held it in the air. "As for your manager, Kristen, she and I will have a long discussion over why this situation was not handled correctly and why stronger measures weren't taken."

Shelly looked like she was about to cry, and I knew it was from the relief of knowing that someone believed and cared about us. "Thank you for listening to us, Mr. Hudland. We felt we didn't have a voice, and for the first time tonight, you allowed us to say what was needed."

"Yes, thank you," I said. "For a long time, I was too scared to come forward, like Shelly. I guess after Kristen handled Shelly's case so poorly, I felt the same issues I had with Brad would just fall on deaf ears. So, thank you for listening. It feels good to get this all off our chests."

"As unfortunate as this situation is, I am glad to help in any way possible. And ladies, I do wish you the best for whatever your future holds. Again, I am sorry for your terrible experience here." While we grabbed our purses and coats, Mr. Hudland asked, "Will it be all right to contact you if I have any further questions?"

"Sure," we chimed in before saying goodbye.

We exited the office and walked straight out of the building without looking back. We didn't even say farewell to our coworkers. Stopping to say goodbye would have raised questions, and we didn't want to leave Mr. Hudland with any more drama than needed.

Only when we had reached our vehicles did Shelly whoop, "We did it! Finally, we found someone who would listen to us!"

We gave each other a high-five before I laughed out loud. "That was seriously intense, Shelly, but I'm glad we did it. I think Brad's ass is grass, not to mention Kristen's."

"She has a lot of explaining to do, that's for sure." Shelly squeezed my shoulders. "I thought this day would never come, but it looks like we are moving on to greener grass."

"Cheers to that," I said, hugging my arms. With the freezing temperatures outside, my adrenaline started to wear off when my teeth began chattering, "I still can't believe we did it."

"Kid, I can't thank you enough for getting me this new job."

"Hey, you got that job all by yourself. I just turned in your resume. Hell, we should have tried turning it in sooner."

"Well, I'm just happy we had each other at this dump-of-a-place. Without you, it would have been unbearable."

"Definitely," I said. "And if anything good came out of this, it was that I found a good friend for life."

"Same!"

"I'm going to miss seeing you every day, Shelly." I could no longer stand the cold and gave Shelly a bear hug. "And I wish you the best of luck with your new job. Don't be a stranger, and keep me posted on how well it all goes with your new man?"

"Yes, and you keep me posted, too, on your new career with the Air Force."

I didn't want to ruin our high for the night by telling Shelly I wasn't so sure the Air Force was the right decision. "I will," I said without divulging anything else.

Before Shelly got into her car, she pointed an angry finger at me. "And, Sammy, don't let anyone push you around, you hear? If you learned anything about men bullying us women, you give them hell, you hear?"

I laughed, "Damn straight, my friend."

Before I turned to go, a small snowflake fell from the dark sky above and landed on my nose. "It's snowing," I exclaimed, feeling a sudden lightness in my chest.

Shelly smiled. "I'd say that is a sign of good luck."

"I hope," I said. "I really hope so."

Chapter 29

Sam 2006

I started my day out hopeful.

For the first time in a long time, it felt amazing to be without any obligations—no work, no school, no problems—unless you count having to wait to hear back from the recruiting office. I woke up for only two minutes to see Liam off in the morning, as he still had classes to attend, and then went back to sleep until noon. At one, while I was still lying in bed, I saw a missed text from my mother. I bolted upright when reading that the official recruiting papers I had signed had arrived in the mail, and they were ready for viewing at my house. It had started snowing again, but I quickly dressed and drove to my parents' place.

The house was empty—everyone at work and my sister at school. Not wanting to leave a wet mess, I removed my boots at the door before plopping down alone at the kitchen table with our dog Otis breathing heavily at my feet. He was a fat little pug with a smashed, smelly face that made him snore so loudly that the floors vibrated. And, if you squeezed his belly just so, you were almost guaranteed a fart too. A one-of-a-kind dog that I had missed since I started living with Liam.

"Okay, Otis," I said, scratching his head. "Let's read the fine print."

I tore open the manila envelope and pulled out the documents—which, this time, were almost two inches thick. "Otis, what the heck? There weren't this many papers at signing."

He looked at me, offended that I had yelled at him. "Sorry, buddy. I'm not mad at you." I scratched his belly before digging into the document, and after an hour of deciphering a bunch of jibberish technical terms, my heart dropped. I found the terms I was looking for—the AFSC, Air Force Specialty

Codes, which more or less discussed protocols for assigning jobs and training to enlisted airmen after basic training.

I was taking in short, quick breaths, which might have contributed to my sudden dizziness, but when the room began to move, I blamed my stupidity for everything else. I double-checked to make sure what I read was correct. Nowhere did it guarantee any specific job would be available to me after camp. In fact, it confirmed that if the choice of career I selected was not available, a waitlist was the next option. I would have to choose a different job, and how long a person had to wait for what they really wanted, it didn't say.

"*Mother of Pearl*," I groaned as I dragged my finger across one sentence, the one that seemed to pound the final nail into my coffin. "Oh, this is just my luck. If I don't find an alternative job on the list that I like, *they* will choose a job/career *for* me?" I slammed the paper down on the table and argued with no one: "How would you ever know if the military deliberately omitted a specific job someone wanted, just so that they could first fill all the jobs that benefited them? *Huh*?" When the dog tilted his head sideways, I begged, "Please trade spots with me, Otis; you human and me dog?"

I wanted to tuck my tail between my legs and run, but instead, I collected myself and forced myself to call my recruiter. He owed me an explanation as to why he had not been honest with me about my career choices. And Shelly was right; if I had learned anything about shady men, I was determined not to go down without a fight.

I practically punched in the phone numbers, and when the receptionist transferred me, Keith enthusiastically answered, "Hey there, Sam. How did the testing go this weekend?"

I didn't want to be on a first-name basis with this man, nor did I wish to have a friendly chat until *after* I knew whether he had set me up. "Hello, Mr. Thompson," I said, wanting him to understand that our phone call meant business. "Yes, it went fine. But, I was calling because—"

"I bet you did great. I'm excited to see your test results and your placement."

His chipper tone suggested he cared about my future, but I wasn't so sure. "Me too. They said we won't know the results for a few weeks."

"That's all right. I'm sure your aptitude and physical tests will come back with flying colors."

I rolled my eyes but answered anyway, just to shut him up. "The doctor was able to give me my immediate scores on hearing and eyesight, saying they were exceptionally high for a girl like me and that I'd be a great sniper." My laugh came out sarcastically. "I don't think that's for me, though. And actually, I was thinking about this whole thing, and—"

"Oh, don't worry about what he said. The odds of you becoming a sharp-shooter are slim to none. In the country, only one CPEC, Close Precision Engagement Course, trains women snipers. That facility is in Fort Bliss, Texas, and has had less than six women accepted since it opened in 1999. It's a rarity. So, no need to worry."

I gave a halfhearted laugh. "Good to hear, I guess." I knew I was jumping off from my main point, but I couldn't resist. "You know, even though sharp-shooting isn't something I'd ever want to choose, it's a shame the chances for women are so slim, like you say. It makes me question what other programs would be unlikely for me to achieve, since I'm a woman and all?"

"I'm not sure I know what you are referring to."

Realizing there was no point in discussing the inequalities women faced, I cleared my voice and got to the task at hand. "Mr. Thompson, I am referring to the dental hygiene program. I called because, as you know, I received the enlistment documents that I signed."

"Oh, yeah. That's good to have on hand."

"Yes, well, I've looked over the fine print, and I was unaware that if the dental hygiene program was not on the list after basic training, either I'd have to pick another career, or they would choose one for me."

"Yes. That is true. But you can ask to be put on a waitlist for that. Easy peasy. "

"Sure, but you told me verbatim that the dental training *would* be available, not maybe. And you never mentioned any waitlists, nor did you mention for how long a person would have to wait if their career choice was unavailable."

Mr. Thompson remained silent longer than typical for such a talkative guy. "Samantha, I apologize if I was unclear at any point, but moving forward, I don't think there is any need to worry."

"Why? Why wouldn't I worry? The whole point of my joining the military was the pretense that the job I wanted would be there for me after basic training. I am more than worried now. And actually, I am kinda freaking out."

"There is no need to freak out, Sam, trust me. Worst-case scenario, you pick something else and get added to a waitlist."

I gripped the phone tightly. "Okay, Mr. Thompson, so if there is no job guarantee, what could be the longest I would have to wait for the specific job to open?"

"It all depends on many factors, like how many others are on the waitlist for that same program or if the program is already full of trainees. And it depends on if that program has already filled their positions for the many military bases throughout the country."

I rolled my eyes. "*Wow*. My chances seem to be getting slimmer by the minute. Is there a possibility I'd have to wait longer than a year?"

"Maybe."

"I guess I'm having a hard time imagining that the government would want to spend time and money for me to train in one profession, only to transfer me into another profession six months to a year later. Seems a waste, no?"

"I understand your point, and honestly, I imagine the wait could be anywhere from six months or longer."

"Like, longer than a year?"

"Perhaps."

"Longer than two years?" I asked.

"I'm sorry, Samantha, but I don't have an exact answer for you. And to be frank, no promises are made for any specific job available after basic."

"Well, I really wish you would have been frank with me from the beginning, Keith. This is my life we are talking about. So now what?"

"What do you mean?"

"I mean, I've signed up for something being told one thing when, in fact, the truth is the opposite. Why would I want to join the military if you've started this whole relationship by being untruthful? Where is the transparency? Where is the trust?"

"Now, wait a minute. I don't think I lied to you, if that's what you are suggesting. I merely stated at signing that, when a job becomes available, they will train you immediately for that, and afterward, you can take even more college courses if needed."

"No, that's not what you told me."

"Ms. Carey, this all sounds like a little misunderstanding. If I made a mistake of not being fully transparent, then I apologize."

I wanted to cry. Not because Keith was no longer using my first name or that his tone suggested we were no longer buddies, but because I got myself into this predicament. "I understand what happened and everything that was said at the signing, Mr. Thompson. I was there. But I'll be the honest one here and say that my first mistake was not reading all the fine print *before* signing the contract. My second mistake was trusting you too much, which is also on me."

"What would you want me to do, Ms. Carey? You already signed legally binding papers and are enlisted as we speak."

I held a hand to my chest, trying to stop it from exploding. "Surely, there has to be a way out of this? I don't want to spend the next four years training for whatever job you folks give me and then have to take two more years for the program I was originally promised at signing. That's six years of my life. Surely you understand?"

"Unfortunately, Ms. Carey, you made a commitment, and moving *forward* is the only option."

Hanging up the phone sounded like my best option, but I was at Keith's unwilling mercy. For a moment, I contemplated begging but stopped myself short. Begging was never my style. I cleared the tightness closing in around my esophagus. "So you're telling me I have no choice here?"

"Unfortunately, none that I can think of," he said point-blank.

I slumped into my chair, a melting puddle of lost hope, wondering how I got into this situation. I searched my mind for a way out that would keep my dignity still intact. Then Shelly's words came to mind.

Maybe she was right, and perhaps I needed to be the bully for once, instead of allowing others to push and pull me wherever the wind blew. And if I did not stick up for myself now, I was doomed. Sure, I'd survive working under false pretenses, but what made me angry was suspecting that the military had lacked principles from the start.

Boldly this time, I asked, "Keith, since you sound like you cannot help me with this matter, I need to know who your supervisor is. I'll need their name and phone number, please."

"My supervisor? Unfortunately, Ms. Carey, I don't think they can help you either. It's a done deal in my book."

"Not in mine, it isn't. I didn't sign those papers with blood. I'm sure I have rights. Especially if I've been lied to just so that you can meet your recruitment quota. So, please give me the name of your supervisor so I can respectfully decline our skewed agreement."

After Mr. Thompson rudely put me on hold, he came back sounding much less chirpy than he did at the beginning of our call. However, he did give me a name and number.

Why did life have to be so complicated?

My stomach twisted in knots and audibly growled. I realized that I had not eaten in over nineteen hours. I ransacked the entire kitchen and ate everything in the house that offered edible comfort. I downed a bunch of chips with salsa, a plate of cheese and crackers, and a peanut butter–honey–pickle sandwich with dark chocolate milk to wash it all down. And only then did I dial the most important phone call of my life. With a name like Mr. Dankworth, I hoped he would be worth the call.

He answered immediately, and I paced the room, speaking to this faceless man on the other end of the line, praying he would sympathize after hearing my ten-minute complaint. Otis followed me around the room like the supportive dog he was, and I made a mental note to buy him a bone the size of a football for helping me feel not so alone in my hour of need.

When I finished explaining my delicate situation to Mr. Dankworth, he spoke soothingly, as if coaxing me off a ledge. "All right there, Ms. Carey, how about we just take a deep breath here for a moment? I understand what you are saying, and I am sorry for your unfortunate experience; I really am. We strive to ensure our potential recruits have the best experience before signing, but sometimes Mr. Thompson can be, well, let's say, overly passionate about his job. He means well. He does. That being said, I believe this is all a simple misunderstanding."

I stopped walking mid-stride. "*Mmmkay*, no. I'm sorry, but I can't entirely agree with this being a simple misunderstanding."

"Sam? May I call you Sam?" He asked me in a strangely slick tone, like a stranger offering me a piece of candy when I knew I shouldn't take the bait.

"Sure. Why not."

"I've been in this business a long time," Mr. Dankworth said, "and sometimes young chaps or young girls like yourself get cold feet. They find themselves a little trigger-shy, you know what I mean? I can assure you that these negative emotions you feel will pass. You are doing the right thing by joining. Your future is promising with us."

I wasn't sure if it was due to the unharmonious array of food I had eaten, but a sick feeling was boiling at the bottom of my stomach. His tone suggested a familiar talking-down-to. I was unimportant, no more than a crumpled piece of paper shoved deep inside an endless filing cabinet of forgotten nobodies. It seemed he was about to shut the drawer and say, "Be gone with you, little lady," because I was just a number to these people.

With my head held high, I took a deep breath and tried once more. "It's not nerves, Mr. Dankworth. I'm telling you; I don't feel comfortable being lied to, and I have this odd feeling I'm not the only one who has been in this regrettable situation."

"Sam, I was not there at the signing, so I cannot confirm nor deny what was said between you and Mr. Thompson." I bit my fisted knuckle so as not to cry out loud and allowed him to finish. "And, despite this slight setback or oversight, I believe you are the kind of young lady who sees through on the promises she makes."

Minus me breaking the promise to myself to refrain from having sex before marriage, well, I thought I was that girl too. I swallowed. "Yeah. Sure, I mostly am a person who makes good on her promises," I said, wishing my voice didn't sound so high-pitched, "but I never thought that the military's promises would be a sham and that I'd have no voice in this type of situation, nor did I ever think that the military forces people to join against their will."

"Well, now, let's not go *that* far. We don't force anyone."

"But that's just it; I feel like I am being forced, and I feel no one is listening to me."

"All right, Ms. Carey. If you are serious and want to *renege* on your legal contract, I have to advise you that the process of discharging someone can be lengthy." His tone of voice changed, and I didn't like the sound of it as he said the next thing. "First, we would have to file a case against you for backing out, and then those documents would have to be sent to the courts for viewing and approval. I hope the judge approves the dismissal in your case since this is your desired outcome," he said in what sounded like a threat.

Court and judges again? Was I on some déjà vu time loop? Or was he bluffing just to scare me into staying in contract? I took a moment to reflect before responding. With the irritable tone in his voice, I thought of all the possible reasons why this man *and* my recruiter sounded so angry with me. One, they were losing out on a commission; two, I suppose they would now have to fill out all kinds of tedious legal paperwork; and three, maybe they would now have to disclose the purpose of me backing out of my contract. I doubt it looked good for any recruiter to be flagged as dishonest with their recruits.

I hoped this man's scare tactic was the case, but either way, I shook my head in disbelief and tried not to laugh at my luck. I had already encountered the pleasant life of courtrooms and judges, so what was another trial anyway? "Yes, please. File away. Thank you."

"If you say so. But just so that we are on the same page, Ms. Carey, you *are* requesting to proceed with the paperwork for dismissal?"

"Yes. Yes, I am," I said boldly.

"All right. But there is no guarantee. You may be forced to honor your commitment, which you should prepare for if it happens to go in that direction."

"Would it help if I wrote a personal letter to the judge explaining my side?"

He cleared his throat. "If you feel this would help your case, *sure*."

He did not sound happy at my suggestion, but I asked, "And, last question. How long before I know the outcome?"

"A week at the earliest."

"And the latest?"

"Maybe a month."

Because I already knew what this man would say next, I spoke the words with him simultaneously, "But we make no promises."

Chapter 30

Sam 2006

I needed a straitjacket, a padded room, and a sedative. Or I needed to vent to someone. Since Liam was still in class and my parents were at work, and because I sure as hell didn't want anyone to tell me that they'd known all along I shouldn't have joined the military, I grabbed my keys and purse and left to see the one person guaranteed to be home before I exploded.

Sweet Alice.

When I arrived at Alice's home, I found her sitting comfortably beside the window, wrapped in a thick blanket as she read her Bible. Snow was falling thickly outside, and the tall lamp glowing above her produced a shadow of her on the wall, a picture-perfect image of an angel. She was a sight for sore eyes.

"Hello there, Alice?" I called out.

Alice looked up and beamed. "Sammy girl. What a treat." She set her Bible down on her end table and motioned me closer. "Come, have a seat next to me, love."

I grabbed a tall chair from the corner and pulled it closer so she could hear me. "How are you, Alice?" I asked and plopped down heavily.

"Sammy, can you believe it's snowing? Don't you just love it?"

"It's beautiful," I said, looking out the window and dreaming of a blissful time when I was a kid. I missed playing in the snow with my sister, back when our only worries were not getting our socks wet and whether our mother would make homemade hot chocolate when we went inside.

After Alice and I admired the scene outside unfold for a long, silent while, she apparently read my mind. "Should you be driving in this stuff?"

"I was thinking the same thing. Probably not. I can't stay long if the heavens keep dumping at this rate. Icy roads for drivers in Washington are never a good thing."

Alice pointed to her phone on the table. "Do you mind if we use the phones again to talk to each other? I'm afraid my ears may never heal. Of course, I remain hopeful, but who knows when or what will come of these dang things on my head."

"Sure." It still struck me funny that we talked through phones when Alice was only two feet away, but I pulled out my phone from my purse and dialed her home number. Not a moment later, we watched her phone light up, blinking red to let her know someone was calling.

Alice picked the phone up and mashed it close to her ear. "Hello?"

"Can you hear me better now, Alice?"

"Wonderfully! Thank heavens for technology. So, now, what's cookin'?"

"Well, quite a lot, and nothing great. But first, how are *you* doing?"

"This old bird? Thank the good Lord above, I'm doing *just* fine! I've got myself a warm home, food to eat, decent health, and good company. Maria came to visit yesterday, and now you are here. What more could a gal need?"

I smiled. "I love your outlook on life. Maybe I need to take a page from it."

"Speaking of life, whatever came of our talk about joining the Air Force? Did you talk to your parents about it?"

Had it really been that long since I spoke to Alice? "I did talk to them. At first, they were a little hesitant, but you were right; they eventually supported my decision. Same with Liam. I ended up signing papers a few weeks back."

"Well, that's wonderful! But what's the long face for? We should be celebrating."

"I'm kinda in another pickle." I told Alice everything that had just transpired before asking her, "Anyway, you always have good advice, Alice, so I just wondered what your thoughts were."

"I am confused. They lied to you?"

"Lied or omitted facts, same thing, but yes."

"Well, now, that just doesn't sound right."

"Yeah, I know. They told me I'd have to go to court again to appeal my case in front of a judge to determine if I can be released from my commitment."

"Court again? What in the world?"

"I know, and yes, I feel like I'm being punked."

Alice looked confused. "What does *punked* mean, dear?"

"Oh, sorry. It means that someone is playing a mean joke on me. I never imagined I'd spend a year in court. I mean, I'm only twenty-one."

"Oh, my child. This sounds terribly unfair. But you know what? If you tell your truth, surely they must release you? I've never heard of the military forcing people to join. Well, unless they drafted you like they did back in the day." She shook her head. "Something just doesn't add up."

"I agree. But I don't quite know what their procedures are exactly. And the bitter truth is that I was naive to the whole process. I took my recruiter's word for what I was signing, so part of it is my fault for not doing more research. I feel like a complete idiot. I'm so mad at myself."

"Samantha, you are not an idiot. It sounds like this guy was trying to pull the wool over your eyes. He's nothing more than a sheep in wolf's clothing."

"Well, it has been a huge lesson for me. But I feel cursed or something. First, the kid I hit with my vehicle tried to lie and sue me for an outrageous amount, and then this guy at my work lies all the time about his real character. And now, my recruiter lied to me. He obviously doesn't care about my future."

"I see. And yes, the lies of men without morals often feel never-ending. But we can't always hold them up to higher standards; otherwise, we'll only find ourselves disappointed at every turn. All men are sinful, says the bible."

"I guess I should count my blessings with Liam. He would never lie or do anything to hurt me. He cares about my future."

"Liam is a gem, a keeper, through and through. That type of man is rare, and you are a very fortunate young lady. But as far as your worries go? Pray about the situation, then speak your truth, and *all* will be revealed in the end."

"That's all I've been trying to do this year, is speak the truth." I closed my eyes and rested my heavy head on the back of my chair. "I don't know; maybe I deserve all the things that come at me for being so dang naïve."

"I'm sorry you're having such a rough go, but you're not to blame. You don't deserve it. Just remember, unfairness can happen to any of us. It just seems to be happening to you all at once. 'When in Rome,' they say." I looked at her funny, and she shook her head. "Oh, wait, that doesn't sound right." Alice laughed. "I mean, when it rains, it pours. That's what I meant."

I smiled. "Sounds more like it."

Alice pulled her blanket up over her shoulders. "You know, when I came home from living in Mexicali, it was like one bad thing after another happened. You know how they say tragedy strikes in threes? No one knows why, but they seem to. It's kind of like what is happening to you now. But try to remember, this too shall pass."

"I guess. I just feel like I can never trust anyone again, and more importantly, I don't think I can even trust my own judgment again. I always seem to mess things up. I'm the destroyer of my own life."

Alice shook her head. "That kind of negative talk is dangerous. It would help if you were more kind to yourself, Samantha. Even if you have some guilt in any of this, don't be so hard on yourself. It isn't healthy."

"Sorry. You are right. I need to be more positive and believe it will all work out. And I guess if you say tragedy often strikes in threes, then I should be safe after this last flurry of chaos in my life. Just like you, after your three terrible incidents in Los Angeles. Once you moved to Washington, you said life was good to you all."

Alice took a long, somber look out the window before shaking her head. "I did say that, didn't I? And we were happy in Washington, for the most part. I wasn't lying about that." She finally looked at me but couldn't hide the hurt behind her eyes. "I understand it is important to trust people to tell the truth, but I omitted something because I don't like speaking of it. Dredging up the past only brings unwanted pain."

"Alice, you don't have to tell me anything that hurts too much."

"I know this. But I don't want you to go through life thinking that just because you survive a cluster of bad things, your life will be perfect afterward. Tragedy still happens, child. We can be kind to ourselves and have a positive outlook on life, but at the same time, we have to be realistic. I don't mean to scare you, but it is important we women prepare ourselves for anything. That way, whatever the world throws at us, it will be easier to get through."

Chapter 31

Alice 1971

Lying to yourself is one big way to destroy a family, and for a long while, I didn't know this. Yes, it's essential to trust the people around us, but the key to having healthy relationships is being honest with yourself first. The second key is to avoid hanging on to shame when life happens.

Not long after moving to Washington, we discovered Maria was pregnant again. This explained why she had been so tired and moody the last time we were in L.A. We were all shocked since she had seen her husband only a few times back home. But because she had let her guard down, thinking Carlos would change, here we were again. Of course, another pregnancy was hardly ideal when already taking care of a nineteen-month-old, but we rallied as a family and did our best to manage.

While in Washington, we devised an excellent system to help Maria. Greg was still in the military at Fort Lewis, which was a blessing because he provided us all with a home and fed us. I don't know what we would have done without him. Johnny went back to school, met a girl, and kept out of trouble. And Maria found a waitressing job at a local restaurant to help pay the bills. Because daycare was too expensive, I stayed home and took care of Laurel while Maria worked.

For a while, life was great. My children would come home after a long day of school or work, and dinner was always on the table. Our little family seemed normal again, working together after such a long spell of turmoil. For once, we had something to look forward to, and the baby to come would mark a new beginning for us all.

Those eight months passed quickly, and before long, Maria's baby joined our family. My daughter gave birth to our little angel, Lillian Mae, Lily for short. Lily looked just like her little sister—dark hair, olive skin, and brown eyes that could melt the world, and I was lucky to stay home with her and her big sister. When I told you my life calling was to serve, I meant that I felt the same immense amount of worth helping everyone, whether it was raising my grandchildren or helping the poor in Mexico. Being a grandmother gave me a new purpose, and I loved every minute God gave me with them.

Some of my fondest memories are of taking the babies on walks through the park, with trees of every color, shape, and size. That was the best place to teach the children about God's beautiful creations. I would push their stroller along the park trails, showing them all God's wonders—bugs, rocks, flowers, trees, leaves, clouds, and the bright, warm sun above. Lily was only five months old when I picked her her first flower. I let her feel it in the palm of her little hand and told her, 'Flower. Smell the flower, Lily? That is the name of the flower we named you after, sweet girl. It means two things: *pure* and *God's abundance.*' Lily would look up at me with a grin, soaking up all the things her two-year-old sister and I taught her. It is a beautiful thing, seeing God's wonders through a child's eyes—like being born all over again.

And that is what I did with her on the last day I saw her. We started the day looking at all God's wonders just before a dark cloud came over us, and it started to drizzle, forcing us to head home.

I stood by the living room window with Lily on my hip as we watched her momma and big sister leave for an appointment. "Say 'Bye-bye, Mommy,'" I told Lily while showing her how to wave goodbye. "Mommy is getting her teeth checked at the dentist." I smiled wide to show her my teeth. "See? Teeth."

A week earlier, Maria had needed to take a week off from work for dental surgery. It was a big deal. They had to break her jaw and wire her teeth shut together so that her jaw would heal in the correct position. And, because her teeth were wired shut, she was on a liquid diet. She had to drink her breakfast, lunch, and dinner through a straw, which worried us, since she still needed enough nutrients to breastfeed Lily.

Maybe things would have been different if Maria hadn't left that day. Maybe if I had put the baby down for her nap differently, or perhaps if I had not put Lily down for a nap at all, then things wouldn't have gone as they did. I often go back to that day and all the 'what-if' questions. But in the end, it was me who laid her down that day. And it was me who would feel the guilt for many years.

Lily usually napped around two p.m. and would sleep only for an hour or so, never wanting to miss out on anything. I clearly remember covering her with her favorite soft pink blanket, tickling her under her chin, and telling her, 'Try to sleep, baby girl. Grandma loves you.' She sucked on her pacifier wide-eyed, and I wondered how long it would take her to fall asleep. After twenty minutes of fighting it, she finally succumbed and fell into a deep sleep.

When an hour had passed, and Lily was still sleeping, I debated going into her room to check on her but changed my mind, figuring she just needed her rest since she had recently started teething. So, I let her be. But by four p.m., I knew I'd better wake her; otherwise, she wouldn't sleep for her mother that evening.

I poked my head inside the room for a peek and whispered her name. "Lillian Mae? Time to wake up, sleepy girl." Lily didn't stir upon hearing my voice, so I moved to the crib to find she had rolled over on her tummy. "Lillian," I said again. When I leaned further over the crib and rolled her gently over, my heart stopped cold when I saw her delicate profile.

My granddaughter's face—normally a soft shade of peach and pink—looked unnaturally ash-pale, and her lips were grayish-blue, like that day's gloomful overcast sky.

Dread and panic filled my very soul.

My hand was shaking as I touched her soft skin. "Please, Lily. Wake up, baby girl." But the coolness of her skin shocked me. "Lily! Baby girl! Wake up! *Come on now*. You're okay. You're okay."

At that moment, I would have done anything to trade places with her, to have it be my heart that had stopped instead of thundering too lively in my chest. I turned my head to scream for help but forgot I was home alone. Calling 911 should have been my first thought, but my brain wasn't working. I was in a state of panic and disbelief. I could only think of one place to run for help. We lived not far from a church, and I knew the pastor well. I grabbed Lily to my chest and ran there as fast as possible.

The pastor came running out of the door when he heard my screams from down the road, and I threw Lily into his arms. "Save her, Pastor! Save my Lily," I screamed.

He yelled for his assistant to call 911 as he gently laid Lily on the ground. "Alice," he said frantically, "did she choke on something? What's happened?"

"I ... I don't know," I said, wringing my hands, "she only had her pacifier in the crib with her."

I felt horribly helpless as I watched him turn Lily over and pat her hard on the back to dislodge whatever he thought might be blocking her airway. But nothing worked. He flipped Lily back over to peer inside her mouth, only to find it empty. "Alice, I don't know what's wrong, but I will attempt CPR."

I dropped to my knees and began to beg the Lord for a miracle. My faith was strong, and I was sure He would answer and grant me this one last and most important prayer. My heavenly father had saved me in Mexicali when that truck rolled over multiple times, and He saved our family from the many disasters in Los Angeles, so I thought for sure God would have mercy on me again. Surely, He would save my little Lily.

Why wouldn't he?

God's mercy and miracles skipped over us that day in the ER.

I stood bitterly next to the table that held Lily's delicate and lifeless form under a white sheet, a shape that looked like no more than a loaf of bread covered in a kitchen cloth. I begged for her chest to rise and delight us with baby giggles and laughter once again, but she remained motionless.

I tried to imagine her tiny spirit, now in the hands of our heavenly Father, at peace and happy—a thought that should have given me some minuscule assurance that Lily was okay, even though she was not. Nothing could reassure me of anything, and any happiness I had ever known vanished. And because my happiness had been stolen from me, I was angry—so very angry and confused.

Why did God not answer my prayers?

Had we exceeded our quota for miracles?

And why had we all had to suffer more than others?

"How about a trade, God?" I begged Him. "Why not give this child a full life and take mine instead?"

I would have to break the news to Maria and break her heart into a million pieces. I was laying my hands over my grandchild to say goodbye somehow, but I was stopped when doctors and authorities quietly came into the room.

They spoke with a tone I'll never forget. "Ma'am, we are sorry for your loss. This must be hard, but the doctors said you mentioned you were the sole caretaker of this child when you found her lifeless?"

"Yes." I choked back a sob.

"Then we have a few questions for you. Can you explain how this child received these black-and-blue marks?"

I shook my head numbly. And then gasped when they uncovered her. Her pink pajamas had been removed, and now I stared down at her body. There were big blotches of black-and-blue marks that made no sense to me.

The doctors and authorities looked at me for answers, but I had no answers.

Not one.

They seemed not to believe me. The police kept asking questions, interrogating me, to uncover what they suspected was abuse. For someone to question my character at such a time—to think there was a possibility I could hurt my beloved Lily—was like pouring acid into an open wound. I was consumed by guilt and despair, feeling desperately lost and alone. Not knowing what was up or down, I questioned again why God was doing this to me.

Why did Lily have to die?

How would I tell Maria her baby girl was gone forever?

How could she forgive me, when it was *me* she left in her daughter's care?

I was afraid of her reaction. It came not long after the doctors and officials finally finished asking me questions. They escorted Maria into the room. She looked at me first, with my red, puffy, hopeless face before averting her eyes to the small form on the table. She shook her head violently before releasing a soul-ripping cry that could not properly escape her mouth because it was still wired shut. It became even more frightening when the doctors realized she had begun gagging on her fierce tears and feared she might choke to death.

How do you help a mother calm herself after such horrible news?

How can a mother calm herself when her world has been shattered?

And how could I ever live with myself, knowing I had been in the next room as our beautiful Lily died and had done nothing to prevent it?

Chapter 32

Sam 2006

"Oh, Alice. How tragic and heartbreaking," I said, wiping the corners of my eyes. "I am so sorry that happened to you and your daughter." We were both quiet for a long time before I asked, "Did they ever find out why she died?"

"It took hours before the doctors offered us their only explanation. Still, it did nothing to ease our heartbreak when they told us Lily died in her sleep from SIDS—Sudden Infant Death Syndrome. We had not heard of such a thing, how SIDS could happen to any baby from birth to one year old, and that it could happen for no reason at all. As for the baby's black and blue marks all over her body, they thought it was from lack of oxygen.

"For months after Lily's death, even though they said SIDS was the cause, I blamed myself. I kept thinking that, if only I had gone into her bedroom sooner to check on her, then maybe she would be alive today. Those lies I told myself only caused more pain for us all. My relationship with my daughter was strained for a few years, as was my relationship with the Lord. I was so angry with Him. He didn't answer my prayer and didn't bless us with one more miracle.

"But when I finally became truthful with myself, I realized that tragedy and pain can happen to the best of us, and such unfortunate events can happen for no apparent reason at all. I may not understand why bad things happen, but at some point, we must live and let go of things out of our control. *Life. Life. Life.*"

"Life. Life. Life," I repeated.

I handed Alice a tissue, and she patted my leg. "Thank you. So, whether your problems come now and then or in torrential downpours, unexplainable disasters are ultimately out of our hands. Sometimes, there is no one to blame. Not even yourself. If you are honest with yourself and prepare yourself for this, I believe you can survive anything."

Alice's words struck a chord in me.

I will survive whatever it is this life throws at me.

A peaceful calm came over me. "I am glad I came to see you today, Alice. What is happening to me is nowhere near the heartaches of your past, but I think I understand what you are trying to say, and you're right; I know I am a good person, and I know my truth. And even if tomorrow is like a blizzard where I can't see a thing in front of my face, it will be okay. I will survive. One way or another, we women can survive anything."

"There you go. Exactly. You will survive and move on, because that is what we women do."

I stood to hug Alice and whispered in her ear, "I am sorry for your loss, Alice."

She held my face in her hands and stared intently into mine. "Thank you, love. When you get to be my age, you try especially hard to forget the bad and try to see the good. And there is *so so much good in this world*, Sam. You just have to look harder during those strenuous times."

I drove home thinking of Alice and how her stories always seemed to put everything into perspective, just like Jane's stories had when I cared for her two years earlier. It was true that my troubles and worries were minor compared to their life struggles, but I was lucky to have such amazing and wise women in my life. With their stories of overcoming hardships with extraordinary courage and strength, it seemed their threads of wisdom, friendship, and love were the materials I needed to overcome anything.

And maybe that is why, later in the evening, when I sat down at Liam's kitchen island with him and his parents to explain my newest dilemma, my relaxed demeanor wasn't what they had expected.

Liam's eyes flew open after digesting my words. "Another court date?"

"It is what it is," I said, drinking a hot cup of cocoa and letting it warm my hands.

"My goodness, Sam," Susan said. "This is terrible."

Liam leaned forward. "Sam, this *is* terrible. Why aren't you freaking out?"

I shrugged. "I spoke to Alice today, and she helped me realize that, at this point, not only are my problems not the end of the world and that things could be so much worse, but this whole situation is out of my hands. I spoke my truth, and now we wait."

"So that's it? We sit here and wait to find out if your life is not yours?" Liam's face turned a fiery red, and I understood his anger. I felt the same just hours earlier. "They just can't force you, Sam. We have to do something."

Liam's mother turned to her husband. "What if we contact Dan Rennard? He can look into this for us?"

I asked, "Who is Dan Rennard?"

"Dan is our family's lawyer," she explained. "He would be able to see what legal rights you have. We've known Dan for years."

I didn't want anyone to deal with my problems, especially since it was partially my fault for not reading a contract before signing. "Susan, that is kind of you to offer, but I kinda don't have any leverage."

"But, Sam," Liam pleaded, "Your basic training starts next week. That doesn't give you much time to resolve this. We have to take action now."

"I *am* taking action. Tonight, I will write a letter to whoever the judge is. Trust me; I will tell them I've been lied to. I know this seems unfair, because *it is*, but honestly, I will survive, whatever the outcome. I have peace about that."

Liam slammed his cup of water down. "Bull crap! So, you're telling me you are *fine* if you have to work four years doing whatever they sign you up for? For all we know, they could force you to become a cook, and that's four years wasted! And then what, Sam? Another two years in dentistry? That's six years. And don't say there is a good chance they'll station you here for those six years, because there is a *huge* chance they won't."

I hadn't expected Liam's outburst. "Of course, I'm not fine with any of this, Liam, but since I got myself into this dilemma, I have to think positively. It is not off the table yet that I won't have my career choice available immediately, or they won't station me right here at home."

"And you believe that?"

The room fell into an awkward silence when I didn't offer a rebuttal. Liam was right, but what else did he expect me to say? If I could, I would have fixed my mess already. But the hard truth was, I'd made my bed and now had to sleep in it. He needed to accept the reality that I messed up. He needed to move on, as I had.

Liam's mother gave me a sympathetic nod as she tapped her husband on his shoulder. "Honey, why don't we head to bed and let these two talk alone."

When Liam and I had the room to ourselves, I spoke first. "Liam, what would you have me do? My hands are tied right now. Until I find out more, I don't know what to tell you. And just so you know, they could discharge me, and this argument might be all for nothing. I'm trying my best to stay cool about it until we know for sure. Why freak out?"

Liam ran his hands roughly through his hair. "I just think ... I think you should have *never* signed up with the Air Force." At that, he dropped his hands helplessly to his sides. "You made such a rash decision. And why? I had a bad feeling about this at the beginning, but no, you are so damn stubborn and won't let anyone help you. And now look where we are."

I gave him a puzzled look. "Help me? As in, I stay, and you take care of your poor, helpless domestic wife? How does that prove my value? How do I contribute to our future? I don't want anyone to take care of me. I need to make my own money."

"Money isn't everything, Sam."

"Oh, that's rich coming from someone who has never had to worry about their future. Liam, everything you have ever had has been handed to you. Your parents pay for everything, and if, for some reason, college didn't work for you, you'd have an immediate job waiting for you at your father's company. So, excuse me, you have no idea what it is like for me. I will feel small and worthless if I can't somehow prove myself valuable. You have a solid future career plan, so why can't I have that? It may not be what we planned, but shit happened. This is my future now."

Liam shook his head. "Who are you trying to prove your worth to, Sam? Because with me, you never have to prove anything. I want you for you. Not for what you can bring to the table. But by you up and joining the Air Force so quickly, it just proves you only cared about your career. You completely forgot about *our* future together. You left me in the dust."

"Wait," I said, swallowing. "You said you would support whatever I decided. Where is all of this coming from?"

"I do support you, but I don't have to like how you left out my feelings on the matter." Liam threw his hands in the air. "Is it so wrong not to want you to leave me?" The rims of his eyes swelled pink before he said, "I already had a hard time with the idea of you being gone for four years, and now there is a possibility it could be two more years on top of that? I mean, God, Sam, I'll be lost without you. Can't you see that?"

I was an asshole. It was apparent Liam was hurt more than he let on when I initially told him of my plans. I walked over to where he sat slumped over in his chair, and when he swiveled himself toward me with his head still hanging down low to his chin, I closed the gap between us and hugged his bent body close to mine. "I meant what I said that first day you trained me in the woods," I said. "I'm so sorry I screwed this up for us. And this is no excuse, but I didn't see any other way. I couldn't see a way out." I rested my chin on his shoulder. "I am an idiot, and I am so sorry. I love you so much, and it hurts to see that you are this upset. Why didn't you tell me how upset you were?"

"Because I never wanted to stand in the way of your dreams to make something of yourself. Even if it meant I wasn't part of that scenario."

"Look at me." He looked up and I continued, "You will always be part of my plans. No matter where I am in the world, I will always make my way back to you."

He swallowed before he spoke. "You promise?"

"I promise. You are the beginning and end of my story. Forever and always. But the last thing I want is for this mess I made to come between us. We have to look at the bright side of things, okay? Because positive thinking is the only way we can get through this. I need you to be with me on this. I can't do life without you."

"Okay," he said.

"And to make you feel better, how about I promise to accept help? Like allowing your parents to help me dispute my case with your family's lawyer if the judge doesn't release me from the contract."

Liam sighed in relief. "Thank God. For a moment, I thought you'd let your pride get in the way of us helping you out of this mess."

"It *is* a mess, isn't it?" I said, giving him a weak laugh.

He pulled my head to his. "This year has not gone well for you, has it?"

"Nope. Not one bit. But, on a positive note, I still have you, right?"

He gave me the longest, sweetest kiss before I heard what I desperately needed. "Forever and always. Near or far."

Our week of waiting for the judge's verdict went by excruciatingly slowly. I crossed my fingers on Monday after filing a complaint letter for the judge to review. On Tuesday, I managed to watch a whole season of *Friends* reruns. And by Wednesday morning, I could no longer sit idle, twiddling my thumbs, waiting for an answer. To keep myself occupied, I spent a whole day visiting with friends, working out, and researching any rules pertaining to the specifics of my contract. It was slightly comforting when I found nothing stating that the military could force me to comply.

And by the time Thursday rolled around, I was happy to be packing for the ski trip Liam had planned for us the following morning. "Don't forget to pack your toothbrush," I told Liam as he searched under his bed for something.

"Found it."

"Found what?" I asked, sitting on his bed and folding his socks for him.

"This." Liam scrambled out from under his bed and handed me a pink and white polka-dotted gift bag. "In a sense, this ski trip might technically be our last week together, so ... "

"Really? And here I thought you were under there looking for more missing socks for me to fold." I opened the bag and found a small black Kodak camera inside. "*Liam*," I gasped.

"To capture our memories on our trip."

I stood, grabbed him, and flung him onto the bed. "You," I said, smothering him in kisses, "are the sweetest man alive. Marry me?"

He laughed. "I thought you'd never ask."

The shrill phone call startled us, and I looked at the number on my phone. "I don't recognize this number. Do you think this might be them?"

The phone rang two more times before Liam barked, "I don't know, but answer it already!"

For days, we had kept our cool about my fate, up until that moment. I gripped my stomach and squeaked, "I'm too scared to answer. Here. You do it."

Liam grabbed the cell phone from my outreached hands and flipped it open. "Hello?" he answered. I could hear a man's voice on the other end as Liam nodded. "*Uh*, yeah. She's right here." He covered the mouthpiece with his hand and nudged the phone toward me. "I think it's them. You got this. I'm right here. If they say anything negative, you tell them that you have a lawyer, and we will fight this. Together."

I gave him a grim smile as I placed the phone to my ear. "Hello?"

"Hello again, Ms. Carey."

Liam's head was against mine, listening in, and I mouthed to him, *It's my recruiter*. "Hello, Mr. Thompson," I said.

"The higher-ups here received the paperwork we processed on your behalf, along with the letter you wrote. Everything has been reviewed, and you'll be happy to know that you are discharged from any and all service with the Air Force."

Liam yelled out the loudest whoop, and I slapped him on his chest to hush him as Mr. Thompson continued, "Unfortunately, we will have to state on record that you were *dishonorably* discharged. This means you can never be accepted back into the military if you change your mind and want to join again."

I rolled my eyes. "Oh, well, good to know." It was on the tip of my tongue to ask him if one of them would receive papers of dishonorable dishonesty, but not wanting to stoop so low, I waved that thought away and instead asked, "So is there nothing left for me to do, then?"

"No. You're good to go, Ms. Carey."

"Thanks. Have a great day," I said and happily hung up on him. I didn't feel guilty hanging up so abruptly, especially since he would not apologize for lying to me.

I turned to face Liam and found him wearing the fattest grin. "I can breathe again," he sighed.

I didn't hesitate and jumped into his open arms. "I'm free!" I proclaimed as he spun me around and around. When he finally set me down, I shook my head. "Can you believe it?"

"I knew they couldn't force you."

I cocked my head to the side. "*Um* ... a few days ago, you were almost certain I was doomed. If I remember it clearly, you nearly cried thinking you'd never see me again."

"*Yeah, yeah*. That's all in the past now. So, how about we break open a bottle of champagne and celebrate your new future? I mean, *our* new future. And before you start worrying about what career you will have to chase next, remember we're in this together now. We will be okay."

Feeling the weight off my shoulders, I laughed. "But we don't drink, remember?"

"You're right." He lifted my chin with a finger and whispered the words that could melt any girl's heart: "Banana splits instead?"

"Now we're talking. Like always, a man after my own heart."

Chapter 33

Sam 2006

At seven a.m., Liam and I boarded the bus with my friends Heidi, Emily, Matt, and Liam's two buddies. As the bus filled quickly with a dozen other college students in thick coats and beanie hats, we hurried to the back before situating ourselves comfortably for the long haul.

Heidi and Emily, wearing matching green bibs with white thermals, plopped down behind Liam and me while his friends took the seats before us. Matt came in last and sat down next to Heidi. "Last time I was on a bus was when Sam and I were headed to Mexico," he said. His dark, unruly hair poked out of his beanie at all angles, but his robin's egg-blue eyes zeroed in on mine. "Let's hope this trip isn't where my heart gets broken and I never see you again."

After our trip two years ago, I had felt terrible for not keeping closer tabs on Matt. But I didn't know how to juggle a male best friend who was once in love with me while I had found love elsewhere. It wasn't like Liam would have been upset if I hung out with Matt from time to time, but I knew how I'd have felt if Liam hung out with any of his exes. It came down to a respect thing. It was what it was. The dynamics had changed our closeness.

"I'm sorry about that, Matt. Life has been utterly wild lately. I barely even see Heidi and Emily either," I said, which was the absolute truth. I tried to change the subject. "Speaking of hearts, I hear you're dating someone, and it might be serious?"

He let out that deep laugh that I'd missed hearing. "If you mean serious, like debating whether to eat at McDonald's or Taco Bell, well then, no. We broke up a month ago."

Heidi pushed her black bangs to the side. "Really?"

When Heidi pushed her bangs to the side, it usually meant business. And to top it off, there was a gleam in her eyes that meant only one thing.

I should have realized it sooner.

She liked Matt.

I wanted to kick myself. It made sense since they had hung out several times at parties after I introduced them. I suddenly recalled the slight irritation in her voice when she told me months ago that he was dating someone. But it was weird. Usually, Heidi took the bull by the horns when she wanted something; boys were no exception. Maybe Heidi didn't want to pursue Matt because *we* had once been a thing for a hot minute?

Girl code or not, I looked back and forth at Matt and Heidi for a moment and realized the two complemented each other quite nicely. They were both edgy, not ever caring what people thought; funny, wild, boisterous, and fiery with their words. And they both were fire signs; she an Aries and he a Leo.

It was perfect.

"Was she an Aries? The girl you broke up with?" I asked him. "I thought you once said you always wanted to date an Aries because they're more fun." He'd never said such a thing, but I had to start somewhere.

"I don't remember ever saying that."

It seemed as if Heidi's chocolate brown eyes ignited in amber when she looked up at him. "So, you don't like Aries?"

"I'd watch what you say, Matt," I said. This was my chance to hint to Heidi that I didn't care about the girl code and that she had my permission. I gave her a slight wink before continuing, "Because Heidi here is an Aries, Matt. You don't want to piss off a fire sign. It can get pretty ugly *real* quick."

Matt turned a curious look at Heidi, scoping her out as if it was his first time seeing her. "I don't have a problem with impulsive, dramatic, passionate women."

The smirk on Heidi's lips accentuated her sharp features. "I don't think you could handle someone with such energy."

He crossed his arms. "Is that a challenge?"

I nodded an okay to Heidi when she looked at me briefly in question, and that's when she took the bull by the horns. "You might regret challenging me," she told him.

"Or I won't," he squinted, along with a smirk of his own.

Emily's wavy red hair moved in an ocean of waves as she bounced in her seat, clapping. "Oh, this is going to be fun."

"Fun or disastrous," I said, laughing.

"What are we talking about?" Liam asked, finally tuning in.

"Oh, just that it feels a little hot on this bus," I said, removing my oversized white ski jacket.

"I was trying to think of the last time we all got together like this," Liam said.

"I'm not sure," I said, "but this couldn't have come at a better time. I'm sick of adulting."

Heidi broke away from Matt's intense stare. "I'm with you on that. If someone had told us this adulting thing was so shitty, I would have enjoyed our high school years a little more."

Heidi always put on a front that suggested she could handle anything life threw at her, but she had recently confessed how she'd been struggling at the veterinary clinic. She had assisted the vet in euthanizing seven animals in just one week. She had thought she was tough enough for the assistant job, but she admitted it was wearing on her. Deep down, Heidi was a softy.

"I couldn't agree more," Emily agreed. She handed out a bunch of Snickers and added, "I'm glad we're doing this. All I ever do is study, study, study."

"We all needed this," I said with a mouth full. "Em, do you remember the last time we rode the school bus together? I think we were with our seventh-grade class and on our way to see the state capitol in Olympia."

"How could I forget? Jimmy White sat right behind me and threw up after sneaking a Zima drink on the bus. I had a huge crush on him because he always wore rocker t-shirts that smelled like Axe Body Spray mixed with pepperoni sticks. He lived down the road from us forever."

"I wonder whatever happened to him," I pondered.

Heidi tossed her wrapper at us. "Have I met this Jimmy, and is he available? He sounds like *my* kinda guy."

Matt nudged her. "Already chickening out and moving on to someone else?"

"Nope. Just seeing if you're paying attention. I like to keep my men on their toes."

My toes came off the floor when the bus hit a giant pothole, but Liam quickly pulled me to him. "*Whoa*. Do I need to request a seatbelt for you?"

"No," I laughed. "But I forget how bouncy these seats are."

Heidi bounced up and down. "You know, Sam, these seats *are* great. Maybe you and Liam want the back seats to yourself?" she hinted, with eyebrows moving like caterpillars.

"We're good, you sicko."

An hour and a half passed before I wished we had sat closer to the front of the bus. I sounded like a child, begging, "Are we there yet?"

Liam squeezed my leg. "I think so. You okay?"

"Yes and no. Just a little bus-sick," I said, pulling my knees to my chest as our bus continued snaking its way through the never-ending switchbacks up the mountain.

"I'm sorry."

"That's okay."

"So, I'm guessing road trips are out? Because I thought it would be fun to drive to California next spring break."

"Car rides, bus rides, you name it; you know I hate them."

Emily leaned over the seat. "Why do you hate road trips?"

"Well ... obviously, there was that time my senior year when I went on a mission trip to Mexico. It was horrendous. It took us a bazillion sickening hours on a bus to get there. Matt can attest to that. But the worst sickness I had was when my mother and auntie thought it would be fun to drive my sister and cousins to Las Vegas—that was a seventeen-hour car ride. I'm scarred for life."

"So, Cali is out?" Liam asked.

"I'm sorry, but we won't be that couple that bonds over long road trips and sightseeing across the country. I'm *not* that girl."

Liam patted my leg. "Don't worry. I won't force you to go on road trips. We will just have to fly everywhere, I guess."

I had never been on a plane and wondered if they made people sick, just like cars. I gave a weak smile and leaned my forehead against the cold window. "Just tell me when we're almost there, okay?"

Liam tapped my shoulder and then pointed to the front. "You don't have to wait too long. I think we are here."

Through the bus windows, we watched as the wet, narrow, and heavily forested road opened up to reveal every skier's dream. We gaped at this winter paradise, thickly blanketed in white, and the mountainside flooded with skiers racing down in every direction. I sighed, "Oh, thank God we are here."

Liam's face scrunched in sympathy. "Maybe you need food?"

"Yeah, that's probably it."

"And hopefully, a little afternoon skiing will refresh your senses."

"Let's hope." I hurried forward and anxiously exited the bus. A brisk mountain chill slapped my face when we stepped outside, and I finally smiled after taking several deep gulps of the pine-scented air. "God, that smells and feels good."

"No, it doesn't. *Holy cold*," Liam shivered, bringing his arms around his shoulders.

We gathered our luggage from under the bus and made our way toward a tired-looking lodge the color of dirt and crowned with two feet of powder on its head. I was apprehensive that the roof's entire sheet of snow might tumble down onto us. But once inside, I was relieved to find the building well-maintained, uncluttered, and spacious—perfect enough to accommodate our group. Everyone would sleep in a European-style way, like a hostel with bunk beds placed in one massive dorm room and shared bathrooms down the hall.

While everyone arranged their sleeping bags and stored their belongings under their wooden beds, I asked Emily if she had Tylenol for my headache. She produced two precious tablets, which I downed before proceeding to dress for the occasion.

"I love the all-white," Emily commented on my ski outfit.

"Thanks. After I got the call yesterday that I didn't have to go into the Air Force, Liam and I hit the mall and splurged. I picked white to represent a new beginning."

"You guys coming?" Heidi asked as everyone made their way to the front doors, with Matt beside her.

I was about to tell Emily how cute they looked together, but Liam interjected. "It's kind of a small trek to the ski lifts, so how about we all head out to grab lunch at a restaurant down the road and then hit the hills?"

"You don't have to persuade me to eat. I'm always hungry," I said.

We walked for ten minutes, sat down, and ordered immediately before Liam turned to me. "How's the head?"

"The headache has subsided, so that's good."

"I'm starving. Anyone else?" asked Emily.

"Me too," Heidi agreed. "I hope they make our food fast. I'm about to chew my arm off; that's how hungry I am."

Matt tilted his chair toward her. "So you're into cannibalism? Cuz I need to know these things before we move forward."

"If I were stranded in the mountains and needed to survive, I suppose I could chew someone else's arm off." She squeezed his biceps. "Yours looks beefy enough."

Liam's friend Justin chimed in, "I heard a group of mountain climbers got lost once, and the only way they could survive was by eating the frozen flesh off of a few climbers that had died. A friends-eating-friends kinda story."

"It's a true story, I offered. "They made a book or movie about it. Some rugby team's plane crashed, and they had to make some disturbing decisions to survive. I think it was called *Live* or *Alive,* or something like that."

"Sick," commented Emily. "Tell me now, but I hope we aren't all a friends-eating-friends kinda group."

"So? Tell the truth. You'd really eat someone?" Matt asked Heidi.

"Don't get scared of me, now," she said, laughing, "but, push comes to shove, yes. I would totally eat someone's dead flesh without thinking twice."

Emily wrinkled her nose. "Not me. Can't do it. Plus, I'm vegetarian."

Liam laughed. "Yeah, I agree with Emily; although I am no vegetarian, I think I'd rather starve to death than eat Sam's leg."

"Hey!" I barked out. "Why am I the dead one in this scenario?"

He looked at me, intrigued. "Okay, then. Let's say I died first. Would you eat your own boyfriend to stay alive?"

I thought about it briefly before answering, "It's our human nature to try and stay alive. I mean, if you were dead already and didn't feel any pain, then maybe just a small nibble wouldn't hurt."

Liam gasped, "*Oh great!* Hannibal Lecter here, everyone!"

"Wait, I said *maybe.* I mean, if this exact scenario presented itself, who knows, maybe my heart couldn't go through with it. Maybe I'd wanna die with you so our souls are together in a happier place."

"So you would be worried that your soul would go to hell if you ate another human?" Heidi asked.

"Yeah. Don't you ever wonder if there is a heaven or hell?"

She shrugged. "Well, sure, we all wonder that, but I think if you are somewhat religious, then you would have to wonder if your God was the forgiving type that He claims to be."

Matt added, "You mean, as long as you don't *kill* that person before you eat them, right?"

He said this explicitly, looking at Heidi, and she laughed. "Obviously. No harm, no foul, and no guilt."

Heidi's response seemed to reassure Matt, who finally sat relaxed in his seat. "Phew," he said. "I have my limits when it comes to dating hungry women killers."

Liam nudged me. "Well, in that case, I guess I'd have to do my part and not let Sam go to waste."

"But first," I said, "please make sure I am totally dead. I don't want to wake up from a coma and find half my leg missing."

We all engaged in the topic further, discussing everything forgivable and dismissed due to unique circumstances, until our food finally arrived. Everyone began devouring their food, but I had lost my appetite.

"Why aren't you eating?" Liam asked as he vigorously shook the bottle of ketchup over his fries.

I leaned back from his wild ketchup pouring. "Careful. I'm wearing all white here."

He handed me the bottle when finished, but I looked down at my burger, with its meat looking almost too pink inside. "I don't know if it's all the cannibalism talk or if I'm just still nauseous from the bus ride, but I guess I'm not that hungry."

"Well, you should force yourself to eat at least half of it. We're about to hit the slopes."

I sprinkled my fries with a massive dose of salt instead. "I think you just want me fat so you can have more of me to eat when we find ourselves stranded in the mountains."

"Dang it. You guessed my plan."

Heidi must have heard all this and patted Liam on the back. "After Sam's story about you feeding her cake in bed, I believe it, Liam."

"Heidi!" I said after picking up my jaw from off the floor. My face felt red hot when I faced Liam, who was holding an uneaten fry halfway to his mouth. "Sorry," I said, wincing. "I sorta tell my friends everything about us in hopes they pretend to know nothing at all." At this, I glared at Heidi.

Liam finally bit into his fry before looking at Heidi dead on. "I'm thinking of trying apple pie next."

She nodded. "Wise choice, my friend."

After lunch, we headed to the ski lodge, purchased our tickets, and suited up. Once we snapped our bootstraps into place and clicked our feet into our skis, Liam handed me my poles. "Ready?"

My stomach still felt queasy, but I hoped to forget it once we started skiing. "Ready."

Crystal Ski Resort was a little over two hours away from Seattle—home to famous musicians like Jimmy Hendrix, Pearl Jam, Soundgarden, and the Foo Fighters—and the resort prided itself on having an eclectic style that brought in the 'cool' factor. So it was normal when we got in line to find a mix of dreadlock hipsters wearing '80s and '90s attire with overgrown facial hair that bobbed and swayed to the loud grunge music that played loud above the speakers.

"Lively group here," Liam commented.

Matt adjusted his gloves. "These are my people. If you think this crowd is wild, we should all return in the spring for their Crystal Mountain Ski Fest. Everyone brings their dogs and barbecues outside. It's a huge party."

"Then I should start practicing the ski *slanguage* here." He looked down at my skis. "Like, *dude*, your K2s are totally tubular."

"*Shh*," I laughed. "You're so embarrassing." But then I played along. "But *bro*, these are *so* last year." I looked up to the sky just as a ray of light glinted onto the surface of my goggles. "The sun is coming out. We may have a BlueBird Day after all. I was worried it would drizzle like the previous day's forecast."

Heidi looked at Matt behind her when she and Emily were next in line for the lift. "Three can sit here. Wanna keep me warm on our way up?" she asked him.

He batted his eyes. "Only if you sit on my lap."

"You two are moving way too fast for my comfort," Emily joked. "I don't think I want to sit with you animals." She turned to one of Liam's friends. "I'll sit with one of you instead."

After everyone had taken flight, and Liam and I were the last to hop on the lift, I told Liam about how I pushed Matt and Heidi together on the bus. "But now, I may have caused the Earth's axis to tilt a little too far with those two," I said, nodding toward Heidi and Matt ahead of us.

"At least it will be fun for us to watch. It'll be like watching *Animal Planet*. With Heidi as the praying mantis, she'll devour him."

"I think Matt will be able to control her. *Maybe*," I laughed. "Speaking of control, you think you'll conquer the hills today?"

"What? I thought I handled it pretty well last year," Liam said, adjusting his poles so they wouldn't fall to the ground below—the mistake he made the last time we skied.

"Pretty well, huh?" Liam could never admit defeat. He was good at all sports except skiing. It was hard for him to struggle at anything when he had such raw talent in all things pertaining to sports. "Um ... " I said, "as I recall, last year, you were more on your backside than your feet."

He rolled his eyes. "It was a rough go at first, yes, but then I got it. Didn't I?"

I pointed to the guy on the slopes below us. "See that guy? The one on his back down there? That was you last year."

"*Nah*. This time, it will be different. I'm going to nail this thing if it kills me."

"Well, it *can* kill you, so don't go crazy and show off just for me. Just take it slow."

"Yes, Mommy," Liam said, batting his eyelashes.

The lift up the mountain was one of the best rides. We sighed in unison as we took in the picturesque landscape around us, enjoying the view from above, level with the tops of the snow-capped pines and firs stretching as far as our eyes could see.

"I just love this," I said. "Whether you can ski or not, you must admit it's pretty spectacular up here."

He scooted closer to me for warmth. "I can see why you love it up here so much."

"Right? It's a winter paradise up here. It is hard to imagine how some people from faraway countries have never seen the snow or this many trees. I could never live anywhere else."

"You almost did."

I gave him a guilty glance and nudged his arm. "I'm here—not going anywhere."

We came to the end of the line, and I knew how scary it was for beginners to come off the lift and onto a short and straight downward slope.

"Okay," I said before jumping off, "remember, stand up as soon as your feet touch the ground and quickly point your toes into a wide pizza shape."

"Got it."

When a small inkling of fear crossed Liam's face, I couldn't help but smile. "You know, you're so cute right now."

"Why?"

"Because you look vulnerable for once. You are always trying to help me, and now I get to return the favor. Plus, I love knowing I am better than you at something. I'm sick of you beating me at cards all the time."

Liam didn't have time to comment when our skis touched the ground. I slid to a quick stop at the bottom and looked up, ensuring Liam wouldn't run into me or anyone else. Instead, he skied toward me at a plodding pace, with his knees wobbling awkwardly like Jello in a bowl. His tall frame hunched forward as low as he could, as if he felt it was safer being closer to the ground.

"That's it," I said. "Now, just bend your knees a little more."

He adjusted his form before coming to a stop in front of me.

"Good job," I said, patting him on the back.

"Thanks. But it's a little slick."

"Yeah, remember I said it rained a bit last night? Well, it makes the snow a tad icy."

Liam rearranged his goggles and looked at the signs pointing in every direction. "So, where to first?"

I pointed to the green sign with a circle labeled Tinkerbell Trail. It was skilled for beginners and led to another main accessible junction. "That way. We'll take the easier route down." Liam didn't argue, and I knew I needed not to frighten him with the more daring routes if I wanted him to continue skiing with me. But I had to remind him, "Remember the last time when I took you on the wrong trail? The one that was listed for experts?"

"How can I forget? It took us nearly forty minutes to slide down on our asses."

"Yeah, you weren't happy with me for the rest of the day. I won't make that mistake again."

"All right, I trust you. I think."

We took the first junction easily, but as we came to the second part, a steeper slope, Liam looked down it and said, "Okay. You go first. I wanna watch how you maneuver this."

"All right, but remember, if you start to speed up too fast, slow down by angling your feet into that pizza shape again. And it also helps if you ski from side to side down the mountain, mainly with long bouts like this." I went down the hill to show Liam how to take longer strides, moving side to side. I yelled up, "See? Long, drawn-out runs, almost as if you are hugging the side of the mountain. And take the turns quick and sharp, not slow and wide." I stopped halfway and looked up the hill. "Go ahead when you are ready."

I watched his chest fill with air before he came down, making an A-shape with his feet. He turned his body to follow along the side of the hill like a champ, but when it was time to pivot and turn in the opposite direction, he turned too slowly and didn't lift his knees high enough, just as I had warned him not to do. He realized his mistake and tried to adjust his angle, but the downward momentum caused him to pick up too much speed. It must have surprised him, making him panic, but he chose to fall onto his side with a soft, grunting thud into the snow rather than barrel down uncontrollably—an intelligent choice.

"You all right?" I called up.

He looked irritated with himself and didn't answer, and even though I knew he wasn't hurt, it was hard to watch him fail. It was so foreign to see him suck at something, since he pretty much won at everything in life. *Lucky* was what his parents called him.

I offered, "You'll get it sooner than later. You got this."

He tried to get up but fell again when he lost his footing due to the angle of the slope. I cringed, realizing it was going to be a long day. He grumbled something under his breath as he tried to stand again, but with determination, he succeeded. I watched like a proud mother when Liam finally made his way to me without falling.

He stopped in front of me, breathing hard. "*Crap.* I've forgotten how hard this is." Liam wiped the sweat off his upper lip and unzipped his coat halfway down to cool off. "And I think the most challenging part is just trying to get up after falling."

"I know," I said. "But you'll get it quickly, like you did the last time. First runs are always a little iffy. Also, it doesn't help that today's slopes are icy. But let's continue."

It took us thirty minutes to make it to the end of the route with three trails. When we made it to the base of the resort, where we had begun, I gave Liam a high-five. "Awesome. See? You did it!"

"If you call falling three times not bad, then sure."

I pointed to the ski lodge. "Let's get a drink of water. I'm quite thirsty from all the salt I put on my fries."

"You know," he said, as we trudged toward the lodge, "all that salt isn't good for you. I've never seen such a salt fanatic as you. I'm surprised you don't shrivel up and die like the slugs in my mother's garden when she kills them with salt."

"Well, what can I say? I like to live dangerously on the edge."

"Seems to be your motto this year." He chuckled.

Chapter 34

Sam 2006

We made our way inside an A-framed lodge, where a crowd of people were ordering food and drinks from the three concession lines. With all the warm bodies surrounding us, we stripped our coats off while waiting for our turn to order. Liam pointed to the front door. "Hey, there's your friends."

I followed his gaze and found Emily and Heidi walking in ahead of Matt. "Looks like *your* friends are still on the slopes." I jabbed Liam with my elbow and spoke under my breath, "How long do you think it will take Heidi to make her first move on Matt?"

I cleared my throat when they approached. "Hey, all!"

"What are you guys ordering?" Heidi asked.

"Just water. I'm parched." I tilted my head toward the back of the line. "Want me to order something for you guys? The line's too long, and I doubt the crowd would be happy if all three of you cut in line."

"Yes, please," said Emily. "If you don't mind, could you bring me some water?"

"Me too," said Heidi. "We'll be upstairs in the lounge area, so just meet us up there."

"All right." Before Heidi turned away, I whispered in her ear, "I heard they have some comfy couches up there, perfect for getting cozy with someone?"

She smiled. "My sentiments, exactly."

After Liam ordered a few water bottles and handed me mine, I didn't waste time guzzling the entire bottle. "I needed that," I told him.

"Down the hatch, all in one go? Wow, I guess you were thirsty. You're like a camel with two humps. Should I get you another water for later?"

"*Nah*. Let's head upstairs. Five bucks says Heidi is sitting on Matt's lap already."

"You're on."

When I found my friends at the top of a balcony, sitting on soft caramel-color leather couches overlooking the happenings of the lodge below, I nudged Liam. "You owe me five bucks." I took a seat beside Emily. "So, how did you guys do out there?"

Emily sat in an oversized chair with her arms crossed. "I did okay. I ended up by myself most of the time, which sucked."

"Where were you, Heidi?" I asked.

Emily fired a glance at Heidi with her eyebrows raised. "That's a good question. One minute, she was there, and then the next, *poof*. Gone."

With a nonchalant wave, Heidi mumbled, "I thought you'd catch up."

Emily made an unladylike snort but didn't press. She looked at Liam and me. "How about you guys? How did you do?"

"Pretty good," I said.

"How many runs did you guys get in?" asked Heidi.

I looked over at Liam and gave him a playful smile. "*Um* ... we're kinda taking it slow, but we'll get in at least two more runs today."

"*Hey*," Liam scolded. "You're the one who wanted to stop and get water. I had a few more laps in me."

I laughed. "*Sure*."

"Does anyone have any chapstick with them?" Matt asked, smacking his lips. "I feel my lips chapping."

We all shook our heads no, but Heidi opened the flap to her ski jacket and dug around. "Let me see." Her hands scoured the bottom of her coat, but she came up empty-handed. "*Crap*. It must have fallen out earlier. I just put some on less than an hour ago."

That's okay," Matt said, "I'll just buy some at the equipment store before heading out again."

The mischievous smile Heidi gave him was priceless. "Or, I can just smear some gloss off my lips and onto yours?" she purred. "I mean, I put a ton on earlier, enough for two people; that is, if you don't mind strawberry."

I could have bet a million dollars that there was chapstick in that coat of hers, but Matt was oblivious. "You're not afraid of getting cooties?" he asked.

We were all laughing when Liam joked, "Matt, how do you know it isn't *her* who has the cooties?"

He didn't waste a heartbeat. "Guess I'm willing to take that risk."

They didn't have a shy bone between them. Matt bravely leaned forward toward Heidi, and she met him halfway with a smug smile plastered to her face. The kiss only lasted three seconds, but they shared more than strawberry chapstick.

Emily clapped at their performance, but I didn't. At that precise moment, I oddly felt sick. I shook my head and stood up, saying, "*Uh*, sorry. I think I'm going to be sick."

Heidi gave me an offended glare. "*Really*? We're just having some fun; nothing to get queasy about."

"No, I just—"

I frantically scanned the room, only to realize the bathrooms were downstairs.

"Sam?" Liam questioned me with a concerned look, but I quickly turned away just as my mouth began to water, a familiar sign indicating what was about to happen. But it was too late when the bile hit the back of my throat. Just in time, I bolted to my right, grabbed a small trash bin from the floor, and hurled into it.

Liam rushed behind me. "Sam. What the heck?" I put my hand over my mouth, unable to answer his next question. "Could it have been the burger you ate? Although I noticed you barely touched it."

I shook my head when I was finished. "I don't know, but I'm mortified."

Liam handed me a napkin that seemed to appear out of nowhere. "Who cares? No one is really looking at us," he said.

I turned around to look behind him and found every single one of our friends looking at me with worry. "*Right*," I said before giving them all a weak smile and a small wave. "I'm all good now," I told them all.

"Do you think you have the flu?" Emily called out.

"I don't know," I said as Liam guided me back to the couch. "I think I got sick from guzzling my water down all at once. Also, I don't think it was from the burger. You all had the same thing I ate, and you aren't sick."

Liam rubbed his hand between my shoulder blades. "True."

When Liam's two buddies made it back from skiing and joined our group, I felt awkward having all eyes on me.

Emily stood and leaned over to squeeze my leg. "You gonna be okay?"

"I'm fine," I said, waving for her to sit. "It must have been the water." I looked at Heidi and Matt and gave them a good head shake. "And no, your makeout session did not make me sick. I promise."

"Well, good. I'm glad we weren't the ones causing you to toss your cookies. Anyway, we're all ready to head back outside for some more fun. You feeling up to it?"

Everyone began to put their coats on, but I gave her and Liam an uneasy glance. "How about you all go without me? I think I'll just sit here for a bit to ensure I'm feeling one hundred."

"No. I'll stay with you," Liam offered.

"Seriously, I'm fine. I'll be mad if you sit here with me. Go and have fun with your friends. Plus, you might benefit from someone else's perspective on ski lessons."

Emily interrupted. "Actually, my boot is hurting my left toe. How about I stay with you, Sam? I could use a longer break."

I felt like a child who needed watching. "*You guys*, I swear I'm fine sitting here alone."

She shook her head. "I know I don't have to, but I want to sit with you."

"Only if you're not doing it out of pity. And Liam, please go and have a good time. You never get to do this with your friends."

He waited a beat before answering, "Fine, as long as Emily is here with you. But can I get you anything first? More water?"

Heidi finished zipping up her coat and handed me an unopened water bottle. "Here, Matt and I can share the other bottle."

"I'm sure you will." I opened the bottle and took a small sip, worried too much water would make me queasy again. Liam leaned in for a peck, but I stopped him and gave him a sideways whisper, "Better not, just in case. I don't know if I have a bug or not."

He tapped my nose. "Well, then, you and Em behave yourselves."

"We will. Go have fun."

When all the others had finally left, I tore my boots off, pulled my knees tight to my chest, and groaned. "*Ugh*. I think I might have the flu or something. I didn't want to allude to that and freak everyone out."

She gave me a look of concern. "How do you know it's not something you ate?"

"I don't. But just in case, you should stay a few feet away. Also, let's keep this between you and me. I don't want everyone to treat me like a walking virus."

"Gotcha."

I pressed the chilled water bottle to the side of my temple and groaned again. "This just sucks. I was looking forward to this trip with you all and with Liam. I swear I have the worst luck."

"I'm sorry, Sam. But now that you're no longer committed to the military, we'll have plenty of time to plan more of these ski trips. We have all winter."

"True, true. I love how you always see the positive side of things, Em."

Emily took her boots off and laughed to herself.

"What's so funny?" I asked.

"I don't mean to laugh about this part, but when you were barfing in the corner, Matt joked, 'Maybe Sam's preggo.'" My mouth dropped open, but Emily threw a hand up. "That's not the worst part. Heidi told him it was impossible because you and Liam were saving yourselves for marriage." My mouth opened further, and Emily continued, "I know; rude. But I'm laughing at the part where Heidi quickly says, 'But not me, I'm not saving myself!'"

I shook my head. "That girl! She doesn't know how to keep her mouth or legs shut. And could she not even *try* to play hard to get with Matt?"

"Right? At the same time, I don't think Matt has a problem with her being so bold and in your face." Emily laughed.

In the back of my mind, I made a mental note to remind Heidi that my personal lifestyle choices needed to stay private. Sure, no one knew how Liam and I broke our promise weeks ago, so with Ms. Blabbermouth Heidi, I was definitely not going to tell her. Besides, she would only laugh, saying she knew all along I had no self-control.

Emily took a swig of her water. "Did you bring any extra tampons? I swear I'm about to start."

"No. Sorry. But I saw a tampon machine in the women's locker room."

The mention of tampons prompted me to think back to when I'd last had my period. By my calculations, I should have already started. I interrupted Emily mid-sentence, "Em, what's the date today?"

When she told me the date, my stomach and the water bottle I held dropped to the floor.

I was late, and I was NEVER late.

But there was no way I could be, not from just that one time with Liam.

"Sam? You're white as your snowsuit. You gonna be sick again?"

I stood up, nodding while my hand shook, and pointed to a paper bag someone left next to her chair. Emily quickly grabbed it and shoved it into my hands just in time. For the second time that day, I threw up. But this time, I knew it might not be from food poisoning or the flu. The thought of being pregnant was ludicrous.

Emily handed me a tissue, and I wiped my mouth. "Thank you."

"Maybe you need to go to bed?"

I contemplated whether or not to confide in Emily. Or, maybe it would be best to find Liam? After thinking about it, the latter seemed pointless. Why get Liam all worked up without knowing anything for sure?

"How is this even possible," I said under my breath.

"What's possible?"

"Emily?" I said, "I don't know exactly if it's the flu or food poisoning."

"Okay. And?"

"And, it's just that, Liam and I ... well, uh ... we slipped up, just once, like a few weeks back." Emily tilted her head in confusion, and I swallowed back more bile. "Like, we had sex. I was leaving to join the military, and I guess ... I don't know. I'm weak!" I yelled, throwing my head into my hands. "Pathetic and weak is what I am!"

"*Nooo*, for real?"

I looked up at her. "Yes. I just realized I'm late. With everything going on lately, I didn't realize."

Emily's hand flew to her mouth. "Oh my God." She nudged closer to me on the couch, putting her arm over my shoulder. "You know for sure?"

My breathing had become ragged, and I pushed the thought that it was even possible. "Here's the thing, I don't. This *could* be from the flu or food poisoning, or neither."

"Do you have body aches, a fever, or chills?"

"No."

"How about diarrhea or watery stools?"

Emily was already asking questions a nurse would ask. She would one day become a great RN.

"*Um* ... no, I don't have flu symptoms. Just feeling super nauseous."

"When did you first start to feel sick?"

"On the bus. But I always get carsick."

"Well, then ... throwing up may not be from your lunch today, since you felt sick *before* you ate."

I took another small sip of water as Emily continued, "Do you normally feel sick hours after a car ride is over?"

I squeaked out, "No. I usually feel better around ten minutes after we arrive."

"And you know for sure you're late?"

A cold chill ran down my spine. "Yes."

"Okay, look, there's no point in freaking out right now, or at least not until you've taken a test. We can walk to the mini-mart down the road to see if they have a test?"

"No!" I said, shaking my head vigorously. "I'm not ready to know this information, nor am I ready to talk to Liam about anything I *might* suspect."

"*Okay, okay*. I get it. Not right now."

"Yeah, not right here, not on this trip, and not with everyone around. If I find out I am pregnant, you know I won't be able to hide my feelings, and then Liam or Heidi will start to ask what's wrong. They'll know something's wrong just by looking at my face."

"Like the face you're making now?"

I slapped my face before forcing a smile. "See? I'm okay. I can fake it better."

We sat quietly, our minds racing with the possibility before Emily interrupted my thoughts. "So what will you do if you know it's true?"

Tell people I'm fat and ignore the truth?

Tell people I'm a surrogate for the sweet gay couple down the road?

Run away to a nunnery?

Give it up for adoption?

Those were the things I wanted to say but didn't. "I don't know, Em. I'll keep my suspicions to myself until I get home to take the test." I bolted upright. "Emily, *please* don't say anything to anyone, *please*?"

"Sam, of course not! I would never betray you like that."

"Even to Heidi?"

"Are you kidding? I promise."

"Sorry."

"Don't be."

When Emily's face edged with worry, I touched her leg. "Look, Em, I don't want you to think twice about this, so how about we pretend we never had this conversation? Hell, people are late all the time. There is nothing to worry about. Maybe my boobs hurt because I'm going through a hormonal change, like menopausal women do when they transition from forties to fifties. So, let's stop worrying. How about you head back out there and ski with everyone? Go and have some fun. I'm fine."

"You are not fine."

"Really. I am fine. Besides, I want to return to the lodge and rest my head, which feels like it's splitting in two. Can you find Liam for me and let him know I'm okay? Just let him know I was tired and needed a nap. Tell him to stay and play and have fun with the guys."

"Okay," Emily said, miserably hiding her worried frown.

"Sorry," I said again and stood to gather my things. "I just need to lie down."

"Okay. Text me if you need anything. And your secret is safe with me. I am here for you, no matter what happens, Sam."

I found the solitary walk back to the lodge insightful. As an enormous snowplow roared by, I quickly moved out of its way before staring at it in wonder, watching it push aside the fallen snow to the side of the road, creating massive mounds taller than my head. The mounds reminded me of my never-ending problems, and I contemplated digging a hole in the snowbank—deep enough to fall asleep inside forever. Sure, the snow would be painful at first, but after a while, after hypothermia took over, and my extremities numbed, and my heart slowed to a barely perceptible beat, there would be a pleasant emptiness of worries, a quiet void leading to a blissful and peaceful end.

But I was too tired to dig a hole. Instead, I trekked the rest of the way to the lodge with the weight of a thousand pounds pressing on my brain, feeling as though the snowplow had parked itself right on top of me. Once inside, I tore my boots off and climbed inside my sleeping bag, still wearing my ski clothes, praying I would die miraculously in my sleep.

I woke to the sound of voices and peeked an eye open to try to remember where I was. I spotted Liam walking through the door at that moment, and he waved when he saw I was awake. It would be hard to keep this massive secret from him, especially for one more entire day that remained on this trip. But I had to. It wasn't the time or place for such life-altering news to invade the beautiful, worry-free spirit of the weekend.

I faked a smile when Liam dropped his jacket on the floor and squatted beside my bunk. "Hey."

"Hey, yourself."

"You feeling better?"

"Yes," I lied.

"You missed the rest of the day. I came back here just a bit ago to check on you but didn't wanna wake you. You looked so peaceful sleeping."

If my head didn't hurt, I would have laughed. My dreams were the opposite of peaceful. I wanted to tell Liam he should have woken me up from the dreadful nightmare where an unnaturally oversized baby with a bowling ball–sized head wouldn't stop crying. The dream continued when a large group of people grew impatient, waiting for me to quiet the baby's cries, but I couldn't stop the screaming. I just stood there, frozen, unable to move a muscle.

"Oh. I guess I was just tired," I said. "Did you have fun? I'm glad your friends brought you back to me in one piece."

"I did have fun, but it would have been more fun with you out there with us."

"I'm not gonna lie, but I worried your friends would take you on a black diamond trail just to mess with you."

"Nah, they know better. Kyle knows I can't risk getting hurt and missing basketball season."

"Right." I bit my lip. *Basketball.* Would Liam be able to continue his beloved sport if we kept the baby? What about college?

"Speaking of basketball," Liam said, "while Kyle and I were up on the lift, he said he heard some good news. His dad is friends with one of the coaches from Seattle Pacific, and they mentioned my name last week. It sounds like there is a strong possibility they will be asking me to join their team. Can you believe that? It's finally happening."

Guilt consumed me, and I swallowed the lump inching its way to the top of my throat. "Really? SPU, huh?"

"Yeah. The university is a division two. Depending on how well I do, there could be a change to an even bigger college, like a D1 school. Wouldn't that be fricken awesome, Sam? My dreams are happening! And the best part is, I would be close to home. To see you on the weekends."

"You know what?" I said, sitting up all too quickly. "That would be awesome, but I think I might be sick again."

"Oh!"

Liam quickly helped me stand, and I patted his hand away. "No. I can do it."

I walked down the hall alone, towards the shared bathrooms, and locked myself inside one of the stalls. Sitting heavily down on top of the toilet lid, I threw my head into my hands and cried softly. I could NOT be with child and ruin Liam's chances of achieving a future in basketball. It was one thing to destroy *my* future, which I was so good at, but not Liam's. He would be devastated. Shattered. Broken. I couldn't destroy everything he had worked so hard at achieving.

I grabbed a tissue and blew my nose before someone called, "Sam? Are you in here?"

It was only Emily. "Yes, I'm here."

I spied Emily's feet under my stall and noticed she was no longer in her ski boots. She now wore soft pink slippers with a kitten's face embroidered on them, the kind Heidi got us both for Christmas. "Are you throwing up again?" she asked.

"No," I said, blowing my nose again.

"Are you crying?"

"Maybe."

"*Oh, Sammy.* Let me in."

I unlatched the door and looked up at her when she stepped inside. "I just can't be, Em. I can't! It will ruin everything if it is true. And my gut tells me it's true. My boobs hurt."

Emily entered the stall and grabbed more tissue. She handed me a long strip. "Here."

"Thanks."

"You know, you could be wrong."

"Nope. Not with the shitty year I've had. Someone from the outside might say, 'Oh, that girl has the worst luck,' but the truth is, I bring all the bad upon myself. I'm the culprit. I'm my worst enemy. Me. Numero uno."

"Stop."

"Maybe some of us are just born flawed, you know? Maybe I should seek some mental help."

Emily crouched low, meeting my eyes as she held my hands. "Your DNA is perfectly made. Unless you have murderous tendencies, you don't need psychiatric help. Sure, you might have made some mistakes, like everyone makes occasionally, but you are not born flawed."

"I just wanna go home and take the test. And I want my mom." I cried even harder, thinking of my mother. "See? How pathetic am I, Emily? I can't have a baby and still want my mother."

"Sam, you are not pathetic. So, stop this nonsense talk. And I would want my mother too if I was in this situation."

I looked down at my hands and shook my head in disbelief. "Women aren't supposed to have babies until they've aged at least a little, and my hands don't even have any wrinkles yet. I'm too young for this. Look," I said, throwing my hands up for her to see.

She grabbed my hands and squeezed them. "I'm not a nurse yet, Sam, but I know wrinkles and babies are not a thing."

"Fine, but I've never wished more than anything that this was just some bad dream. I want to wake up like it was yesterday, when my life was all mine." I stood and wiped my eyes with the tail of my shirt. "I need to get my crap together and come to get food with you all. I have to pretend nothing's wrong."

Emily backed out of the stall to let me pass, and once at the sink, I gripped its sides. "Look at me. I'm a wreck and don't even know if it's true yet. You're right. I'm totally overreacting." I turned the cold water on. "I just need to calm down and wash this ugly-cry face off me first, and then I'll feel better." I splashed myself and tried to control the hiccups as the water's chill slapped my face.

"Now, doesn't that feel better?" she said.

"Yes."

Emily handed me a paper towel to dry off. "Here, you're going to be just fine. It will be *fine*. Just breathe."

I repeated her words: "Yes, everything will be *fine*."

"What's going to be fine?" I heard Heidi ask from the doorway.

Emily looked at me, and I hurried to the rescue. "I was saying how ... how that maybe I will hopefully feel better tomorrow." I let out a nervous laugh. "Yeah. I'll be fine tomorrow."

"Exactly. She will be fine," Emily repeated.

"You two are acting weird," Heidi said, giving us an odd look. "You two were talking about something else. I just know it. And Emily's the worst liar. Her eyebrow twitches when she is hiding something. You guys are talking about me and Matt. You're not fine with it, are you, Sam?"

I didn't have the energy to lie. I took a deep breath and allowed the words to spill into the universe. "I think I'm pregnant, and nothing is going to be fine ever again."

"*Ha-ha*. But *really*, what were you two talking about."

I held my hand up to stop her. "We weren't talking about you, I promise."

"Heidi," Emily said softly. "Sam *really* thinks she's pregnant."

"Okay, come on. Now you two are annoying me. Just tell me the truth."

"We are!" Emily and I said in unison.

Heidi looked dumbfounded. "What the flack? How? You said you and Liam don't have sex. You're supposed to be the born-again virgin, remember?"

I shrugged. "Well, I guess we are sinners. Are you happy now?"

The look on Heidi's face said she still didn't believe me, but after ten seconds, as she saw the red rims on my eyes, her shoulders sagged. "Oh, *shit*."

After filling Heidi in and answering her endless questions, mostly about our sexual encounter, I also informed her that Liam knew nothing and that it would stay that way until I knew for sure.

"*Wow*," is all she could say.

"Look, we can't talk and stay in this bathroom any longer. Liam will worry and come search me out."

"You're right; we better leave," Emily said. "Let's go and see what everybody else is up to."

"Wait." I grabbed both of their arms before we headed out. "So, again, to verify, we all agree to pretend none of this information exists?"

Emily nodded. "Agree."

Heidi stood quiet, and I barked, "Heidi?"

"Sorry, yes, I agree." She shook her head. "It's just ... a baby, Sam? *Wow*. Just *WOW*."

"Wow, she is all she says?" I said, looking at Emily. "I never knew what could make her speechless. I guess we know now."

When we exited the bathroom arm in arm, I could breathe better knowing my girls were by my side. However, I was still a little worried that Heidi couldn't keep a secret. She was often unpredictable—a loose cannon, a bomb with a faulty detonator. My relief came as soon as Matt came into her line of view. Either she was an excellent actor, or the news I had just shared in the bathroom was not of epic proportions when compared to her newest love interest. So, when the remainder of the evening passed uneventfully, I was thankful that Heidi was able to keep her mouth shut.

After we all decided to order in, I sat in my bunk and picked at my food while watching everyone around me making jokes and having fun. What they were all talking about, I didn't know, not when my thoughts were entirely elsewhere. In a way, I already began to envy them and how they easily lived carefree while my entire life was hanging at the edge of a cliff. So, when I shut my eyes to sleep that night without really knowing or believing in heaven or hell, or if God even existed, I prayed to anyone who would listen; prayed they'd save me from falling. I was lucky enough that whoever had been watching over me lately had saved me from all my worst-case scenarios. Whoever was still watching me, I considered, maybe they could do me this one more immense favor.

But I had a feeling, a feeling deep within my gut, that I'd end up like Alice. Because, faith or no faith, some prayers in the most profound, life-altering moments in a person's life go unanswered.

Chapter 35

Sam 2006

The next day, I didn't feel sick at all. I even wondered if maybe I was wrong about being pregnant. I dressed in all my gear and told everyone I was ready to join him on the slopes.

Emily pulled me aside, and Heidi followed her. "You sure you want to ski? What if you fall? It could be bad for the ... you know ... the baby?"

Heidi snorted. "Emily, you're so overdramatic. The baby is literally the size of a pea right now."

"Technically, it's the size of a grain of rice, Heidi," Emily snapped back, "but still, she should be careful."

"Well, if something happens to it, then maybe it was meant to be." Heidi looked at me sideways. "Sam, don't listen to her. Go have fun today, and don't worry."

Emily's eyes shrank to two small slits. "How can you be so callous, Heidi? She is carrying a human life."

I quickly patted Emily's hand before she grew two heads. "I might not be preggo, and I'll be fine. But thank you for caring so much, Em."

When Heidi was out of earshot, Emily grumbled, "I swear she is missing a sensitivity button."

"It's fine. I'll be careful skiing, just for you."

We went outside for the first time that day, and everyone began to whoop and holler at the scene before us. Three inches of freshly fallen snow had blessed the grounds overnight, making the conditions perfect for skiing. As my friends talked about no more icy trails and all the new fresh powder, I couldn't help but think about what Emily said and wondered if there was any truth to the possibility of an injury affecting my unwanted predicament.

Part of me almost hoped for a so-called accidental fall, while the other part wondered if I was sick in the head to hope for such a thing. Either way, I was a mess, and I couldn't wait for the day to end. It was hard to pretend normalcy when I was screaming inside.

There was no fall, but I couldn't have been happier when we boarded the bus at 5:00 p.m. I was prepared this time for the carsickness and bought limes with a large cup of ice chips before we boarded. I chewed on that ice and sucked on those limes for hours until my lips were peeling raw, but it worked and helped tremendously. I just needed to get home as soon as possible.

Home, as in I needed my mother.

It was 7:00 p.m. by the time we arrived at Liam's. After I put away my luggage, I grabbed my keys and faced him. "Hey, babe. I know it's late, but I wanted to say a quick hello to my mom. It's been forever since I've seen her. And because she works tomorrow, I thought I'd catch her before she heads to bed."

"You want me to come with you, or do you want some mommy-and-me time?"

"Um ... mommy-and-me time?"

"Okay. Then I'll see you later. Tell her hello for me."

"I will."

Liam walked me to the car and kissed me. "I'll keep your side of the bed warm for you. Just wake me if I'm sleeping, because I don't know how long I can keep my eyes open."

As I drove to my parents' house, I dialed my mother's cellphone instead of the house phone. She was the only person on earth I wanted at this very moment. It was just like whenever I was sick. As much as I loved Liam, I still wanted my mother over anyone else when I felt sick. Call it a mother's instinct or intuition, but she always knew how to make me feel better. When she picked up, I tried to sound calm. "Hi, Mom."

"You guys back?"

"Yeah."

"How was your ski trip?"

Just the sound of my mother's voice brought on a child-like ache for her to comfort me. I wasn't little anymore, but I still needed her to hold me. "It was fine. But, Mom?"

"Yes?"

"I need your help," I choked out.

"Help with what?"

I scrunched my face into a tight ball, barely seeing the road before me. "I think I could be pregnant."

There was silence on the other end before I could sense her panic set in. My mother tried to keep her voice even but failed. It came out sounding like a canary. "Okay. *Um* ... all right. It's okay. When did ... I mean, do you know for sure?"

"That's the thing. I don't know. But I think so. I just have this weird feeling."

There was more silence on the other end until my mother finally said, "So you have *not* taken a test?"

"No. I'm driving over to see you right now. I was nervous about taking the test by myself. Can you help me?"

"Yes, of course. *Of course.* I'm here for you. I am right here for you. How far away are you, and do you have the test with you?"

"I'm driving now. I'll be there in fifteen. And, no, I didn't buy a test. I kinda hoped you'd do it for me."

"Okay, listen. I will quickly run to Walgreens to grab you a test. I should be right back."

"Okay."

As I neared our house, I hesitated before pulling into the driveway. I didn't want my father to see me, nor did I want to have to explain why I was there. So, instead, I parked my car across the street and down near the stop sign, where, back in high school, I had always met Heidi and Emily when I was sneaking out. While I waited until my mother came, I couldn't help but wish for the time when my friends and I were young and carefree again and still sneaking out to parties. It is funny how I thought getting caught would have been the end of me back then, when in actuality, birthing another human being would be the true end of all ends.

I watched my mother drive in from the opposite direction and pull into our driveway. I got out of my car and closed the door behind me.

"Sam?" she said, squinting in the dark. "Is that you?"

"Yeah. It's me," I called out.

She met me halfway and embraced me with a ferocious hug. "Hi, Mommy," I barely said as she squeezed all the air out of me.

"Hey there, sweetheart." She pulled back and took hold of my shoulders before piercing my soul with her eyes. "Look at me. Either way, it's gonna be okay."

I didn't expect less from my mother. She had more than once found herself in the same predicament, but sadly, at a much younger age than I was now. She would never be the one to judge. She was like Alice in so many ways, with their selfless love.

"Mom, I don't want to see anyone inside yet. Could you let me in through the back door? We can take the test in your back bathroom?"

"Sure. Sounds like a good idea. Your father is glued to the TV in the living room, and your sister isn't home. She's at a friend's for the weekend, so you're safe from any social contact tonight."

"Good."

I walked to the back of the house and waited for her to let me in. She opened the back door and smuggled me inside toward the bathroom before locking the door behind us. I watched her unpack the scary contents from the plastic bag and onto the counter, along with a Snickers bar and a packet of gum. "I'll pay you back," I said.

"Nonsense."

When she picked up the pregnancy test, I felt a fleeting flutter in my heart. "*Oh, man*. Do you feel the room tilting?"

My mother stopped unpacking the box and gently placed it on the counter. "Now listen to me," she said, facing me. "Whatever the answer, positive or negative, I'm here for you. We will figure this out together. Won't we, Sammy girl?"

When I didn't answer her, she continued. "Sam, accidents happen, and I'm not here to reprimand you for not being more careful. Lord knows I've been here a time or two. Once with your older sister, whom I had to give up for adoption at age fifteen, and the other time when I found out I was pregnant with you, at nineteen. Your younger sister was the only one we planned. But, like all those other unplanned times, it wasn't the end of the world, and it isn't over for you now, either. Everything's going to be fine. I'm here, and like I said, we will figure this out together. Won't we?"

My heart swelled at the intensity of her words. I couldn't have felt any prouder to call the woman before me *mother*. There was indeed no one like her. I replayed her words in my mind like a soft bedtime melody and wiped the corners of my eyes. "You're right," I said, "whatever the test says, it's not the end of the world."

"That's right. We got this."

"Thank you, Mom. For ... for just being here with me."

She squeezed my hand. "I always want you to feel like you can come to me for anything. No matter what. Now, shall we proceed?"

I nodded.

She opened the box and read the directions out loud. "Okay, sounds easy enough?"

"Yep," I said.

I sat on the toilet, and she handed me the stick. After I followed the directions, I returned the test to her. "Here. Now what?"

She gently placed the stick on the counter, hanging slightly over the side of the sink. "Now we wait two minutes." She smiled.

"The longest two minutes of my life." I laughed, on the verge of hysteria.

She gave me a sympathetic smile.

"Mom? What will I do if it says positive?"

"Well, I suppose you can move back home with us, and even though I work during the day, I'll be home in the evenings to help you. Raising a baby isn't easy, but you're perfectly capable. Heck, if you wanted to, you could get an evening job, and your father and I can help while you work just a few nights a week or even on the weekends."

"I guess. But what about Liam? Would he live here, too?"

"I suppose while Liam finishes college, you both could live here until you eventually have your own apartment or a little rental. It's not impossible and not the worst thing to happen. But by any means, your circumstance is not ideal. This isn't what we wanted for you kids. Your father and I always hoped you would be smarter and wouldn't follow in our footsteps. But even though I was nineteen, too young, when I had you, it all worked out. You're two years older and already way more mature than I was then."

"I wouldn't be so sure about that," I said, rolling my eyes. "I've done some stupid things lately." I nodded toward the stick. "Is it time yet?"

She picked up the stick without looking. "Here, you take a look first."

"No. *Please*, just go ahead and tell me."

It felt like my mother was holding a crystal ball in her hand and was about to tell me my future. While I waited for her to decipher what she saw, I held my breath, praying for a miracle of happily-ever-afters. But she let out an unexpected squeal of excitement, confusing me. "Looks like we're having a baby!"

My eyes went wide as she jumped up and down and hugged me. I stood frozen, arms to my sides, and mumbled listlessly, "Why are you so excited? How is my mistake good news? Once again, I've ruined everything."

"*Honey*. First of all, mistakes do not define a person. What you do after a mistake is made and how you move forward to better yourself is what defines us. You may not realize this now, but this baby *will* be a beautiful blessing in our lives, so you should always remember this as a happy occasion, not a sad one. The first two times I found out I was pregnant, not one single person offered me a word of encouragement or a show of excitement. My broken family just showed their utter disappointment in me, while my boyfriend all but forgot who I was the moment he heard the news. Those are not the sad memories a mother should hold onto forever. But with me jumping for joy, knowing I will be a grandmother, well, this is the memory I want you to have."

I let out a sniffle and wiped my eyes again.

"Oh, Sam, don't cry. This is good news! Everything always has a way of working itself out."

"Oddly, I'm not crying because of the news. I think I might actually be okay. And maybe I'm just numb about it all right now, but I'm mostly crying because you are the best mother in the whole gosh-darn world." I hugged my mother tightly. "I just hope one day I can measure up."

"Sammy. You will. You will be an absolutely wonderful mother."

"How do you know for certain?"

My mother took my head in her hands and pressed her forehead to mine. "A mother knows these things. Trust me."

Chapter 36

Sam 2006

It was late when I left my parents', and Liam was asleep when I returned. I would have to tell him the following day that our lives were about to change. As I climbed into bed without waking him, I knew I couldn't sleep. I kept thinking of how exactly I'd break the news to him. Was there a way to deliver the news to lessen the blow? Like how my mother did with me? Maybe I should make a banner or find a baby picture of him and give it to him? Perhaps I'd wrap the EPT test like a present? I thought about writing a letter, packing my bags, and heading out of town to live a secret life, but I knew this was the coward's way out. I was past running away from my problems like I did back in high school. There was no more running for me.

Somewhere between my thoughts about how to break the news, I fell asleep. I woke to find Liam at the end of the bed, dressing. "Hey."

"Hey, yourself."

"Where are you going?" I asked.

"Sorry. I tried not to wake you. I have class. It's Monday, remember?"

"Oh, yeah."

"Some of us still have priorities," Liam joked, squeezing my toe underneath the thick blankets.

Priorities, I thought to myself. I still had to tell Liam we had a new list of priorities.

I stared out the window, watching the sky shift from blue to grey. "Liam, is there any way you could skip today's classes?"

Liam sat down on the edge of the bed and moved a few messy curls away from my eyes. "I don't necessarily have anything I'd miss out on, but why do you want me to skip?"

"I just want some alone time with you. We didn't get that on the ski trip."

He looked down at his watch. "Well, I guess I could skip just this one day. I'm super tired anyway."

He removed his layers of clothing and climbed back into bed with me. I curled up next to him, spooning him to stay warm. I knew I was stalling, but I also wanted some normalcy, just this one last time before our lives would forever change. As Liam sighed in what sounded like contentment and fell back asleep, I could only lie there, feeling like a helium balloon full of anxiety. It didn't help that there was a lingering, familiar nausea, letting me know there were three of us in that bed.

I imagined a make-believe world where we were already married, in a little house of our own, and as I gave him the news, he would pick me up and throw me around—so thrilled with our discovery. Of course, I knew the odds of him having a fairytale reaction were far-fetched, but it was a lovely dream to have.

When Liam's eyes fluttered open an hour later, I cringed, knowing I sounded overly chirpy, like a puppy waiting for his owner to finally offer her some attention. "Hey, good morning!" I figured if he saw *me* in good spirits, then maybe he, too, would follow suit. I tousled the top of his matted hair and kissed his nose. "I love you. You know that?"

He laughed, "You're in a good mood this morning."

He gave me little kisses all over my face and asked, "So, what do you want to do today? Do you want to go to the theater or watch a movie? Or we could just stay here and play some cards and hang out?"

Ignoring his question, I asked, "Do you ever think about having kids?"

He gave me an odd expression. "Sure. We've talked about it before. If I could choose, I'd want two boys and maybe a girl someday. I love kids."

"When did you know you liked kids?"

"Maybe when I started coaching little league basketball. It was something the school made our basketball team take part in, and I loved that."

"What about babies?"

He laughed. "I suppose I'd like babies, although I've not been around any since my cousin had his daughter, back when I was twelve." He shook his head. "What's with all the questions? Are we babysitting someone's kid today or something?"

I knew I needed to spit the words out before I exploded. "Well, would it be so horrible if we had a baby of our own, soon?"

"A baby? *Soon*? Hell no. That would be terrible. I have to finish school first, then work for my father for a year or two before we get married, and then we could talk about the kids. But in that order. Seriously, that's a silly question to ask me. Did you hit your head on the ice or something?"

What did I expect? He was right, but his comment hurt nonetheless.

When I remained quiet for too long, Liam sat up in bed and asked, "Sam? What's up with the questions? You're acting weird."

My fingers traced his arm hairs playfully, as if I weren't about to plant a landmine. "Well, I don't know any other way to say this, but well, I ... I mean, *we* are having one." Liam sat motionless, saying nothing while his face looked perplexed. "Liam," I said, clearing my throat and sitting up to meet his wide eyes. "Don't freak, but I'm asking these questions because, well, we are pregnant, Liam. Or technically, *I* am pregnant."

Liam laughed nervously. "Yeah, right."

"I'm ... I'm not joking. I am really pregnant. I took a test last night at my parents' house. It explains why I was so sick on our ski trip. I had a weird feeling about it but kept it to myself until I knew for sure. I *now* know for certain." I took the positive test from under my pillow, placed it on his lap, and winced. "Congratulations?"

Liam picked it up and stared at it in dazed disbelief for the longest time. When the color slowly drained from his face and his hand holding the stick visibly shook, he finally dropped his head into his hands.

Alarmed at the sudden way he reacted, I touched his shoulder. "Liam, I—" Liam had always been the strong one, always there for me. He was always the sensible one. So, to see him react like a helpless, cornered, frightened animal scared me. "I'm sorry. It's not what I hoped for us, either."

"How?" he asked without looking up.

"How? Like how this could happen with one go? I know. I was in shock, too, when I found out. I thought we were careful enough." I rested my head timidly on his shoulder. "Please say something."

"What are you going to do, Sam?"

I repeated his question in my head. *What are* you *going to do?* Feeling a larger-than-life lump in my throat, I tried to swallow the rock down. He was not reacting positively like my mother did. And what did he mean by, what was *I* going to do? I needed to hear him say the words I so desperately needed from him, like: What are *we* going to do? I mean, we were in this together, were we not? I bit the inside of my cheek. "I don't know what you mean; what will *I* do?"

"Do you ... do you want to keep it?"

I barely registered those words until a sick feeling crept into my bones. His question came with a tone that pierced my soul. "Liam, I can't *undo* this. Do you actually mean I should ... "

He still could not meet my eyes. "So, you do want to keep it, then?" Again, the way he said the last sentence, it seemed to come from someone ready to jump off a cliff. With shoulders slumped, Liam suddenly stood and walked to the bedroom door. He didn't even look back at me when he said, "I ... I'm sorry. I need a moment to myself. I can't do whatever this is right now."

The landmine had been detonated, but it was me left in pieces.

After Liam walked out the door, and as I sat there utterly flayed open, bare, and alone, exhaustion set in. I wanted to sleep for weeks, if not for eternity.

For me, born into a family, who mostly communicated by yelling, Liam's silent exit felt worse than all the screaming I had ever endured.

The silence was deafening.

But the silence didn't stop me from filling the empty space with the words I thought he really wanted to say to me: *What about me finishing school, Sam? What about my basketball dreams? My parents will hate me. They can't find out, Sam! How can we support a baby? I'm freakin' too young for this, Sam! I don't even have a job, and you've quit yours. People will look at us forever as a pair of losers. My life will be over! We can't do this. Don't do this to me. If you love me, don't do this to us.*

The truth was simple. If I didn't want this baby without Liam's full support, and if I couldn't have him as my rock to see this through, I couldn't do it alone. Sure, Liam didn't say it in exact words, but I knew what he wanted me to do, and it cut me to the core. But could I do such a thing and get rid of it? Or would it be worse if people looked down on us for destroying our futures? Would Liam's parents disown him or hate me? Would Liam resent me? Or could I do it alone? Could I have this baby in secret and give it up for adoption?

The answer to my last question came too quickly. No, I could not go through what Alice or my mother went through—having a child, giving it to someone else, and then forever knowing that my child was out there in the world, wondering why they weren't wanted. At the same time, all this stress over a tiny dot of nothing inside me made me wonder. Maybe Heidi was right; perhaps the thing inside me was only the size of a pea or a grain of rice or even something smaller—like a speck of dust, a substance lost without purpose in space and time, and none of it really mattered at all.

And what would be the difference between that and a tiny bug crawling across the floor, that we kill without thinking? We couldn't just let these little things wreak havoc in our lives. So, what was holding me back, and why was I hesitating to save Liam and me from dreadful consequences that would follow us for the rest of our lives?

My thoughts ran wild as I sat there alone for what seemed like decades.

Who would judge me if I went through with ending things? Maybe my mother? But she would never actually *really* judge me; mothers loved unconditionally. Sure, she would be highly disappointed, but she would never disown me. So, who did that leave? My friends? They couldn't possibly hold it against me.

Was I worried about not going to heaven?

Did hell even exist?

What if there wasn't even such a place, and we were freaking out over nothing?

Was I honestly expected to have some kind of blind faith without questioning it?

Believing something greater existed is one thing, but if there was something greater than us that loved us unconditionally, we wouldn't be judged solely on our mistakes, right?

While Liam continued to leave me thinking the worst, the weight of it all bore down on me. Exhausted, confused, out of place, lost, and feeling completely alone, I numbly put on my shoes, threw on a coat, and grabbed my keys. I didn't know where I was going, but Liam wasn't the only one who could leave.

Besides, thanks to my never-ending mistakes, maybe everyone was better off without me.

Feeling utterly hollow, I drove around town aimlessly for an hour. As tiny morning snowflakes misted my windshield, I wondered if they were heaven's tears—frozen in shock from my thoughts about throwing it all away. But it didn't matter. I felt nothing for it or myself. I couldn't even cry or even be mad that Liam wanted us to take the easy way out.

Could I even blame him?

However, it didn't stop me from feeling let down, disappointed, and rejected by the man I loved. I couldn't believe it. Liam wasn't who I thought he was. In a sense, he was just like Alice's Frank. Hell, I didn't know who I was either, and knowing that I had been willing to do anything for Liam only made me hate myself more. I wanted to be a strong woman who thought rationally, but at that moment, I couldn't seem to find this courageous girl.

Like a cord snapping when stretched to its limit, I felt my old self emerging—lost and spinning out of control again. I wanted to disappear forever, somewhere where expectations, responsibilities, guilt, disappointment, and hurt no longer existed. With my mind in a dark chasm, I drove my car carelessly around an outer curve on a steeply inclined ridge road. My wheels came close to the edge, and the gravel pulled me in. It was as if the deep dropoff on the side of the road was calling to me, beckoning me closer.

It called me to end it all.

In a frail state of mind, I turned the wheel slightly toward the edge to see the canvas of trees below more clearly.

How pretty the trees are from way up here, all covered in white.

How lovely would it be just to swerve and let go?

Such an easy way to go out.

As I peered down through the window, I worried the hill was not quite steep enough to guarantee me the peace I strived for, so I drove farther up the hill to gauge the best spot that would promise an easy end to it all. But when a perfect spot on top of the hill finally came into view, so did a familiar house on its right corner. A rueful laugh escaped me when I noticed I happened to be aimlessly driving in Alice's neighborhood. I pictured it then: the sick thought of Alice finding out that I had killed myself in her neighborhood, just a few houses from hers, and it seemed terribly cruel to do such a selfish thing to her.

I quickly snapped out of my morbid thoughts, and instead, my wheels miraculously carried me straight to her driveway. I shut the engine off after parking and stared at her front door for a long time. I don't know how long I sat in the car or why I was there, but I finally forced myself to get out and enter the house. Shutting the entry door behind me, I called out Alice's name. She wasn't in the living room, though the TV was on, so I called out again, more loudly, then realized it was pointless.

I wandered around the house looking for her. When she wasn't in the kitchen, I tried her bedroom next but found that empty, too, and her bed unmade. I wondered where she could have gone, since it was only a little after ten in the morning, though she'd always been an early bird, sometimes waking up as early as five. I wondered if someone had picked her up or taken her to run errands. But why did she leave the TV on? Maybe Alice's family was with her at the hospital. But why would they leave the front door unlocked?

With my mind already in a dark place, I panicked and envisioned something terrible. Just my luck—as with Jane, when I needed someone the most, they always left me. I had grown to love Alice as much as I had Jane, and I couldn't lose her too. When I was just about ready to give up, I heard a toilet flush coming from the guest bathroom. Relief flooded me.

It only now made sense why I had mindlessly driven to Alice's. The clarity and wisdom I needed were something only she could provide. So I sat on the couch and waited patiently. When Alice finally entered the living room, using the cane I bought her for support, she almost didn't see me there until I waved hello.

"*Ah!*" Alice cried out while holding her hand to her chest. She laughed then. "You gave me a fright, girl."

"Yeah, it seems I've been doing that a lot to people lately," I said.

Alice sensed my mood and frowned. "Now, if that isn't the saddest face I ever saw." She still wore her morning clothes, a long yellow cotton nightgown with a ruffled scoop at the neck and sleeves, like something characters wore in *Little House on the Prairie*. Her heels came out an inch from a pair of grey foam slide slippers, and I made a mental note to buy her a new pair that actually fit. She shuffled over to me and slowly swiveled her body to sit beside mine. "Something must be wrong," she said. "For one, I have never seen you this early in the morning, and two, you look like a lost soul."

I shrugged, not wanting to tell Alice just yet. Plus, the ball in my throat made it unbearable to speak.

When a tear finally escaped, Alice frowned, nodded, and patted my hand. "*Life, life, life*; it gets to us sometimes, doesn't it?" I nodded a silent yes, and when I still didn't divulge my pain, she continued, "When I feel lost sometimes, I try to remember how God wants me to lay my burdens at His feet. It's His way of saying my troubles are also His, and we are wearing these shoes together."

Alice was always quick to insert her beliefs into our conversations. It was what made Alice *Alice*. Like the fast-beating wings of a hummingbird, her faith beat its own unwavering rhythm, and nothing could stop her from speaking what was in her heart. Of course, I never minded her talks and had grown to expect her religious bouts, but at that moment, I didn't want to hear about God or religion. I wanted to believe whoever created us didn't actually exist. I wanted to feel the absence of guilt, with nothing to weigh me down, when I erased the growing mistake inside me.

I couldn't help myself and asked, "What if God doesn't exist? How do you know He isn't just a made-up folktale, a story told since the beginning of time? I mean, if you read the Bible, it doesn't seem to favor or even like us women very much. Really, I think it was written by men and only men," I said bitterly.

Alice tilted her head, giving me a sympathetic look. She tapped her hearing aid. "Did I hear correctly, or is this thing broken again?"

"Yes," I said. I spoke much louder, almost yelling, "What if there isn't even a God, and we are all freaking out over nothing?"

Alice was quiet for a moment, looking out her living room window, watching the snowfall. For a second, I thought she was mad that I had questioned her God's existence. Surely, she understood why it was so hard for people to believe or trust with this so-called 'blind' faith. Or maybe, if I was being honest with myself, it was that I wanted to be blind, without faith, for only a little while. I crossed my arms defiantly like a child, waiting to see how Alice would respond.

"I've been at that very question once. Heck, more than a few times," Alice said. "I've wondered the same thing myself; does God exist? So, you are not alone in asking that question. It's a question meant not for solitude but for solidarity. We all ask the same questions, but it's only after we share our ideas with each other that we find our beliefs coming together and taking shape. And since you asked, I can only share with you my own personal experience.

"Of course, everyone knows that, for as long as people have existed on Earth, the number one question is: Why are we here, and what or who brought us into existence? Sure, the Bible was written by man, hopefully with guidance from above, but because all people are sinful, the Bible may have its inconsistencies. I get that. So, how can we trust what's been written or believe what has been passed along to us for as far back as thousands of years? How can we know what the real truths are?"

Alice clearly knew my mind, and I nodded in agreement. "Exactly. It's the uncertainty that makes it so hard to believe."

"We will never know all the truth, but ..." She looked at me and asked, "Do you remember me telling you about the time when I was at one of my lowest moments? When I was pregnant with my youngest, and I felt completely abandoned, exhausted, and full of despair?"

Alice hit too close to home for my liking. "Yes, I remember," I said, my voice barely audible.

"And do you remember I said a presence came to me that very evening by tapping my shoulder repeatedly?"

"Yes."

"You are right; maybe it wasn't something holy, but whatever that unique presence was, *for me*, it felt holy—something greater—something bigger than you and I. There is no other way to explain how, after that experience, I did not feel alone anymore. A peace came over me like no other. And the image I saw the next morning, the image of my father's white Bible that I had seen a hundred times growing up, I saw it in my mind clear as day. So, I knew I was supposed to find a Bible, for a reason. Because, let's face it, I was without hope and lost in my life."

"I can relate," I said, but Alice didn't hear me.

Alice laughed. "I read my Bible from front to back, and sure, there were things in there that didn't make any sense, and some completely outdated or unrelated to our times, but there was one message repeated constantly, which brought with it the purpose and hope we all need—one word I kept hearing over and over, time and time again. Do you know what that one word is?"

Not having ever really read the Bible, I guessed, "Forgiveness?"

"No. It's the word mentioned more than any other in the Bible."

"Thou shall not kill?" I asked, with a small stitch in my heart.

"*Love*." Alice smoothed out her floral nightgown and folded her hands in her lap, entirely at peace with her words. "I'd like to believe the basis of my faith, with who we are, what we are, and why we are here on this Earth, all relates to *love*. Why are we here? It's to love others, Sam. And why were we given a life full of choices and experiences? It's because we are learning the meaning of love. And guess what? We all have free will and the choice to choose what we do with our love. That is all that really matters. It's that simple."

"Then why can't we hear or see this God that loves us so much?"

"I can't explain it, Sam, but I know because I *feel* this kind of love deep inside my soul. Sure, I can't see love physically or touch it, but I sure can feel it there," she said, tapping one wrinkled finger over the yellow gown above her heart. "You just have to trust it, and you have to want it. That's the beauty, though; it will always be our choice as to how and who we choose to love. Love cannot be forced."

"You make it sound so easy, Alice."

She laughed. "It is easy, and yet it isn't, mostly because I think we are creatures of habit who must see something before we believe it is there."

Like this child I carry? I wanted to say. I couldn't see it; hence, I pretended it wasn't worth loving or keeping. To me, it was as insignificant as a pebble in the sea. I shook my head, fighting her words. "I don't know."

"Sam. Look at me. I can tell you are struggling with something in your heart. Just know that whatever it is, there's nothing that love can't handle. You have to have faith and hope that there *is* something bigger out there. As long as you have that confidence, you can overcome anything. Only then will you find the peace you seek. This old bird knows this from experience. Trust me."

I looked away from Alice so she couldn't see me wipe a tear. "It's just hard to believe it's real," I said, referring to both God and the life growing inside me.

"Sam. Tell me this. Have you ever, in all the time you have known me, believed me to be a liar?"

"No."

"Exactly. Anyhow, at the end of the day, I'd rather not press my luck by not believing in this unseen faith or thinking that this kind of love doesn't exist. Instead, I'd rather take the chance that I am right about it being true. What do you have to lose by choosing to believe? Personally, I believe you have more to lose without faith."

I whispered under my breath, "By choosing faith, I'd lose everything."

Liam.

I knew I could lose Liam if I had this baby.

Alice's statement made me question everything about myself, about my future. If I were to go through with not having this baby, I wondered if I could ever forgive myself or even love myself afterward. I wouldn't judge anyone for whatever choices they made for themselves; after all, it was their body, their choice, but as for myself, Alice was right about one thing: what was I without love? This question made me think of all the women who had brought a child into this world. My mother came to mind, and I doubted very much that she regretted having me.

"Alice?"

"Yes, child?"

"Do you remember when you gave up your first child?"

"How can I not? I think about her all the time. I'll never stop regretting that choice."

"So, if you could do it all over again, would you have chosen the baby over your husband?"

Alice didn't even blink. "In a heartbeat. No question about it. A woman's love for a man simply cannot compare to a mother's love for a child." Alice sighed. "Unfortunately, I didn't know that kind of wisdom until it was already too late. So, if I could go back and I had the faith that I have now, I'd be strong enough to stand my ground and tell that husband of mine to go shove it where the sun doesn't shine, if you know what I mean."

I laughed and cried in one big hiccup. "I know what you mean."

Alice wagged her finger at me. "Now, my child, you have *yet* to tell me why you are so upset, and you don't need to tell me, but I could bet my pinky toe this is about a boy and not so much about who, what, and why we were created?"

I shook my head, yes. It was mostly true.

Alice clucked her tongue once, sucking the air between her teeth. "*Men*. They are often the root of our sorrows. A woman will one day find that even without a man, she has an incredible amount of strength and fearlessness the minute she decides her worth. So, if there were ever any advice I could pass along, it's that *we*, as women, are in control of our destinies, and *you* are stronger than you think, especially if you have so many women who rally beside you and love you. *I* love you."

"I love you too, Alice," I said, wiping my tears.

"Now, give me a great big hug, because I think you need one." For an old bird, Alice's hug was stronger than a lumberjack's. "Yep," she said before singing with a voice that moved high and low, "Love is the glue that binds us all. Love is what makes the world go round and round and round. Love is what makes the world go round."

It's funny how people are placed in one's life at the right time. Whether it was coincidence or by grace, I thought about that as Alice's words of love sang their way to me, a melody that soothed and filled the holes of doubt in my heart. And I thought about my other relationships with all the women in my life: my mother, who had showed me what unconditional love was; my sister Stephanie, who, as much as we fought, secretly loved me; my newly found half-sister, Tina, a lost puzzle piece that I knew we were meant to find again; my bold friend Shelly, who was showing me what strength and endurance looked like; my friends Heidi and Emily, who, despite being polar opposites, each revealed a bit of myself; and especially Alice and Jane, my wisest confidants, my *fidus Achates* sent from another time and place, who paved the way for me to see the world in a different perspective.

As to whether there was a heaven or hell, I still didn't know, and I realized I would never know for certain. But the love I received from all my womanly friends, in some way, in some shared solidarity, was all I ever needed, and that was a kind of faith I could believe in. However, there was one big part of the picture still missing. I needed to boldly stand and begin a new chapter in my life, starting with whom I chose to love in return. And as hard as it was, the choice was simple.

I had to love myself before I could love anyone else unconditionally.

Chapter 37

Sam 2006

The drive back to Liam's not only brought clarity but also an overdose of resentment and anger. Just like Alice and Jane had felt with the false-hearted men in their lives. I resented Liam for lying when he said he would always be *my person*—someone who would never let me fall alone. He had said he would always be there for me, when in fact, it seemed he wanted to bail the minute shit got real. As for the anger? That was towards me alone, for allowing the lies of all the men in my life to make me question my faith in myself and my self-worth as a woman. I was so sick of men making me feel small and worthless.

The liar Randy Jergins, who made me fear being in debt for the rest of my life. My boss, Brad Rapp, who humiliated me and made me feel less than others. The male recruiters in the military who looked at me as just a number. The fifteen-year-old neighbor boy who tried to steal my virtue and innocence at age five. And my father, who, from the start, was unable to be an example or show me what fatherly love looked like.

It seemed not just Liam but *all* the men in my life had left me feeling some sort of injustice. But unlike Jane and Alice's choices in men, I realized that I did not need to fear the worst about myself. I was worthy of love, and I was worth way more than the little breadcrumbs the men in my life left me. The real heart of the problem wasn't that Liam didn't want me to have this baby but that I thought I needed a man to give me the happiness I was seeking.

But I didn't need a man.

Not when only *I* could make *myself* happy.

Besides, I had my mother, sisters, and friends Shelley, Heidi, Emily, and Alice there to support and love me. They truly wanted what was best for me.

And even if I didn't yet know what role I was to meant play in this world, even if it was only to become a mother to a child who needed to be shown what love meant, then hell, that in itself was a kind of faith I could believe in. But I *had* to start believing and having faith in myself before I chose to love anyone else.

As I drove through the thickening shower of white flakes that melted the moment they hit my windshield, I picked up the alder leaf I had found in the treehouse, the one I had placed on the dash of my car to remind me who I was. Liam was right about one thing: my story wasn't over. Not by a long shot. But this time around, I had finally found myself.

I was a confident woman who knew who she was and where she was going.

By the time I reached Liam's house, the rage in me could have fueled a caged grizzly. It was good that Liam's parents were still at work, as I didn't want anyone to hear what I needed to say. I swung open the front door to the family room to find Liam sitting on the couch, waiting for me. He sprang up from the sofa but hesitated to move forward when he saw the serious look on my face. "Sam! Where the hell did you go? I called you like twenty times. I was worried."

When I moved my wet, snow-covered hair away from my eyes, I noticed Liam's face was no longer white as a sheet, but there was a slight pink puffiness around his eyes. Even so, and not ready to be close to him, I moved purposefully across the room and stood opposite the kitchen island. He followed me anyway. "Sam, you just dropped the biggest bomb and left me. I—"

"No, *you* left *me*. You left me when I needed you the most, so I did the same. You got up and left me sitting there, scared by poisonous thoughts that had no place existing in my mind in the first place. You made me doubt everything. You made me doubt myself."

"Sam, about that—"

"Let me finish." His face cringed as if he had just bitten into a sour grape, but I looked away to avoid meeting his eyes. "I get that you are smack in the middle of college, and our little mistake puts your basketball dreams at risk. I am mortified and embarrassed that we are in this situation, too, especially because we're not married. And I am equally embarrassed that neither of us currently holds a job. You can also tally up the embarrassment of neither of us having a degree yet and the fact that I'm living in the basement of my boyfriend's house. So, yes, this totally sucks. I get that. We are in the worst predicament possible."

Liam thought I was done and went to say something, but I put my hand up to stop him. "And yeah, we screwed up, Liam. But I can't dismiss the child we created out of love. I am not taking a chance by questioning what is right or wrong, not when something profound inside me says that our lives and souls are worth something. I have to believe we are here on this Earth for a reason and for a purpose. I can not go through what you wanted me to do. I am so angry you made me even consider it. That alone made me realize something today. I want to be with someone who wants what is best for me, and this morning, you weren't that person."

"But, Sam—"

"I'm letting you know right now that I am *more* than willing to figure this out all on my own. I don't need any man in my life, especially one who is not going to back me up or be the person I need them to be to make this work. I love you, but right now, I have to do what's best for my heart. I don't want to live with regrets or hate you for what you want me to do. And I don't want to stay in a relationship that will only make me hate myself in the end.

"And sure, without relationships, we deprive ourselves of the most important part of being human—experiencing love. But relationships are like a dance, Liam," I said. "Some of us are intuitively good at it, while others, without guidance, will step on toes. But eventually, with a bit of time and practice, hopefully we can meet and dance a beautiful waltz together. So, yeah, I'd rather dance with you than sit it out, but don't get me wrong, I will survive and dance without you, either way."

My heart was beating with pride and fear all at once when I said what came next. I wanted to lift my eyes to meet his, but some internal courage wouldn't let me, so I looked anywhere but at him. "So, I leave it up to you. You can either be a part of this, or we can go our separate ways. And I'm perfectly okay with that decision." The last sentence was a lie, but it needed to be said because I was done with men backing me into corners and making me feel small and worthless. Still, I had to know if he was in or out. As much as he was the beating pulse I wanted to move with, I also knew I'd survive by thrumming to my own song.

"Okay. Are you done speaking?" Liam asked, sounding exasperated.

I finally looked up at him and glared. "Yes, I'm done."

"Good." Liam moved along the island to be closer to me, but I held up my palms to stop him in his tracks. He stood five feet away from me instead. "Fine. I won't any come closer," he said, running his fingers through his wild hair. He let out a shaky breath, "First off, I am so, so, *so* beyond sorry for what I hinted at earlier. And I am sorry for how I acted by getting up and leaving you to sit alone. *Truly*, I am. But in my defense, I panicked. I had a moment of weakness. I don't know how long you've had to mull over this news, but I assume longer than me?"

I didn't answer, so he continued. "Either way, I handled the news terribly. In fact, I don't know if I am more mortified that we are having a baby or how I acted this morning. I was thinking of only myself. I didn't think about what you must have been feeling. I should have stayed sitting beside you, and we could have been sitting scared together. All I can say is I am sorry, and I am especially sorry for suggesting we do anything other than raise this baby together. I'm a shit for putting you through that this morning, and if you give me another chance, I will forever make it up to you. I love you, dammit. But I would understand if you wanted to throw me out the window and never see me again."

The tears welling behind my eyes wanted to escape with relief, but I was still angry and not totally satisfied with his apology. An hour ago, I had nearly contemplated killing myself because I didn't think he cared about me enough. So, his one-minute apology hadn't made a dent yet. Even though I was standing with my arms crossed, Liam bravely closed the gap between us and reached for my fingertips. That made me uncross my arms. His hands shook as he held both my hands in his. "I'll tell my parents. I will. And yes, they will be disappointed, but they'll get over it; they have no choice. As for me finishing college? I'm just not going to."

My back straightened in shock. "Why? Why wouldn't you finish college? I'm the one pregnant, not you. *Your* dreams are still waiting for you."

"What's the point? We both knew I'd eventually work for my father's company. I was only attending college for the opportunity to play basketball and see if it led anywhere, but basketball isn't everything. Basketball isn't a career. Also, I need to provide for us now. I need a job, not a sport."

I was torn that he had to choose at all. Part of me knew he was semi-correct about him needing a job and not a sport, but I also knew his dreams would never come to fruition. "But you love basketball, Liam."

"Yeah, well, I love *you* more. I choose you. I choose *us*," he said. At the last part, he brought our hands together and held them over my flat stomach. The look he gave me conveyed that he was speaking the truth and any doubt I had ever had about his love for me all but vanished.

Still, I looked down at our entwined hands and whispered, "But your dream was to play basketball. That big college is about to offer you a great opportunity."

"Let's be real. It's not like I would ever go pro. Besides, dreams change. My dreams are changing as we speak." I stood in the quietness of his last words and held them close to my heart. Unable to answer, I could only nod in agreement. He brought one of my hands to his lips and kissed my knuckles. "I'm not going to lie. I am super scared," he said. "That part I can't hide from you."

I looked down at the floor and dug my socked foot into the grouted tile. "I know. I'm scared too."

"Then we will be scared together." Liam wiped a fallen tear from my cheek. "You will never have to do anything alone ever again."

"You promise?" I asked, looking up to finally meet his eyes.

"I promise. I will *always* be here for you." Liam pulled me into a tight embrace and, in a taut voice, whispered what I needed to hear into my ear. "I can't live or breathe without you, Samantha Carey. You have to know this. You are *mine*, always and forever. We will figure this out. I don't know how, but we will. The three of us will figure this out together."

Epilogue

"Liam! I can't find her other pink shoe," I yelled from the living room in our new two-bedroom condo. "I swear they purposely mislabel baby shoe sizes so that we have to buy more."

"I'm on it," Liam barked from upstairs. "And I could have told you those shoes were too big for a seven-month-old, but no, you said they *had* to match her dress." I could imagine him rolling his eyes at the last part, and he was right, but I would never admit it. Just like I would never admit to secretly loving the ring he chose to surprise me with.

I had told Liam it was pointless to buy me a ring when I was already knocked up, and spending money on a stupid rock seemed so wasteful when we had a wedding to plan. But that didn't seem to stop him. And it wasn't like I didn't know he would eventually propose to me, since I was indeed knocked up, but that was beside the point. Still, the evening that Liam asked me to marry him was one I would never forget.

"Where are you taking me?" I had asked him when we arrived in downtown Seattle. It was just the beginning of summer and still slightly warm before the sun set to our east behind the Cascade Mountains. I rolled my window down to take in the rainbow colors of the hundreds of rhododendrons that grew in green spaces between the tall building blocks and skyscrapers and breathed in the new smells of the bustling city.

"I'm taking you to dinner at a special place I once took you before," he said, pulling into the valet parking for the Space Needle.

I looked up at the tall, narrow tower with its golden elevators running slowly up and down between its three legs until my eyes reached the flying-saucer crown on top. "You plan on taking me up there and then pushing me over the edge, don't you?"

"You read me so well." He opened my side of the door and helped me out. "Ready?"

My high-heeled black pumps hit the ground. "Are *you* ready?" I asked him with a grin.

He gave me a curious look, suggesting he thought I might have already guessed his surprise, which, of course, I already knew or guessed. How could I not? It wasn't my birthday, and it wasn't our anniversary. I laughed. "Liam. You told me to dress in the nicest dress I had," I said, gazing down at my black baby-doll dress dotted with tiny pink flowers, "and for no reason at all, here we are now at the Space Needle, with the world's *only* rotating glass floor, where dinner is *very* expensive, and we only come here on special occasions. *And* I'm six months pregnant."

He wore all-black attire—a button-up collared shirt, slim-fitting slacks, and shiny laced-up black oxfords. The shirt was tight-fitting around his arms from him hauling tile and flooring for the past few months at his father's shop. His shoulders slumped in defeat. "Can you at least *pretend* to be surprised when it happens?" he asked.

I don't know why I would ruin his surprise. It dawned on me that I was a little nervous and, as always, talked out of my ass whenever too much anticipation loomed. I smiled warmly and squeezed his arm as he escorted me through the building's automatic glass doors. He looked deflated. "Liam, I think it is so sweet of you to bring me all the way here so that we can retake our photos. As much as I love our first-year anniversary picture—the one I keep in a frame on my nightstand—the wind blew my hair over both our faces that night. So, a new photo means a lot to me."

Liam coughed. "I mean, yeah, a picture re-do is the least I could do."

As the glass floor rotated us in a circular motion ever so slowly, allowing us to enjoy a full 360-degree view of the city from the observation windows, we ate our dinners of tender prime rib au jus and fingerling potatoes with baby carrots. Next came the famous misty voyage dessert called the Lunar Orbiter 2.0. The dry-ice vapors that poured out and around the tall martini glasses filled with berry sundae made the experience truly out of this world. But for once in my life, dessert wasn't my main focus. It was Liam's red cheeks and his shy downward glances at his sweaty-palmed hands over mine on the table that suddenly left me feeling warm and fuzzy inside.

He was nervous, too, and I loved him more for it.

"Now that the sun has set, you wanna go outside and look at the city lights with me?" he asked, his voice cracking.

I was relieved he wasn't going to do it right then and there at the table, inside a room full of stuffy diners. I took his damp hand in mine. "Of course. Outside is perfect."

"Like you," he said, kissing my cheek.

Once we were outside on the glassed-in viewing deck, observing the endless city lights below and the stars above, I sighed. "Six hundred and four feet is a long way down."

"That it is," he said, standing closely behind me as I leaned my back against his chest, listening to his fast-beating heart. His arms were wrapped under mine, with his hands resting protectively on top of my growing belly. "But I could never allow my girls to fall. Never in a million years."

We had found out a week earlier that we were having a little girl, and there was something in the way he said *my girls* that made my toes tingle. "Did you like the view better at sunset or now, in the evening, with all the twinkling lights below?" I asked him. "I don't know which I like better."

Liam slowly turned me around to face him and threw my arms over his shoulders before he pulled me to him in a dancing stance. "I didn't notice the sunset or the city lights. And if I did, neither could ever compare to the view I see now," he said, looking straight into my soul.

His gaze shot hot love through me like a searing arrow, and I nearly turned to liquid. I wanted to squeeze him tightly to me, but my belly, or should I say, our daughter, wouldn't allow it. "I do," I said in a dreamy tone.

"You do what?" he asked, cocking his head to one side.

Crap. He hadn't asked me yet. "I ... I do love you. More than you can ever know," I said, hoping I hadn't blown it for a second time.

He shook his head and clicked his tongue disapprovingly. "I see you are not going to make this easy."

I laughed. "Do I make anything easy?"

When Liam swiveled his head over his shoulder and nodded to someone behind him, I glanced around him to see who he was silently communicating with. It was our lady server, holding a small boom box. She smiled warmly at me before pushing the play button. When the song came on, I roared with uncontrollable laughter. "You just *had* to bring Montell Jordan into this, didn't you?"

"Of course. Sam, you once declared you loved *both* of us, and both of us you shall have. Plus, 'this *is* how we do it.'"

I looked around me at the handful of visitors on deck who had stopped peering at the view and now gawked curiously in our direction. I laughed. "Then get to it. Make me an honest woman already."

"With pleasure."

When Liam stepped back a foot and nearly dropped to one knee, I hurried and pulled him back up to a standing position in front of me. "Wait. What are you doing?" I asked him.

"What do you think I'm doing?" he whispered awkwardly so the others didn't hear.

"Don't you think your chances would be better if you serenade and sing along with Montell before you ask me something important?"

Liam's eyes did a shifty look from side to side at all the people staring at us before his mouth dropped open. "You're kidding, right?"

I crossed my arms, remembering when he made me profess my love for him *and* Montell in the car. "Paybacks are a bitch. I'll need *you* to show me how much you truly love me this time."

Liam slowly ran a hand down his reddening face as if he couldn't believe the turn of events. He looked at me with glistening beads of sweat appearing above his top lip. "You're really going to make me do this, aren't you."

"Oh, hell yes."

"In front of all these people?"

"Affirmative."

After a slight hesitation, it was as if someone switched on the bright stage lights to cue him in. And there stood a white-boy rapper who took over my soon-to-be fiancé's body. As Liam danced and rapped to the lyrics with his hands and arms flailing about in the air, as well as singing terribly off-key, I stood there smiling and laughing with my hands over my heated cheeks as everyone around us cheered and clapped, watching him do his thing. When the song finally finished, Liam took a bow for his fans and thanked our server before he faced me.

"Wow," I said. "Just wow. Better than the first time."

He was out of breath when he took my hands in his. "Samantha Carey?" When I cleared my throat and took a suggestive glance down at his left knee,

Liam laughed. "Right. Almost forgot that part." He got down on one knee then and tried again. "Samantha Carey?"

"Yes, Liam Becker?" I said, smiling from ear to ear after some woman in the crowd gasped in pleasure and other random strangers murmured excitedly.

"Sam, I know we haven't had the easiest of beginnings, but with fate on our side, I know with absolute certainty that you were made for me. And now, with a little faith to guide us, I believe together we can conquer the world together. Anything is possible with you by my side. So, please, will you and our little girl walk down the aisle and marry me? Because I love you so damn much, Samantha. It physically hurts to think of my world without you in it. Please say yes."

At this, the server behind Liam handed him a palm-sized trinket box, shaped like the silver pumpkin-shaped carriage, like the one Cinderella rode in on the night she met her prince. Liam flipped open the top of the carriage, revealing a dark blue velveteen cushion holding a gold band with a sparkling diamond set into it. His eyes never left mine. "Will you marry me? Will you do me the honor of spending the rest of your life with me, Samantha Carey?"

I didn't even realize I was holding my breath during his whole speech. I finally let out a shaky breath and wiped the tears that appeared out of nowhere. "Yes. Of course, I will marry you, Liam. Of course, I will spend the rest of my life with you."

The crowd around us burst into applause just as Liam stood, grabbed my face, and pulled me to him, giving me the wettest, hottest kiss he had ever given me. "It's you and me, forever and always," he said.

I looked into his eyes, which held mine and our baby's future in them. "Forever and always."

Our baby girl was born on a sunny Tuesday afternoon. We named her Faith A.J. Becker. Because I wanted my little girl to one day grow up with the knowledge and wisdom of my wiser friends, we gave her the middle names Alice and Jane. I shifted little Faith onto my other hip and swooped down to grab her pink blanket off the floor. She squealed in laughter from the swift movement. "Never mind, Liam!" I called out. "I found her shoe. It was under her blanket."

I nuzzled my nose into the soft, fat folds of Faith's neck and asked her, "Did you hide your shoe from Mommy? Did you?" Our daughter could not answer, nor was she truly capable of hiding shoes, but she already showed signs of cleverness and spunk. It wouldn't surprise me if she had already figured out how to kick her shoes off for pure entertainment, just to see me run around looking for them every time.

Faith made a sour face as she tried to pull the sapphire blue bow out of her thick, curly brown hair. It matched her eyes perfectly. "Now, now. Leave the bow in your hair," I said. "Don't you want to look pretty for Miss Alice today?"

I distracted Faith with the keys in my hands and walked over to the bottom of our stairs, calling up to Liam, "Hey, are you ready to go yet? We don't want to be late. The phone call is supposed to be at exactly 2:00 p.m."

Liam sprang down the stairs with his eyebrows rising. "You forgetting something?" he said, holding a grey diaper bag.

I had picked out this bag when my friends took me to Babys R Us to register for the shower they were throwing for me. I had my eye on a pink bag that Emily held up until Heidi immediately scolded both of us. "Please don't buy that godawful pink one. Leave some dignity for your man, Sam." She was totally right, and I ended up choosing a more sophisticated, 'manly' grey. My friends took my pregnancy as an opportunity to prove which of them was most supportive, and to show I loved them equally, I allowed Emily to pick out all the pink frilly shoes a girl could want.

Liam stood at the bottom step, dangling the grey diaper bag over his head, too far up for me to grab it from him. "What would I do without you?" I said sarcastically.

"After seeing you give birth to this little one with a head the size of a cantaloupe, I know you can do anything without me. But I'd like to believe that without me, you'd panic, curl into a ball, and feel lost for eternity," he said with a smirk.

"Let's just say I would do all of the above without you." When he handed me the bag, I went to kiss him but paused. "Would you like a finder's fee?"

"Yes, please," he said, bending down with his eyes shut.

I went in to kiss his lips but tricked him and grazed his cheek instead.

"What? You missed," he said.

"I'm teaching Faith not to give boys what they expect." But I laughed and stood on my tippy-toes to give him a saucy kiss on the lips. "Happy now?"

"Yes. Thank you, *wife*."

"You're welcome, *husband*," I replied.

Liam and I were still in the obnoxious newlywed stage where we said *wifey* and *husband* too many times to count, as Heidi had pointed out one day. We told her to get used to it, since the PDAs she engaged in with Matt were just as over-the-top and ridiculous. I'd even had to pull her aside at the wedding to tell her to tone it back a little. "Geez, Heidi, there are children in the room," I had said jokingly. She looked at my six-month-old daughter in my arms and laughed. "Well, whose fault is it again that they had to bring a baby to their wedding?" I smothered Faith with kisses and shot back, "All mine, and I'd do it again. Some mistakes end up being the biggest blessings."

When we first told Liam's parents the news of our pregnancy, they had tried to talk us into getting married right away—a shotgun wedding. I wasn't too thrilled with the idea of people thinking we were getting married just because of our circumstances. A shotgun wedding sounded like a terribly unromantic way to begin our lives together. Plus, wearing a wedding dress while pregnant seemed un-fairytale-like. And because I was determined to believe fairytales could come true, I dug my feet in, insisting we get married when Faith was six months old.

The day we said our I-do's felt like a dream come true. Our wedding was beautiful, with sage green and white peonies to symbolize new beginnings. Although Liam was sad that his basketball dreams were over, his parents supported the idea that he drop out of college and immediately start learning the family's flooring business. The money they had saved for Liam's college tuition went towards a down payment on a small, brand-new condo down in the valley, where we made the tiny place into a happy home for the three of us.

"Ready to go, Faith?" Liam asked as he held his arms out to her. She reached anxiously towards him, and he sighed, "*Ah*, there you go, baby girl. Let's get you in your car seat." Liam was a natural father, already talking about how many more kids he wanted. I told him that when he grew a uterus, then we could talk about future babies.

While Liam ensured Faith was strapped in tight, I checked the diaper bag. "You grabbed the camera, right? Don't want to miss the big moment."

"It's in there. Don't worry. We will capture the big moment." Liam straightened his back and shook his head. "It's crazy to think how everything turned out. I mean, look at us. We didn't plan for *this* to happen," Liam said while playfully tapping Faith's nose. She responded by giving him the stink eye, and he laughed. "But here we are, as if this was all meant to happen exactly like this. So tell me, Samantha Becker. Would you want it any other way?"

I looked into his eyes, which seemed to say so much. "Nope. I like us just like this—like we were always meant to be. Now, let's go and make someone else's dreams come true today. We can't be the only ones living out a happily-ever-after."

"Speaking of happily-ever-afters, I almost forgot the celebration cake. Be right back."

When Liam finally returned holding a box of our favorite chocolate cake from our favorite place, I asked him, "What took you so long?"

"I had something important to do."

When he opened the box, revealing that a corner of the cake was missing, I gasped. "You seriously went inside and ate a piece?"

He laughed, "No. I was worried everyone would eat it all, leaving us nothing for later. No one will even notice it missing." When I continued to look at him in confusion, he finally elaborated, "I saved us a tiny piece for *tonight*, my wife."

The wicked grin he gave me and the roguish look in his eyes let me know exactly what he intended to do with that cake. I couldn't help but laugh and shake my head. "Oh, wow. Only *you* could have your cake *and* eat it too." I winked at him before crawling inside the truck. "I look forward to *tonight*, husband."

When we arrived at Alice's home, I spotted my mother standing outside her car in the driveway. She waved at us excitedly as we parked.

When I opened my door, she called out, "Well, can you believe this is happening today, Sam?"

"Honestly, no." I gave her a giant hug and confessed, "We couldn't have done all this without you. Thank you for all your help in making this happen, Mom. And I'm glad you can be here for the surprise."

"Me too, honey, me too. And Alice still doesn't know?"

"Nope. No clue."

Liam unstrapped Faith from her car seat, and my mother's face lit up like it was Christmas morning. "Give me that baby, Liam, before I burst."

We made our way inside and found Alice visiting with her youngest son and daughter. A week prior, I had found their phone numbers and called them so as to include them in the celebration. They needed to be a part of this as much as Alice.

"Sammy!" Alice said in shock when she saw me. "What good timing. You can meet my son Johnny and daughter Maria." Alice didn't know that I had already talked to them by phone a week ago, but I played along like it was our first meeting.

"How wonderful," I said. I also brought Liam, Faith, and my mother for you to meet. We all just wanted to drop in and say hello."

After everyone made introductions, Faith was the star of the show.

Alice clapped her hands. "Well, this is a splendid day! To have all my favorite people here."

Not *all*, I thought.

Not just yet.

I looked at the clock above Alice's television, and my heart began to tick faster. We were only a few minutes away before the big surprise.

Alice asked my mother, "I don't suppose you could relinquish that little one to me for a bit, Julie?"

"Oh, I suppose I can let her go for a few minutes." My mother laughed. "Although it's hard to share her."

We all watched as Alice held Faith and began to bounce her softly while singing the nursery rhyme, "Old Macdonald." We couldn't help but laugh when Alice made the silly animal sounds and then added in a verse about a hippopotamus, of all things. Who knew a hippo sounded just like a cow?

Alice's daughter, Maria, leaned over and whispered, "Samantha? Are you nervous?"

"Yes, but you guys must be more than I am."

"A little," she said. "I still can't believe this is happening. The work your mother did to put together all the clues is just absolutely wonderful. I'll never know how she fitted the puzzle pieces together."

"My mother just knew the right people from her own experience, I suppose. Everything happens for a reason. Sometimes I wonder if Alice was brought into my life for certain reasons, and then I think maybe I was brought into her life just for this exact moment today."

"It sounds like you both were brought together for all kinds of beautiful and unexplainable reasons."

"Yeah. I like that theory too," I said.

I looked around the room at all the joyful smiles and thought of Jane at that moment, how much she would have loved to be a part of Alice's experience. For a moment, my heart dropped with that familiar guilt I held. Whenever it came to Jane, I would forever regret what part I played those last six months of her life. She might have still been here if not for the fight we had before her son sent her to that awful nursing home. Even though we made peace, and out of that negative came a positive—our friendship, I still held onto the 'what ifs'. Whether it was keeping my word to Jane and befriending Alice like she requested, or helping Alice resolve this one regret, I would forever be searching for ways to make it up to Jane. To prove I would become someone she was proud of.

Liam leaned in with a whisper, snapping me out of my thoughts, "Hey, there's less than a minute left. Should I take Faith now?"

"Good idea," I said and hurried to grab the camera.

We stood up together, and I nodded to everybody, speaking quietly so Alice didn't hear, "Okay. It's time. Is everyone ready?"

With fervent nods from all, I faced Alice and spoke up loudly. "Alice?" Faith looked up with a sad expression, as if upset I had interrupted all the fun. "Alice, Liam is going to take Faith now. But you can have her back in a few."

"*Oh, darn.* So soon already?"

Liam laughed and held his hands out to take Faith.

"Alice," I said, feeling nervous about such a momentous speech. I had practiced what to say to her earlier, but then emotion took me by surprise. My voice wavered, and it sounded like a frog lived in my throat, "We *all* have something to tell you. There is a reason we are all here today, and it isn't by chance or coincidence."

Alice looked at each of our faces, with anticipation and worry. "What do you mean?"

"Well, you see, we all have worked together to find someone for you. Someone especially important." Alice tilted her head in question as I continued, "There is someone who wants to meet you, and you met her once, long, long ago."

"I don't understand."

"Well," I choked back my happy tears. "Alice, you met her almost sixty years ago. You have waited such a long time to meet her again, and this is it. The time has come. We found her, Alice. We found *her*."

The confusion in Alice's eyebrows lasted a few seconds before they smoothed out with the possibility of hope. Her chin shook, and her glistening eyes widened.

With perfect timing, the phone rang. We all jumped before Alice's daughter Maria picked up and held out the phone for her mother. "Mom? I think you'll want to answer *this* call."

Alice threw her hand over her mouth and almost sobbed. "Oh, sweet Jesus. My God!" The phone rang again, and Alice's voice shook. "This ... this is *my* baby?"

There wasn't a dry eye in the room when we all nodded.

Alice's hand shook as she delicately cradled the phone close to her ear. She hesitated only for a moment before she answered with a cry of joy as if no time had ever passed, "Hello! Hello, my dear, *dear* child!"

Alice's long-lost daughter lived six thousand miles away, but she had already purchased a plane ticket to see her mother for the first time, next month.

I looked over at Liam and sniffled. "Looks like life is full of surprises, huh?"

As he held our beautiful daughter in his arms, he winked and pulled me tenderly into his side. "Yep. It looks like we just had to have a little faith."

"Yes." I beamed, resting my head on his shoulder. I gave my daughter's tiny hand a little squeeze. "Yes, faith and a little love."

Sneak Peek into the Final Book in the Trilogy.

The Caretaker of Secrets {Freed)

Olongapo, Philippines, 1953

They say water buffaloes don't cry.

As my nine-year-old self stood on the edge of the riverbank, opposite the side of where I desperately needed to be, my mother, my Nanay, my only friend and pet, made an ungal howling sound, one that I had never heard before.

And I knew all of Nanay's sweet noises.

A low grunt said Nanay was calling for me, usually because I had wandered too far again, and she had grown bored and lonely without me. A high grunt meant she was annoyed or needed to warn me, like the time I climbed a tree, not realizing a hornet's nest lay on a branch a foot from my grasping fingers. Or a moo sound was Nanay's way of saying she was angry or hungry, which was often on the days my drunk and forgetful father had pushed Nanay too hard on the sugarcane press. If it weren't for me, Nanay would have died nine years ago, along with my mother, whom I had never had the chance to meet.

But this new, soft panting, this ungal noise that Nanay made, was different. It sounded as if Nanay was crying, and her eyes said so, too. One might have said it was just the rain dripping down her face that gave the impression of tears, but I didn't think so. Before I left for school that morning, no one had warned me that a monsoon was coming. And no one could have predicted that the river would rise so high and stretch its mouth so wide that it threatened to wipe anyone out who dared get in its way.

I looked across the roaring river at Nanay's big, smooth body of slate grey pacing back and forth, still making that sound. Her big dark blue eyes, with eyelashes as long as the wings of a green skimmer, said she wanted to come get me, like she always did after school. She had smooth horns the length of my arms that curved up and outward like the legs of the bow-legged boy at my school, the one who had taunted and chased me up a tree that day and was the sole reason I was late from coming home safely. I noticed how Nanay's ears flattened behind those horns now, as if worried or scared or both.

As was I.

Again, Nanay cried out for me, and my heart raced. When she took a step closer to the torrent angrily rushing along the edges of our property, I contemplated the risks. Water buffaloes, or carboas, were strong swimmers, but so was I. The problem was, I didn't want her to try to come get me. It was too dangerous. I could see that. We could not survive this.

But when Nanay moved closer to the river's edge again, and her foot slipped, and the earthen bank crumbled under her weight, I knew I had to stop her. "Huwag!" I yelled in my native Tagalog language. "No!" But she did not listen.

I was her baby.

She my mother.

Nothing would stop her from reaching me.

My heart stopped when she leaped out toward me and plunged deep into the murky brown current, leaving me no choice.

They say water buffalos don't cry.

But mine did that day I died.

Afterword

Dear Reader,

Thank you for reading The Caretaker of Secrets (Faith). If you enjoyed this book and the others in this trilogy, please don't forget to leave a review on Amazon and Goodreads. Your reviews help us Indie Authors more than you could ever know.

*Links to my newsletter, social media, and upcoming books can be found at atgeiger.com

Author's Words and Acknowledgements

It's funny, but when I started writing this three-book interconnected trilogy about a young woman coming into her own with the help of her three strong, wise, senior friends, I never quite imagined it would all come to fruition. It was an idea, a hopeful thought, a dream, and I didn't think I had it in me to become an indie author. I laugh at my doubtful self now, but if you listen to the lyrics from a famous song called "Creep," written by Radiohead, that is precisely how I often felt while writing these stories: "I'm a freak. I'm a weirdo. What the hell am I doing here? I don't belong here." Thank goodness I didn't believe those dream-shattering negative words that swarmed in my head, because here I am, with book number two published. I still can't believe it.

I want to thank you first, **my readers,** from the depths of my soul, for supporting me as an indie author. Having a group of bookish friends in my corner means so much to me! I am forever grateful that you gave me, a new author, a chance. I hope you stay tuned for the final book, book number three in this trilogy, or whatever else I have planned for future writing endeavors.

But the absolute truth is, I could not have accomplished this book all alone! As hard as it was to overcome my fears and tackle the first two books in this trilogy, I love the end product, mainly because it was written and inspired by actual events. In honor of the three extraordinary women in my life: **Jane** in *Fate* (book one), **Alice** in *Faith* (book two), and **Malaya** in *Freed* (book three), these women are the heart and soul of what pushes my pen to paper. Without these three invincible women, with their tenacious voices urging me never to give up, I could not have accomplished my dream of becoming an author. My only hope is that in retelling their stories of hardship, of love, heartbreak, and betrayal, that I have done so in a way that would make them happy and proud.

So, most importantly, and for this particular book, *The Caretaker of Secrets (Faith)*, I thank you, my dear, sweet, passionate, spirited, and resilient **Alice**, for all the stories you have instilled in me over the years. I will forever cherish and hold dear to my heart every one of your timeless tales. Besides your joy of storytelling, your infectious laughter and positive outlook on overcoming life's never-ending challenges, you give us all the faith and hope to continue forward, one step at a time. So thank you for being one of a kind, Alice. Thank you for being a light in my life. I am forever changed by your grace and selfless love.

There is someone else dear to my heart that I must thank. To my faithful daughter, **Ms. Emily Geiger**, thank you for all you have contributed to this book. For someone who hates having her picture taken, not only did you allow me to capture your beautiful face for the cover of this book, but you, my girl, are the only person in the world I can trust to keep it real and honest when it comes to reviewing my manuscript in progress. Without you as my number one beta reader, I could not have had the insight and critique I needed to improve this book. Thank you for pushing me to bring more excitement and passion to all the romance scenes. Even though I prefer romance scenes to be more on the PG side, you were not wrong by taking me by the shoulders, shaking me hard, and begging me to add more depth and spice to these scenes. Because of your determination to make it real, I love this book even more. So, thank you, my baby girl. You truly are gifted as the ultimate romance beta reader! I love you to the moon and back. Forever and always grateful for you.

To my editor, **Doreen Martens**, how lucky am I to have found you! You saved me. Not only have you gone above and beyond to help me polish this manuscript with your expertise and wisdom, but you are also from our favorite neighboring country, Canada, which part of this book was written about from Alice's POV. When I hired you, I didn't even realize where you were from until *after* we exchanged details. Coincidence or fate? I'd like to believe it was the latter. Thank you. Thank you. Thank you.

Let's not forget, but I could not have done this without all my amazing **friends and family**. There are too many to list, but to every single one of you who holds a special place in my heart, thank you for all of your encouragement over these last few years. Thank you for being my fans and for having my best interest at heart. I have learned so much about myself through our love and friendship. I couldn't be more blessed. So, coming from another Amy, I find this quote accurate. "Find a group of people who challenge and inspire you; spend a lot of time with them, and it will change your life."—Amy Poehler—"The Art of Inside Out."

I must give a special thanks to my writer/lawyer friends **Barry K. Shuster**, MBA, JD, MSB, and **Matthew Cragg Martin**, reformed trial attorney, soap maker, master chef, gardener, and lobster man from Maine. Thank you both so much for helping me hone the legal jargon in this book. You both kindly and selfishly helped me in an area that I was so unfamiliar with, so thank you for your wisdom and expertise!

Other special thanks must go to the unstoppable and determined badass boss lady, **Ms. Sena**, who would take a bullet for me. I want to thank you for your help with some of the language I needed for a particular section of this book. Thank you!

Last and finally, I want to thank my thoughtful and endearing husband, who just gets me. **Sean**, not one day goes by that you don't ask me how my writing is going. Not one day goes by without you calling to check in on me to ask if my sanity has slipped through the cracks and if I might need a coffee or a hug to bring me back to earth. Your shoulder rubs, encouragement, attentiveness, and concern for my well-being are genuinely something I cannot wrap my brain around. How did I get so lucky? How did you become my person? Every day, I thank my lucky stars for you. Every day, I pinch myself to remind myself of the unbelievable way that fate made you mine. This book could not have existed without my person, Liam. I love you *and* Montell Jordan. And I love you more than chocolate cake.

Much love,
A.T. Geiger

www.ingramcontent.com/pod-product-compliance
Lightning Source LLC
Chambersburg PA
CBHW061335310726
48974CB00001B/62